BONES

A collection of monsters.

Four stories
written by Andrew Cull

with an Introduction
by Eddie Generous

Special thanks to:

Kerrie
Eddie Generous
Frank Errington
Noel Osualdini
Silvia Brown
Mary Papadakis
Silke Templeton

Published by Vermillion2One Press 2018

Introduction.

Though I'm not wholly versed in technology and the various gadgets and applications I supposedly need for an easier life, I have taken to using a social site to track my reading habits. Not just my own. Goodreads is an interesting preview into someone's interests without having to talk to them, hell, you don't have to interact with them at all. In fact, you can simply trail their likes and dislikes and everyone's cool with it because it's books and books are the baseline for what's good about intelligent, uh, society. Or something.

However, it's not the reading habits of others that will get my rambling point across, it's my reading habits. Last year I read one hundred eight books, most of which were horror. The year before that, I did not use the social site, but I know I read closer to one hundred fifty because I'd filled much of the time I spend dealing with Unnerving and Unnerving Magazine by picking up and reading books. Again, primarily horror. The years before that… who knows? Hundreds of horror books.

I don't know what that tells you.

Probably a few things.

One thing it suggests to me is that I'm a student of horror. Another thing suggests that maybe I know a thing or two about horror stories. Perhaps that even makes me a halfway decent judge of good storytelling.

In my adult life, I've read more than sixty books by King, nineteen by Barker, fourteen by Koontz, a dozen by Straub, handfuls or more from JCO, Hill, Little, Saul, and SGJ. I've delved into many suspenseful novels from Atwood and Flynn and Thomas Harris.

Andrew Cull is none of these authors.

On top of what I read in published form, I read mounds of stories submitted to me for publication. One common trait amidst many authors sending stuff out is, be intentional or unintentional, regurgitation; that space where inspiration sinks teeth too deep and becomes facsimile. It's something that many budding authors start out doing and eventually grow beyond, if they write long enough to gather their *own* voices that is.

Andrew Cull is not one of these writers either. This despite being relatively new to publishing fiction.

For the past couple weeks, I've racked my grey meat trying to figure out what to say here. I've read most of Andrew Cull's short fiction, I've read his novella (included here), and I look forward to his novel on the horizon. His stuff I know fairly well, but for quite a while still couldn't quite place how to describe it.

And then it hit me.

Andrew Cull is a writer unlike most because if I had to guess, he might have much more to say on the topic of Hitchcock or Fincher than he would about King or Barker. His stories flow like visual scenes.

Andrew Cull is a writer who understands storytelling and writes like there's a movie playing in his head.

He gets the Hitchcock adage that the suspense exists in the ticking of the bomb and not the explosion. He understands that describing scary things is not the same as writing scary situations. He understands that in the fascinating and fantastic worlds of suspenseful genre writing, story is first and stands miles above all else in importance. For me as a reader, and an experienced reader with demands, it's paramount that the writer understands good storytelling, otherwise I'm bored and frustrated. Now and then, I even feel robbed of my time.

Not with Andrew Cull.

When it comes to distinctive, spine-tingling, truly thrilling, commercial-style terrors, you can do a lot worse than to read this guy, a hell of a lot worse. Methodical and purposeful, Andrew Cull doesn't waste words and makes good use of a reader's time. The stories included here are rich in atmosphere and heavy-duty in follow through. This is a dude who can take you on a journey with nothing more than paper and ink, and what more do you really need from an author?

Eddie Generous
2018

Contents

DID YOU FORGET ABOUT ME?

He had written to me a month or so before he died. I'd ignored the letter the same way I'd ignored all the others.

It had rained ever since we'd left Oxford that morning. I'd stayed with Kelly and Jack the night before, played uncle to Milly and Seth before being dragged *against my will* upstairs to read them bedtime stories. In truth I loved reading to them. Living in London I only got to see them once or twice a year. I was acutely aware that each time I saw Milly and Seth they had changed dramatically and I was missing large chunks of their childhood.

Since I'd moved to London, to 'concentrate on my acting career', I'd played a supply teacher in a soap (two lines) and a cab driver in an ad (good pay but no lines). Oh, and I'd shared a lift with Christopher Lee once. I'd been in London for seven years, and that had been the extent of my acting success. Even those around me, who had initially cheered me on, had seen my enthusiasm wane and had begun to ask if it wasn't time that I thought about another line of work. But what else was I going to do? I'd be thirty in two months' time. If I gave up now I was a failure. Ironically, it was through one of my non-roles that he'd found me.

It had been a three-story marathon. An hour of jumping from Charlotte's Web, to the Cat in the Hat, to the BFG, before Milly had begun quietly snoring and Seth had finally given in to sleep. Kelly had met me coming down the stairs. "I was just coming to rescue you."

"No need," I smiled, "they're out for the count."

"I brought reinforcements." She pressed a large glass of red wine into my hand. She hooked an arm through mine and led me down into the lounge.

As soon as I smelled the wood-burner I felt the muscles in my shoulders relax. A whole year's tension, melting from my body, breathed into the smoky air in a deep sigh. Had it really been that long since I'd last left the city? When I hated it so much why did I continue to stay there? "So, little bro? Any gossip? Any ladies you want to tell me about? Anyone special you'd like your big sis to vet for you?"

I slumped into one of the large green armchairs. "Jack?"

Jack refilled his glass. "Don't look at me. I'm just here for the wine."

"Thanks!" I took a big mouthful and laughed.

We'd stayed up until one in the morning talking. All the time we'd avoided discussing the trip. It wasn't until I was smoking my last cigarette of the night that Kelly followed me out onto the porch.

"Christ! It's freezing!" She disappeared back inside the hallway and returned wrapped in a throw from the couch. "You should pack that up." She punched me in the arm. "Here, give me a drag."

Kelly reached to take my smoke. I waved it away from her. "Jack would kill me"

"Who's the oldest here, huh?"

"Jack. And he'd kill me."

Kelly growled at me. While I smoked, she tried to blow smoke rings with her breath condensing on the freezing air. "You OK about tomorrow?"

*

When we'd finally left, it had been under the cover of darkness. Kelly had told me about it years later. I'd been seven. Apparently I slept through the whole thing. Mum had put me to bed in one house and I'd woken up in another.

*

It was quiet, so quiet. And dark. Away from the town, Kelly and Jack's house backed onto fields. At night, the most sound came from the occasional fox crying. You never heard a car or a shout. No screaming laughter or fighting in the street to rip you awake. Just silence. Hours of glorious silence. I never slept as well as I slept at their house. Warm with wine, I sank under the heavy covers. I was asleep in minutes.

I'd heard the movement. It started in a dream I was having and edged into the real world as it grew closer. The face materialising from the darkness made me start.

"Sorry Uncle Cam. I was scared."

"It's OK mate. There's nothing to be scared of."

Seth climbed up into the bed next to me. He lay on my arm and his breathing quickly fell into a gentle rhythm. I thought he had fallen asleep. I closed my eyes.

"Uncle Cam… Are you and Mum going to Grandad's house today?"

That word stopped me. Grandad. I guessed Kelly had had to find a way to explain it to Seth and Milly. I would have chosen different words.

"Yes. We are."

"Was he really a bad man?"

*

He'd left me the house. Not Kelly and me. Just me. I didn't want it. I didn't want anything from him. Kelly had offered to loan me the money to hire someone to clear the house, throw out everything he'd touched, then we could sell the place and move on with our lives. Initially I'd agreed, but then a week ago I'd changed my mind. Maybe it was for the same reason that she'd called him Grandad to Milly and Seth, even though they'd never met him, but I couldn't let strangers empty the house.

At six Milly had joined Seth at my side in the bed, and then taken over the whole bed, and then, at 6.10 I gave up and got up. It was still dark. I could hear the rain on the roof. Kelly was already up, drinking coffee, when I went downstairs.

We ate breakfast without talking about the day ahead. Kelly would drive. I'd never learned. That was on a to-do list somewhere that grew longer each year.

*

That morning I'd gotten a letter from Authentic Films. They were holding second auditions for a new thriller and they wanted to me to attend. I remember thinking that my luck might be changing. The next letter was from the solicitor with the news that he was dead.

*

It had rained ever since we'd left Oxford that morning. We pulled off the A4 and onto the Newbury road. From there the roads had grown thinner, tighter, the hedgerows closing in around us until, finally, the tree canopy had intertwined its fingers over our heads and blocked out the sky altogether. We had been funnelled back into the village we'd fled 23 years ago.

"Do you remember any of this?" Kelly asked.

We passed St Mary's Church. "You were baptised there." She pointed.

I shook my head. None of it was familiar.

"That's probably for the best."

*

The bruises had healed in the first few months but it would be years before Mum stopped looking over her shoulder. She'd triple check that she'd locked the doors at night and the slightest sound would send her racing to the bay window at the front of our house, peering through a gap in the curtains, checking the street to make sure he wasn't standing there.

*

Thatcham under a slate sky. The roads had grown so narrow that only one car could go in either direction at a time. We passed a tractor pulled off to the side of the road. The driver watched us as the rain lashed at his cab.

Eventually, the road ran out. The house, a two-storey red brick farmhouse, sat on land large enough that you'd neither hear nor have to see your neighbours unless you chose to. A mix of fences and tall firs further isolated the house. Our way onto the drive was barred by a large wooden gate, locked with a padlock.

"Shit!" The rain was freezing! I hurried from the warmth of Kelly's BMW over to the gate. The chain was heavy, rusted, the links bit at my fingers as I felt along them for the padlock. I stopped with the key in my hand. I stopped watching the house.

I didn't have to do this. I could turn away now, never look beyond the black windows, stop asking questions. We could drive back to Oxford, Kelly would understand. Spend a few days with Milly and Seth. Stop asking questions before…

"You OK?" Kelly shouted from the car.

I hadn't read his letters. I hadn't thrown them out either. I kept them all, an elastic band wrapped around them. I had them in my bag.

I heard Kelly shut off the engine behind me. Why had he left me the house? Had he wanted me to come here? I turned the key and the rusted lock popped open in my hand. I unthreaded the chain. I had already asked too many questions to turn around now.

*

Dust and cigarette smoke. I could taste them both on the stale air.

"Watch out! It's wet here." I held out an arm to stop Kelly going any further. The hallway lino was wet with rain. "Must be a leak somewhere."

We edged around the puddle of water and headed further up the hall. Ahead, a staircase led up to a landing halfway between the ground and first floor. A large window looked out of the back of the house. I climbed the stairs to look out of the window.

Kelly poked around downstairs behind me. "Looks like he gave the maid the past couple of years off," I heard her grumble as she disappeared into one of the downstairs rooms.

A thin lace curtain hung over the window. It was yellow from the cigarette smoke. Mum had ones just like it in her house. I wondered if she'd hung this one all those years before. I pulled the curtain aside. I could feel the cold pressing against the glass outside, wanting in.

I'd been here before. I knew that because I'd been told, but this was the first time I remembered it. I remembered the garden. Out through the kitchen door, racing through the grass, day into night as you ran under the shadows of the apple trees. First to the gate! Through the little wooden gate and out, out into the fields beyond.

I'd stood on the landing above, listening. Cold feet on the thin carpet, confused, scared, listening to them arguing in the lounge below. I turned from the window to look behind me. "Kelly!"

The shadow moved, fast across the stairs, as if my turning had startled it.

"What?"

Behind me, a break in the clouds shifted the darkness on the stairs. It was slow, but it might explain what I'd just seen. "You OK?" Kelly stood at the foot of the stairs.

"I remember. I remember being here."

"Good thing I packed the booze then!"

*

By the time I got into the room for the audition they were going through the motions. I'd arrived early. Early enough to see an actor I recognised from EastEnders shaking hands with one of the producers on his way out. That producer had left shortly afterwards and when I finally got in an hour and a half later, the director was talking on his phone at the back of the room and the assistant left to audition spent most of her time checking her email while I read the piece they'd sent me. Even largely ignored I'd thrown everything I had into it. The audition was recorded so I hoped that, if they reviewed the tapes, I might get noticed. A day later they'd announced they'd cast the actor who'd played a cabbie in EastEnders.

*

Kelly had packed wine. Not one bottle.

"Reinforcements?" I'd asked.

"Bugger the reinforcements, I brought the whole army!" she'd laughed as she'd carried the box of bottles in.

We measured out the rest of the afternoon in mugs of wine. Kelly hadn't thought to bring glasses and neither of us felt comfortable using his, so she'd gone back to the car and brought in a couple of travel mugs she'd had in the boot.

"Cheers!"

"Here's to…" Kelly stopped to think about it. "Here's to something good coming out of this shit!"

"I'll drink to that!"

Outside it rained, with no sign that it would ease up any time soon. There was an ashtray, one of those tall ones that you could drop the butts into, by the armchair I was sitting in. I broke out my smokes and lit one. As I flicked the ash I realised that I was likely sitting in *his* chair.

"Hand 'em over." Kelly had her hand out. "What? Jack's not here now." She kept her hand out. "And I brought the wine so no mucking around!"

I handed over the pack. Kelly lit one and grimaced. "Oh, horrible!" She chewed down her disgust and took another drag.

"How long has it been?"

"About a year. Since we last had a night out." Kelly took another drag and blew smoke out of her nose. "Like riding a bike! What did you remember? When you were on the stairs?"

I poured more wine. "I remembered the garden. Running through the garden. The fields out the back. Through that gate in the fence." A thought occurred to me "Shit! Do you think they've built houses all over them?"

"There's one way to find out!" Kelly was already on her feet.

*

Neither of us needed the other to guide us through the ground floor. Right out of the lounge, along the corridor, another right into the dining room, left into the kitchen. We stood in front of the back door looking out into the garden.

"You first!" Kelly had already pulled her coat up over her head. I found the latches and threw open the door. Running on nicotine and red wine, we raced through the garden. I remembered the grass being long but maintained. It was almost knee high now, knotted, wet fingers catching at our ankles as we ran. Kelly squealed and laughed, almost going over a couple of times before we hit the orchard at the end of the garden. The smell of rotten fruit stopped us dead.

A carpet of decaying apples spread in every direction. Dead fruit, left unpicked it had fallen from the trees and now lay, brown, liquefying on the wet earth.

"Christ!" The smell was overpowering.

Kelly put a hand over her mouth and we tried to step around the rotting fruit, through the dark orchard and on towards the end of the garden. But there were too many to avoid them altogether. I felt the apple underfoot. It was too late. I'd already pressed my weight down to step. The apple's skin split with a muffled pop and the flesh inside spread around the sides of my Converse.

"Shit!"

I heard Kelly shout from behind: "Shit!" The same thing had happened to her. "Whose idea was this anyway?" she called.

"Yours!"

We arrived at the gate. The fir trees surrounding it had grown together, forming an arch over the small exit. We'd have to crouch down to pass through.

"Think of the spiders!" Kelly grumbled.

I took a grip on the gate. The wood was slippery, coated in a thin layer of slime. I almost snatched my hand back in disgust. I'd expected the gate to be stiff from lack of use; it certainly didn't look as if anyone had been down to the end of the garden for some time, but it swung open easily. It hadn't been latched either. I ducked and stepped through the gap in the trees.

*

Nothing had changed. The fields, some fallow, some stubbled with the stalks of this year's crop, stretched away in front of us, sloping down almost to the edge—I'd forgotten they even existed—to the edge of the lakes. Three large gravel pits, huge to a seven year old boy, flooded in the late '60s. Reclaimed by the land they'd been cut from, they were a nature reserve by the time I'd known them. Seeing them again, filled with dark water, stopped me in my tracks.

"The den in the reeds." The words dropped from my mouth.

Kelly's hand on my arm made me start.

"Sorry." The concern in her voice was clear. "Let's go back inside." Gently but firmly, she began to turn me away, back to the small gate, back to the 'haunted' house we'd come from.

Before we ducked through the gap in the trees, I stopped and looked back to the lakes. A memory had begun to surface, as black and as cold as the water that crawled on the shore behind us.

*

I was soaked. We were both soaked. Kelly left me in the lounge and went looking for some towels.

"Have a look at the fire. See if you can get it going."

She'd pointed at the open fire and then to a rack of newspapers in the corner of the room, joining the dots for me. She'd have been better off Googling for instructions. I'd seen plenty of open fires roaring in pubs but I'd never had to light one. When I reached to pull a paper from the rack, I realised how much I was shaking.

This had been his house. After we'd left, he'd lived here, alone, for 23 years. And then he'd died, alone. The solicitor hadn't given me many details but he'd let it slip that a neighbour had found him. He'd been dead for some time.

He'd made no attempt to follow us. That was what Mum had feared the most. But after that night when we'd fled, we'd never seen him again. In what I'd read of the first letter he'd sent me, he'd apologised repeatedly. He'd admitted he'd been a drunk, that he was filled with shame… I'd closed the letter and put it away. Now I wondered if I'd owed him at least a conversation before he'd died.

"Shit!" I heard Kelly shout from upstairs. I wandered to the bottom of the stairs.

"You OK?"

Kelly appeared at the top of the staircase. "I'm fine. Stay down there."

"Why?"

I was already on the stairs and heading up. "Cam! No!"

She moved in front of me, blocking my way onto the landing.

"What is it?" I looked past her. I couldn't remember in any concrete way; right now all the memories I had were jagged pieces, dropped and picked up out of order, but I knew that the room behind Kelly had been my old bedroom.

"What?" I edged around her onto the landing heading for my old room. Kelly joined me at the door. I pressed it gently open.

"Shit!"

It was the same. Not how I'd remembered it—glimpses of a child's room that I could just have easily imagined as recalled—but actually the same, exactly the same, as it had been on the night Mum had carried me to the car, when we'd run. My Superman bedspread, the Honey I Shrunk The Kids poster above my bed, my books, my toys, all still where they'd been abandoned that night 23 years before. Time and nicotine had aged them. The room smelled of smoke, the same as the rest of the house. A small wooden chair had been pulled into the middle of the room. I was struck with an image of him, sat smoking, waiting, alone.

"Why would you do this? Leave the rooms like this?" Kelly's voice brought me back.

"Yours is the same?"

Kelly nodded.

"Shame. He left the rooms like this because he was ashamed."

"Ashamed? Fuck him! So he should have been!" Kelly was livid. "Cam, you were seven, you don't remember how bad it was. I'm glad that's the case, for your sake, but, fuck…" Her words caught in her throat. "It was really bad."

"I'm sorry, I'm not defending him. You're right, I don't remember."

"I know. But, fuck it! This place! I need another drink!"

Kelly was already on the stairs heading down but I lingered in the doorway. For 23 years the boy who'd lived in this room had been a stranger to me. Now, a lifetime later, I had a chance to get to know him, for better or worse.

"Where'd you put your lighter?" Kelly shouted from the lounge below. I looked down. I had it in my hand. I noticed the carpet where I was standing was wet. We'd probably walked water all through the house when we'd come in from the rain. I turned, expecting to see my dirty footprints leading up the stairs, across to my room. There were no footprints on the carpet.

*

We got drunk. And lit a fire. It seemed like a good idea at the time. It wasn't exactly a roaring hearth but after a great deal of persistence, and swearing, we had enough of a fire to sit a few inches away and dry out. The wood was waterlogged. That was my excuse and I was sticking with it. Everything felt damp. It was an old house, it leaked, it was to be expected. Kelly mumbled something about bad workmen. I feigned a scowl and we cracked open another bottle of wine.

"You really don't remember much about living here, do you?"

I shook my head and lit another smoke. "I remembered being on the stairs. I think I remember them fighting. Was this house always this cold?" I shivered and leant closer to the fire, trying to force the chill out of my bones.

"One night—I was 9, you would only have been 6—I'd been woken up by their arguing. I pulled the pillow over my head to start with, hoping it'd be over quickly, but I couldn't muffle the noise. It was a bad one. Mum was shouting too. When that happened it always ended the same way. I pulled that pillow tighter and tighter. I wanted to pass out, black out, for it to be over. I heard her hit the table as she fell. I've never heard a sound more terrible in my life. Then the front door slammed and I heard him start the car and drive off. I'll never forget the silence that came afterwards. I remember pulling the pillow away from my face, expecting to hear her crying, to hear something, anything. I stood on the landing. The house felt empty but I knew she was down there. I was terrified. I called out quietly to her, pleading her to answer me back." Kelly took a deep drag on her cigarette. "I found her on the floor over there." She pointed. She wiped a tear from her cheek.

"He'd punched her and she'd fallen backwards. She'd hit her head on that table." She gestured at the heavy oak side table against the wall. "I thought she was dead." Kelly gritted her teeth against her anger. "He didn't fucking know if she was alive or not! He'd just left her there, like rubbish, like she was meaningless. And he'd gone out! Maybe to drink more, maybe he was going to run away. Maybe we would have woken up to find our Mum lying dead on the lounge floor. He really cared that little about her and us."

"I didn't know. I… I just don't remember it."

"You know we stayed for another year after that happened? I begged her to call the police, to take us and leave, but she just made excuses for him. Every night I thought he'd kill her. I took a knife from the kitchen and kept it under my pillow. I'd lay in bed holding that knife until I fell asleep. You know, I'm glad he died alone. I'm glad that he didn't have anyone in the end. He didn't deserve to have anyone after what he'd done."

"We should burn it."

"What?"

"The table. We'll take it outside. He must have an axe around here somewhere for the wood. We'll chop it up and burn the fucking thing. God knows it's cold enough in here!"

"You're not wrong. That's a terrible fire!" Kelly smiled. It was just a small smile but enough that I knew my idea to burn the table had helped to bring her back from the awful memories the house held for her.

"Thanks!"

"Don't mention it."

And so we hauled the table out into the rain, found his axe and set about chopping it into pieces. Drunk and starting fires, now drunk in charge of an axe. Again, it seemed like a good idea at the time. I took the first shot, missed, and then swung the axe again. This time I hit the top of the table dead centre, splintering the varnished wood, cracking the table top. Then I gave Kelly the axe. It was her memory to destroy. And she did. She swung the axe again and again, tearing into the table until it lay shattered, hacked into pieces at our feet.

And then we threw it on the fire. The wood popped and cracked, its varnish bubbling, embers spitting against the grate. We weren't going anywhere in a hurry. The rain fell harder than ever and Kelly had already drunk too much to drive. So we drank more. We fed the table to the fire piece by piece and we talked.

Night came early, creeping up to the windows of the farmhouse as we talked. By 5pm it was dark. Still the rain fell constantly. We listened to it in the gaps in our conversation, when we smoked in silence, trying to work through the hundreds of questions being in his house raised.

"How did he find you?"

"He saw me in EastEnders. He said he'd recognised me straight away. That it was like looking in a mirror thirty years ago. When he checked the credits he saw I was using Mum's maiden name and that confirmed it."

"The perils of being famous!"

"Hardly. Supply Teacher 2: Cam Miller."

"That's still more than most people."

"Yeah, I know. Anyway, so he Googled me. Got my address through my agent. He told me all this in the first letter. He told Todd he had a script to send to me. Dickhead gave him my address. Just like that."

"What else did he say? In the letter?"

"Do you want to read it?"

Kelly didn't hesitate. "No."

"Just a lot of apologies really. How ashamed he was. How he'd stopped drinking. He'd been dry for fifteen years apparently. Said he felt he deserved everything he got. He said he didn't expect to hear back from me."

"That was it?"

"Pretty much. I thought that would be it. Two weeks later another letter arrives."

"And you didn't open it?"

"No. Once was enough."

Kelly was on her feet. She crossed the lounge to a cabinet by the chair where I was sitting. She bent down and pulled open one of its cupboards. "There…" It was full of half-finished bottles. "Lot of booze for someone who's been dry for 15 years"

"How did you know?"

"He always kept his booze in there. I guess old habits die hard." Kelly leant in to look. She'd noticed something behind the bottles, at the back of the cupboard. "What's this?" She reached into the cupboard. I could hear the bottles shifting around her hand as she reached in. "Got you!"

Kelly pulled her hand out. In it she was clutching a bundle of photographs.

"What is it?"

Kelly separated the shots, old Kodak prints, glossy squares, sepia with nicotine. "You." She flicked through more of the shots. "And me." She handed me the photos as she leafed through them. I was five, ice cream all over my face, in another Kelly had pigtails standing by a bike that was too big for her, in another we were at the beach. He'd written the dates on the back of each shot.

I knew the boy in the shots was me but I couldn't remember any of the photos being taken. In the next one I was older, seven maybe, and I was holding a fish between myself and another boy, our catch, by the looks of it. I was squinting, the sun in my eyes, but smiling. "Who's that?"

"I thought you remembered. When we were outside when you said, 'The den in the reeds.' I thought seeing the lakes had brought it back"

"No, I…"

"That's Sam… Adams. He was your best friend when we lived here."

I looked down at the smiling boy holding the other end of the fish. He beamed, a huge grin, the kind of excitement only a seven year old could muster. "He died Cam. That summer we left."

"I can't believe I don't remember."

"The two of you were inseparable that year. Cam and Sam. The Magnificent Sevens. That's what Sam's dad called you. We barely saw you all summer. If Mum had started taking your dinner down to that den we probably wouldn't have seen you till the summer holidays were over. As it was you came home every evening to eat, sleep and to complain that you weren't allowed out after 7 at night. Then at just after 8am every morning Sam's face would pop up at the kitchen window to see where you were. Same routine every day. Then one morning he just wasn't there."

"What happened to him?"

"The police came round to talk to you. There was a search. Went on for over a week. Then they found him, tangled in the reeds, washed up against one of the banks of the lakes. Mum never said anything more about it."

"There was a service, at school."

"That's right. An assembly to explain to us what had happened."

I lit another cigarette. It was all in pieces, hard to tell if it was my imagination but, "I think I remember the den."

"After Sam died you'd disappear down there for hours. Scared the hell out of Mum. You'd come back talking about Sam as if he was still alive. Talking about what you'd done

19

that day. You took it really hard. Mum was going to try and stop you going down there but, in the end you stopped going of your own accord."

"What happened?"

"We were sitting, eating breakfast, waiting for 8am, when you'd get up, head to the back door, just like you'd done every day when Sam came calling, and you'd go out, go to the den on your own until dinner time. That day you looked up to the window but you didn't move. You just sat there. Mum asked you if you were OK. You said, 'Sam doesn't smell nice now. I'm not going to the den anymore.' That was it. You didn't go to the den again and we didn't talk about it any further. I think Mum was just glad that you seemed to be moving on. Looking back, I'm not surprised you don't remember any of it, people have forgotten much less traumatic things."

"And they never found out what happened to him?"

"We left not long after that. Until coming back today I hadn't thought about it."

I could see it. At a distance. I was standing on the edge of the fields. Tall corn behind me, I could feel it on the back of my legs, swaying against my back, pressing me forward. The den was on the very edge of the lake, a concrete bird watching station. One doorway in and one long window across its front, a thin slit, no glass, looking out over the lake. Now the corn scratched at my skin, it was cold and I wanted to get away from it. I climbed the short flint wall and stepped down into the mud on the other side. The earth squelched, I could smell the rotten apples. Decay. My memory and the day just past blurring.

It had begun to rain. I wasn't sure how much I remembered and how much I imagined. I trod through the mud. It was summer: the ground should have been harder, drier. The den was hidden, you had to know where to find it. It had been built to disappear into the landscape, surrounded

20

by trees and thick reeds, camouflaged so anyone in the den wouldn't be seen by what they were watching. It was filled with darkness.

"You OK?" Kelly's voice found me, standing in the freezing rain, trying to see into the den.

"There was a door, a metal gate, but someone had stolen the padlock from it. That was how we got in."

I looked down at the smiling boy in the photograph. I felt his eyes meet mine. "I'm sorry Sam."

"Right! Time for another bottle." Kelly was up from the arm of chair and over to what she'd called her "Box of Delights". This time she produced a Pinot Noir and a box of chocolates. "What? I packed for every eventuality."

Kelly set about opening the chocolates. "Today you get all the orange creams for dragging me here."

"Thanks for bringing me."

"You didn't really drag me, Cam. I came here to make sure the fucker was actually dead."

*

We didn't drink everything in the Box of Delights, but we gave it our best shot. In the end, Kelly had fallen asleep halfway through a mumbled sentence, her words trailing off into a gentle snore. We'd put our coats over a chair in front of the fire to dry. I tucked her in with hers.

I was drunk. Either the house had begun to lean or I was, as I pulled myself, still carrying my mug of wine, through the doorway and out into the hall. The walls in the hallway were papered with woodchip wallpaper. My fingers slid over it like a blind man reading Braille instructions to get him to the toilet. I leant into the wall as I climbed the stairs. It was cold, wet, everything in the house felt damp.

As I turned the corner onto the first landing I stopped. Just for a moment I thought I'd seen myself, seven years old, standing at the top of the stairs, cold and scared, listening to my parents fighting underneath me.

It wasn't me. Just shadows shifting as I swayed unsteady on my feet. My tired, drunk eyes playing tricks on me. The sense of foreboding that I'd felt outside seemed to have followed me into the house. Now it waited in the shadows, stronger, darker than before, as if I was closer to remembering, closer to giving it form.

After I'd peed, I poured away the rest of the wine from my mug and filled it with water. I downed the water and filled it again. I leant on the sink. Both Kelly and I would suffer in the morning.

The bathroom was next to my old bedroom and, although I'd intended to go back downstairs, I'd found myself drawn into the doorway of my old room. The light from the hallway picked out the small white chair in the middle of the room. Had he really sat there, in his empty house, mourning our loss? If he'd lied about the drinking, had he lied about everything else? Why leave me the house if he wasn't sorry? Surely he'd known I'd come back, find out the truth?

Kelly had tried to stop me, protect me from seeing my room, from the memories. Now there was no one standing in my way, no one to protect me. I stepped through the doorway and into the bedroom.

I didn't switch on the light. Doing that felt like it might somehow spook the truth, scare away the answers I was seeking.

Time had stood still in my room. It hadn't been abandoned, it wasn't covered in dust, it had been kept, cleaned, he'd looked after it. If he hadn't hoped we'd return one day, why go to such an effort to preserve it? I stood over the white chair. I knew he'd been wrong, knew he'd been a monster, but now I wanted to know if there was more. I wanted to know his perspective, to see from his point of view. Maybe then I'd get the answers I needed. I lowered myself into the chair.

It was wet, a thin layer of water coated the small wooden chair. It soaked into my clothes, spreading, reaching like icy fingers around my legs. My Converse slipped on the carpet in front of me and water, pressed out by my weight, slithered around my shoe. I raised my other foot and dropped it back to the floor. My legs were heavy, booze adding kilos to them. More water spread around my foot. The carpet was waterlogged. I looked around the room. I'd not noticed it before but a sheen of water seemed to cover everything. From my low perspective I could see the moon's light reflected on the water covering the surface of the shelves that held my books, my toys. All the time the cold bit deeper into my legs.

I pushed hard on the arms of the chair, trying to lift myself up, to get away from the cold. Drunk and awkward, I lost my balance. My feet slipped on the wet carpet and I fell forward against my old bed. I threw out a hand to break my fall. It took my full weight, pushing hard down on the Superman bedspread, pressing into the mattress beneath. Freezing water spilled from the bed, pouring between my fingers, spreading and swallowing my hand.

Panicking, I snatched my hand back. The bedspread, the mattress, were soaked, filled like a sponge, with icy water. I fell against the side of the bed, its frame jamming into my ribs. The pain winded me. I hauled myself backwards over the slick carpet, away from the waterlogged bed.

I sat in the doorway trying to catch my breath, watching the bed. Water dripped from the bedspread onto the floor, spreading out a black pool on the carpet.

*

By the time I could breathe again, the shock of the freezing water had begun to wear off. The dripping from the bed had slowed and eventually stopped, the water I'd disturbed falling still once more. Leaning into the door frame for support I pulled myself off the floor. I was soaked, shaking from the cold. I grabbed a towel from the bathroom and threw it onto the pool of water that had spread under my old bed. Then I closed the door on that room and headed back downstairs.

The fire was fading in the lounge. I threw the last of the shattered table on it in the hope it'd produce enough heat to stop my shaking. Kelly had thrown her coat/makeshift blanket off in her sleep. I tucked it around her once more. I wanted to wake her. To tell her what had happened, but what *had* happened? It'd rained solidly for at least a day and the old farmhouse's roof had sprung a leak? Was that really a surprise? And was it worth forcing Kelly to face her hangover any earlier than she really needed to?

I pulled my chair close to the fire and wrapped myself in my coat. I felt the warm fabric slowly drawing the cold from my body, my clothes drying, my shirt no longer sticking to me. I watched the pieces of table glow and smoke in the hearth, the smell of the wood burning took me back to Kelly's house. I felt my body relaxing, my eyes closing, booze rocking me gently to sleep.

*

About an hour after I'd fallen asleep, I felt Seth pull himself up onto the chair with me. He climbed under my coat and fell asleep against me.

*

When I woke, Seth had gone. My shirt was cold, clinging to me where I'd dreamt he'd been. The warmth had gone from my coat and the fire had reduced the pieces of the table to smouldering ashes. But it wasn't the cold that had woken me. Booze had eased me under but it had been *his* letters that had dragged me back to the surface. If I wanted answers, if I wanted to understand, I had to read them.

*

I sat at the kitchen table looking at the pile of letters. I'd doubled an elastic band around them; it pinched into the envelopes, tearing them at the edges. They might be full of lies, like the lie that he'd stopped drinking, but I'd never know unless I read them. I'd never be able to have that conversation with him now, this was the only way he could speak to me. I pulled at the band, stretching and unwinding it from the bundle of letters.

I'd read the first one so I put it to one side. I tore open the second. I could smell the cigarette smoke as I pulled it from its envelope.

It began in a similar tone to the first one: apologetic, remorseful. He'd moved on to describing his life on the farm. Maybe he'd hoped to strike up a conversation. He asked if I had more roles on the horizon and told me he was proud of me. I stopped. The rain beat constantly against the kitchen windows. It had been relentless since we'd arrived. I watched it stream against the black glass and I thought of Sam. I thought of his face pressing against the dark pane, looking in. Are you coming out to play?

I looked back to the letter. He'd finished the second one much the same as the first, saying he was glad he'd found me and he'd write again soon. He didn't. The next letter had come six months later.

Something was different about this one straight away. I'd not noticed it before, because I'd only given it a passing glance when I'd received it, but the handwriting on the envelope was larger, untidy. It looked rushed. I tore open the letter.

It began with another apology. This time for not being in touch for a while. He said he'd been ill. In hospital. He didn't go into details. He told me he'd been waiting to see my character again on EastEnders and told me that, if they had any sense, they'd make me a regular. He'd hoped I was well and that everything was going well for me. About halfway down the page the letter changed.

His handwriting changed. It was larger, messier, like the writing on the envelope. *Son, you won't believe what I have to tell you.* My first thought was that he'd been drunk when he'd written that. The rest of the line was blank, as if he'd debated what to write and returned to the letter later. *He's found you.* He'd written it twice. *Maybe when I found you.* Outside the rain hammered against the kitchen window. *Maybe I did something. Somehow made him aware.* It wasn't the drink fuelling the letter, it was fear.

On one line he'd written: *I've seen him in the house.*

Then underneath he'd written: *PLEASE SON. I'VE SEEN HIM AT NIGHT. I WAKE UP IN THE NIGHT AND HE'S HERE!* The line was scrawled. All caps. Fast. He'd been terrified. I wondered if he was sick from the alcohol. If he'd been hallucinating.

He wants you to come home. He says he's been waiting all these years. He says you left and you didn't tell him where you were going. The cold at my side made my skin crawl. It seemed to spread from where my shirt clung to me, wrapping itself around me. I pulled the shirt away from my skin but it was too late. The cold had already eaten into me. *Sam. It's Sam Adams, Cam! He's been here. At night.* My heart hammered in my chest. The horror that I'd first felt when we were outside, that had followed me back to the house, had a name now. The letter ended abruptly, the last line scrawled, desperate. *Oh God! He's terrible! I can't bare it!*

I sat at the table staring at the letter in silence. I wanted to bolt. To race to the lounge, shake Kelly awake and run. But I couldn't. I daren't move, daren't look up from the letter in front of me. I read the last line again and again. I could hear the rain beating on the glass of the kitchen window. *Are you coming out to play?* It hurled itself at the glass.

I folded the letter closed, as if hiding his words could somehow take back what I'd read.

He'd written to me twice more before he'd died. I looked at the next letter sitting on the table. My name and address had been written all in uppercase. It reminded me of the single, desperate line he'd written in caps in the letter I sat holding. I should have stopped, ignored the rest of the letters.

I picked up the fourth letter and opened it.

I thought about how I'd dreamed of Seth climbing up next to me on the chair. How I'd woken with my shirt wet, clinging to my side.

The fourth letter was short. Two paragraphs scrawled on the paper, two weeks after the last letter. *He finds a way in. Every night. He's there in the darkness. Any patch of darkness. I'm drinking again son. I can't sleep without it. He hides. He waits until I'm asleep. I can smell him before I see him. The smell of rot. He's death. He's death come for me! Please! I'm sorry!*

My stomach turned over. I felt the night tighten its grip on the farmhouse. There was so much darkness in the house. So many places to hide. The last paragraph he'd written was neater. Like a moment of calm in the middle of his insanity. But what it said terrified me more than anything else I'd read.

We've done a deal. Done a deal. He says if you come home he'll leave me be. Son he says if you come home he'll leave me be. It's you he wants. He's here now.

I dropped the letter on the table. I jerked back, my chair screamed on the tiles of the kitchen floor. I stood up, I had to be away from those letters. My eyes darted around the room. Was he here? Could Sam really be here now? Before I realised what I was doing, I was looking straight at the kitchen window.

"Sam?"

*

I heard Kelly stir in the lounge; the sound of my chair scoring across the tiles must have woken her. I looked away from the black pane. I'd expected to see Sam's face, see his sad eyes looking in at me. But it couldn't be! Not after all this time! Sam was dead. He'd been dead for 23 years. Whatever my father's booze-addled mind had seen. Whatever he'd hallucinated. It wasn't Sam. In the lounge, I thought I heard Kelly mumble something. Was she talking to someone? Then Kelly started to scream.

I ran from the kitchen into the hallway. The door to the lounge was shut. I hadn't shut it when I got up to read the letters! I made to grab for the door handle. And I stopped. I couldn't do it! I couldn't open it! After everything I'd just read, I couldn't open the door, couldn't face whatever was in there with Kelly!

"Kelly!" I shouted. In the same instance her screaming stopped.

I stood in the hallway watching the door, desperate to hear Kelly's voice, for some reassurance that she'd just had a nightmare, that everything was OK, that I'd just scared myself with the letters he'd written.

No sound came.

"Kelly?" I called quietly at the door. "Kelly, please…" The lounge stayed silent.

He's terrible! I can't bare it! His words held my hand back from the door handle. What had he meant? He'd said that Sam hid in the dark, waiting for him to go to sleep. Had he been watching us? The light from the fire had lit less than half the room. So many places to hide. I could feel the panic rising through my body. I forced myself to grab the doorknob.

It was freezing cold. So cold that I had to stop myself immediately snatching my hand back. It burned my skin, bleeding into my fingers, spreading. I twisted the handle and pushed the door quickly away from me. It swung into the darkness that filled the lounge.

I stood in the doorway holding my numb hand in the other, trying to work the cold out of my fingers. It clung to me though, the same cold I'd felt at my side when I'd woken up.

"Kelly?" I called, my voice small, afraid of what might hear me.

No one answered.

I stepped forward into the dark lounge. The smell stopped me in my tracks. *I can smell him before I see him. The smell of rot.* That was what he'd written. Spoiled meat. It made me want to gag. I'd smelt it before. Sometimes you'd be walking by the lakes and it'd find you. The smell of something dead, a rotten fish washed up against the bank. I remember one time it was a deer. Fish had eaten its eyes from their sockets. It was the smell of something bloated, swollen with water and decay, peeling skin and putrefying flesh. The smell hit the back of my throat. I turned away, holding a hand over my mouth and nose, trying to stop myself from retching. Panicking, I swept my hand fast along the wall trying to find the lounge light switch. The wall was wet, slippery.

Come on! Come on! I hugged the wall as if somehow pressing myself into it might protect me from the darkness.

Finally I found the switch and hit it. The bulb flickered on above my head, sending the darkness scurrying for the edges of the room. Kelly's coat was on the floor in front of the chair she'd been sleeping in. Kelly was nowhere to be seen.

*

I sat in the kitchen, at the table, with the letters folded away, back in their envelopes. Out of sight, definitely not out of mind. Once I'd realised Kelly wasn't in the lounge I'd been through the house switching on every light, every lamp I could find, checking every room. Her car was still in the driveway. She hadn't driven anywhere. How could she have gotten out of the lounge? I'd heard her screaming! She'd been right there! I was by the door and no one had come past me.

I sat there for hours. I thought about calling the police, but what would they do? Would they even believe me? The whole thing was madness! Just a day ago I'd been arriving from London, staying with Kelly and Jack. Everything had been so normal. And now this?

The smell that had overwhelmed me in the lounge had spread. It seemed to fill the whole house. It wasn't as strong as it had been confined to that small front room but now it was everywhere. Now it waited for me in every room of the house.

It was almost seven. It'd be at least another hour before the sun came up. I hoped that with it would come answers. That Kelly would somehow be back, with an anecdote about a drunken adventure that would perfectly explain what had happened. I sat at the table, entirely still. A part of me believed that if I stayed perfectly still he wouldn't find me. That he'd pass me by. That I'd somehow blend into the background for long enough to escape him. It was the thinking of a seven year old boy. The terrified seven year old I'd left here 23 years ago. *It's not my fault!* I wanted to shout. *They took me away. It's not my fault!* I knew he was coming. It was just a matter of time.

*

Still the night held the house in its black grip. Still the rain fell without ending. I'd read four out of the five letters he'd written to me. The final one sat, unopened on the table in front of me. I must have looked at it for almost an hour before I finally picked it up.

The envelope was damp to the touch. The ink on the front, my address, my name, were smudged and barely readable. If I'd just read the letters when I'd received them none of this would have happened! We wouldn't have come back! Kelly wouldn't be missing—I felt my stomach flood with cold water, the terrible horror of the situation demanding I face it. Panic wrapping its black fingers around my heart, I tore open the final letter.

I held the wet paper in my hands. The feel of it repulsed me. I wanted to rip it to pieces, to tear it to shreds. Instead, I pulled the wet folds apart. What I saw made me cry out. I dropped the letter onto the table. Scrawled on the page was a single sentence in handwriting that resembled a child's. It read: *Come out and play.* It was written again and again. *Come out and play. Come out and play. Come out and play.*

I screamed when I heard the voice: "Come out and play!"

*

Kelly was at the kitchen window.

"Come out and play," she called. Behind her, the sun had begun to rise, just enough light to outline her, just enough that I could see her expression. Utter terror. Her eyes were wide

31

with fear. Tears streaked her cheeks. "Come out and play" she called again.

"Kelly?" I got up from the table, the same place Sam had found me every day during that long summer, every morning at 8am when he'd stood at the kitchen window and called. "Come out and play!" Kelly's expression scared me but her voice, her voice was haunted, terrible. It was filled with an awful resigned calm that was completely at odds with the fear her face portrayed.

Kelly looked off to her side. Was someone out there with her? Were they forcing her to say the words? If they were they were hidden, beyond the edge of the window. I watched, terrified, waiting for them to reveal themselves. Kelly's tortured expression looked back to me. "Kelly, please!" Did she even recognise me?

Kelly spun slowly away from the window, turning her back on me, and began to make her way across the garden towards the orchard.

"Kelly, no!" I shouted after her.

"Come out and play." Her words drifted lazily on the air, blending with the sound of the rain. Her arm was stretched out to her side, reaching out as if she were holding an invisible hand. Kelly looked down, her eyes connecting with the unseen figure that led her away.

"Kelly!" I shouted, "Kelly, stop!"

But she didn't turn back.

Whatever led her into the orchard, it was the height of a small child.

I stood at the kitchen door. I was completely paralysed by my fear! I watched Kelly disappear into the darkness under the cover of the apple trees. I had to do something!

But I did nothing. I watched her slip away. I was so utterly terrified that I couldn't force myself to open the door, to confront whatever might have waited for me in the orchard.

Like father like son, I thought.

Two cowards.

The thought crushed me.

I stood in the doorway as the sun slowly rose, looking into the orchard. I watched the darkness that swelled between the apple trees, diluted to a sunless grey. I watched, waiting for Kelly, but I didn't see her again. Was she watching me from the orchard, her face twisted by unimaginable fear? What had been controlling her? What had she seen that had driven her to such wide-eyed terror?

An hour must has passed before I dropped my hand from the back door's handle. I looked away to the kitchen clock. *No, it couldn't be!* It was almost 9am. I didn't want to believe it! Sam had come, just like he had every day that summer, at 8am.

*

As dawn stretched into morning, the words from his letters buzzed in my mind, growing louder, until I hunched, sat at the kitchen table, unable to hear anything else. *We've done a deal. Done a deal. He says if you come home he'll leave me be. Son, he says if you come home he'll leave me be. It's you he wants.* I balled my hands into fists. *It's you he wants.* Stop! Please stop! *It's you he wants.* Every muscle in my body was spring loaded, ready to explode. The buzzing grew so loud it became a scream, his words filling my skull, drilling, screamed by an awful, shrill voice. They filled the whole room, they filled the whole house! I couldn't hear if someone was coming. I couldn't hear if he was coming, I couldn't hear anything but the words!

It's you he wants.

I slammed my hands on the table. Stop! I swept the letters onto the floor. STOP! The letters stuck to the wet lino; the thin layer of water that covered the kitchen floor bled into them, smearing the ink, warping his words. I knew what I had to do. I started to laugh. It was insane! The whole situation was insane! That just made me laugh harder. It was a black laughter. It rose up through my body like a breath released underwater, forcing itself to the surface and exploding. It hurt but I couldn't stop it. He'd done a deal with some thing that had crawled out of the lake! That was impossible, wasn't it? Wasn't it? "Well, it didn't work for you! Did it? *Did it?*" I shouted. He'd done a deal and no one had listened. Had it come for him? Had it sucked the life from him in return? Its terrible form torturing him, lurking in the dark, night after night until he drank himself to death?

Had it killed him to get to me?

I couldn't remember. I couldn't remember the end of that summer. Sam's disappearance, his body being dragged from the lake. Had I seen him again, after he was dead? Had I seen the same thing that had haunted my father? Something decaying, something rotting but yet still somehow alive? Had I blocked it all out because it was too terrible to face?

I shivered. Where had all the water on the floor come from? It seemed to be growing deeper around my feet. As I moved, ripples spread away—or were they following me, trailing after me, waiting to drag me down to some dark, airless place?

It's you he wants.

It might not be too late for Kelly.

I knew what I had to do. I knew and I wasn't laughing any more. Now I was just numb. Resolved. I walked to the back door, opened it and headed out into the rain.

*

34

I followed the path that Kelly had taken. I walked to where I'd seen her disappear among the trees. Rotten apples split beneath my feet, their flesh oozing from their skins, the smell of decay was thick on the cold air. I could taste it as I breathed.

I looked between the trees for any sign of Kelly. I didn't expect to find her. Sam had led her away. She was his to bargain with. He wouldn't give her up so easily. All that lurked between the trees was the sullen grey air of another waterlogged day.

The rain had eased to a seemingly endless mist that hung in the morning air. It followed me through the gate like a ghost and stretched out over the fields before me. It spread over the lakes, making it impossible to see where the sky ended and the water began.

I trod through the stubble remains of the year's corn crop until I found myself standing by the low flint wall. The last barrier between me and the den in the reeds. I stood behind the wall and scanned the shoreline in the distance. At first I thought it had gone. It'd been two decades. It was entirely possible that it had been knocked down, moved to make way for a visitor centre. When I finally saw it the numbness I had felt was gone immediately. I cried out in fear.

The den had been overtaken by the reeds that had surrounded it. They had massed around it, much thicker than I remembered them being, a thousand slender figures converging on our den. They had grown so tall, they twined and twisted around one another, completely covering the front of the building. They had stretched up onto the roof of the den, as if they were slowly inching to consume it, drag it back down into the lake where it could do no more harm.

I focussed on the reeds, trying not to look at the den itself. Trying not to allow my eyes to draw along the moss covered walls, to the doorway, to the darkness that swelled beyond it. The voice was quiet, slick, it seemed to slither through the mist to find me, "Coooome and plaaay," it called. It wasn't Kelly's voice. "Cooome and plaaay."

I wanted to cover my ears. To stop the voice getting in. I wanted to turn and run as fast as I could back to the house. But if I ran, what would happen to Kelly? I couldn't leave her behind. I'd no choice but to go on. I was crying as I climbed over the flint wall and stepped down into the mud. Now nothing stood between me and the den. Nothing stood between me and whatever called to me from inside.

I looked at my feet as I approached, trying not to look up through the doorway into the den. I was seven again, a terrified child even now trying to deny what was happening. Ahead of me, something moved in the darkness. *Slithered?* "Please…" I pleaded pitifully.

The metal gate still stood ajar in the doorway. It was covered in rust now. It reminded me of metal hauled up from a shipwreck. I stopped in front of the den.

"Please, Sam. I'm sorry." My voice was weak. "I'm sorry that I left. I didn't know…" My words were hoarse and broken. Another movement came just beyond the gate, something wet squelched in the dark.

I could smell the same rotten smell that had filled the lounge. It grew stronger, closer. The mist seemed to be growing colder, thicker, closing in around me, the rest of the world ceasing to exist, only the den ahead of me now, only the inevitable in front of me.

I stepped forward through the doorway and into the black.

*

The reeds had completely covered the slit of a window into the den. I stood in the cold, dark room. The ceiling was low, I could feel it close above me. The room stank of death. Somewhere I could hear dripping. I couldn't move.

I waited for my eyes to adjust to the darkness.

I saw it move, low, close to the wall. I heard its rotten feet stick to and peel off of the concrete. Sticking and sucking as they carried its weight around the edge of the room. "Youu caaame." Its words were distorted, slow, wet air sliding over what remained of its rotten voice box. "I kneeew... I kneeeew..."

"I'm sorry Sam. I'm sorry."

I couldn't move. I stared at the wall hoping that it would stay away from me. "Plaaaay now... Plaaaay wiiith uss". It slurped at the liquid that spilled from its mouth.

I could see it on the edge of my sight: a black mass, moving awkwardly, low to the ground like a hunched old man. I stared straight ahead. "Plaaaay with usss" it hissed. As it moved its rotten joints cracked, bone scraping on bone in wasted sockets.

Then it was in front of me, its stench so overpowering that I couldn't breathe! *Please! Please, anything but this!*

I couldn't help it. I looked down. I looked down at Sam's animated corpse, his swollen, rotten form watching me with milky, dead eyes. But it wasn't the terrible bloated thing that had once been my friend that made me scream. It was the second form, the second thing that pulled itself from the darkness. This one was larger, older, it had been in the water even longer than Sam. It had pulled him from the bank all those years ago. Held him under. Kept him for itself. "Plaaay nooooow... Plaaaay nooooow!" Sam demanded from the ground.

As the larger one wrapped itself around me I started to scream.

*

On the 28th October 2016 Kelly Reeves was found wandering on fallow farmland below Lower Way in Thatcham, Berks. She had no memory of how she'd arrived there and was taken to the Royal Berkshire Hospital where she was found to be suffering from hypothermia.

She later gave a statement to police where she explained that she had been visiting her late father's house with her brother. That they had consumed a large amount of alcohol, after which she had no recollection of further events. The whereabouts of her brother, Campbell Miller, are currently unknown.

<u>A bit about the true story behind Did You Forget About Me?</u>

I grew up in Thatcham, Berkshire. The places in this story are all actual locations from my childhood. I remember, when I was about the same age as Cam and Sam, Glen (my best mate at the time) and I used to play in our own 'Den in the reeds'. It was a birdwatching station like the one in the story, a cold concrete box, with a slit of a window in its front and a metal gate in the doorway that someone had broken the lock off of. In the early evening we'd wander along the paths that ran along the banks of the lake, stopping to try and skim stones off the water. I could never get the hang of skimming. Glen was a natural at it though. Sometimes during our dusk strolls we'd find something the lake had washed back in, bobbing in the shallow water against the bank. Cam mentions seeing a deer once. That really happened.

For a long time there had been stories of a black figure who'd hide along the bank, something that slithered among the reeds, waiting to pull passers-by into the lake and drown them. I'd heard it called The Bloated Man and The Shore Creeper. There were stories that it was a construction worker who'd killed himself while the gravel pits were being flooded and turned into lakes but there were also much older stories that said that the Bloated Man had drown in the River Kennet and had hauled himself into the lakes years later because they constituted a better 'feeding ground'.

I'd forgotten all about those stories until last summer when I read an article that claimed that a drone, shooting for Google maps, had photographed something black, larger than a dog, moving along the shoreline of Jubilee Lake at sundown on a summer's evening. The images are intriguing and also pretty inconclusive, however, they transported me immediately back to those warm summer evenings, gnats swarming over the water of the lakes, the smell of the insect repellent I kept in my bag and the occasional, creeping sense that we weren't the only ones walking the bank at sunset.

Andrew Cull, Melbourne, December 2016.

HOPE AND WALKER

1.

We were both 10. But he was dead. And I sat drawing him.

I grew up in Hope, NT, a small town founded in the dying days of the gold rush. The gold rush had died but Hope had, stubbornly, refused to.

"If you live in Hope, stubborn's in your blood," Dad had once said.

We had a pub, the Clayton Family's General store, a servo and two funeral parlours. The school run was a 20k drive to the closest town, or a "bus and blisters" as Old Man Clayton used to laugh and say when we stopped in to buy a bag of Redskins on the way home.

You might think that having two funeral parlours in a town didn't speak well of your prospects in Hope but, save for some notable exceptions, which I'll come to in a bit, we had a pretty healthy mortality rate. We'd had our fair share of successes too. We had a movie director hailed from Hope, and Old Man Clayton had been an Olympic swimmer in his day. I guess if you grow up in the desert you're going to want to get into the water as often as you possibly can, and that had certainly paid off for him.

You might also be thinking that having two funeral parlours had come from the dying days of the gold rush, but if you were thinking that you'd be wrong again. Twenty years ago, Grandpa Walker and Bob Ryan had had such an almighty blue (it'd been brewing for some time) that the *Walker/Ryan Funeral Directors* had split apart and become *Walker and Son Funeral Directors* and *Bob Ryan's Family Funerals*.

After that, save for firing daggers at one another across the room at Town Hall meetings, the Walkers and the Ryans had had little to do with each other. When Grandpa Walker retired, Dad had taken over the business and when Grandpa Walker passed away (some two weeks after retiring), the town had held the biggest funeral it had ever seen. Even Bob Ryan showed up to pay his respects.

Being funeral directors was all I'd ever known our family to do, so it never seemed strange to me when the van pulled up to the back of the house and I'd look down from my bedroom window to see Dad and Pete unloading the stretchers and bags. I'd watch them opening the cellar hatch and then carrying the bodies solemnly down into Dad's workshop under the house.

There were two entrances to the workshop, one from outside via an old wooden bulkhead, and one from a small door under the stairs in the main hallway of the house. Both were kept locked at all times. Ever since Grandpa Walker had converted the house into his business it'd been a home secondary to being a funeral parlour. We lived upstairs for the most part with the downstairs divided between Dad's office, the casket showroom and the Chapel of Rest.

Downstairs wasn't out of bounds but Mum would often shoo me upstairs if she caught me on the ground floor during office hours. Dad, on the other hand, encouraged me to stop by when I got home from school, to tell him about my day and, if I felt generous, to share my Redskins. We'd sit in the office, chatting and laughing. For a family that dealt with death every day, we were generally a happy bunch.

Mum and Dad never argued much. Although… they did have a huge row one time when I was seven. I'd been playing hide and seek with Dad when he'd gotten a call from a customer. He'd been on the phone so long that he'd forgotten all about the game. Two hours later Mum found me, asleep in a casket, where I'd hidden, while she was giving a tour of the showroom. It hadn't helped matters when I'd woken up with a start, sat bolt upright in the coffin and screamed. Mum and Dad lost that sale to Bob Ryan and it was quite a while before I showed my face downstairs again.

Dad was always happy to talk about the business with me. He didn't want me to be afraid of what he and Mum did, the way some of the kids at school were.

"Death's just a part of life, Em," he'd say. "No one knows for sure what happens to us after we die, but it's a difficult time for everyone, and me and your Mum try to make that time as painless as we can for the people who hire us."

Grandpa Walker's explanation was a bit more blunt: "No one stuffs up dying. That's the easy part. But it's easy to stuff up a funeral. We make sure that doesn't happen." I'd heard him telling Dad once.

Sometimes, when Dad and I were sitting chewing Redskins on the porch (we'd stopped our office meetings after the whole casket incident), Dad would look off into the distance and say, "You know, I should really update that old sign of ours. *Walker and Daughter*. What do you think?"

"She can make that decision when she's a bit older than eight!" Mum had called out through the open office window behind us.

Dad was never going to get rich being a funeral director. Especially in a small town like Hope. Hope people were sure stubborn. They'd refused to move and let the town die after the gold rush, and most of them refused to go ahead and die themselves until they were a ripe old age. When they did, their families would either come see us or Bob Ryan's boy to get a funeral worked out. Who they went to see depended on who they'd sided with in the big Walker/Ryan blue. Yes, even years later we could generally predict who'd come to see us when someone in their family died and who'd go see Danny Ryan when the time came. Hope people were stubborn but they were loyal too.

Occasionally someone broke ranks, like that time I woke up in that coffin, or like the time Greaser Davies' son got killed in a motorcycle accident. Greaser Davies came to see Dad. Then he left to go see Danny Ryan. Later than night, Dad told me what had happened in their meeting.

Greaser Davies' boy Tommy had been a Hell's Angel. Greaser had wanted Tommy displayed in the Chapel of Rest in full leathers. That wasn't a problem, but when he'd continued on to say "…and on his Harley", Dad had stopped him.

"On his bike? In the Chapel of Rest?" Dad had repeated back.

Now, Greaser Davies loved his boy and his boy Tommy loved his bike, probably more than anything else in the world. The two of them had spent hours working on that Harley. They might have been Greaser's fondest memories of his son. So, it was understandable that he wanted the bike in some way involved in his son's service, but Dad just couldn't do it. It felt wrong to him, displaying Tommy's body propped up on his bike for the town to come look at. Dad didn't say it to Greaser, but it felt morbid, ghoulish to him, and he'd apologised but politely refused.

That might have been just as well because Danny Ryan accepted and, the day before the funeral, when Tommy'd been on display on his Harley, a group of his friends had broken into the Ryan Chapel of Rest, fired up the bike and taken Tommy for one last drunken two-up ride down Hope's Main Street. That would have been bad enough but, just as they turned off of Batman onto Main, Old Man Clayton had reversed out of his drive right into the path of Tommy's motorcade.

Well, Bear Adams, with Tommy on the bike behind him, swerves off the road and down the bank outside of the Stevens' place. The bike shoots back up the other side of the bank and slams into the fence in front of the house. Bear gets himself two broken legs out of this and Tommy's body gets thrown through the front window of Cal Stevens' house where his wife is sitting watching 60 Minutes. You can imagine the chaos that ensued after that.

For the next couple of months it seemed that no one went to see Danny Ryan to arrange a funeral and our phone never seemed to stop ringing. Now, Dad and Danny Ryan didn't hate each other the way Grandpa Walker and Bob Ryan had. They didn't talk, but the reasons the funeral home had split into two weren't really their reasons. Time went on and people in town had begun to suggest there was a very real chance that the whole Greaser Davies disaster could spell the end of *Bob Ryan's Family Funerals*. Danny had taken a loan at the bank but couldn't keep up the payments.

About the same time, I overheard Dad telling a family that he was very sorry but he was just too busy to take on their funeral, and recommending they ask Danny if he had any free appointments available. We didn't have anything booked in that week. The next week I heard Dad saying the same thing to another couple. We tightened our belts for a month or two and Danny started being able to meet his payments at the bank again.

A couple of months later, I saw Dad and Danny standing at the end of our driveway talking. I couldn't hear what they were saying but at the end of the conversation, when I thought Danny was going to make to leave, he stopped and held out his hand. Dad took it, and a Walker and a Ryan shook hands for the first time in 20 years. Unofficially, that was the end of the great Walker/Ryan blue. That didn't mean that Dad and Danny would become friends—too much time and water had passed under that bridge—in fact, we didn't see Danny around our place again until the winter when Mum died.

2.

No one knew about my trips into the Chapel of Rest.

I was seven the first time I saw an actual dead body. That might seem odd considering that for years I'd seen the van arrive at the back of our house and unload the many stretchers and bags that had passed through Grandpa Walker's, and then Dad's, workshop.

When Grandpa Walker died, so many people from Hope wanted to come by and pay their respects that Dad had to ignore the usual two hour slots for viewing a body, and in the end, he'd kept the Chapel of Rest open for two days straight to accommodate everyone. The first time I saw Grandpa Walker's body I was in a queue of family that couldn't move fast enough for Mum. I remember that the Thompson twins, Mary and May, had the same floral patterned dress on. I remember a curtain of fuchsias blocking my view, and then they were gone, and I was eye level with Grandpa.

Before I could say anything, or really register what was going on, Mum had gently but firmly taken my hand and pulled me along the queue away from the casket. The next thing I knew, we were back in the corridor outside the Chapel of Rest. Mum handed me a large paper bag filled with Redskins and told me I'd done really well. Well, that wasn't good enough for me, so I waited until the last people had left and I snuck back downstairs and into the empty Chapel of Rest to see Grandpa.

I pulled up a chair by the casket and started talking with Grandpa. It was a pretty one sided conversation, but, given that he had never been a great talker when he was alive, it wasn't much different to many of the chats we'd had before. Firstly, I apologised for having left so abruptly earlier in the day, then I told him I hoped he was OK with how things had worked out and that I'd miss him being around. Then I told him about my day and about the days that he hadn't been around to see. I told him that, under the circumstances, Dad was doing OK, so he needn't worry about that, and I told him that we'd never seen crowds like the ones who'd turned out to pay their respects. Then, and I don't know exactly why I did it, I raced back up to my room and I grabbed my sketchbook. I returned to Grandpa's side and I began to draw him. I drew him for hours, until I had what I thought was a good likeness of him, and then I said goodbye, stood on my chair, kissed him on the forehead, and left.

From then on, I drew every person who passed through our Chapel of Rest. I'd wait until the last mourners had left and I'd sneak in with my book and grey leads and begin to draw. As time went on the pages of my sketchbook grew thick with my portraits. While I drew, I talked to the person in the casket, and when I was done, I'd stand up on my chair, kiss them on the forehead and wish them well.

The dead always smelled the same, of the same flowers. I'd no idea what those flowers were but it got me to thinking that heaven was a huge field of blooms spreading as far as the eye could see. Dad sprayed the scent into the caskets before he lay the bodies into them but still that image stayed in my mind. One night, when I'd finished my drawing, I climbed up onto my chair and a voice shouted out from the back of the Chapel of Rest.

"What do you think you're doing?" Bailey Baker glared at me across the dimly lit Chapel.

"I… er…" How long had she been there? How long had she been watching me?

"What's that you're holding?"

She must have just come in. I wobbled on the chair, grabbing the backrest to steady myself. Bailey was in the aisle and approaching fast. It was her mum in the casket. Bailey's mum had had Bailey and then some years later she'd bought a dog which she'd also called Bailee. We all thought that was strange. I guessed she just *really* liked the name. Now Bailey was face to face with me. Standing on the chair I was tall enough to look her in the eye. "What were you doing?"

"I was saying goodbye." I told the truth.

"What's that?" She prodded at my sketchbook. And so I showed her.

And she started to cry. Then she hugged me.

Now *everyone* knew about my trips into the Chapel of Rest.

Word quickly got around about my portraits, and people who arranged their funerals with Dad began, quietly at first, to ask if there was any chance I might draw their loved ones before they were gone for good. Mum didn't like the idea but Dad asked me what I wanted to do. Now, I still don't know why I started to draw the dead, but I do know that my portraits seemed to help ease the pain of those who'd lost someone, and so I'd often be found in the evening, after I'd finished my homework, in the Chapel of Rest talking to our latest guest.

I never expected them to start talking back to me.

3.

A silence had fallen over Hope. A choked silence, as if no one knew what to say, or maybe talking made it somehow more real. It was shock. And all but one of us felt it.

Dad had given Pete the night off. He'd driven out to the hospital on his own and returned two hours later with the short stretcher and the bag that was too big for the body it contained. I watched him unload the bag and gently carry it in his arms down the bulkhead steps into his workshop. I crept downstairs and leant against the heavy wooden workshop door. I heard Dad crying while he worked. The only other time I'd heard that was when he'd had to get Mum ready for her funeral.

I'd not known Billy Jenkins all that well. I knew he had been a popular kid. So popular, that someone had stolen him away from the Saddler Memorial Park, done things to him, as Dad had said through gritted teeth, and then hit him on the head until he was dead. He'd been found propped up on the swings in the park. It'd been a still, quiet morning. Going to be 40 degrees by 11am. Old Man Clayton said he could hear Kelly Wilson's screams from his backyard. That was the morning mayhem had descended on Hope and the morning that struck the town mute.

Hope locked its doors. Old Man Clayton shut up his shop when he saw the reporters pull up out the front. The same went for the servo, the pub, and when Dad saw them swarming up the path outside our house he locked the door, pulled down the blind and we went upstairs for an early lunch. Hope didn't want to talk about it. Hope couldn't talk about it.

That evening Dad had gotten the call from the hospital. He'd explained and sent me off to bed early. He asked me if I wanted him to call Sally Barber to come babysit. I told him I was 10 now and I could look after myself. He'd smiled and kissed me goodnight. He watched me for a long time from the doorway before he left that night.

I must have fallen asleep leaning against the wall next to the door to Dad's workshop because I remember him carrying me back up to bed when he was finished for the night. He smelled of the flowers. I dreamt of Mum chasing me through those endless fields of blooms.

Once they realised that no one in Hope was going to talk to them, the news crews left town "to chase the next ambulance", as Old Man Clayton had put it, and Billy Jenkins' parents had come by to see Dad. There were no child-sized caskets in our showroom, we'd never needed one before. Dad would have to make a special order from the city. He set out straight after the Jenkins had left and drove the six hour round trip to collect the coffin himself. When he got back at 5pm, Danny Ryan was waiting for him. Between them they had little Billy Jenkins ready in the Chapel of Rest by 5.30pm, just as Dad had promised his parents. Danny hadn't just come to help. He'd brought with him a cheque. And he wasn't the only one. Hope didn't bury its children. It buried the old buggers who'd hung around too long anyway. Over that evening the town's people delivered enough money to Dad to pay for Billy's burial three times over. Dad gave every last cent to Billy's parents.

Billy's parents stayed with him that evening until 10pm when Dad closed up the Chapel. I could hear Billy's dad thanking him through my open bedroom window. I'd put my grey leads and my sketchbook under my bed and, once I heard Dad in the lounge room watching TV, I gathered up my tools and snuck downstairs.

This was different. It was different to all the times before. I stopped at the door to the Chapel. I didn't know why yet, but I was scared.

We were both 10. But he was dead. And I sat drawing him.

I'd dragged my chair as quietly as I could across the tiled floor of the Chapel of Rest, and, so as not to give myself away, I'd only turned on the lights right above the casket. Everything a foot or so behind my chair stayed in darkness.

It wasn't right. It was one thing to die of old age when you'd lived your life, but Billy was the same age as me. Even the smallest casket Dad had been able to buy seemed too big. It *was* too big. Children didn't belong in coffins.

Even after the cancer had taken Mum, after it had eaten her away to nothing, death still felt like it was something that happened to other people. But, seeing Billy lying there, it was suddenly in everything. It was in the darkness that had crept from the back of the Chapel of Rest, that now wrapped around me, like a great black hand, waiting to close over my mouth, stifle the scream I could feel welling in my throat. My heart hammered in my chest, like a tiny animal, alive inside me, trapped inside me, looking for a way to burst out. I almost dropped my grey leads and my pad and ran. But I didn't. Something stronger held me in the chair. I didn't run. Instead, I opened my mouth and began to talk to Billy.

"I'm sorry about what's happened to you, Billy," I said in a hushed voice. I wasn't being quiet because I was worried Dad would hear, it was fear that had stolen my voice. I flipped through the pages of my sketchbook looking for a fresh page to begin my drawing, but the book opened at one of my drawings of Mum and I found I couldn't turn the pages any more. I couldn't look away from my portrait of her. I could feel my face was hot, my throat tightening, tears welling in my eyes. Why couldn't she be here now? Why did the cancer have to kill her the way it did? It wasn't right.

Suddenly, I was struck with an overwhelming sense that someone was watching me. I spun around to look into the back of the Chapel of Rest, sending all my grey leads clattering onto the floor in the process.

The noise seemed huge. Had Dad heard that? The pencils hit the tiles and rolled, scattering, disappearing under the empty pews, like mice scrambling for the darkness. Then they were gone.

"Shit!" I sat on the chair watching the darkness that filled the back of the Chapel. The sense that I was being watched had faded, but I was still going to have to venture into the black that swelled around the rows of pews if I was going to get my pencils back. I should have left them there, left the Chapel and gone to bed. I would have done that if I'd known what was good for me.

I didn't.

I'd already done enough to draw attention to myself. I'd not heard any movement from upstairs, but I daren't turn on any more lights for fear of getting caught, so I climbed down from my chair and, with goose bumps and white knuckles I stood facing the darkness. I kept thinking of the night that Bailey Baker had caught me in the Chapel and half expected her to step from the pews in front of me, materialising out of the darkness, with an accusatory finger outstretched and ready to prod me, demanding to know, "What do you think you're doing?" That sense of being watched hadn't gone completely.

I took a deep breath and stepped into the dark.

I knew roughly where the pencils had rolled and so I

edged towards the pews until I caught sight of the first one. It'd come to rest a way underneath the first row of pews. I got down onto my knees and swept my hand across the dusty floor trying to reach the grey lead.

"Watch out for that huntsman!" the voice shouted. I tore my hand back, jumping away from the pew. Then I jumped up onto the pew. Spring-loaded, ready to run, I watched the tiled floor, waiting to see the spider emerge from beneath the seat.

The laughter that followed made my face flush. There was no spider! I'd been tricked! I turned to the voice, to Billy in his casket. "You... you dick!" I said, and then felt immediately bad that I was swearing at a corpse. "Sorry! Sorry!"

Well, that just made him laugh more. "Gotcha, didn't I?"

I didn't know what to say. Although I could hear Billy's voice, and he seemed to be able to hear me, the boy in the casket remained still, his eyes closed.

"How did you know I was afraid of spiders?"

"Isn't everyone?" Billy's motionless corpse replied. "Do you want to hear a story about spiders?"

"No, I, er..."

"OK, well, we were up in the woods, you know behind the Saddler Memorial? Yeah, well we see this huge spider, hanging, you know, in a web that's so thick you can't see all the way through it—you know spiders' webs never rot? They're the only thing on earth that doesn't. Anyway, we see this huge thing, it's the size of one of his hands. And he's got big hands." I could feel my skin twitching just thinking about it. I checked the tiled floor just to make sure no thick black legs were reaching out from the pew beneath me.

"Well, he reaches up and he grabs this thing in his hand. Its legs are reaching around his fingers, it's wriggling, but he keeps a hold on it. And then, he raises it up to his mouth and he takes a huge bite out of it! He bites this thing clean in half!"

I let out a small squeal of horror. "Yuuuuk!" and then again, "Yuuuuk!" as the thought of what Billy had just said played across my mind a second time. "No way! That didn't happen! Did it?"

Billy laughed again. "No! Ya goose! Who'd do something like that? That'd be messed up!"

"You're an idiot!" I said, and we both laughed.

"There was a huge spider though. Never seen one that big before. Weird how they get like that. When you think they're so small to start with. He said the same thing, you know. Never seen one like that before. It was a bit like seeing a single crow, you know how they're meant to bring bad luck."

The darkness in the Chapel felt like it had crept closer to us. The room seemed to shrink as Billy talked. His voice had changed. He wasn't laughing any more.

"Hey, you don't have a blanket about, do you? I'm freezing here." I didn't, but I took off my jacket and crossed to Billy's casket.

I really wasn't sure what to do. If Dad came in now and found me laying my coat over Billy, I didn't know how he'd react. But I couldn't ignore him, I couldn't do nothing after he'd asked. I tucked my jacket around his shoulders. I hoped it would keep him warm.

Billy didn't speak again after that. I sat with him for another hour until I couldn't keep my eyes open any longer. I drew him with a pen we kept for the Visitors' Books. I didn't want to go into the darkness to try and rescue the grey leads. They could wait until tomorrow. All the time I expected him to burst into conversation again the way he'd done before, but the Chapel stayed silent. Eventually, when I found my head nodding and my eyes closing, I pulled myself from my seat and headed over to the casket.

"Billy?"

Nothing. I leant in and kissed him on the forehead.

"Goodnight, Billy."
I left my jacket so he wouldn't get cold again.

5.

The thought had found me in the dark. I'd closed my eyes and it had been waiting for me. If the dead could talk, why talk to me now? Why not before? Why didn't Mum have anything to say to me? I'd drawn her. I'd snuck into the Chapel of Rest when Dad had thought I was asleep and I'd drawn her. I'd drawn her again and again until my eyes were sore from crying and my throat burned. I'd talked to her for hours and she hadn't said a thing. She hadn't had a thing to say to me. Why? Why didn't she have anything to say to me?

I cried myself to sleep.

The screaming woke me.

Dad! I ran into the corridor.

No, it wasn't Dad. His door was ajar. I heard him shift, rolling over in his bed and settling again. Couldn't he hear it? Couldn't he hear… it was Billy!

"Help! Oh no, help! Help!" he cried.

I raced to the top of the stairs, grabbing the bannister to stop myself from skidding over the top step and tumbling down to the next floor. I gripped the handrail as I jumped down the stairs.

"It's so dark! Help Em! Help me, please!"

"Billy! It's OK! I'm coming! I'm coming!"

I raced into the Chapel of Rest. I reached out to hit the light switch but it was already on. I'd thought that maybe Dad had turned the light out and Billy had woken scared in the dark. No, that wasn't it.

I turned to look and the coffin was gone. Oh no! Dad must have taken Billy back down to his workshop!

"Help me please! You've got to get me out of here!"

I raced across the corridor but I already knew there was nothing I could do. The door would be locked. It was always locked. I didn't even know where Dad kept the key.

I tried the door. I shook the handle. Let me in! But it was locked. All the time I could hear Billy screaming for help.

"Billy I'm sorry! I'm sorry Billy!"

I leant against the heavy wooden door listening to Billy's cries. I put my hands over my ears but I couldn't block the noise out. There was nothing I could do!

Get Dad. Wake Dad! That's what I'd do. I turned, and was about to race back up the stairs when I heard it. A window. One of the old ones in the Chapel of Rest. It had a metal frame that had warped over the years and it always made the same screech when anyone tried to open it. We knew about it and left it alone, but, when people came in for viewings, and it was hot, they always tried to force it fully open, and that was when it screamed.

I stopped dead. Billy had stopped screaming too.

In the darkness Billy's voice came, quiet, scared. "He's here, Em! Watch out! He's here!"

I didn't know what to do.

"Em! Hide, Em! Hide!"

I ran for the stairs. I'd just made it to the top when the door to the Chapel of Rest opened. I collapsed into a ball. Trying to press myself into the bannister, make myself as small as I could, hoping that whoever had broken in wouldn't look up the stairs.

I could hear him moving about in the corridor below me, agitated, pacing the hallway in the dark. I was sure he was going to round the foot of the stairs, look up and see me, then there would be nowhere for me to run. I couldn't move! I couldn't move!

I heard him try the door to Dad's workshop. He rattled the handle, gently at first, then with more force when he realised it was locked. Then he really shook it, with a violence that made me start and hug at my legs even tighter, willing myself to disappear. He must have known we were in the house. Maybe he didn't care if he woke us.

"Em?"

I spun to the voice. It was Dad! He'd been woken by the noise. Dad, stay there! Don't get up! Don't get up! Below me I heard *him* trying the lock again. Jerking the handle back, trying to force it open.

"Em? Is that you?" Dad's voice came again but this time it was right behind me. As I turned to look at him he must have seen how frightened I was because his tone changed completely. "Em? What is it love? What's wrong?"

Without turning back, I listened in the dark for the sound of the handle turning. I was sure that if we disturbed *him* trying to get to Billy he'd hurt us. Dad sat down on the top step next to me. He put an arm around me. "Is this to do with Billy?"

Dad could feel I was shaking. "It's OK Em. It's OK."

"No" I said quietly. I knew it wasn't.

"I found your jacket earlier. On the casket. You know that what happened to Billy has never happened in Hope before, don't you? It was something very, very bad but it isn't going to happen again. You understand that, don't you? You don't need to be afraid."

Downstairs I heard the window in the Chapel of Rest creak, grinding against its frame. Dad heard it too. "I could have sworn I closed all the windows earlier." He made to get up. I stopped him, hugging him, until I was sure that whoever had been in our house was long gone.

Billy didn't make another noise that night. I don't know if it was possible but it felt like he was hiding. Either way, I lay awake in bed, dreading his screaming starting again.

By morning my fear had gone. It had been replaced by another emotion. Anger. I was angry. I was angry about what had happened in our house and I was angry about what had happened to Billy. And it was that anger that drove me to do something really stupid.

6.

I was 10, so stupid was allowed. That morning, once it was light enough to see, I'd gotten on my bike and I'd ridden to the Saddler Memorial Park.

I didn't have a plan. I'd packed my grey leads (rescued from the floor of the Chapel) and my sketchbook and that was as far as thinking it through had gone.

It was another still morning, silent except for the hollow sound of the hoist rope knock, knocking on the flagpole as it shook in the breeze. The flag was down; it only got raised once a year as far as I knew, and that was on Australia day, when the whole of Hope descended on The Saddler Memorial for a huge BBQ. I sat on the swings and waited.

Before Billy had been found, where I was sitting, the park had been a popular spot for Hope people to walk their dogs. Since his death they'd found other routes to get their exercise. For the first two hours I didn't see another soul.

I was scared.

"Being scared's good," Grandpa Walker had told me once. "Stops us from doing stupid things."

It hadn't stopped me.

What did I think was going to happen? Did I think that Billy was somehow going to lead me to the killer? I was sure that what he'd remembered had been from the day he was taken. I was sure the *he* in his story was the same he who'd broken in our house the night before. So, what was I doing? Why come here? I was setting a trap. That was the plan I didn't want to admit to myself. I was setting a trap with me as the bait.

I heard the gravel under his feet before I saw him.

If you're going to start talking again, Billy, now would be a good time.

When Old Man Clayton reached the top of the hill and walked into the park, my heart sank.

"What are you up to, Missy?" he smiled.

Is it him, Billy? Is it him?

"You OK, kid?" He wandered over to the swings and sat down next to me. "Been a tough few days, huh?"

Is it, Billy? Don't let it be him.

"You know, I come up here every day Em, get my morning swim in the quarry. I hadn't missed a day in twenty years, but that morning, Maddie, she'd been crook in the night and so I stayed home to make sure she was OK. We're getting on now, so being sick's a bit more serious than it used to be." He looked down at his feet.

"That should have been me, Em. It should have been me that found him. Not Kelly. She's got young kids. How's she supposed to get that out of her head now?"

Billy didn't say anything. That was OK. I was sure it wasn't Old Man Clayton. He got up from the swing next to me. "You should go home, Em. Way things are at the minute, your Dad'll be worrying about you."

"I will, Mr Clayton," I lied.

Old Man Clayton wandered off along the path, down the hill, taking the long way round to get to the quarry. In the summer the teenage boys took a much shorter route to get into the water. Straight off the highest point at the back of the park, dive bombing into the cool depths below. Dad said they were idiots. One day one of them was going to hit the bank going in and that'd be the end of them. It was a fifteen foot drop. One time I'd stood on the edge and looked over. I'd felt like I was about to jump out of a plane. I was with Old Man Clayton, happy to keep taking the long way round.

It was early but already I could feel the heat of the day making me sweat. I fidgeted on the swing. I was a pale kid and being in the sun too long just made me red and raw. I wouldn't give up, though. I just felt sure that he'd be here, that he'd come back, back to where he'd snatched Billy, back to… the spider! The story that Billy had told me, if it was true, there was a huge spider in one of the trees in the woods behind the memorial. If it was true, that was the route he'd taken Billy before… I got up from the swings. *Come on, Billy. Talk to me. Tell me where to go.*

Nothing from Billy. I looked around the park. Trees on three sides of me. If they'd headed towards the water, they'd soon have run out of woods. It was pretty thin, you could see the edge from the path. He would have taken Billy deeper. *Think, Em, think!*

It wouldn't be to the left, that was where the boys went, with the girls, after they'd been in the quarry. I knew that because one time Bobby Flack (nickname: Plop) had said he'd take me up there. Dad had overheard and slapped him round the back of the head. He hadn't suggested it again after that. It wasn't left, so it had to be to the right.

Armed with my grey leads and my sketchpad I stood on the edge of the tree line trying to work up the courage to go in. I was afraid. Grandpa Walker would have told me that was a sign not to do something stupid. Actually, no, no he wouldn't. He would have been as angry as me, as everyone else in Hope. He would have been angry enough that he'd have marched into the woods in the dead of night if it had helped to catch the man who'd hurt Billy. It was morning now, not night. Coming up for nine. It was light and I pulled myself together and I stepped into the woods.

Three feet in and I was wondering if Grandpa would

really have gone into the woods alone. He'd probably have taken someone with him. I should have taken someone with me.

"Billy?" I called under my breath. "Billy? Can you hear me?"

Somewhere deeper into the trees I heard branches snapping. Away from the sun it was cold. I wanted to run.

I hadn't gone much further when I realised that I could no longer see the path where I came in. Trees had closed in around me on all sides. I wasn't lost, but I would be if I lost my bearings. I had to keep going straight so I could just turn around at the end and walk straight back out. But had I already turned off a straight course? I looked around trying to work out which way I'd come. Above me, the canopy had blocked out the sky. I spun a circle, panic jumping up from my stomach into my chest, then into my throat. When it made it to my mouth it'd be a scream. I stopped dead when I saw it.

Billy had been right. It was a huge spider. Its body was the size of a mouse, its legs seemed as thick as my fingers, only they were longer, they could reach further. It was so big it had caught a bird in its web. I couldn't take my eyes off it. I was afraid that if I did it wouldn't be there when I looked back and I definitely preferred knowing where it was.

"Fuckin' huge, isn't it?" I didn't turn around straight away. "Never seen one that big before." That was what Billy had said. Still I didn't turn around. If I did, would the spider be gone when I looked back?

"That was what Billy said," I said without thinking.

"What? What did ya say?"

Now I turned around. "That was what Billy said, wasn't it?"

I'd expected a man, old like most of Hope. But twisted. I'd imagined a monster. He couldn't have been more than sixteen. I doubted he'd even started to shave yet.

"Wha'?" He looked surprised. No, he looked scared. "Fuck you!"

I'd seen him about town. I think he was Pook Wilson's boy. He was skinny, wiry, his neck looked too thin to hold up his head. "You don't know what you're talking about!" he shouted.

I hoped someone had heard him.

Out of the corner of my eye, I thought I saw the bird twitch in its web cocoon. I turned to look, and that was when he dived forward and grabbed me. Locking his arms around me, he ripped me up off the ground. My legs ran in the air, the world stolen out from underneath them. Panicking, I kicked at his shins.

"You bitch!" he shouted.

He tried to dodge my kicks, shifting his legs, spinning around. I managed to catch the trunk of a tree as we spun. I stamped hard into it and we fell backwards… into the monster's web.

I felt the silk wrap around us. Panicking, he dropped me straight away. I fell awkwardly, my leg twisting underneath me, I slammed onto my knees. The pain made me cry out.

Behind me, I could hear him wailing. "Where is it? Where is it?"

I could feel the silk of the web on my arms. Was it on me? Both my knees were raw, blood and dirt where their skin had been. I was crying as I pulled myself up, peeling my knees from the forest floor.

I stumbled, grabbing at the nearest tree. My fingers gripped at its bark. I hauled myself around the trunk. Pushing off from it, I ran.

I didn't know which direction would take me out of the woods. I didn't care. I just ran. My blood thundering in my ears, my heart shaking my whole body, I ran. But he was faster. I heard his feet hammering into the hard ground behind me. I tried to dodge between the trees but his fingers caught at my waist, then they were his hands and then he'd rugby tackled me to the ground. We hit the forest floor hard.

He threw me over, spitting the words at me: "You fuckin bitch!"

He was winded, wheezing, trying to catch his breath. When he pulled himself together he was going to kill me. I was sure of it.

I realised that throughout everything I'd been clutching one of my grey leads in my hand. I'd dropped my sketchbook when he'd first picked me up but throughout the whole chase I'd gripped a single pencil tightly in a fist. Its end had snapped when we'd fallen but it was still sharp enough. I swung it as hard as I could, slamming it into the side of his face. I felt it stab right through his cheek, pinning his tongue like a fat slug.

I'd never heard a scream like that before. It was terrible. He jerked backwards, fast and awkward, as if he was trying to escape the pain. He was too late.

He seemed to scream blood. It poured from his mouth along with an awful wail that almost made me stop to help him. I didn't stop. I scrambled back to my feet and I ran.

If he got up now, if he caught me now he'd tear into me, his pain driving him, wild and cruel. Behind me, his terrible screams chased after me through the trees.

Then they were gaining on me. I couldn't help myself, I turned back to look. I couldn't see him for tree trunks but I could hear him. He was on his feet and running, his horrible, distorted cries reaching me first. Soon they'd be his fingers, then his hands pulling me down. Then he'd crack me open on the hard, cold ground.

I looked back ahead of me and that was when the ground ran out.

*

I'd run to the edge of the woods. The dirt floor dropped away in front of me, a cliff edge over the quarry below. But this wasn't where the boys ran and dive-bombed, laughing and shouting, showing off to the girls. This was higher, it wasn't sheer, rocks reached out from the bank, jagged, waiting to catch and shatter the bones of anyone stupid enough to jump.

I couldn't stop! I'd seen the drop too late. I screamed as I hit the edge… and I fell.

Dad had always said the kids jumping into the quarry were idiots. That one day one of them would hit the bank going down and that that would be the end of them. When he'd said that, he'd never imagined that that kid would be me.

Epilogue.

Before that night, I wouldn't have believed that the dead could speak either. Let alone tell stories.

Billy's story had led me to the Memorial Park, led me to find the giant spider, and when I'd heard his words come out of Pook Wilson's boy's mouth, I'd known they'd led me to his killer. Perhaps the dead couldn't choose when they spoke, or maybe they could only speak to put things right when something terribly wrong had happened to them. Maybe that was why Mum never said anything to me. Maybe she just couldn't.

The police picked up Pook Wilson's boy when he'd stumbled into the path of their car on the road outside the Memorial Park. At first they'd taken him to the hospital to patch him up but, when he couldn't explain why the doctors were pulling one of my grey leads out of the side of his face, they'd searched the woods and found my sketchbook. Then they'd searched his house and found Billy's cap in a box under his bed.

As for me? I'd hit the rocks falling down into the quarry. My arm had shattered in three places. Even if the fall onto the freezing water hadn't knocked me out, there would have been no way I'd have been able to swim to the shore.

If it hadn't been for Old Man Clayton, I'd almost certainly have drowned. He'd been getting set to go home when he saw me fall. He dragged me out of the water and performed CPR until I woke up briefly on the shore. I didn't wake up again until the hospital. I was two doors down from Pook Wilson's boy when I came to a second time.

My grey lead had taken such a chunk out of his tongue that he never spoke properly again. He never explained why he did what he did to Billy that day in the woods.

I got out of hospital on the morning of Billy's funeral. Dad had wanted me to stay in till I was fully recovered but I was Hope through and through, stubborn, pig-headed, and there was no way I was missing out on giving Billy a proper send off. The whole town turned out that day to pay their respects.

I'd hoped Billy might speak to me again, but I never heard another word from him after that night in the Chapel of Rest. After the service, I'd gone to Mum's grave and I told her all about what had happened. I guess I'd hoped she might have something to say once she'd heard my story.

I got home later that day to find a bunch of flowers on my bed. I still didn't know what they were called, but I knew their smell, that same smell of the endless fields of blooms I imagined running through with Mum.

No one ever owned up to buying those flowers for me. Dad had bought me a new set of grey leads and Billy's parents bought me an easel. It would be a while before the cast came off my arm, but they'd be waiting for me when I was ready to start sketching again. As to how the flowers got there... Well, you can talk amongst yourselves on that one.

Before that night in the Chapel of Rest, I wouldn't have believed that the dead could speak. Let alone tell stories. It'd be a long time before the dead would speak to me again. But that's another story for another time.

THE TRADE

1991.

That summer should have been filled with laughter, with slip n' slides in the yard, lazy afternoons lying watching ice cream clouds swirling through the blue sky, melting in slow motion. I watched a plane rising high above our house. From the ground it looked completely still, as if it hung suspended in the air, a model on a string. I wished I was on it, I wished I could escape. I was seven and that was the summer death stalked our home.

It began with the offerings.

Dad had opened the back door to have a smoke. I heard his swearing from my room,

"Jesus Christ! For fuck's sake!"

I put down the book I was reading, switched off the fan that whirred noisily, and edged towards my bedroom door. I leant against the door listening. This was how their fighting often started. I didn't want to get caught in the middle of it.

No one responded to Dad's shouts. After a time, I twisted the handle on my door and cracked it open enough to look out. I could see Dad standing by the backdoor. He was stood, wrapped in cigarette smoke, looking at something on the path outside.

He spotted me and raised a hand to stop me.

"Stay there, son."

I didn't stop. I saw the flies before I saw the thing lying by the back door.

It might have been a cat once, but now its body was

broken, mangled beyond recognition. Bones tore through grey flesh, the fluids of decomposition had spread a putrid outline around the carcass. Its intestines and stomach had been pulled from its belly and stretched like bloated worms across the path. The stomach had either swollen and burst as it had rotted, or something had eaten into it.

Dad waived the flies from his face. He lit another cigarette off his last. Normally I hated the smell of smoke, but that morning I was grateful of it. Underneath it, the smell of the thing baking in the sun, the stench of spoiled meat, caught in my throat. Looking at it, I noticed that the thing on the doorstep didn't seem to have a head. Instead, each end of it came to an abrupt, raw stop.

"Probably foxes dumped it. They eat the rotten meat. Bury their catches, come back later to dig them up and eat them. Bloody grave robbers."

I watched Dad take a shovel and scrape the remains of the corpse from the concrete. He carried it along the path, the smoke from his cigarette chasing behind him as if it were afraid he'd leave it behind, to the edge of the woods. There he threw it back in.

Our house was long and thin. It only had one storey, and so the rooms had been lain one after another in a trail stretching from our drive to the woods behind. Our yard was thin too, lasting as long as a cricket pitch before the woods stepped into its path and claimed the ground for their own again. Dad had always said he'd put a fence up around the yard, but he'd never gotten around to it. It wasn't unusual to be woken at night by the sound of a stray deer or foxes scratching around by the house.

I'd seen a documentary once where a wood had caught fire, and the animals of the forest had stampeded from the cover of the trees, tearing away from the danger. I imagined waking one night to find those woodland beasts charging through the corridor that was our house, a procession of all the animals the forest held. I loved being so close to all that wildlife. That was until I learned what else lurked in the woods behind our house.

*

I switched off the fan. I'd fallen asleep on top of the covers. It was too hot to lay under them. The fan wound down, its fins slowing, no longer churning the stale summer air that filled my room. Something moved outside. I heard it trampling the dry leaves that piled like yearlong snow drifts along the sides of our house.

The fan rattled to a stop and my room fell silent. I sat listening. The window by my bed was open: an attempt to draw some cool air into the room. Outside it was almost thirty degrees. There was no cool air anywhere. I leant close to the window and looked out into the darkness.

I sat watching the darkness for almost an hour. No further sound came. I lay down on the bed, the silence and darkness calling me back to sleep. I closed my eyes. That was when I smelt it.

The same awful smell of rotting flesh that had spread from the animal corpse Dad had found on the path. It poured into my room, reaching in through the window like a black hand, trying to force itself into my nose, my mouth! I clamped a hand over my mouth to keep the smell out and to stifle the scream that welled in my throat.

I kept my eyes shut tight, terrified of what I might see if I opened them. Eventually the smell began to fade. I waited for what seemed like hours before daring to open my eyes again. When I did the night had begun to recede. The sky had begun to lighten above. I shut and locked my bedroom window. That had been its second visit.

*

It would be at least two more days before there was a break in the heat.

Mum and Dad had been sleeping in separate rooms for some time. At first, they'd tried to hide their fighting from me. To begin with, maybe even they had thought that the feelings that drove them to anger might pass; the confusion and jealousy might fade. It didn't. Their fighting became more frequent, until the only thing holding them together was me.

Mum's scream jolted me awake. I jumped out of bed and ran to my bedroom door. I opened the door, just in time to almost run into Dad who came racing along the corridor to see what was going on. Mum stood by the back door, sheltering behind it from what she had seen outside. The smell stopped me in my tracks. This time it had left a dog.

Dirt pressed into its flesh, the dog had been buried, left to rot before being placed outside our back door. Its fur had shed, leaving large patches of bare skin, swollen against the liquefied meat underneath it. The head had been pulverised.

"Aaron, no!" Mum yelled to Dad when she saw me coming. Dad quickly grabbed me and whisked me back to my room.

He knelt to talk to me man to man, "Stay here buddy. Please." I nodded, wide eyed and terrified, and then I threw up.

*

Mum threw my old clothes in the wash basket. I stood in my underpants in the middle of the bathroom, quarantined to the centre of the room.

"I just got really hot" I said, embarrassed.

"It's OK to be scared. I was scared."

"You didn't throw up."

Mum put her hand on my forehead, "Maybe you've picked something up." She smiled, a warm, comforting smile. "You can't be sleeping well. I know I didn't last night. I heard you moving about."

I hadn't gotten out of bed the night before. I thought of the stench, of that awful smell reaching in through my window. Mum could see how scared I was.

"How do you think it got there?" I asked.

"Your Dad thinks it's foxes. They bury their kills, dig them up later on to eat them. Maybe it got scared off, left its dinner behind."

"Yuk!"

"Yuk indeed! They pick their noses too you know…" She smiled. She washed my face with a cool face cloth. "… and they eat that too!"

I screwed up my face in disgust.

"Eeewww!"

Mum laughed. I laughed too.

*

Outside the fly spun, a spiral flight path, bouncing off the window one, two, three times. Even it wanted out of the heat. There was no respite in my room. The fan churned the sweltering air. Despite the heat I kept my window closed and locked.

The wood surrounded our house on three out of four sides. We had trespassed into its domain. A path ran from the yard, past the sunroom, alongside my bedroom to the shed where Dad kept his tools. The sun was high and bright, casting black finger shadows through the shifting canopy onto the path below. They scratched back and forth, waiting to catch any unwary prey that should stray beneath them. I tried to picture a fox dragging the dog's corpse from the woods, along the path.

After Mum had cleaned me up, I'd gone into the lounge and taken the encyclopaedia (volume D – F) from the TV cabinet. I'd carried it back to my room and had begun reading everything I could find about foxes. The heat made my head swim. The words on the page seemed to sway as I read them. Foxes did bury their kills, to stop other animals stealing them. If that was the case, why would they bring them to our house, leave them for us like an offering?

I heard Mum shout at the other end of the house. Her shout was followed by Dad's, the heat making their already short tempers flare quickly. My head had begun to pound. I couldn't listen to them fighting again. If I stayed in my room, I was going to be sick for the second time that day. All I could think about was the cool shade of the wood. How even in the height of summer it was always cooler under the cover of the trees. I ran for my door, out into the corridor, and before I knew what I was doing, I was standing where Mum had been when she had screamed a few hours before.

Dad had cleaned away the remains of the dog. Likely thrown it back into the forest where it had come from. I could smell the bleach he'd used to wash down the path. The water had long since burned away in the heat. I hurried along the path into our back yard. There I stopped on the edge of the wood.

I could feel the sun burning the back of my neck, an angry voice urging me into the cool shade of the trees. I looked back to our house. I could hear Mum and Dad shouting, the hate they hurled at one another. I stood on the edge of our brown, dried up lawn and looked into the wood. And the wood looked back at me.

I froze. The heat of the summer day immediately drained from my body. I looked at my feet, too scared to look up and see what eyed me from the trees. I could feel its gaze locked onto me. Had it been waiting for me?

I couldn't move! I wanted to turn and run but my body wouldn't listen to me! In the split second we'd locked gazes, I was sure that what I'd seen wasn't a fox. Those eyes. The shape was wrong, they were too high off the ground to be an animal on all fours. Something moved in the trees in front of me. I stumbled backward and fell onto the lawn.

The pain of the fall brought me to my senses. I rolled onto my front and, grabbing handfuls of grass, I pulled myself to my feet and ran.

I ran for the house, tumbling down the path and slamming into the backdoor. I burst into the house, spinning and slamming the door behind me. I tried to pull the bolts shut, but they were old and stuck. Dad was standing in the corridor. The house seemed hotter than ever.

"What's going on?"

"I… I…" I managed that much before I passed out.

*

I remember the cold, the gentle pressure on my forehead. I thought the cool change had come, that the heatwave had broken. But, when I moved I could feel the heat returning, my clothes sticking to me. Mum looked down at me and smiled.

"Hey you."

She took the face cloth from my forehead and dipped it into the bowl of cold water on the arm of the chair.

"It's OK. You've got a fever."

We were in the sunroom. The amber light of the dying summer day poured through the large windows. The air was heavy and stale, the windows specked with dirt and dust, the history of our summer baked onto the panes.

When I try to remember Mum's face, we are always in that room. The setting sun is so bright it hurts my eyes. I can still see its glow through my eyelids. When I open my eyes again, Mum has leant forward, her red hair a curtain of gold protecting my eyes from the glare. I can remember every word from that evening but, no matter how hard I try, I can't remember her face.

"How are you feeling?"

"Hot."

Mum wrung out the face cloth and placed it back on my forehead. I closed my eyes again.

"Well, I guess this proves that it takes more than a fox's lunch to shake your nerves of steel. I think you were sick earlier because you're, well, sick."

Somewhere in the dark I could hear pipes knocking, a rattling approaching. I opened my eyes.

"That's the heating. It blew a fuse while you were asleep. It came on and it's stuck on. Your Dad's trying to fix it now."

The sunroom was the only room in the house without a radiator.

"Until it's fixed you and me are camping out in here."

The old, wire framed camping bed that Dad hauled down from the attic each Christmas, had been set up in front of the sunroom's floor to ceiling windows. Mum helped me down on to the bed. My thoughts were a jumbled mess, a fever dream. As I lay on the bed, watching the night creeping from the woods all around us, I remembered the eyes that I'd seen watching me from the cover of the trees. I tried to pull myself from the bed, but I was too weak. I thought I called out, but my cries were swallowed into my dreams.

*

I woke to the sound of muffled crying. It wasn't the first time I had heard Mum crying in the night. She sat on the couch looking out of the black panes of the sunroom, a hand held over her mouth to try and stifle the noise. She was trying not to wake me. I could get through their fighting, the shouting and screaming at one another, but the quiet, mournful sound of Mum's weeping filled my heart with ice. The terrible sadness she carried with her filled me with more fear than any creature I might have glimpsed in the woods. I rolled onto my front, burying my face in my pillow. I could feel my chest heaving, sobbing taking hold of me. Then I felt her hand on my back.

"It's OK" she whispered.

Fortunately sleep stole me quickly back into its darkness.

*

The next time I awoke, I was facing the mottled windows of the sunroom. Outside the darkness pressed tight up against the glass, watching us. I lay looking into the black. The room was stifling. My mouth was dry from the heat. My throat hurt from crying.

I could hear a TV on in the distance. Even with the broken heating, Dad would stay out of the sunroom tonight. In the darkness, I could hear Mum quietly breathing. She'd fallen asleep by my bed. I pulled the sheet off of me and placed it over her. I sat on the edge of the folding bed and looked out into the yard.

As my eyes became accustomed to the dark I began to be able to make out the outlines of the trees that lined the yard. I watched their huddled forms, rows of dark figures surrounding us on all sides, and I thought of the eyes that had watched me from the woods. I was sure that they had been the eyes of whatever had dragged the putrid animals to our back door, whatever had been outside my bedroom window the night before.

I needed to pee. I didn't want to leave the sunroom, but more than that I didn't want to pee where I was sitting. Slowly, feeling my way across the dark room, I made my way to the sunroom door. I stood, listening at the door. Now I really needed to pee, so I had no choice but to venture in to the house.

The sunroom door was further up the corridor than my room. I would have to pass the backdoor to get to the toilet.

I edged along the dark corridor. Ahead, at the far end of the house, was the lounge. The sound of the TV was louder now, reaching along the hallway towards me, drowning out the other sounds of the night around me. The door to the lounge was ajar, a thin beam of light escaping to stripe the hallway carpet.

I stopped by the backdoor for a moment. In the darkness, I leant against the door and listened. The night was still; hot and quiet. All I could hear was the sound of the television behind me. I thought of the cat's corpse, how its stomach had been pulled from its belly, how it looked like something had chewed on its entrails. I turned my back on the backdoor and hurried for the toilet. I locked myself in and switched on the light.

When I was done, the sound of the cistern filling crowded the room. Slowly it faded, leaving me alone in silence. Out of habit, I switched off the light. I was about to unlock the door when I heard it.

At first, I thought it was the heating. It was distant, quiet, it took a moment for me to realise where the sound was coming from. The wheeze came through the vent in the wall above the toilet.

I froze, terrified, listening in the dark. The sound came

again, a wet breath, air rattling through mucus. The breathing, laboured, painful, drew closer. Something was moving along the path on the other side of the vent.

I had to stop myself from screaming. I was sure that the breathing belonged to the thing that had watched me from the woods. Slowly it drew closer, along the path, until I could tell that it was right on the other side of the vent. Even though there was a wall between us, I felt its breath moving over me, as if it were in the room with me. I tried to hold my breath, as if that might hide me, but my asthma meant I could only manage a few seconds before I spluttered the air from my lungs. I slammed a hand over my mouth. Had it heard me?

I could taste its foul breath in my mouth. The stench of decay reached into the toilet with me. I pressed hard, back against the door, trying to get away.

And then it moved off. The breathing began to fade. I could hear it heading along the side of our house. I stood, my hand clamped over my mouth, until the sound had faded to a murmur.

*

I stood in the dark for what felt like hours, terrified, locked in the toilet, watching the vent and waiting. My mind squirmed with terrible images of what had been circling our house. Finally, I turned back to the toilet door and quietly unlocked it. Trying to be quiet, I turned the handle and slowly pulled the door towards me.

The corridor was black, still and stifling. I edged out of the toilet trying to take in all of my surroundings at once, fearing those eyes tearing from the darkness towards me. No movement came. The sound of the TV no longer drew along the corridor. The light in the lounge had been turned out.

The pipes rattled, making me start, as the heating fired

again. The air in the corridor was thick and sticky. It clung to me as I moved along the hallway. I was unsteady on my feet. I felt sick and dizzy. I needed water. I couldn't take much more of the heat. I felt my way through the dark hallway to the kitchen.

The cupboard where the glasses were kept was too high for me to reach. Normally, I'd climb on a chair, but I felt too dizzy for that, so I took a mug from the cupboard by the sink. I lifted the mug up to the tap to fill it. That was when I saw it.

The kitchen window was open! Wide open! Mum or Dad must have opened it in the hope that some cooler air would get in. If the thing that had stalked our house had seen it! It might already be in the house! I grabbed a chair and climbed quickly up onto the bench. The pane angled away from me reaching out into the night. I had to hang over the sink to try and reach the handle. I stretched my arm out into the darkness… and stopped.

Something moved outside. I froze with my arm reaching into the night. No, please! Then the whole world rolled over. The heat and my fever got the better of me. I almost fell into the sink. To steady myself I reached out and grabbed the window's handle. I tore it back, slamming the window closed.

I gripped the handle on the window; gasping, hanging over the sink waiting for the spinning to stop. I was too scared to look back up, out of the window, into the night. It had almost certainly heard the window slamming.

I slid down from the bench back onto the chair. There I sat facing away from the window, too frightened to look behind me. As I sat there a terrible realisation overtook me. This wouldn't have been the only window in the house that would have been opened to let cool air in!

I stumbled off of the chair and raced from the kitchen. I ran into the dark lounge. Dad was asleep on the couch. The lounge was surrounded by windows. They were all open! I set about trying to slam them all shut as quickly as I could.

Dad stirred on the couch.

"Wha… what's going? Andy? What are you doing?"

I didn't have time to explain. I grabbed at each of the windows, tearing them closed. Behind me, Dad got to his feet. He knocked over an empty beer bottle. It collided with another and a third; glass dominos scattering across the floor.

"Son?"

I couldn't let him stop me. I raced across the room, closing the windows as fast as I could.

Before I knew what was happening Dad had grabbed me.

"Son? Son! It's OK!"

"No!" I wrestled against him. "It'll get in! It's going to get in!"

Mum shouted from the other end of the house. "Andy?"

I struggled against Dad. There would be other windows in the house that were open!

Mum appeared in the doorway. "What's going on?" She was immediately angry at Dad.

"Put him down!"

"It's his fever! I thought you were looking after him!"

"Me? I fell asleep! It's two in the morning!"

Straight away, they were in to a fight. I felt Dad's grip around me tighten. It was subconscious, his anger making his whole body taut. There was no way I would be able to get away. All the noise! Surely it could hear us! Surely, it could find its way into the house through one of the open windows!

My panic grew till I screamed: "Stop yelling! Stop yelling at each other! You won't be able to hear it if you're shouting all the time!"

Mum and Dad fell silent. Dad's grip on me softened. After a time he spoke quietly, "Sorry son. I guess it's the heat. Got us all worked up." He let me go.

"Why don't you go with your Mum? She'll take you back

to bed."

Mum stepped in to take me from Dad. I'd barely heard Dad's words. I was listening in the silence, listening for the sound of its approach.

"You have to close the windows. You can't let it get into the house!"

I think Dad thought it was all a nightmare brought on by my fever.

"I will son. You go back to bed." I was too young to realise he was lying to me.

Mum led me back along the hallway towards the sunroom. We passed the backdoor. I turned to look, straining to hear if it was there, waiting, its foul breath hot with the spoiled meat it had left at our doorstep. I stopped, listening.

"Come on you. Back to bed. You'll feel better in the morning." Slowly Mum edged me away from the backdoor.

The lights were off in the sunroom. Mum had run from the room when she'd heard me shouting. She hadn't stopped to switch on the light. The room was thick with shadows, a hundred hiding places for a seven year old's nightmares.

Mum tucked me in. She sat by my bed waiting for me to fall asleep. I closed my eyes, pretending to doze off. Once she was happy I had gone back to sleep Mum climbed back onto the couch and, within a few minutes, I could tell from her gentle breathing that she had fallen asleep once more.

I climbed off of the folding bed and headed to the sunroom door. I leant against the door listening. I pressed my ear to the painted wood, closing my eyes, concentrating, listening to every vibration, every whisper the house made. I didn't know at the time, that after he'd seen me and Mum head to bed, Dad had gone through the lounge reopening all the windows I had closed.

*

My eyes started open. I'd dozed off leaning against the door! It was 7am. The sun was already up and the temperature was rising for the fourth day in a row. As soon as I moved I could feel my clothes clinging to me. I didn't care about the heat. I was only thinking about the backdoor.

I left the sunroom and made my way along the hallway. I stood in front of the door, small. I reached for the handle and pulled it open.

*

Now the dog had been torn in half. Its entrails dragged after it, as if the headless dead thing had hauled itself along the path to our door, its stomach and intestines pouring from it as it crawled. Flies swarmed the rotting meat that had spilled a wet trail behind the corpse. Back then I didn't realise what it meant. What had been an offering at first was now a demand.

*

I heard them talking about the dog. Mum had found me at the backdoor. I'd been quickly ushered away, back to the sunroom, where Dad had shut me in. I sat in the window watching the woods, standing guard. My eyes were wide, flicking across the trees, trying to watch everywhere at once. I knew it would be back. It was just a matter of when.

Dad had found its collar. It had fallen out of the remains when he had moved them. It hadn't been around the dog's neck. It no longer had a neck to speak of. It had been inside the corpse. As if something had crammed the collar in to the open cavity where the dog had been torn in half.

It was Digger. Digger had been our neighbour's dog. Finn

and Sal's from the Wilson farm. They lived about a mile from our house, the closest thing we had to a main road running along the front of their property. Digger was always running off from the farm. He'd hare across the fields, chasing a fox, a rabbit, something he might have stood a chance of catching when he was younger. Then, when he'd finally given up on the chase, he'd get confused and often wander out of the woods into our yard.

When he'd disappeared, the Wilson's had pinned posters to the trees that lined the road in the hope that someone would see Digger wandering in the woods as they drove past. I'd heard Finn tell Dad that he thought he'd heard Digger howling in the woods one night, but Digger never found his way home. Months of sun bleached the posters. One had blown into our yard on the hot wind. The photocopy had faded until it was only a memory, the ghost of the Wilson's hope that Digger would one day come home.

I cried as I watched the woods. The carcass that had been left outside our back door bore no resemblance to the affectionate blur that had loped from the woods in search of water and friendship. I was terrified, terrified of the thing that had murdered Digger, but I was angry too, furious that anything could do the terrible things that it had done to Finn and Sal's dog. Outside, the conversation had turned into an argument. The sun that scorched us drove Mum and Dad to anger even quicker than usual. As they fought, I watched the woods, their shouting growing louder and louder.

I heard Mum run back into the house. She ran towards the sunroom door. I could hear she was crying. She stopped outside the door, and after a long moment, turned and headed back along the corridor. She was trying to protect me.

High above the woods a plane crept across the perfect blue sky. I wished we were all on it, I wished we could escape. I knew that, with the night, something terrible was coming.

The day burned away until all that was left of it was the red haze that bled between the tops of the trees. I had watched the woods all day.

The heating groaned behind me. Dad had called a plumber. A few minutes later, he had been shouting at the plumber. They couldn't come out until the next week. The call had ended with Dad slamming down the phone.

The sun had risen to its highest point, looking down at us like we were ants under a magnifying glass. Still I had watched the woods. I watched for any movement. I watched for the eyes that had fixed on me. Nothing moved. I was sure it was biding its time, waiting until the sun had set.

The day had been punctuated with arguments. The hotter it became, the more frequently they started. I had never heard Mum and Dad arguing like that. They screamed at each other until I sat holding my hands over my ears, watching the light draining from the day.

Soon the red sky melted to deep grey and the shadows of the trees once more spilled across the dry yard. Soon the distance I could see would shrink, until the night drew right up to the large windows of the sunroom. I leant nearer the glass, focussing, straining to see if anything moved.

*

Mum had packed a bag. She'd sat it by the side of the sunroom couch, thrown a coat over it. She didn't want me to see it. I didn't find it until almost a week after that night.

*

I sat in the sunroom in the dark. Now the night had swallowed us whole. Even in the heat I felt cold, I could feel the hairs on my arms standing up, the electricity of fear running down my spine. I leant against the glass, squinting to see. I knew it would be coming and I had to be able to hear its approach. I took my hands away from my ears.

Outside the stagnant air had begun to move, a wind, growing stronger swept through the trees, they cracked and strained in its wake. Still I could not hear or see the thing that stalked us.

I had to be somewhere I could hear its approach and the only place I could think of was the toilet where I had listened to its breathing the night before. Gently, I opened the door to the sunroom and stepped out into the corridor.

I made my way along the dark corridor. A light was on in the lounge, but tonight I couldn't hear the TV. I had no idea where Mum and Dad were, but, for now, their arguing had ceased. I held my breath as I approached the backdoor. I slowed, but did not stop as I passed it. I arrived at the toilet and I shut myself in.

I locked the door and turned on the light. I could smell the summer air, the flowers on the vine that curled along the wall on the other side of the vent. I could hear the wind outside, it rushed against the house. Finally, the weather was changing. And with it, the thing crawled out of the woods.

*

I heard its laboured breathing, the wet wheezing drawing along the side of the house. Immediately I was terrified. Even though I'd been sure that it would come back, that its leaving the gutted dog outside our house meant that it hadn't finished with us, I had hoped I would be wrong, that the night might be still and quiet, that the devil that haunted us might have found some other prey to hunt.

I didn't know what to do. Could it tell that I was in here, on the other side of the vent? Panicking, I slammed my hand on the light switch, plunging the room into darkness. I hoped that the darkness might hide me.

Still the breathing grew louder, closer. Now I could smell its foul stench, the terrible smell of rotten meat. I tried to be quiet, although I knew I was whimpering, more afraid than I had ever been before. I hoped that it would move off, the way it had the night before. It didn't. It stopped on the other side of the vent.

I crouched down, curled myself up into a corner by the door. I watched the vent, the foul smell of the thing making me want to wretch. I listened to it sucking in the night air on the other side of the vent. Was it watching me? Could it see me through the thin slats that hatched the vent?

The wind had grown stronger. In the distance, I heard a roll of thunder. The heat wave was going to end with a storm. Behind me, in the house, Mum shouted. The noise made me start, a small scream burst from my lips. Oh no! I'd given myself away. Now it would know where I was hiding! Dad shouted back, their fighting starting in earnest. I struggled to hear the breathing. Was it still on the other side of the vent?

I couldn't hear it! I climbed up and stood on the toilet seat, straining to hear, close to the vent, trying to tell where it was. The thunder was getting closer, the storm gaining on us fast. Mum and Dad's shouting drowned out any chance I had of telling where the thing was.

Panicking, I jumped down from the toilet and unlocked the bathroom door. I leant out into the dark corridor, up towards the backdoor. The hallway was surprisingly quiet: a lull in the fight, while either Dad or Mum thought of what to say or do next.

I could hear rain drumming on the roof above me, the

droplets growing heavier as the storm closed in around us. Suddenly, there was a huge crack of lightning and the whole house lit up. In the instant before we were plunged back into darkness, I looked to the back door.

It was still closed. The deep bass of the thunder that followed shook the house. I heard Mum gasp in surprise. That seemed to be the cue for their fighting to start again. As I stood in the doorway and listened, their shouting seemed to be getting louder. I'd never heard them arguing like that before. It was ferocious, as if all their fighting had been building up to this.

I didn't know what to do. I ran to the place where I felt safest. I ran to my room and slammed the door.

The hot air took my breath away. The window was closed, the stifling air had been baking, left to stagnate ever since I'd slammed the window on the thing two nights before. I looked up to the window, the pane was black; I could see myself, small and lost, reflected on its surface. Rain, hurled by the wind, beat against the glass, looking for a way in. Suddenly I knew what I needed to do.

I climbed up onto my bed and slowly, gently, unlatched the window. Immediately the sound of the storm was in the room with me. It barged in, loud, rain slamming on the path outside my room. I leant close to the small gap that I'd created between the pane and the frame and listened. Was it circling our house as it had the night before, looking for a way in?

A gust of wind tried to pull the window from my grip. I held on tight, struggling to keep it from blowing fully open. Cool air poured over my hand and into my room. The frame was slippery with the rain. Another lightning strike exploded in the sky. For a moment the whole world was blinding white. That was long enough to see it.

Along the path, no more than a few feet from where I held the ajar window, was the figure. It stood on two legs, although it was hunched forward. It looked at first glance like an old man. It had what resembled an old coat wrapped around it, but it was torn and hung loosely on the thing's gaunt form. Patches of marbled flesh protruded through gaps in the torn material. Something moved beneath the coat and it looked as if it might be carrying something smaller, huddled close against its body. Its arms were wasted, bones loose inside its sagging skin.

But, it was the face of the thing that made me scream out. It watched me with milky eyes, bulging fluid filled orbs that sagged from their sockets. The centre of its face was a large raw wound stretching from its temple down to its teeth. It looked as if its nose had been ripped from its face. The skin of its face was bloated and formless, it looked like a mask, like the thing was wearing someone else's skin. Its teeth were bared and its jaw constantly cycled, chewing on the air, sucking in my scent, imagining how I might taste.

I fell backward away from the window. In an instant, the flash from the lightning was gone and the room was pitch once more. The deafening sound of thunder almost drowned out my cries. The wind tore the window open. I didn't stop to try and close it.

I burst into the hallway and ran shouting for Mum and Dad. I expected someone to race from the lounge to see what was happening, but no one came. As I ran I realised that I could no longer hear their arguing either.

I threw open the lounge door and what I saw stopped me dead in my tracks.

A lamp had been knocked from the table by the couch; its broken shade spread an angular, awkward shadow over the room. Dad stood in the middle of the lounge, still and silent, looking down at the floor. Mum lay on the floor beside the couch.

The shame was written deep into Dad's face. He couldn't

even look at me as I stood taking in the terrible scene. Mum edged backwards towards the door. She wiped the blood from her nose and struggled to pull herself to her feet. All the time, her eyes were fixed on Dad, wide, scared. Without saying a word, she backed out of the room.

I don't know what I expected Dad to do, to say, but I stood watching him. Maybe I was hoping for an answer, something that might make sense of what I'd seen, but he just stood in the middle of the lounge looking at the floor.

When I heard the backdoor opening, I spun to see what was happening. I saw Mum walk out of the house and disappear into the thick darkness beyond.

"NO!" I ran along the hallway shouting after Mum, "NO! STOP!" By the time I made it to the backdoor, she was nowhere to be seen. I knew it was out there, knew it had been waiting, its foul mouth chewing the air. "MUM!" I screamed at the door hoping she would appear again from the darkness, have heard me, changed her mind and come back into the safety of the house.

"MUM!" I screamed into the darkness. "MUM! Please!" I felt Dad arrive at my side. I wanted to go after her, wanted to run into the darkness, but I was too scared. All I could do was stand at the door and call after her.

*

I stood at the door for hours; until I was so tired I leant against the frame to hold myself up. Dad took a torch and went out after Mum. I knew he wouldn't find her. She hadn't been thinking. She hadn't taken the bag that she had packed, that she had planned to take when she left. She had been so shocked by what had happened that she had just walked straight to the backdoor and walked out of our lives.

Long after the storm had passed, after wind had died

down and the night had fallen silent, as the sky had begun to lighten, Dad closed the backdoor of our house.

"Don't worry son. Your Mum'll be back" he said. He was never the same after that night.

*

Dad went to bed, but I stayed by the backdoor. Eventually, when I couldn't stand any longer, I sat leaning against the door.

I woke to the sound of movement outside. I jumped to my feet and grabbed the door handle. Had she come back? Had Dad been right? At the last moment I hesitated. I remembered the offerings, the broken dead things we had found rotting outside the door. My hand slipped away from the handle.

KNOCK
AND
YOU
WILL
SEE
ME

1.

We buried Dad in the winter. It wasn't until the spring that we heard from him again.

People say I'm "sensitive", on account of the fact I drowned when I was five. I was dead for nine minutes and forty four seconds. That's always been the story. Not that I remember any of it.

Anyway, there've been times in my life I've seen things, known things. Like that time Kitty Burke disappeared and I just knew she was down the creek. Don't ask me how. They dragged her out two days later.

Or that time I saw the *thing*. Strode through our house as sure as if it lived there. Hooved feet but it stood up like a man. And its face! That face. Like it had borrowed it from a corpse. Cut out and stuck on top of its own. I caught it looking in on me through the sliding doors of my bedroom.

Never want to see anything like that again. If that's what being sensitive entails, you can keep it. I was twelve when that happened. Now I'm thirty five, got three kids and I'm pleased to say that I'm a lot less *sensitive* these days. At least that's what I thought.

Dad had been sick a while. We knew the end was coming. That didn't make it any less painful. He'd moved in with us

101

after I'd found him lying on the floor of his unit, bleeding from where he'd fallen and cracked his head. He couldn't get himself back up again; he'd pissed his pants. Age takes everything from you in the end.

I said, "I'm not coming round here and finding you dead like this."

In the end, he'd just fallen asleep in a chair on our porch and not woken up again.

That time of the year, the ground was frozen solid. They used a *grave blanket*, a heated blanket they put on the ground to thaw it out, before digging Dad's grave. I liked that idea, warming the ground for him. It felt somehow kinder, like putting the electric blanket on in his bed one last time.

It was a small service. Dad had outlived most of his friends. He'd been a stubborn bastard in life. He'd refused to give up on me when he'd dragged me out of the pool that day I drowned. He'd performed CPR till his arms screamed and his whole body shook, but he didn't give up.

Thanks to him I'd survived. He'd passed that stubbornness right along to me. When it came to dying, he was too stubborn to give up on life and he'd clung on till he was almost 90 years old, long after Mum and most of his friends had passed on.

Yeah, Dad had been 54 when he'd had me. That'd never seemed strange to me. He'd met Mum at the County Fair. Never thought he'd get married. Never thought he'd have kids. Both of those things happened within a year of meeting Mum. I won't tell you which came first.

Mum had been 40, Dad almost to his fifty fifth birthday when I arrived. I asked him once if I'd been a mistake.

"A mistake's something you regret. So, no, you definitely weren't a mistake. You weren't planned. But that's different altogether."

Including the Pastor, there were five of us at the funeral.

Me, Tommy, Max and David Jnr (named after his grandfather, not his father.) Tommy's twelfth birthday had fallen three days before Dad had fallen asleep in that easy chair, and David was due to turn eight in another month. Max, my middle boy, would be ten in June. They were smart kids, smarter than I was at their age and smarter than their Dad had been when he'd left us. And by left us, I don't mean in the way their grandfather was leaving us that day. I mean running away when he'd found out I was pregnant for a third time.

Tommy and Max barely remembered their father and David Jnr had never met him; and that was fine by me.

We huddled together by Dad's grave as the Pastor read back the notes he'd scribbled when we'd met. He hadn't known Dad. Dad hadn't been a religious man. Truth was, he thought it was all bullshit, made up to make death seem less like the end it is. Me? After what I'd seen and felt, I wasn't sure. Which is why we hadn't dumped his body in the forest in a black plastic sack as he'd once suggested I should. He also didn't catch fire when he was lowered into the consecrated ground. I thought he'd be pleased with that.

I'd gone to the service that morning focussed on my boys, on making sure they were okay, keeping them safe from the grief of their grandfather's loss. I held their hands, checked their scarves were wrapped tight against the cold, I smiled to reassure them I was okay, but as Dad's casket dropped out of sight, the thoughts I'd been trying to protect them from swallowed me whole.

In my mind the darkness was pitch, tight. The Pastor's voice faded as sure as if he'd stepped into another room and closed the door. A second sound took its place: a muffled thud, thud, thud. I was back on the porch when I realised that Dad wasn't breathing. I was standing at his side when we buried Mum. I was standing over him that day when I found him lying on the floor of his unit. He'd been so strong when I was a kid! Now he was broken at my feet. I was watching him slipping away, dropping inch by inch into the ground, and all the time the thud, thud, thud, like the voice of my panic, grew louder, stronger. *No! Please no! Please stop! Please don't go!*

I felt Max tugging at my hand. The service had ended. The Pastor stood: awkward, shuffling from foot to foot, trying to keep warm. I couldn't even feel the cold. I forced a smile for Max, my jaw clenched tight against the sob that waited in my throat. Tommy took my other hand and between them they led me away, back to our car. That morning I'd set out to protect my boys and, in the end, they'd been the ones to save me. I didn't tell them about the sound I'd heard. Had I imagined it? The building thud, the growing sound of someone knocking, trying desperately to be heard.

2.

Spring is like that friend who you love to see but who always arrives when your house is dirtiest. You spend their entire visit following them round with a cloth and everywhere they go seems to be dustier than the last spot.

It had been a long winter, made harder and darker by Dad's passing. I admit I'd neglected the house during those months. The boys had helped where they could, but Max's idea of tidying away his toys meant building an ever-growing stash of them behind the couch. Yes, they weren't *out*, as he'd tried to argue with me, but hiding them behind the couch didn't really count as *away* either.

Sally Peterson and her husband Jim ran the diner in town. She knew I'd taken Dad's death pretty hard so once a fortnight, on a Sunday, she'd drop in with a casserole to make sure we were eating right. She'd take over the kitchen, feed me an endless supply of tea and listen to me talk, mostly about Dad. Outside, Jim would make sure we had enough firewood to get us through and give the boys lessons on building a fire and chopping wood. Tommy got to handle the axe (while Jim was there), much to the envious awe of his younger brothers.

Afterwards, we'd load up the fire and all sit down for a family meal. David Jnr liked to write his name in the thick condensation that formed on the dining room windows. He'd

105

learned that if he wrote it backwards he could read it in the mirror, hung on the wall opposite him, while he was eating his dinner. Max would tidy away a few more of his toys (behind the couch) before we sat down to get started.

Those were the brightest days that winter had to offer. The days we laughed the most. The days I could almost forget, for a few hours, that Dad wasn't with us.

Those hours didn't last though. It didn't take long for the condensation to fade. For David's name to melt and for me to find myself once more looking out to the porch and the chair where Dad had died.

One evening, I was standing out on the porch with Sally while she had a smoke. She'd seen how my gaze was drawn again and again to that chair.

"You should throw it out. Throw it out or… put it in the garage out of the way. Somewhere you don't have to look at it the whole time. It's not good for you, you know."

I wasn't ready to do that. I wasn't ready to admit that Dad had really gone.

But, when spring came and I followed it through our house, I realised just how much I'd neglected our home over those winter months. I was ashamed. And that shame drove me to empty the cupboard under the kitchen sink, pull out and load up my cleaning caddy (thanks, Mum!) and set out to put things straight again.

I decided to start with Max's toy stash behind the couch. On more than one occasion during the winter Max had commented, with pride, that his room was the tidiest it had been in a long time. Initially I'd explained to him that simply moving the contents of his room to another location in the house (behind the couch) didn't count as tidying. He'd countered that all tidying was moving stuff from one place to another, wasn't it? At that point, I'd realised I wasn't going to win that argument.

At the start of the winter, there'd been a big enough gap behind the couch that Max could comfortably crawl from one end to the other, disappearing in on one side of the room, tunnelling through, and then popping out on the other side. By the end of the winter he'd bricked up the tunnel with toys.

I'd originally intended to climb behind the couch and pull the toys out one by one, but it wasn't until I got down on my hands and knees and began to unstack the top toys that I realised there wasn't just one stack, there were two. Two stacks of toys, one on either side of the couch with a slim gap trapped in the middle. I'd always thought Max was just piling his toys, without giving much thought to what he was doing, but now I started to wonder if there was some method in his bricking up the tunnel behind the couch.

As I pulled the couch away from the wall I expected both stacks to collapse, toys to rain down on one another, scrambling to get free after a winter of confinement. But the stacks didn't collapse, and when I'd pulled the couch right out so I could see behind it, still both of Max's stacks stood tall, Buzz Lightyear balancing on Scooby Doo, on Lego, on Spongebob, like some kind of toy totem pole or those stunt guys who do the pyramid by climbing on one another on their motorbike.

But, it wasn't the two, seemingly gravity-defying, stacks of toys that stopped me in my tracks. It was what I found, caught in the gap between them, that signalled the beginning of the series of terrible events that followed.

3.

I recognised it straight away. Basildon Bond: Dad's choice of writing paper.

"A hand-written letter, on good quality writing paper: that'll open more doors and get you more respect, than any e-mail or typed note that someone's printed or tapped out on their phone." He'd spat the word *tapped*. He'd hated cell phones. Truth be told, he'd not been a fan of phones in general, but I think that'd come about after the call he'd gotten that night when we found out about Mum.

Sure, handwriting a letter might seem *old school* but Dad had been right. Every time I'd written a letter by hand it had opened a door for me. It'd gotten me my first job, gotten me a second chance at high school after I'd given Sully White that black eye, and even kept Tommy in school after he'd done the same to Sully White's boy all of fifteen years later. That White family never learn.

It was Dad's writing paper alright. A single piece of champagne-coloured Basildon Bond, screwed up into a ball, caught between the two piles of Max's toys. Had Max packed his toys around the note? I wondered if he'd put the piece of paper there. If so, why had he screwed it up?

I knelt down and picked up the paper. The familiar watermark was just visible in the creases folded into the paper ball. When I was a kid I used to pretend that the watermarks were secret messages left for me by a spy, that if I held the sheets of paper up to the light their real meaning would be revealed. It never was.

That hadn't stopped me looking.

Slowly, I unfolded the note. Finding something of Dad's I'd not known was there, that had been abandoned all winter, that I likely would have found if I hadn't been so absorbed in my grief, made my face flush and tears well in my eyes. I was ashamed. Ashamed that I'd let the house go. He'd have kicked my arse if he'd been around. That just made me miss him more.

The writing on the paper was definitely Dad's. He'd written a single word:

WHY?

That was it. WHY? Sitting on the couch I spread the note out on my leg, rubbing the paper, doing my best to flatten it out. WHY?

Towards the end Dad had been a drinker. I didn't blame him. Way I look at it, you get to a point in your life when you turn a corner and realise that's about all you're gonna get. If you can face down that knowledge and not crack open a bottle, well, you're a better person than I am. If I make it to eighty I intend to start smoking again. As far as I was concerned, Dad could drink as much as he wanted if it made him happy. And most of the time it did. But he had black moods too. They'd started after Mum's accident. I tried to make sure the kids never got to see him like that.

I guessed he'd written the note during one of those black times. Dad had been so strong and so proud for as long as I could remember. But, during those last few months, he'd grown frail, he knew he was losing the fight, and occasionally desperation would seize him. I did what I could for him, made him comfortable, tried to calm him when the panic overtook him. Mum hadn't had the chance to consider her death. It had come fast, an eighteen-wheeler on a badly lit road. The driver had fallen asleep at the wheel. I wondered if that was kinder than shrivelling away to nothing the way Dad had. Given enough of it, time screws us all in the end.

Carefully, I carried the note to the dining room table. I took down two volumes of the Encyclopedia Britannica set that Dad had bought us when I was growing up, and placed the letter between the two books to press the creases out of it. I'd leave it there for a few days and then put it away with the rest of Dad's things. I rested my hand on the top volume. WHY? I wish I could answer that for you, Dad.

That evening, I sat on the end of Max's bed, and I asked him if he'd built the two stacks of toys on purpose behind the couch.

He looked confused, and then said: "Mum, is this going to be another one of those conversations about tidying versus moving things? I thought we'd already addressed this."

I couldn't help but laugh. He was ten going on thirty alright. My brilliant Max. I was going to make sure he joined the debating team as soon as he was old enough. They'd never lose with him on their side.

*

I didn't find the second letter until almost a week later. Well, I didn't find it at all. Max did.

I was a pretty good swimmer when I was a kid. That didn't stop me from almost drowning that time though. So, as soon as they could wriggle, my boys were in the local pool, and every Friday became Fishy Friday. We'd go practice being fish in the pool and then have fish and chips from Manny's afterwards.

I was unpacking dinner when Max came out of his room holding the note. I thought it was the one I'd found behind the couch. I guessed he must have found it between the encyclopedias.

"I found this in my room." He handed it to me. It was written on the same champagne Basildon Bond paper, screwed up same as the first letter. "It was on my bed."

I was about to call him out on that when I turned it over and saw what was written on it.

DID YOU LEAVE ME HERE?

It was Dad's writing alright. I shivered. The paper was cold in my hands. No, it was more than that. Like someone had opened the door on a freezing winter night. I looked over my shoulder, back up the hall, to see if someone had just stepped into the house.

But I didn't see the hallway, or the door, I was back in that same darkness I'd found myself in at the graveside. And the noise was back too: the thud, thud, thud. It was getting louder all the time. I could feel it, as sure as if I was hammering on a door myself. Was someone trying to get in?

"Mum? Mum? Are you okay?" Max pulled me out of the darkness again. I could feel him tugging on my arm. I was back in the kitchen, the smell of fried food and vinegar thick on the air.

I tried to shrug it off. I don't think I was fooling anyone. "Where did you find this, honey?"

"It was on my bed, on my pillow."

It hadn't been there when I'd left to pick up the boys from school. I knew that because I'd been running late and I'd only just finished changing Max's bed before I left.

"Is that really where you found it?"

Max looked genuinely taken aback, confused that I was questioning him.

"Is that from Grandad?" he asked.

I smiled at him. "Yes, I think it is."

*

I let the boys watch TV while we ate dinner that night. I knew Max had more questions about the note but I didn't want to talk about it in front of David Jnr. I had more questions too.

Later, after the boys had gone to sleep, I lifted the encyclopedia off the first letter. I sat at the dining table. Dad drank Jack. He'd left a bottle and a half when he'd died. We never just had one bottle in the house. If you've got more than one, you can't run out so easily. I poured myself a glass. I took the second letter from my cardigan and placed it next to the first.

WHY   DID YOU LEAVE ME HERE?

I couldn't understand when Dad would have written the notes. It wasn't something I'd ever known him to do. Even when he was at his lowest. He'd drink. Sometimes he'd shout. Only one time I'd found him crying.

I looked out the dining room window to the easy chair on the porch. I still expected to see Dad sat there. If Max hadn't put the letter on his pillow, who had? Were there more letters? I'd sit Max down and talk to him about it in the morning. If he'd found letters his grandad had written, I wanted to see them.

I poured another glass of whisky. The chill that I'd felt in the house earlier had lingered. I couldn't shake the feeling that something was wrong, that something awful was coming.

Ever since Dad had died I'd felt it. I knew I'd grown overprotective of the boys, stopping them from staying out late, demanding to know where they were at all times. Sally had said it was normal, that while you're grieving it's easy to see how everything else could go wrong. Suddenly life seemed very fragile and fleeting.

I'd hoped the Jack would help. It hadn't. I collected the two letters and gently placed them back between the encyclopedias. I stopped at the window and looked one last time out to Dad's easy chair. "Night, Dad." I raised my glass to him, downed what was left of the whiskey and then flicked off the outside light and headed to bed.

I checked in on the boys first. David Jnr had fallen asleep on his back and was snoring. Tommy always kicked his covers off. I picked them off his floor and laid them over him. Max had dozed off while he was reading and dropped his book on his face. That was a regular occurrence too. Max read a lot. He kept a large stack of books on his bedside table that we topped up every Saturday with a trip to the library. That was, by far, his favourite part of the week.

As I reached out to take the book from his head, I noticed he was lying flat on his mattress. His pillow sat on the floor in the middle of his room. I wondered if discarding it had had anything to do with finding the note earlier. I gently lifted *The Wizard of Earthsea* from Max's face and placed it on top of his bedside pile. I'd remind him of these times when he was eighteen. I picked up his pillow and was about to tuck it under his head when he stirred and waved the pillow away.

"No. Smelled bad. Like the dog last summer."

I knew what he was talking about. One evening last summer, when we'd been out for a walk, we'd stumbled across a dog on the bank of the creek. Its legs had been broken. Probably hit by a car and had limped down to the creek and died. It'd been dead for some time, its stomach had swollen, flies swarmed around it and its muzzle was alive with maggots. But the thing I remembered the most, the worst thing about it, had been the smell: the sickly smell of rotten meat, of something dead.

4.

The next day, Saturday, all the boys had plans so I got the house to myself. I'd wanted to corner Max about the letters, but David Jnr had clung to me from the moment he got up to the moment he got picked up by Crystal for his play date with Jack. If Max did have a secret, he was going to keep it a while longer. We could talk in the afternoon on our weekly library trip.

I stripped and washed Max's bed again. To me, his room smelled just of him, but I opened the windows and aired it all the same.

I stood at the window, looking out at the woods, at the path through the trees down to the creek. Way I look at it, there are two types of people: ones who dream of living by the sea and ones who want to live in the woods. I'm definitely in that second group. I've loved those woods since I was a kid. I love the smell of them, the sound of them.

Summers growing up, me and Billy Finch used to play in the creek. Covered in mud, lizard skins baked on by the sun, our bare feet would hammer along the track through the woods, a flicker of sunlight sparking in the canopy above us as we rushed up towards what was then the Varney's backyard. Cutting through to get to the main road and the bus home. I'd never dreamed that, years later, it'd be my back yard.

About six months after David had left us, the Varney house came onto the market. Turns out that the Varney kids, Jim and Jen, were the type of people to dream of living by the sea and, pretty much as soon as Old Man Varney was in his grave, they put the house up for sale with a plan of splitting the money and moving upstate to the coast.

There was no way I could afford the house: we were three, soon to be four, living hand to mouth in a trailer. Anyway, about the same time Dad puts his house up for sale. I don't know whether he did it because he could see we were struggling. He told me he'd always been planning to get himself a smaller place. That was his story and he was sticking with it. With the money he got for his house, he had enough to buy the Varney place outright and, I thought, the unit he moved into. I wanted him to move in with us but he wanted to keep his independence for as long as he possibly could.

It wasn't until after he'd died that I found out he'd put all the money he'd made on his house into buying the Varney place for us. He rented that apartment of his month on month with the money he got from his pension checks.

You stupid, stubborn old bastard. Why can't you be here now?

The third letter was waiting for me when I turned back from the window.

It sat in the doorway to Max's room. It hadn't been there when I'd carried Max's bedding in to his room only a few minutes before.

"Hello?" I called out. Were the boys back? I hadn't heard a car pull up to drop them home or the clatter of a bike dumped on the front porch. They were hardly good at keeping quiet.

"Max? Tom?" No one answered.

The paper was the same as the first two letters: champagne Basildon Bond. I knelt down to pick it up.

"Dad?"

116

The cold was waiting for me. As my fingers closed around the crumpled note, I thought of the dog we'd found the year before. Of the maggots spilling over its face, writhing in its decay.

A single word had been written on the page.

CAN'T

Looking up from the paper, I noticed another note, screwed up, waiting on the hallway floor. I was sure it hadn't been there a moment before. I edged out of Max's room and into the corridor. Was someone else in the house?

The second note was equally as cold as the first.

YOU

It was Dad's writing. All caps, scribbled, like it'd been written fast. His voice getting louder, more desperate.

A third letter lay in the middle of the hallway floor, closer to the front door.

This one was different. It had been screwed up tight. No, it had been *crushed*. Before I opened it, I could see where the words had been written with such force they'd torn through the page.

HEAR ME

Dad? I looked down at the scribbled note in my hand, at the words torn into the paper. What had started as a whisper had grown louder, more desperate. The words had been *screamed* onto the page.

Dad? Please. What's going on?

The corridor was freezing, like I'd stepped out of Max's room and into one of those walk-in coolers. The ones you see on TV filled with hanging animal carcasses.

I looked across the hallway to Tommy's room, to see if I could see who was dropping the notes. No sign of anyone there. I turned to my room, on the left. Everything remained still, silent. When I looked back, a fourth letter lay by front door.

This one was different. It bulged. It hadn't been crushed as much as *wrapped*. As I picked it up its contents shifted, it felt wet to the touch. As I opened it, they spilled from the note: a mass of squirming maggots, pouring over the paper onto my hands. I screamed and dropped the paper. I shook, rubbed, wiped the maggots from my hands on my shirt and jeans, onto the hallway floor.

I felt fat grubs popping under my feet as I stumbled back from the note. What was happening? I'd been standing in the hallway the whole time. The notes hadn't been there and then they were. I would have seen if someone had been placing them.

CAN'T
YOU
HEAR ME

I could read the single word on the last letter from where I was standing.

KNOCKING

Oh no! No! It couldn't be! I grabbed my car keys, tore open the front door and raced out to the pickup.

*

I swung the truck up onto the verge, narrowly avoiding

slamming head on into a tree. The truck skidded to a stop and I jumped out. There was a shovel in the back that I kept in case I broke down when it snowed. I grabbed it and raced into the cemetery.

I'd heard the knocking. I'd heard it in the house, in the darkness. But the place I'd heard it clearest and loudest, the place I'd heard it first, was at Dad's graveside as he'd been lowered into his grave. *Dad, I'm so sorry! I didn't know! I didn't understand what I was hearing!*

I thought I'd been mistaken. That the sound was in my mind. Maybe it was. Maybe it was like before. Like the time I'd known Kitty Burke was dead in the creek.

Dad's grave was at the back of the cemetery, behind the chapel. The pastor had called the area *secluded*. Truth was, it was cheap. But, it was the best we—and the owners of the twenty or so other graves in the *out of sight, out of mind* area of the cemetery—could afford. The grass was longer and a short wall ran round three sides of the second graveyard, further cutting it off from the rest of the dead. The wall had once run all four sides, but the settlers who'd built the church hadn't counted on the ancient oak tree that leaned from the neighbouring wood over the churchyard. It had leant against the wall when they'd built it, and, over the years, it had continued to lean till it had toppled the wall back into the cemetery. Now it leant over Dad's grave.

I stood at the foot of the grave, my whole body shaking, gripping the shovel with white knuckles. "Dad?"

I listened for the knocking.

"Dad?"

I could hear my blood rushing in my ears, my fast breath, but I couldn't hear the knocking.

I stepped forward and drove the shovel into the ground.

*

The digging was slow going. The spring thaw had begun to set in but still it felt as if I was chipping away at stone. Soon my hands were wet with sweat and more than once they slipped on the rough wood of the shovel, burning my fingers and palms. I stamped down on the back of the blade to cut into the ground. *Come on! Come on!* The pile of earth at my side grew painfully slowly.

As I dug, I became more and more sure that someone was watching me from the woods, their gaze burning into me from between the trees. I stopped and looked up, my eyes searching in the darkness between the trunks, looking for a figure, looking to catch my watcher in the act.

The wood seemed empty, still. *Watch all you want, I don't have time for games.* I slammed the shovel into the earth once more. Time and again I hacked at the hard ground, pulling the earth from Dad's grave. *I'm sorry, Dad! I should have realised sooner!* Time and again I drove the blade into the ground, fighting to get to Dad. I was knee deep in the grave when I heard the voice behind me.

"Ellie Ray! What in the hell do you think you're doing?"

The pastor had been watching me from his office in the back of the church. Being a man of God, he'd decided that, instead of leaving his office and heading to talk to me, he'd call Sheriff Weaver to have me kicked off the church's property. Seemed like the Christian thing to do, I guess. I stamped down on the shovel once more.

"Don't try and stop me, Al."

I could hear Al Weaver approaching me. I pulled another shovelful of earth from the grave.

"I've heard him, Al! I've heard him knocking, trying to get out!"

Al stopped next to me. "He's dead, Ellie. No one's knocking." His voice was quieter, kinder.

I buried the blade in the earth again. "No! Al, I've heard him."

"Ellie, please." Al reached out a hand and took a hold of the shovel. I wanted to tear it out of his hands but I was exhausted. I wanted to argue, to fight and tell him he was wrong. But I knew he was right. In my heart I knew Dad was dead. No one could have survived being buried alive for more than a few hours. A day maybe. Not the months it had been since the funeral.

Al and I stood in silence, holding the shovel between us. *Please Dad! Knock again! Knock now and I'll keep digging. Knock now and I won't give up.*

No sound came. I let the shovel slip through my fingers. I sat down, in the hole I'd cut, and wept.

*

Al Weaver had one of those old Thermos flasks. The ones with the tartan pattern on them, with the plastic cups on the top. He twisted the lid open and the squad car was filled with the smell of minestrone soup.

"Sorry, I don't have any coffee. Can't really drink it any more, not with my blood pressure the way it is. That and Maree thinks carrying soup will stop me picking up snacks in the day." Al poured a cup of soup and handed it to me. "What's going on, Ellie?"

We sat in the church's car park. I looked back up to the graveyard, towards Dad's grave. My shovel, still covered in mud, lay across the back seat of Al Weaver's patrol car.

"You said you'd heard him? Your Dad? You said you'd heard him knocking?"

"I think… somehow… we might have buried him alive,

Al."

Al didn't respond straight away. I guessed it wasn't every day he was called to the cemetery to haul away a grieving daughter who was attempting to dig up her dead father. He took a slow, deep breath, weighing up his response. His voice was gentle, full of fatherly concern. "You know that's not possible. Don't you, Ellie?"

"I know what I heard."

"Look, Ellie, I know you've taken your dad's death pretty hard, but what you're saying, it's just not possible. When did you hear him? Today?"

"Yes… and at the service, when we were burying him." I knew how that sounded. "What if someone made a mistake? What if the coroner got it wrong?"

"No one made a mistake, Ellie. There are tests the doctors do, checks to make sure. People don't get buried alive any more, hon."

"I heard him, Al."

"Drink your soup, Ellie. You must be freezing." Al turned up the heating another notch. I took a sip of soup. He was right. I'd run out of the house in my jeans and a t-shirt. I hadn't even noticed the cold until Al had handed me the soup. Now all my muscles had tensed against it.

"I'm going to drop you back to your car. Can you promise me you're not going to try anything like this again?"

My hands were filthy, covered in mud. I looked like I'd been down on all fours clawing at the grave with my bare hands.

"Ellie?"

I nodded.

"Think I'm going to hold on to your shovel for a bit, okay?"

I nodded again.

"Don't worry about the pastor. I'll talk to him. He won't

be taking this any further. That would be a decidedly unchristian thing to do, don't you think?"

"Thanks, Al."

"No problem. Now drink that soup before it goes cold."

*

Max was waiting on the doorstep when I pulled up. All the way home I'd had the heating up full blast. Still I had to clench my jaw against my chattering teeth. I jumped out of the pickup and hurried up to the house.

"Are you okay?" Max asked as I climbed up onto the porch. "Mum? What happened to you?"

"I'm sorry, hon. I didn't…" I fumbled for my keys to unlock the door. How long had he been waiting outside in the cold?

"What happened to your hands, Mum?"

I grabbed at the handle and the door swung open. It wasn't locked. It had just been pulled to.

I turned back to Max. He had edged behind me.

"The smell… that smell was back. So I came out here to wait for you."

*

I held an arm behind me, wrapping it around Max as best I could, as I pressed open the front door and stepped into our hallway. I would have been happier if he'd waited outside but he wasn't having any of that.

I waited for the smell to hit me, the smell of death, decay, but the air in the house smelled cold and clean. I expected to see the letters on the hallway floor where I'd dropped them. I expected to see the maggots, fat, squirming on the floorboards. The letters, and the maggots, were gone. Max and I edged into

123

the house.

"I put Grandad's letters on the dining table. So you could put them with the others. What's going on, Mum?"

"Nothing, honey. Nothing to worry about."

We stepped deeper in to the house.

"Where did you smell it, Max? The smell, like the dog."

"I put the letters on the table, then… It was weird, like it was coming from David's room, but it wasn't there when I got home. It got really strong. Like it followed me. That was when I went outside to wait for you."

The door to David Jnr's room was closed. "Stay here, hon." I felt Max tense as I stepped away from him. "It's okay. I'm not going anywhere." I should have made him wait outside. What the hell was I thinking? I reached for the handle to David Jnr's door.

My hands were still covered in dirt, mixed with blood from my blisters. It smeared on the handle as I turned it. I pushed David Jnr's door open.

I expected the smell, but it didn't come. I thought a window might be open in David Jnr's room. That might have explained the cold, gone some way to explaining where the smell might have come from, how the letters had gotten into the house. I stepped into the room. I only looked away from Max for a second.

"Mum! Mum!"

I spun back to see Max hopping on the spot, his eyes wide with fear, pointing into the kitchen.

"What is it, Max? What's going on?" I raced out of David Jnr's room. Without thinking, I put myself between Max and whatever he'd seen in the kitchen.

From where we stood in the corridor, I could see the blood on the floor. A chair had been flipped onto its side, coming to rest in the doorway.

"You stay behind me, Max. Okay?"

He didn't say anything, but I could feel him nodding as he pressed himself into my back. I stepped closer to the kitchen.

Looking past the chair, I could see the remains of eggs, smashed and scattered across the floor, a milk carton burst open as if it'd been stamped on. The fridge door had been swung wide. One of the shelves had been pulled out, its contents cast across the kitchen tiles. The butcher's paper that'd held our Sunday steaks and been torn into. Blood from the steaks had been smeared across the tiles, streaking pink in the spilled milk.

Then the smell hit me. I felt Max grip me tighter. He'd smelt it too.

"It's okay, honey."

Rotten meat. The stench filled the kitchen.

"That's the smell!" Max whimpered.

He was right. It was how the dog had smelled that summer night. When we'd gotten home I'd made the boys strip off and I'd washed all their clothes there and then. Even afterwards, I'd still felt I could smell it, as if something dead had followed us home.

I took another step towards the kitchen. I could feel Max clinging to me, gripping my jeans, holding me back. The voice gave us both a hell of a start.

"Mum? Max? What's going on?"

Tommy was standing in the front doorway. "Stay back there, Tommy!"

"Mum?" Tommy made to step into the house.

"You do as I tell you, young man!" Tommy stopped dead in his tracks. I tried to keep my voice down so as not to be heard by whatever might be in the kitchen. My voice might have been quiet, but that wasn't hiding my fear. That came through loud and clear.

"Max, go to your brother."

Tommy knew I was serious. He didn't ask any more questions.

"Max, come on." Tommy waved Max to him. "Come on!"

Reluctantly, Max began to back up the hallway.

I'd hung Dad's cane up on one of the coat hooks in the hallway. I grabbed it and headed for the kitchen.

"You two go wait in the pickup."

Tommy and Max didn't move. They weren't going anywhere. There was no point in arguing. If I'd been in their shoes, I would have done the same.

I raised the cane up ahead of me and gripping it tight, ready to defend myself, I rounded the corner and headed into the kitchen.

I stopped by the overturned chair, trying to take in the whole room, trying to look everywhere all at once, expecting whatever had broken into our house to tear from cover and attack me.

The kitchen was a mess. The contents of the fridge had been pulled out and thrown around the room. The bench was filthy with dirt. Something had climbed up onto it. The kitchen table had been shoved across the room. It had come to rest against the wall. I looked underneath it, to see if anything was hiding there.

The room seemed empty. The back door was wide open. The awful smell had begun to fade too. Whatever had broken into our house had been big, strong. Strong enough to shove the heavy kitchen table from one side of the room to the other. It'd been hungry too. Although, when I set about cleaning up, I realised the only thing it had actually eaten had been the raw red meat I'd bought to cook for Sunday dinner.

It had also pissed on the kitchen floor, leaving a puddle of stinking, dark yellow fluid in the middle of the room. I locked and bolted the back door. I kept the boys out of the kitchen until I'd finished cleaning up. I didn't want them seeing the mess. I didn't want them any more afraid than they already were. That night, I checked every door and window in the house. Then I checked them all again. I told David Jnr he was camping in my room for the night, and Tommy and Max bunked together too.

I don't think I slept for a moment that night. If I hadn't run out of the house, leaving the door wide open, whatever had come through our home wouldn't have gotten in. What if Max hadn't left the house and, instead, had come face to face with it? It had been strong enough to throw the kitchen furniture around. What might it have done to my boy?

5.

"Sounds like a bear to me." Jim Peterson had brought over the check for dinner. "Maybe something woke it up early. We sometimes get 'em fishing round in the dumpster out back. How the hell'd it get in your house?"

"You want me to come check it out for ya? Be happy to make sure it's not under your bed," Mac Thompson leered from the next booth.

"Mac!" Jim growled.

"What? I'm just offrin' to look after Ellie."

I couldn't help myself. "Mac, you can't even look after yourself. Did your mum dress you again today?"

"Fuck you!"

David Jnr started laughing. "My mum dressed me today!" Pleased with his input into the conversation, he nodded to Max and then returned to spooning in large mouthfuls of cookie dough.

Tommy looked over from the pinball machine. He'd spent most of the night feeding it instead of himself. His meal sat pretty much untouched where Sally had put it down almost an hour ago. "You okay, Mum?"

I smiled and took the check from Jim. As our Sunday dinner was *in the bear,* I'd decided to treat the boys to some burgers at the diner. The diner gave out their checks in little black wallets. You know, the kind you get when you go to an expensive restaurant. The kind where they're hiding what your meal cost so you don't get a scare and run. Well, the diner wasn't expensive, but Jim and Sally liked to do things properly. The diner was always spotless, the tables always set perfectly and the food was the best in the county. Jim and Sally waited the tables and they cooked the food. They could have charged a lot more than they did. Those little black wallets were just another example of the pride they took in doing things right.

"Have you got a gun, Ellie?" I could see Jim was worried. I shook my head. Dad had had a rifle years before but he'd given up hunting well before any of the kids were born. I think he took an ad out in the paper and sold it.

"I've got a spare shotgun. I'll bring it up tomorrow. You keep your house locked up in the meantime, okay? You want Tommy's dinner to go?"

"Thanks, Jim." I passed Jim the plate and he headed off to get a take-out box. Jim and Sally had been good to us. I couldn't repay them for the kindness they'd shown me after Dad had passed. They'd helped drag me through the winter. I might have gone off the rails without them.

It was waiting for me underneath the check.

There was dirt on the paper. Champagne Basildon Bond. It was wet. It looked like it had been pulled out of the ground. I looked across the table to Max. He was watching me. He'd seen my expression change.

"Mum? What is it? What's wrong?"

I didn't want to touch it, but I had to know what was written on the page. I lifted the note from the plate. It was cold, so cold. I peeled the paper open.

WHY DID YOU STOP DIGGING?

I stood up fast. The world was spinning. Max was on his feet too. He was watching me, trying to predict what I was going to do. He grabbed David Jnr and David Jnr's ice cream. I emptied my pockets onto the table. There would be enough there to cover the meal.

"Come on." The words sounded like someone else spoke them.

Max edged David Jnr out of the booth. I was already headed for the door. Tommy saw me coming.

"Mum? You okay?"

By the time we hit the door I was running. Tommy scooped up David Jnr. Max followed behind with the ice cream.

"Mum? What's going on?" Tommy strapped David Jnr in and we took off for the cemetery.

*

The gates to the car park were locked. I pulled over in front of them. We'd have to jump the fence to get in. Al Weaver had taken my shovel. I'd need to find something else to dig with.

"Mum? What's going on? What are we doing here?" Tommy wanted answers. I noticed a light blink on upstairs in the pastor's house.

"Mum and me found some letters from Grandpa" Max started to explain.

"What?"

"I found one in my room. Then they were all over the floor when I got home yesterday. When the bear got in."

I was pretty sure I could get myself over the fence. I wondered if I should take Tommy with me.

"What? What letters? Are you talking about what happened Friday night?"

"Yeah, that's right."

"No! That's bullshit! I don't know what you thought was going on, but I didn't see any letter. I looked between those two books Mum's got on the table. There's nothing between them."

"Bullshit!"

"Max!" I scolded him.

"Sorry, Mum. But that's not true! I saw that letter. It was on my pillow. They were all over the floor yesterday. Like a trail of them. I put them on the dining room table."

The letters had been where Max said he'd left them. I'd put them between the encyclopedias along with Dad's other letters. "Tommy, what are you talking about?"

"I'm sorry, Mum. I looked between those books you've got on the table. There's nothing between them. I know you miss Grandpa, but there aren't any letters."

I didn't understand. I'd seen them. Max had seen them. I had to get out of the pickup. I had to get to Dad.

WHY DID YOU STOP DIGGING?

"Tommy, stay here with your brothers. Okay? Wait here for…"

Al Weaver's squad car pulled in behind us. I thought about running. About jumping the fence before he could catch me. I turned back to Tommy. I think he knew what I was considering. He put a hand on my arm

When I turned back, Al was looking in through my window. He knocked on the glass. Reluctantly, I wound the window down.

"Ellie. I hadn't expected to see you here tonight." He shone his torch into the cab, sweeping the beam over the boys. Tommy raised a hand up to shield his eyes. "Boys." Al nodded.

"Mr Weaver." Max waved hello back.

"Pastor called me. Said he'd seen your car pull up. You

can understand he's a bit wary of you, after yesterday. What are you doing, Ellie?"

I've never been a good liar. I always thought of that as being a good thing. Right then, though, I wanted a lie, wanted to be able to come up with something plausible, something that would send Al away so I could get on with what I had to do. I had nothing.

Al leant a bit closer. "It's a cold night, Ellie. Don't you think your kids should be at home?" That wasn't a question.

WHY DID YOU STOP DIGGING?

Someone was watching us. I could feel it.

Maybe I could drive round the block. Find another place to park. Jump the fence after Al had gone...

"Take the kids home, Ellie."

"Mum." Tommy tugged at my arm. "Let's go."

What was I supposed to do? Just leave Dad there?

"I'll follow behind. I hear you might have had a bear at your place. I'm going to check around, make sure the house is properly secure. Okay?"

I knew what Al was doing. He was going to make sure I went home, make sure I stayed home.

I gripped the steering wheel without moving.

"It's okay, Mum."

I'm sorry.

I'm sorry, Dad.

"I'm sorry, kids."

What was I thinking, dragging them into this? I locked my jaw against my anger, the frustration and the shame I felt. A tear streaked my cheek. I cast it off my face. I wouldn't give in.

Behind us, Al Weaver flashed his headlights. I started the pickup and we pulled off with the squad car following us home.

All the time we'd been parked up I'd felt it. I was sure

someone was watching us. I could feel their eyes burning into me. Not from the pastor's window though, from the darkness beyond the graveyard gates.

*

Al had patrolled the house for over an hour. I heard him on the porch talking to Tommy.

"Your Mum's been through a tough time. You've got to look after her, son."

"Yes, sir."

I poured another glass of Jack and looked out of the window. When we'd gotten home, I'd headed to the encyclopedias. I'd taken off the top one to check on Dad's letters.

They weren't there.

"She needs you right now. You're the man of the house. Don't let your Mum do anything stupid, okay?"

"Yes, sir."

Al had sat for another hour in his patrol car in the driveway. He could have his soup. I'd have another Jack. And after that, I'd had another.

The boys had put themselves to bed. I fell asleep on the couch, watching Dad's chair on the porch.

6.

Death is silence. It's not the crying and the grieving. It's not
the condolences or the pastor's patronising words. It's not the
pain, like a heart attack, that seizes you in the dark when you
close your eyes. No, it's the never-ending, fucking silence of it.
It's never hearing their voice again. Not a word.

Not a sound.

Not *ever* again.

That silence took hold round my neck. It hung there, a
dead thing that I carried with me wherever I went. A constant
reminder I'd failed Dad.
No more letters came.

A few days later, Al Weaver called. I stood in the hallway

listening to him talk. I remember bits of the conversation, the silence drowned out the rest of it.

"…had a hard time with this, Ellie. It's been tough on you."

I watched the dust spiralling on the beams of morning sun that stretched into the lounge. It had only been a week ago that spring had shamed me into tidying behind the couch and finding the first letter.

"…might like to know I spoke to Doc Kellerman. He issued the death certificate for your Dad. He… well, he confirmed his death, Ellie. He was definitely dead. No one made any mistakes."

I looked in through Max's doorway, up over his Superman bedspread, to his pillow. I willed a letter to appear. Some word. Anything.

"…thought that might, you know, help."

I think I thanked him for calling before I hung up. With my gaze, I traced a path from Max's doorway, where the third letter had appeared, through the hallway, picking out the spots where I thought I'd found the trail of notes. Nothing but Max's discarded gumboots on the floor now.

I headed back into the lounge. I grabbed the side of the couch with both hands and pulled it out from against the wall. I sat on the floor and looked at the empty space left behind. I sat there until Max got home from school.

*

Couple of weeks passed. I'd tried to keep news of our *bear* visit from David Jnr. That had worked okay until one afternoon when I'd caught Max and Tommy arguing over whether it had really been a bear or not. That, in itself, wouldn't have been a problem if they hadn't been doing it across the room from their *now likely never-to-sleep-again* eight year old brother. That night David Jnr moved into my bed.

Now, David Jnr was a small boy but he had a big snore. It wasn't always loud, he snored worse when he had a cold. Recently, he'd had a cold. I had no idea where the snoring had come from. His father hadn't snored and, as far as I was aware, I didn't either. I don't even remember Dad snoring when I was a kid. Either way, David Jnr got a good night's sleep in my bed. And he was the only one.

I didn't mind the noise. It helped keep the silence at arm's length. I wasn't going to be sleeping through it though, so I got up, fixed myself up a Jack and spent most of the night watching Dad's chair through the dining room window. Over the next few nights I finished up that bottle. I bought two more from the store. Just like when Dad had been with us. David snored his way through the night and I found my way to morning from my lookout in the dining room with a long glass of Jack.

During those nights, I'd raise a glass to Dad and talk to him, more noise to keep the silence away. I didn't really mind being awake while the boys slept. I'd not slept well since the bear had gotten into our house. Being up meant I could watch over them, stand guard. Being up meant I could watch for more letters.

Night after night I'd talk with Dad. I'd tell him what had happened at the graveyard that night. I'd tell him about the bear. I'd ask him why the letters stopped, what it had meant. I'd imagine him sat in his chair on the porch. I'd pour two glasses out. We'd drink Jack together and, as the nights drew on, I'd ask him again, why did he stop writing? Then I'd demand to know, then I'd plead for another letter, just one more, so I'd know it wasn't all in my head. *Knock again, Dad, and I'll come running*.

No more letters came.

I'd drink both glasses and toast Dad's health. For all the

fucking good that would do now.

*

When the kids were around the silence left me alone, or at least, they made enough noise that it couldn't keep up, so over the next few weeks, I tried to spend as much time with them as I could. We went out to the diner, we went to the movies, Fishy Friday became Fishy Thursday and Even Fishier Friday. On Saturday mornings, I took the boys to the graveyard to visit Dad's grave. Al Weaver had spoken to the pastor and, as long as I checked in with him first—I guess so he could check I wasn't carrying any concealed shovels—he'd let me visit Dad's grave without calling the cops. To the outside world it would have looked like we were getting on with our lives.

Still, no more letters came.

I filled my days with noise and my nights with Jack Daniels.

I brought Tommy's curfew forward for a second time. From eight in the evening to seven. I wanted my boys around me. I wanted them home: to protect me from the silence, but also to make sure they were safe. Tommy was out almost every night; he was twelve, just discovering the world, starting to break away. He didn't want to be cooped up with his Mum and brothers. We fought. I won. Nothing was going to come between me and protecting my boys. Even my boys themselves.

I didn't mind that we fought. It was more noise to keep the silence away.

For weeks the silence endured. Until one evening it was replaced by screaming.

*

137

At the movie theatre in town Sunday afternoons were *Kid's Classics* afternoons. They'd show a movie like *The Goonies* or *Raiders of the Lost Ark*, they'd lay on hotdogs, ice-cream, sometimes one of the theatre staff would dress up as Indiana Jones or Luke Skywalker when they showed *Star Wars*. David Jnr couldn't tell that it was always the same guy dressed up. He was in awe. He loved *Kid's Classics*. In fact the whole of his weekend revolved around it.

Max shook his head and shot me a cheeky smile when the same staff member appeared from behind the curtain, this time dressed as one of the ghostbusters, but David Jnr was so excited he threw popcorn all over himself. I wished Tommy was with us. A year ago, he wouldn't have missed it. That afternoon, he'd made his excuses as soon as we'd finished lunch, taken his bike and hurried off. I suspected he had a date with Em Cooper, Deputy Ray Cooper's kid. Max had quietly confirmed I was right. His thinking was, that his big brother couldn't beat on him if he didn't strictly tell me, but instead just gave me enough clues that I could work things out for myself. I told him that was clever thinking, and that no one would be beating on anyone while they were living under my roof.

Well, *Ghostbusters* was a huge hit with the kids that Sunday, and afterwards it looked likely that David Jnr's new hobby would be busting ghosts, as often as he possibly could, for the foreseeable future. He busted double figures just in the car on the way home.

By the time we got back, it was getting on for five and starting to get dark, the world beginning to shrink around us as we sat in the pickup. Max unstrapped David Jnr, who leapt out of the car after another ghost he'd spotted, this one headed for the house. I was about to get out when Max stopped me.

"Mum, the other day, at Grandpa's grave…" he stopped, like he was having second thoughts.

"What is it, Max?"

"Did you feel like someone was looking at us?"

I'd felt it too. I felt it every time we visited. I didn't want to scare him. "You mean the pastor? I don't think we're his favourite family."

"No, from the woods. Like there was someone in the woods."

I could feel panic rising up through me. I gripped the steering wheel, trying to hold it off. It settled in my gut: a pitstop.

"You saw the notes, didn't you, Max? Grandpa's notes. You saw them. They were real, weren't they?"

"Yes, mum. I saw them. Why?"

Night after night I'd slowly convinced myself I'd made it all up. That I'd gone crazy with the grief, that Dad's messages had just been denial, my own desperate denial that he was gone.

I looked up towards the house. The night seemed to have come early, darkness closing in fast on all sides of the pickup. I thought of the bear, of whatever had come out of the woods searching for meat. Had it followed me home that day? Followed me from the graveyard? I realised I couldn't see David Jnr. The panic leapt from my gut to my heart.

"David?"

I spun to look behind us, trying to take in everywhere around the pickup. No sign of him. "David!" I grabbed at the handle to open my door.

Just then David Jnr slammed into the side of the pickup, slapping his hands against my door.

"Busted!" he yelled.

"You little shit!" Max yelled.

"Max!" I scolded him, even though I was thinking the same thing.

"Sorry, Mum."

"That's okay." We both had our hearts in our throats.

"Haha! Bustin' makes me feel good!" David called as he raced off after a new ghost.

The next hour was taken up with drinking hot chocolate and hunting through Max's wardrobe for the boiler suit I'd bought him two Halloweens previously, so that David Jnr could complete his Ghostbuster outfit. He'd already repurposed his school backpack and a tube off the vacuum to create his own proton pack. The boiler suit found, he was ready.

"Don't cross the streams, man!" he shouted as he raced off to catch the next spook.

I'd roasted a chicken for lunch, so Sunday supper was always going to be leftovers. I made chicken and coleslaw sandwiches for me and Max. David Jnr wasn't interested in anything but ghosts. He chased ghosts down the hallway, he'd chased them out of each of our bedrooms, he'd even found one in the toilet that he liked to call 'The Floater.' Well, that had had Max in fits.

"They're sneaky. They hide in the shadows," he'd warned us. "You can't see 'em… until they want you to see 'em."

After we'd finished eating, Max excused himself and headed off to his room. We'd scored a second hand copy of *The Tombs of Atuan* from the library's used book sale the day before, and I knew he was excited to get into it.

"Will you go and bust ghosts somewhere else?" I heard him yell five minutes later.

"David Jnr, let your brother read," I called down the hallway. "Go and bust some ghosts in your own room."

"But Mum, there aren't any ghosts in my room," David Jnr protested. "There's a big one in Max's."

Panic flickered in my stomach. I knew David Jnr was only playing but the unease I'd felt in the car, while I'd been talking to Max, had followed me into the house. Having David Jnr race through the house was a good distraction, but things were starting to quiet down now and, as the noise faded, the silence and all its dark questions returned.

I heard Max's door close and David Jnr's feet drumming across the hallway floor. He was back on the hunt. Max had seen the letters. If that was the case, why hadn't Tommy? And, if he had, why lie and say he hadn't? Where was he anyway? It was dark outside. I checked my watch. It was only six fifteen. I tried to shake the sense that something was wrong, convince myself I was overthinking everything. I really wanted to break open the Jack. I'd promised myself I wouldn't do that until the kids were asleep.

When I heard the front door open ten minutes later, I felt like I could breathe again for the first time since I'd thought of Tommy out in the dark.

"Tom?" Max called from his room.

No one answered.

"Tommy?" I called from the dining room.

Still no reply.

Then I saw David Jnr race past the dining room window.

"David Jnr?" I shouted. He couldn't hear me.

I got up and headed over to the window. The blur, that had been David Jnr ever since we'd gotten home, had stopped near the end of the porch. He stood, on the edge of the darkness, looking out across the drive.

I raised up my hand to knock on the window. I didn't want him outside any more than Tommy. But I stopped myself. David Jnr waved his hands in front of him. I knew what he was doing. He got that from me. We both talked with our hands. He was talking to someone. Someone out of sight in the darkness on the drive.

I unlocked the window and opened it. The frozen evening air welcomed the chance to slink inside.

Now David Jnr was pointing. It might have been my tired

eyes, but the darkness in front of him seemed to grow thicker.

"... think I'm afraid of you? I'm not. You don't scare me."

The darkness swelled. Yes, it definitely moved.

David levelled up his vacuum-hose-particle-accelerator to take a shot.

"I ain't afraid of no ghost!"

Max's voice caught me by surprise.

"What are you doing, butthead? I thought we agreed to stay inside the house and wait for Tommy."

Max was heading along the porch towards his brother. David Jnr turned from his ghost busting.

"But I'm busting ghosts here!" He protested, pointing into the thick darkness.

"I'll bust you in a minute!" Max growled. He wasn't messing about and David Jnr knew it. He shrugged his shoulders, huffed and stomped back along the porch. I stayed watching the darkness where he'd stood.

As he passed it, David Jnr jumped up onto Dad's easy chair.

Max called out, "What are you doin? That's Grandpa's chair!"

David Jnr was already jumping back off.

"Yuk! It's wet!"

"It's not wet. It's just cold, dumbass. Now get inside."

David Jnr turned and waved the now soaking butt of his boiler suit at Max. "Just cold, huh?"

I'd been watching Max and David Jnr out of the corner of my eye but now I wanted to know what was going on. I turned to see Max inspecting Dad's chair.

Cautiously, he pressed down on the seat. Water spread out from the cushion, outlining his fingers. He looked up at me. "Mum?"

It hadn't rained in two weeks, and even then it barely got under the porch unless we had a big storm. Only once while

Dad had stayed with us had we needed to put a cover over his chair to keep the rain off.

Max looked down at his feet. Water was pooling, spreading out around his sneakers. He edged backwards.

"Max? What is it?"

He crouched down in front of the easy chair.

"Mum!" Now there was fear in his voice. "Mum!" When he stood up with the wet note paper in his hands, I ran out of the house.

*

Max and David Jnr stood behind me as I knelt down to look under the easy chair. Black water had oozed from the seat cushion, dripping and pooling across the wooden boards.

"It's that smell again!" Max's voice cracked. He hopped from foot to foot. He'd run at the first sign of trouble.

"It's okay, hon. It's okay." I tried to calm him. He was right though. The stench was back: decay. The water was thick with it. I could feel it seeping into my jeans as I knelt in front of Dad's chair.

Max had found the letter laying in the puddle of water under the seat. It had fallen apart, sticking to his fingers, as he'd picked it up. I'd tried to carefully peel the remains of the note apart. I needed to know what it said, but it had disintegrated to mush. How long had it been there? How long had it been sitting in the stinking water waiting for me to find it?

The underside of the seat cushion had split open. Had the material rotted? Its foam insides, heavy, swollen with black water, sagged through the opening. All around the edges of the split, notes poked through, as if someone had been stuffing the seat with letters. How many were there? What had Dad been trying to say? I thought he'd fallen silent. Night after night I'd sat watching his chair. All the time he'd been trying to talk to me! The letters had been right in front of me the whole time.

I grabbed at one of the notes, trying to ease the wet paper through the opening without tearing it. The bulging foam pressed against the back of my hand. It should have been cold but it wasn't. It felt warm, like something alive.

As I pulled on the note, the split in the underside of the seat began to grow. The material tore, ripping open, the heavy foam insides spilling onto the porch. It hit the boards with a sickening squelch that made me snatch my hand away.

"Shit!" Max gasped behind me. I was afraid he'd bolt, panic and run into the darkness. I reached up and grabbed his arm. In turn, he clapped his hand round David Jnr's arm to stop him running off into the night. I could feel the pair of them tugging against me.

"It's okay. It's okay." I held Max until he stopped struggling. He held onto David Jnr until he'd calmed down too.

The foam was black with rot. The awful smell poured from it. I could taste it in my mouth. Maggots writhed on the foam. They spilled from the empty carcass of the seat, raining down on to the decaying cushion. Maggots and paper.

I snatched up one of the notes. It was soaked, it tore as I tried to open it. I snatched up another, I could barely make out a word written on it: HELP.

I found another note. This one was drier, more recent. Only half of it had been lost to the black water.

…ALL OVER ME! HOW DID THEY GET IN HERE?

I grabbed up another note. Maggots spilled out as I opened the paper.

144

CHRIST ELLIE! I CAN FEEL THEM.

THEY'RE UNDER MY SKIN!

THEY'RE EATING ME!

Another: IT HURTS SO MUCH! WHERE ARE YOU???
ELLIE!

No, no, no! All those hours I'd sat watching the chair. All
the time he'd been screaming for my help and I'd done
nothing!

"Go get in the pickup, kids." I pulled myself quickly to
my feet. Maggots clung to my jeans. Max and David Jnr stood,
stunned, looking at me. "Go and get in the pickup. Do it now!"

"We have to wait for Tommy." Max pleaded. He looked
around. "Where is he? Where is he?"

"Max, listen to me. Go and take David Jnr and get in the
pickup. Do as I say, okay?"

I ran along the porch and down towards the shed. Al
Weaver still had my shovel. What the hell was I going to dig
with? I grabbed the hatchet off the wood chopping block. It'd
have to do. I ran after the boys towards the truck.

Max was standing by the door to the pickup. "Mum,
please. We've gotta wait for Tommy!"

"Max! I don't have time for this. Get in the pickup!"

I dropped the hatchet in the footwell and began strapping
David Jnr in. Max climbed slowly up into the cab. "Tommy'll
be fine, Max. The house is open. He can let himself in. We can't
wait. We have to go. Now put your seatbelt on."

Dad, we're coming! We're coming!

Max grabbed my arm. "Mum, no! Please, mum!"

I should have listened to him.

145

But all I could hear were Dad's screams. Everything was red, everything was wrong, my whole body shook to the beat of my heart slamming in my chest. I couldn't get my breath. I couldn't get my panic under control. I threw the truck into drive and we lurched forward, heading fast for the main road.

It was just before 7pm. Just before curfew.

Max yelled from the backseat. "Mum! Please! We need to wait for Tommy!"

I swung the truck out onto the road.

I didn't see Tommy until it was too late.

The pickup bucked as it ran over Tommy's bike. The front wheels twisted the frame, mangling it till it snapped. I stamped on the brake. *STOP! PLEASE STOP!* We skidded, the bike caught under the pickup's front wheels. We must have dragged it six feet out into the road before I felt it break free and run under the back wheels, crushing what was left of it.

The screams I could hear were no longer Dad's: they were mine.

7.

Tommy had been rushing home to make curfew.

He'd turned in to the drive as I'd turned out of it. I'd been going too fast. I couldn't brake in time. Al Weaver said, seeing that twisted and broken bike was like someone had punched him in the gut. He'd dragged it off the highway himself. Afterwards he'd sat on the side of the road and had a smoke. To hell with what the doctors said, it was the only way he could stop himself shaking.

"Christ, that could have been Tommy."

The pickup had clipped Tommy, throwing him off his bike and out into the road.

I know they say your brain blocks out the worst things, the things you can't cope with remembering. I only remember pieces of what happened next. I remember standing over Tommy, laying there in the road. He wasn't moving. I remember thinking of Mum and the eighteen-wheeler. I remember Tommy lain across the three of us in the pickup's cab, his head in my lap, as I prayed to God he'd be okay. *You can have me. You can do what you want to me. But don't you dare, don't you dare hurt my boys!*

I couldn't tell you the route we took or a single detail of a single thing that took place outside the pickup's cab on the way to the hospital. Next thing I remember was carrying

Tommy into the emergency room. He hadn't moved, he hadn't moaned, he hadn't stirred the whole way there. *Please wake up, hon! Please wake up!*

Jenny Taylor told me later that she thought she was going to have to sedate me just to be able to pry Tommy from my arms so she could treat him. At any moment I thought my heart might explode.

Tommy woke up on a cot in the corridor when they were about to take him in for a CT scan. He wanted to know where he was. I tried to tell him but I couldn't get the words out for crying. Jenny got me a coffee and told me it was a good sign: that Tommy had been talking when he'd woken up. They'd run all the tests they needed to and we'd know more soon enough.

*

The accident had broken Tommy's right leg. He'd gotten a bad concussion and a large, angry bruise the shape of one of the pickup's headlamps across his side. Max thought that was the coolest thing ever.

"You can really see where the truck hit you! So cool!" He got in really close to have a good look. David Jnr hung back. I picked him up and hugged him. I'd caused this. All of it. I couldn't forgive myself for that.

Sally and Jim had agreed to take Max and David Jnr for the night. They picked them up from the hospital at around 11pm after they'd closed up the diner. They brought a plate of sandwiches too.

"It's just leftovers, but I figured they'd be good now or for breakfast too, if you need 'em." Sally hugged me.

"I guess there's no way we can convince you to go home and get some rest tonight?" Jim had bought a Thermos of coffee. He opened it and poured me a cup.

"Would you?"

"Not a chance in hell." Jim smiled warmly and handed me the coffee. He also reached into his jacket pocket and snuck out a hip flask. "Thought you might need this too."

*

About 11.30pm, a nurse came into Tommy's room. She seemed surprised to see me and demanded to know what I was doing in the hospital after visiting hours. I told her, if she wanted me to leave she could call Al Weaver and get him to come drag me out. Or... she could try it herself if she wanted. We didn't see her again after that.

An hour or so later, Jenny Taylor came in with a blanket for me. There was no way I'd be sleeping, but I was grateful of an extra layer for Tommy. It had grown so cold in his room that I expected to be able to see my breath when I spoke. Jenny said she'd see about getting the heating turned up and asked me to try and avoid scaring any more of the night shift staff, no matter how annoying they might be. I made no promises.

Tommy woke up hungry at around 1am. We shared half of one of Sally's sandwiches. I told him again how sorry I was.

He just smiled.

"Who was knocking, Mum? I... can you tell them to keep it down, please?"

CAN'T YOU HEAR ME KNOCKING?

I listened in the silence. "Sure, hon. I'll tell them."

Tommy was asleep again before I'd finished speaking.

I pulled my jacket closed around me. The room seemed to be growing colder all the time.

Knock again, Dad. Knock again and I'll come running. That was what I'd said when I thought the letters had stopped, when I'd sat through those long nights at the dining room table desperate for some word from him. How long had those

149

letters been gathering in the easy chair? Some of them had been legible, but most of them were rotten beyond saving. How long had he been screaming for my help?

I balled my fists against that thought. I couldn't accept it. I couldn't stand it.

But I couldn't leave Tommy's side. Not after everything.

I'm sorry, Dad. I can't leave my boy. Not now. Not tonight. I tried to help. I tried to help and look what happened! I won't leave him while he needs me.

The letters had been terrible. How could Dad be aware? How could he know what was happening to him?

Tommy stirred. He mumbled something before trying to roll onto his side. The pain made him moan in his sleep. He rolled back onto this back. I'd have taken his pain in an instant if I could. I'd gladly have taken his place in front of the pickup to save him from this.

He stirred again. I wondered if he could hear the knocking in the darkness of his sleep?

No, Dad. You can't ask me. You can't ask me to leave Tommy. Not after everything. I can't. I won't!

Somewhere, a way off in the depths of the hospital, I thought I could hear someone crying. I held Tommy's hand and sat tight. Whatever happened in the world outside Tommy's room tonight would be for the world to solve. I was where I needed to be, where I was going to stay.

8.

By 4am I'd read the paper twice. I'd watched two episodes of Law & Order with the sound turned off. I'd paced Tommy's room, read every notice, every note fixed to the magnolia walls. I'd replayed the accident a thousand times over. If I'd just listened to Max, none of this would have happened. If I'd stopped…

And then I realised why Max could see the letters and Tommy couldn't, and how I'd thought I wasn't sensitive anymore, but I was.

That was why Max had been panicking, shouting for me to stop: he'd known. He'd known that if we raced out of the driveway we'd hit Tommy. That was why he was screaming that we had to wait. It was why he'd arranged with David Jnr to stay inside until Tommy got home. He'd known. He'd known in the same way I'd known Kitty Burke was in the creek.

I sat down next to Tommy's bed. I tried to piece it all together, searching for signs, times when I thought Max might have known more or sensed something he couldn't know. That was how it had been for me.

I hadn't ever talked to the kids about it. Hell, even Dad and I only danced round the subject once. That was a couple of months after Mum had died. I was fifteen. Dad had asked how

I'd known where Kitty Burke's body was. I couldn't answer him. Even then I couldn't really explain it. I remember we sat in silence for a long time. I think he wanted to ask me if I'd heard anything from Mum after she'd been killed. He never came out and said that though, and we never talked about it again after that.

I'd read about near death experiences in the library. What had happened to me fit with what they were describing in the books. They said dying and coming back could leave you changed, able to sense things. I had this feeling that the dead had seen me when I'd drowned, before Dad had brought me back, and they'd clung to me. Sometimes I thought I heard them talking, black voices pressed into my ears. Like when you're driving up a hill and you can feel your ears are gonna pop. Other times it was just an idea that wasn't there before. Sometimes I'd flinch when I felt them touch my skin.

Being sensitive was a curse, not a blessing. I'd seen and known things no kid should know. I didn't want it and I certainly didn't want it for my boys. I was glad when it seemed to have faded. When the dead had moved on, left me be.

Had I brought them back now, with my grief?

I sat watching Tommy sleeping peacefully. Whatever had disturbed his dreams earlier in the night had moved on. I hoped I was wrong about Max. That it was just 4.30am talk, the shock of what had happened the night before, me pulling crazy answers out of the darkness. What had happened to me when I was 5, nothing like that had ever happened to Max. The dead had no cause to seek him out. I hoped I was wrong, because the only thing connecting Max to the dead was me.

9.

Jim was going to run the boys to school while Sally opened the diner.

"You didn't sleep at all, did you?"

I shook my head, and then realised Sally was waiting on the end of the line for an answer.

"No. I couldn't." My voice was rough, small. "I tried to sleep in a chair for a bit, but I couldn't get... it was just uncomfortable." That wasn't true but I didn't want her to worry.

"Bullshit!" Sally called me out. "You didn't sit down for the whole night, did you?" I heard her take another drag of her smoke. "How's he doing this morning? You eaten anything yet?"

"I shared a sandwich with Tommy. He's doing better. They're gonna keep him in for another day. I'm about to go home and get him some books and some clothes."

"Alright, but pop in here and get yourself something to eat later, will ya?"

"Thanks, Sal. Thank Jim too, for me."

"You don't have to thank us. We're just glad you're all okay. Now go get yourself some rest. Not your bullshit rest. Some real rest."

"I will. Hey, Sal, how was Max this morning?"

"He was fine, hon. Couldn't stop talking about that bruise."

"Yeah, Tommy says I made him the coolest kid in school. Wants me to make sure Em Cooper hears about it."

"Shit, they grow up fast. Don't you beat yourself up about this, Ellie. It was an accident. Could have happened to anyone."

I knew that wasn't true. If I hadn't been racing to the cemetery, Tommy wouldn't be in the hospital.

"Thanks, Sal."

"Remember, rest and food. That's what you need today. And get yourself some coffee before you drive home, okay?"

"I will. I'll see you later."

"Sure thing. You look after yourself."

*

It hit me all over again the moment I stepped out of the hospital. The screaming messages, the accident. Everything I'd tried to keep at arm's length while I'd watched over Tommy. I'd swung the pickup across three spots when I'd parked it. From where I stood, I could see a ticket stuffed under one of the wipers. It flapped angrily on the wind, like it'd been caught in a trap and was trying to escape.

Jenny Taylor had just clocked off from the night shift. She'd huddled into a corner by the hospital's entrance, trying to keep out of the rain while she had a smoke. I gave her a big hug and thanked her for everything she'd done for us the night before. I also begged a cigarette off her: my first one since I found out I was pregnant with Tommy. It went straight to my head and made me want to throw up, but it was the only way I could face the pickup that morning.

I ground my teeth against my anger and shame as I examined the front of the truck. One of the headlamps had smashed where it hit Tommy and paint had been scored off the grille where his bike had gone under us. It could so easily have been him.

I'd go to jail to protect my kids. That the person hurting them had been me was unthinkable. It'd be a long time before I'd be able to forgive myself for what I'd done. I tore the ticket off the windscreen and pulled myself into the pickup's cab.

It'd been raining since dawn, a mist of thin rain that muted the landscape speeding past the pickup. I'd left the hospital and driven into a grey world with nothing to distract me from the thoughts swarming in my mind. The roads were slick and I was driving too fast.

CHRIST ELLIE! I CAN FEEL THEM.
Every time I'd tried to help Dad I'd put us in harm's way.

THEY'RE UNDER MY SKIN!
First Max had almost run into the bear.

THEY'RE EATING ME!
Then Tommy had almost gone under the pickup.

IT HURTS SO MUCH!
Each time the danger had gotten worse.

WHERE ARE YOU??? ELLIE!
I thought about that as the hatchet slid from side to side in the footwell as I drove. I thought about that as I sped towards the cemetery.

10.

"You can't go up there, Ellie." Al Weaver had put his arm in front of me to stop me. He was stood by his squad car, trying to hear what was being said over his radio. Another blast of static came through loud and clear. He shook his head and threw the radio on the seat. "Bullshit! Ray, go into the pastor's house and call the office. Tell them we need animal control up here."

"Yes, sir." Ray nodded hello as he passed me. Al kept his arm in front of me.

"What are you doing here, Ellie?"

"Just came to visit Dad. What's going on?"

"How're the kids doing after yesterday? That was a damn close call."

"They're okay. Al, what's going on?"

"Sit down, Ellie."

"Al?"

Al pulled open the back door on his cruiser. "It's about your Dad."

I had no intention of sitting.

"What's happened?" I tried to look past Al up to the graveyard, to Dad's grave. A way up the path two more officers stood with their backs to us, a blue wall blocking me seeing any further along.

"That bear that was at your place, well, it looks like it's been here last night, or the past couple of nights. It's been digging in the cemetery. I guess, because the extension's behind the chapel, no one saw it."

"Are you kidding me? We both know the pastor's got x-ray eyes. You're telling me he didn't see anything? What are you trying to say, Al?"

"It'd been digging at the graves. I don't know, I guess it was starving, which is why it broke into your house…"

"Al! What's happened?"

"Ellie, your Dad's gone. We got up there about an hour ago and, well, the coffin's there, the bear must've bust it open. I'm sorry, Ellie. We're getting animal control in. It's possible it dragged him into the woods. We'll track the bear and we'll find your Dad. I promise you that."

Everything was spinning. I grabbed a hold of the door to stop myself from falling.

"Ellie? You okay? You should sit down."

I backed away from the squad car. I thought about trying to run past Al. I think he could tell what I was considering.

"Ellie, you can't go up there. We're not sure where the bear is right now. If it comes back… I won't let you risk your safety. There's nothing you can do. Do you understand me?"

Al held his hands up, ready to try and grab me, but I was already heading back towards the pickup. I stumbled down the path to the cemetery's entrance.

I fell against the side of the pickup. The whole world turned over and I threw up coffee onto the wet earth. I leant against the truck retching until I'd emptied what little I had in my stomach. If I'd brought Max and David Jnr to the cemetery last night, we'd likely have run into the bear. How would I have protected them then? With the hatchet? You fucking idiot, Ellie! I hammered my fist on the side of the truck. At every turn I'd risked my boys.

No more. No more. I was shaking so badly I could barely get the door to the pickup open. I pulled myself inside, started the engine and turned the heating up full blast. My body was exhausted and empty. I sat watching the rain, gripping the wheel so tight my knuckles turned white. I'd drive home and get Tommy's things. Yes, then I'd drive to the store to pick up some snacks to smuggle into the hospital. I'd spend the day with Tommy, wait for news from Al, try to put some of the awful past few months behind us. Yes, that's what I'd do. That's what I'd do, just as soon as the shaking stopped.

I angled the heating so it was hitting me full on. As I twisted the vent, the parking ticket caught in the stream of hot air. The folded paper flipped up and open. That was when I saw the Champagne writing paper tucked inside it.

No more.

I thought about leaving it. About driving home and never reading it. I thought about the awful cries for help that had poured from Dad's easy chair.

Please. No more.

I reached across the seat and picked up the wet sheet of note paper. It stuck to my fingers, clinging, cold as death. I peeled the message open.

Six words. It read:

IT TOLD ME YOU WOULDN'T COME

11.

I parked the pickup round the side of the house. I sat looking at the easy chair on the porch, at its rotten insides spread across the wooden boards. I knew it was impossible, but the rotten foam looked like it had moved, somehow squirmed away from Dad's chair. I remembered how it'd felt warm, alive. No, no! I had to be imagining that.

From where I sat I couldn't see a single piece of paper, a single note.

I'd shoved the latest letter in the glove box as soon as I'd finished reading it. I wanted it out of my hands, off my skin. Its cold seemed to bleed into my fingers, draining what little warmth my body had left. I couldn't look at it. I couldn't understand what Dad had meant. Before he'd been screaming for my help, but now the tone of his words had changed.

I climbed out of the pickup and headed over towards Dad's chair. The rotten foam *had* moved. A trail of black liquid streaked behind it along the porch. Had something dragged it? I knew that foxes would eat decaying meat. Maybe one had come out of the woods last night and tried to drag it off? Its wet surface was alive with maggots. They'd spread through the liquid trail, they'd climbed over the wooden frame of Dad's chair, fat with decay they twisted and pulsed on the seat.

I couldn't look any longer. I had to step back, get back, get away from the rot! I could feel the maggots on my hands, they were on my arms, I could feel them under my clothes.

I ran around to the front of the house. I threw the door open and hurried inside. I slammed it behind me and leant against it, holding it closed, a human barricade. Against what? Maggots? I looked down at my hands: no maggots. I looked at the floor. Had they dropped off as I'd run? Nothing. Was I so tired I'd hallucinated the whole thing?

I was so exhausted I barely managed to haul myself to the dining table. I grabbed the Jack and poured myself a large glass. I sat where I'd sat night after night. I sat where I could see Dad's chair. I knew there was another explanation for everything that had happened. I knew there was an explanation that I didn't want to admit to. I'd lost my mind. I'd lost my fucking mind. Grief had reached up from Dad's grave with two black, terrible hands and it had pulled me down to madness.

There hadn't ever been any letters. That was why Tommy hadn't seen them. Max had been so scared by what was happening to me that he'd played along. He'd played along to appease me, so the truth wouldn't break me anymore than I already was. Christ! He was a ten-year-old boy. How would he react to his mother seeing things that weren't there? Ranting about things that weren't real? I downed the Jack.

My throat was raw from throwing up. The Jack burned it as I swallowed. I felt its heat spreading inside me like something alive. I poured another glass. I took another large drink. It hit my empty stomach and I felt the knot, the red knot of anxiety, a fist closed tight inside my gut, begin to relax. *I'd done this. All of it.*

I'd almost killed Max and Tommy.

Just me.

But I'd find a way to put it right.
Yes, I'd find a way to fix it all.
Yes, I'd do that,

I'd do that just as soon as I'd stopped for a moment to catch my breath.

As soon as I'd rested my head…

on the table…

just for a moment.

*

I could hear them moving around in the darkness. They were out on the porch. I could hear them approaching, shuffling closer. But I couldn't move. I couldn't open my eyes. I couldn't pull my head from the table. I couldn't see them, but I could hear them. Voices. Feet? Something wet, sliding? Then they were at the door.

Now I could smell them. The dead dog, the oozing foam, the bear that had strode through our house. Death, rotten meat. They'd all come to see me. Still I couldn't raise my head. Still I lay slumped, paralysed. I heard the door open and they were inside.

I screamed. I screamed in the darkness but no one heard. I screamed, I thrashed, but my mouth stayed closed and my body still. I felt their eyes on me. Just like I'd felt them at the cemetery. Just like I'd felt them watching from the woods. *Please, help! Someone help! SOMEONE HELP!*

"Mum! Mum!" It was Max. *Oh, thank God. My Max. Help me Max! Help me please.* "Mum!" he called again. "Mum! Grandpa's home! It's Grandpa, he's here!"

161

My eyes started open.

I pulled my head up fast from the table top, the pain in my neck and my skull straight away making me regret it.

The dining room was empty. No sign of Max or any of the nightmares that had crept up on me while I was sleeping. I thought I caught a movement out of the corner of my eye. I spun to look at Dad's chair on the porch. In the dream I'd heard them shuffling along the wooden boards outside. I waited, expecting to see someone or something lurch into view.

Nothing.

While I'd been sleeping, someone had put my head in a vice. At least that was how it felt. Exhaustion and two large Jacks on a recently emptied stomach had left my head pounding. I looked at the clock on the cooker. It was almost 4 o'clock.

Shit! It was almost 4 o'clock! I'd been out for nearly six hours. I had to clean up before the kids got home, get rid of that foul mess outside, get myself together. I planted my hands on the table and hauled myself up. The pain in my head and neck made me clench my teeth. I froze when I heard the front door open.

"Mum! Mum!" It was Max. I stayed watching the clock on the cooker. I couldn't turn to look. I couldn't shake the nightmare. "Mum!" I could hear Max's feet drumming on the hallway floor, racing closer.

"Mum! Can we go see Tommy?" Max ran into the kitchen. I heard him stop by the kitchen door. "Mum? What's wrong?"

I turned slowly to look at him, my focus shifting to look past the kitchen door, to look behind him. Had anyone else followed him in? "I'm okay, honey. Just got one hell of a headache. Where's your brother?"

"He's round by Grandpa's chair. He's poking the

maggots with a stick. He'll be in in a minute. Can we stop at the library so I can get a book for Tommy?"

"Sure. But get changed first." He spun round, spring-loaded, ready to race off and change. "And go tell your brother to leave the maggots alone."

*

The nightmare lingered. It hung on the edge of the woods while we drove to see Tommy. It waited as we found out that Tommy was being discharged and we could take him home. It circled our house as we went to the diner to celebrate. It stood on the porch while we laughed and ate, the four of us back together again. It peered through our windows as I watched my boys joking with each other, my heart full to bursting with my love for them. I'd sworn I'd put things right and I would.

The nightmare lingered, biding its time. It knew we'd be home, sooner or later.

12.

I thought I caught a glimpse of something moving as I swung
the pickup into the drive. I shrugged it off as the movement of
my headlights sweeping across the tree line. The chatter of my
boys warmed me more than the hot air blasting from the
heating vents. I could feel the tension lifting from my
shoulders as I listened to their excited conversation. Maybe it
had been the rain, distorting my view as the pickup's wipers
arced fast, back and forth across the windscreen. Whatever it
had been, it wasn't there now.

I pulled up close to the house. The rain had grown
heavier with each mile we'd driven back from the diner. That
and I didn't want Tommy seeing the mess on the side porch
around Dad's easy chair. I shut off the engine and we sat,
warm in our family bubble, watching the rain hurl itself
against the pickup's windows. I could happily have sat there
all night but I knew the boys would soon get restless to get
inside. "We ready, gang?"

"You bet!" called Max.

"Okay, let's do this!" And we were on a mission... I
threw open my driver's side door. Almost as soon as I was out
of the cab I was drenched. I heard Max squeal with excitement
as he jumped out the other side of the truck.

"Max help your brother!" I shouted over the noise of the

downpour.

But Tommy was already rounding the front of the pickup. He had David Jnr hanging round his neck and was hobbling fast for the house.

"Tommy! Be careful." I called.

"'S okay Mum!" he called back. Max raced after him, skidding in the mud, almost losing his balance. That just made him hoot even more.

I met them at the front door, the four of us soaked and covered in mud.

"Wanna do it again?" Max laughed.

I unlocked the door and we tumbled into the house. Tommy hit the hallway light, sending the darkness scuttling into the other rooms of the house. The boys made to run off.

"Hold it! Nobody moves till their boots are off and they've got a towel. Are we clear?"

A resounding "Yes, Mum!" from all three boys.

David Jnr dropped onto his butt and began trying to wrestle off his boots. I headed off to the bathroom cabinet to fetch some towels.

*

It was already well past the boys' bedtimes. The next half an hour was taken up with David Jnr and Max running around the house with towels over their heads pretending to be ghosts. That came to an abrupt end when David Jnr—unable to see where he was going—ran face first into the hallway wall. I think he was more surprised than hurt but I wasn't taking any chances.

"One concussion in a week is enough!" I told him.

The towels went in the linen basket and the boys went off to bed.

Another half an hour and the house was still. Tommy had

crashed out as soon as he'd hit the pillow, David Jnr snored quietly and Max grudgingly gave up reading his book when I tucked him in and turned out his light.

I was so relieved to have my boys back, safe at home that, for a while, I'd not thought about the bear, about what had happened at the cemetery that morning. Their laughter, their shouting and thundering footsteps had kept the nightmare at arm's length since we'd gotten home. When I sat down at the dining table and poured myself a drink, the nightmare was waiting for me.

At first, I thought it must have been trees reflected on the glass, cross hatching the black panes. But the shadows didn't move, not like the canopy which fought with the wind outside. I got up from the table. I could feel the knot of panic returning, that fist closing in my stomach, as I edged over to the window. They weren't shadows, they were smears.

As he'd promised, a couple of days after we'd talked about the bear at the diner, Jim had dropped in his spare shotgun. I'd put it in the top of my wardrobe in my room. The shells were in a high cupboard in the kitchen. And never would the two meet, unless I genuinely thought the bear might be back. It took several attempts, but eventually I managed to load two shells into the shotgun.

I flicked on the porch light and, holding the shotgun how Jim had shown me, I unlatched the back door and stepped outside.

It was darker outside than it had any right to be. The light from the porch barely stretched a few feet out across the drive. Beyond that, the night was pitch. I was sure I'd been able to see the tree line when we'd pulled in just over an hour ago.

Above, the sky was choked with black clouds. The rain had stopped, for the time being. The silence left behind it felt like a pause in an argument. It wasn't over and there was probably worse to come.

The stench of rot was thick in the night air. It made my stomach turn over. I held my breath and tightened my grip on the shotgun. I headed along the wooden boards towards Dad's chair.

The streaks across the windows were brush strokes, if you could call them that. Someone had taken the rotten foam from Dad's chair and used it to smear huge letters across the windows and wall. It reminded me of the plague houses I'd read about when I was a kid, the way they'd mark them with crosses when the people inside were infected. Our house had been marked. Death had stepped from the woods and spread decay over the walls and windows.

The letters were rough, broken. They read:

IT'S SEEN YOU

"Oh, Christ! Oh, Christ!" I wanted to spin round, turn and run back inside the house. But I was stuck, paralysed as certainly as I'd been in the nightmare. The boys! I had to get back inside. Call Al Weaver. Get help!

The letter pulled me closer.

Sat on the now hollow seat of Dad's chair was a single piece of writing paper. Unlike the ones that had poured from the chair when it had birthed its rotten insides onto the porch, this one was perfect, neatly folded. It was new.

I took my hand from the shotgun's stock, lowering it to my side—*what the hell was I thinking?*—and I picked up the letter.

I should have fought harder to free myself from its spell. I should have left the letter, run back in the house, gathered the boys, got in the pickup and never looked back. But I didn't. I had to know. You understand, don't you?

Just like the letters before, it was Dad's handwriting. As I read the words, my eyes blurred with tears. This letter wasn't like the ones that had come before it. It wasn't a scream. It wasn't a plea for help.

THERE'S A VOICE. HERE IN THE DARK.

IT SAYS I CAN COME HOME.

I HEAR IT

SCRATCHING AT THE EARTH AT NIGHT. WHISPERING TO THE DEAD.
TO ME.

IT SAID IT'S SEEN YOU. SEEN YOU DOING NOTHING.

IT TOLD ME YOU'D LEAVE ME TO ROT.

IT TOLD ME YOU'D LEAVE ME HERE

FOR THE MAGGOTS

TO FUCKING EAT ME.

"Oh no, Dad, no…" I wiped the tears from my face. It wasn't him. It couldn't be. Not any more. It was madness. What he was writing was madness. "I didn't leave you, Dad. I couldn't help you. I tried."

I noticed the track on the edge of my vision as I read. It passed along the side of the porch. A trail of prints in the mud, circling the house. Not footprints though: hooves.

IT SAYS I CAN COME BACK.

SAYS IT'LL CARRY ME HOME.

IT WANTS SOMETHING IN RETURN.

Not a trail of hooves like a horse or a deer would leave. It was made by two feet, not four. Whatever had left the tracks, it had been standing upright. There hadn't ever been any bear, had there?

ITS GOING TO BRING ME HOME

BUT I HAVE TO GIVE IT SOMETHING IN RETURN

JUST A LITTLE THING.

I CAN COME BACK

BUT IT WANTS ONE OF YOUR BOYS FOR ITSELF.

NO, NO, NO! I stumbled back away from the chair. It couldn't be! Dad wouldn't have made that deal! I couldn't believe it! I *wouldn't* believe it! I took one step too many backwards and put my foot down over the edge of the porch. Stepping into thin air, I lost my balance, scoring my shin down the side of the porch, stripping the skin off the bone and making me cry out in pain.

I fell awkwardly, landing hard on my side on the wet driveway. The shotgun slammed into the earth next to me. I lay in the mud trying to suck some air back into my lungs. I could taste dirt, metallic in my mouth. It might have been blood. I knew *it* was around. I'd fallen close to the trail of hooved tracks that circled the house.

I rolled over onto my front. I couldn't get my breath. The whole night had turned red. I could hear my own panicked wheezing, my blood rushing, thundering in my ears. Then I heard something else: a dead branch cracking underfoot, across the drive in the darkness on the edge of the tree line. I spun to the noise. It was here.

I screamed and grabbed at the shotgun. *Move! Move now! I hauled myself onto all fours. It's coming! Christ, it's coming!* I jammed the shotgun into the earth and used it to pull myself to my feet. *RUN! RUN!* Without looking back, I raced for the house.

I could hear it behind me, gaining on me, its muscled legs hammering into the mud, driving its huge shape forward. If it caught up to me, if it brought me down, who would protect the boys?

I leapt up on to the porch and threw myself at the back door. I heard it hit the porch behind me. Its hooves skidded across the wooden boards. It crashed into the side of the house. The porch light exploded out and the night snapped closed around us.

In the darkness, I could hear its breath, blasting, angry. I grabbed at the handle and tore the back door open.

I threw myself into the kitchen and slammed the door behind me. I sat against it, holding it closed, fooling myself that I stood a chance of keeping the door shut if the thing tried to rip it open.

I could hear it outside, moving along the porch, getting closer, a loud clack cutting through the night each time it stamped one of its hooves down on the wooden boards. Clack, clack. I could feel each step through the door. Clack, CLACK. The boards groaned, straining under the thing's hulking size.

I eased the bottom deadbolt closed, hoping it wouldn't hear me. I looked up. Did I have time to reach the top one before it made it to the back door? The door had a bamboo blind covering a window in its top half. I stood up to grab the bolt, just as the huge shadow of the beast stepped in front of the window.

13.

It leant close to the backdoor, lowering its head until it almost touched the glass. Could it see me? Could it tell I was stood on the other side of the door, trying to be still, be silent, trying to control the terrified shaking that had set my teeth chattering in my head? Could it hear that?

I couldn't see it clearly, it just was a black mass, shifting shape on the other side of the blind as it moved. That just made it even more terrible. Its breath exploded against the glass. I gritted my teeth against the scream that had leapt into my throat. Outside, it sucked in the night air, a long, wet wheeze. Could it smell me, taste me like the bloody meat it had torn into when it had broken into our house?

Trying not to move my head, I looked down to my feet for the shotgun. On the other side of the door I heard the clatter of the gun skidding across the wooden boards, kicked away by the thing. *No, no, no!* I'd been so desperate to get inside, I must have dropped it in my panic! Without the gun there was no way I'd be able to protect the boys. I tried to hold myself together but, in that moment, hopelessness loomed as large as the devil on the other side of the glass.

I heard movement behind me, on the other side of the kitchen.

"Mum? Mum? Who's doin' all that hammering?" David

Jnr stood in the kitchen doorway, rubbing the sleep from his eyes.

They say that when something terrible is about to happen, when you're about to die, that everything seems to slow down. I don't think that's true. I think, when you're pushed, you can think a lot faster than you mostly spend your days thinking. And no thought has ever screamed so fast into my mind as it did right then: *You will not hurt my boys! I will fight you until you kill me, but you will never get to my sons.*

In that instant, the hopelessness I'd felt was gone, replaced by anger, anger that sent me spinning away from the back door, racing across the kitchen towards David Jnr. I scooped him up as I passed him, sprinting through the kitchen doorway and out into the corridor.

I didn't have a plan, I was just running. But I knew that I wouldn't give up. I would fight to my last breath to protect my boys. I'd find a way to get them to safety.

When we hit the hallway I'd expected to hear glass breaking, the door smashing in behind us. But no sound came. I'd expected the thing to barge into the house as soon as it'd heard David Jnr, to force its huge form into the kitchen. But it didn't.

I stopped in the dark hallway. Was it still waiting outside the back door?

"Mum? Mum?" David Jnr's eyes were wide with fear.

I pressed us against the wall, hoping the darkness would swallow us, hide us. I gently held my hand over his mouth.

"Shhhh! It's okay, honey. It's okay. It's okay." I whispered, trying to convince myself as much as him. "It's going to be okay, but you've got to be quiet. Do you understand? Real quiet."

David Jnr nodded.

Where the hell had it gone? Was it still waiting on the back porch? If so, what was it waiting for? I snapped to look along the corridor to the front door. Had it gone back to circling the house? I watched the glass panels that framed the door, looking for any movement, a shadow crossing, approaching to attack.

Nothing. I could feel David Jnr's heart racing where I held him against me. "It's going to be okay," I repeated. I felt him grip me tighter.

I'd backed us into the wall by David Jnr's room. His door was open. His window looked out onto the drive, just a few feet along from where I'd stood, facing the beast through the kitchen door. I leant across the doorway and took hold of his door handle. Watching the window the whole time, I eased the door towards me.

Trying to keep quiet, I pulled the door closed. I winced as the latch clicked loudly into the frame. Had it heard that? I braced for it to charge David Jnr's window, looking for a way in.

No noise came. Another thought flashed through my mind: *You did this. Your kids are playing along because they're scared. Of you. There wasn't any demon outside. No letters, no monsters. You did this.*

Part of me wished that was true. If it was all in my head my boys would be safe. I'd take being crazy over what was really happening any day.

Slowly I crossed David Jnr's door. Tommy's room was next. I grabbed the keys to the pickup off the hall table and side-stepped along to Tommy's bedroom door.

My hands were sweating. I pressed down on the handle to Tommy's door. It slipped through my fingers, springing back with a loud *thunk* that made me start and David Jnr cry out. "Shit!"

Please don't have heard that. Please don't have heard that.

Inside his room, I heard Tommy stirring. Gripping the handle, tightly this time, I opened his door and leant into his room.

"Tommy…" I whispered.

"Mum? That you? What's going on?"

I could hear him moving about, he knocked a book off his bedside table as he reached across for his lamp.

"Tommy, no! Leave the light off."

I hurried across the room to stop him.

"Wha…? Mum?"

"Tommy, listen to me. Take your brother." I gently dropped David Jnr down to the floor. He clung to my waist. "Take David Jnr and…" I gave him the keys. "Take these. You know how to drive the pickup."

"Mum? What the hell?"

"I'm going to get Max. Listen, Tommy, when I tell you, I want you to go out the window with your brothers."

Tommy wasn't confused anymore. Now he was scared. "Seriously, Mum, what's happening?"

Standing in the hallway, listening for that thing, I'd decided what I was going to do. At best, it was a shitty plan. But, at best, it'd get the kids away from the house safe.

"Don't stop. Don't look back. Just run. Run to the pickup and…" My voice cracked. I'd realised that, if we all went together and it caught up with us, it might get what it wanted, get one of the boys. But if I distracted it, if I held its attention long enough for the boys to get away… I couldn't fight it, not without the gun. I just had to give them enough time to get to the truck and drive off. Whatever it took. *You will not hurt my boys. I'll fight you until you kill me, but you will never get to my sons.*

"… drive to Al Weaver's. Tell him the bear came back. Tell him to send help. Please, Tommy, I need you to take your brothers and get them to safety."

"Mum? What about you? *Mum?*"

The sound of a window smashing on the other side of the

175

house cut my answer off.

14.

Max screamed. I raced back into the hallway. "Tommy! Go! Go now!"

Tommy tried to follow me out into the corridor. I slammed his door closed and held it. I could feel him struggling to pull it open.

"Mum! I can help!"

I shouted back to him. "Tommy! No!"

"Mum!" He hammered on the door.

"Tommy, stop! Please! Get David Jnr to the pickup. Now!" I held the door until he stopped fighting to get it open.

Across the hallway, Max's bedroom door was closed. "Max? Max?"

"Mum! Help!" Max screamed again.

Stumbling around in the dark hallway, I managed to find what I was looking for: Dad's cane. I snatched it up and raced across to Max's bedroom door. I grabbed for the handle. But the door was already opening.

Max's door swung backwards, swallowed into perfect black. It reminded me of the darkness that had consumed me when I'd first heard the knocking. I was certain now, that that had been the same terrible darkness Dad had found himself trapped in after he'd been buried. It was the darkness of the grave.

I could smell the beast in there with Max. Its stench poured into the hallway. The stench of decay. It burned my eyes, I could taste its rot in my mouth. It was watching me. I could feel it, just as it had watched me at the graveyard.

IT'S SEEN YOU.

"Max?" I called. I could hear him crying quietly in the darkness. "Max?" I felt so helpless. I gripped the cane with white knuckles. What the hell was I going to do with that?

"Mum?" he whimpered. The fear in his voice was terrible.

"Oh, honey, it's okay. It's going to be okay." I took a step closer to the door.

Then Max stepped out of his room.

His eyes were fixed on me, his face streaked with tears.

"Mum, help, please," he pleaded. *I'm so sorry, Max. I caused this.* Max stepped slowly out of the room, but he wasn't in control. A huge black claw held him from above. Three long fingers—with nails that had grown thick and twisted, corkscrewing into filth-caked daggers—were clamped tight around his head. Streaks of blood mixed with his tears as the nails cut into his temples. The grip of the beast was so tight it raised Max up so he was walking on tiptoes. At any moment I thought the thing might crush his skull.

"Let him go!" I demanded, as the thing spilled forward from Max's room. Hunched, it squeezed through his doorway and then unfurled in the corridor, filling the hallway with its awful form. Its full height was over eight feet. It stood on two legs, thick and strong as a horse's, muscles swollen beneath its leathery skin. Its skin was black, coated with wet earth as if it had hauled itself from a grave to torment us.

Standing in the corridor, facing the beast, I knew I had seen it before, or seen one of its kind before. Years earlier, the thing that had eyed me through the sliding doors of my bedroom, the thing I'd tried to convince myself had been a nightmare, had been real, a demon as sure as the one standing in front of me. It pushed Max closer, as if it were parading him in front of me, taunting me,

"Let him go!" I snarled, raising up the cane. The beast leant forward, bringing its face out of the shadows for the first time. It was Dad's face! I stumbled back. *No! No! No!* It wore the skin of Dad's face over its own. Was this the ritual? Some terrible black magic to bring Dad back from the dead?

It brought Dad's face close to mine. It watched me through the empty eye sockets of its skin mask. Its eyes were milky, almost entirely white.

"Dad? Why?" I begged the face for answers. I knew it wasn't Dad, that the thing in front of me just wore his skin, but seeing my father's face again months after we'd lain him to rest, when I thought I'd never see him again, I was desperate for Dad's voice to answer, tell me it was a mistake, that it would all be okay.

The beast's breath fired behind Dad's skin: fast, hot blasts that made Dad's sagging mouth move as if it were about to form an answer.

No answer came. Instead I saw teeth flash behind the death mask. And then the demon smiled. It smiled at my pain, Dad's face contorting in an awful impersonation of the beast beneath. It sucked in a long, wet breath—I could hear it whistling through its mucus filled throat—and then it hissed at me, "Mine… now."

The words seemed to be made of saliva, it spat them at me. I could see spittle on Dad's lips, it dripped from behind Dad's face. The demon was drooling. It was visualising what it would do to my son and drooling.

Then it began to retreat. Dragging Max backwards along the corridor: it headed for the front door. Max tiptoed fast, awkward, trying to keep up, stand up, trying not to fall as the thing pulled him.

"Mum!" Max held out his hands for me to take them, to try and grab him. I daren't. Then he was fighting, trying to pull the black fingers from his head, trying to stop the nails from digging into his flesh. Blood poured from the wounds at his temples.

I followed them along the corridor. If I attacked it, would it drop Max or crush his skull? I couldn't take that chance.

The demon in Dad's face stopped at the door. It reached behind itself and pulled the door open. Standing watching me with its milky, dead eyes, it raised Max up, lifting him until his feet dangled, kicking in the air, until he shrieked from the pain, from the pressure on his skull.

"NO!" I screamed.

Savouring our anguish, the thing smiled and stepped back out of the house and onto the front porch.

A third scream joined Max's and mine. This one was a war cry. It tore along the side of the house towards the demon. Running as fast as he could, David Jnr raced towards the beast. He held the hatchet, that I'd had in the truck, up over his head.

"FUUUUUUCK YOOOOOOU!" he yelled as he brought the hatchet down on the arm the demon was using to hold Max aloft. The blade tore straight through the flesh, cleaving the bone, hacking the thing's forearm clean off. Max, and the arm, dropped hard on to the wooden boards from the porch. The beast howled, stumbling back, grabbing at the air where its arm had been. Blood fountained from the stump.

"Max! David Jnr! Get away from it!" I shouted, running forward, out the front door, heading for the demon. The boys were too stunned to move. At any moment the beast would recover, channel all its pain into anger.

I swung Dad's cane, striking down on the demon's head.

I slammed it down again and again. "Max! David Jnr! Run! Run!" I tried to put myself in front of them, between the monster and my boys. Too shocked to move, they crawled back against the house and watched. If it had a chance to recover, the demon would tear us apart.

I drove the cane down one last time, with such force that Dad's walking stick shattered. Behind the beast's mask, something cracked loudly. It wailed, a broken sound, howled into the earth where I'd knocked it off balance. When it rounded on me again I could see I'd beaten part of Dad's face flat.

The demon rocked on its hooves. Even given its injuries, it was nowhere near beaten. It stamped in the mud, rage driving its hooves deep into the earth. It reared up and roared into the sky, a howl you might mistake for an injured animal if you were out in the woods at night. But there was something else, something more familiar, more human in the cry. I wondered if the thing had once been a man, before some terrible black magic had taken hold of it.

The beast turned to look at me, hot breath firing, blasting smoke into the cold air. Dad's face hung lopsided. Whatever lay behind it was broken. His mouth was wet with blood; it poured over his chin. I gripped the remains of Dad's cane. It had shattered in two. Half of it lay in the mud at the beast's feet. It hadn't broken neatly. The half I held ended in a mass of jagged splinters.

I'd aim for its throat, drive the remains of the cane into its neck. I couldn't see any other way to bring it down. If it saw me coming, it could easily swat me away. Even if I got close enough, I'd no idea if the splinters would puncture its leathery skin. But I had to try. I held the cane out in front of me, the muscles in my arm locked tight, ready to drive my makeshift stake home.

"Mum! No!" I heard Max call out.

The beast turned to look at him. I took my chance and ran at it.

15.

I didn't make it to the devil.

I heard Tommy yell from the pickup, shouting out the driver's side window.

"Mum! Watch out! Watch out!"

The pickup roared over the wet earth.

"Mum!"

The truck shot in front of me, its huge power blurring past only inches away. I could feel the heat radiating from it. The wing mirror clipped Dad's cane, tearing it out of my hand and sending me spinning. I almost fell against the side of the truck.

The pickup slammed into the beast, hitting it at waist height. Its pelvis exploded, white bone tore out of its black skin. Its body buckled, folding over the truck's front end, its head smashing down on the hood.

Tommy must have carried it six feet or more, the whole way its legs cycled in the air, trying to get a footing. The whole way it screamed, twisting, writhing, trying to climb up onto the pickup. I could hear bone grinding on bone in the shattered sack of its body. Eventually one of its hooves caught in the tread of the front passenger tire and it was snatched under the truck.

The pickup bucked high over the body of the thing,

crushing it with the front tires, and then bringing the truck's full weight down on it again as it went under the rear wheels. Tommy had been so focussed on the beast, on its black shape fighting to climb up onto the truck, that he hadn't noticed the tree line coming up fast ahead of him. When it was suddenly gone, he was just feet from the woods.

"Tommy! Hit the brake!" There was no chance he could hear me.

Tommy spun the pickup. The back end swerved, skidding across the wet driveway. A huge arc of mud sprayed up into the air. The side of the pickup hit the edge of the woods, bouncing and scraping along the first row of trees. The truck's wheels had locked, Tommy was standing on the brake, but still the pickup tore along the tree line. A huge branch tore out of the darkness, it slammed into the windscreen, punching through the glass and stopping the truck dead.

"Tommy! Tommy!" I hauled myself back to my feet and ran for the pickup. I couldn't hear my boots pounding on the dirt, or my voice screaming Tommy's name. I couldn't hear my hands hammering on the pickup's shattered windows, or my desperate grunts as I tried to tear the locked passenger door open. The night had been stunned silent, muted—and it could stay that way, until I heard the one sound I needed to hear, that I desperately needed to hear: Tommy's voice.

"Mum?" Tommy called from the cab. "Mum? I'm okay. I think. I think I'm okay."

I pressed a hand against the passenger window. A huge sob of relief burst from my mouth. I could barely get the words out: "Honey, you need to open the door for me. It's locked. I can't get in to help you."

"I think I might have broke my other leg." Tommy called back.

I heard him slide across the seat and pop the pin on the passenger door. I ripped the door open and climbed up into the cab. I tried to hug Tommy and check he was okay at the same time. Something hit the side of the truck and we both spun to the noise.

Max and David Jnr stood by the side of the pickup. They'd run over when they'd seen me race for the truck. Max looked up into the cab, but David Jnr was watching behind him.

"Is it dead?" David Jnr asked.

I looked out of the back window of the pickup to the mangled black form lying motionless on the drive.

"We're not waiting around to find out," I replied, and held out a hand to help pull Max up into the truck. I helped Max, and Max helped David into the cab. David slammed the passenger door behind him.

I managed to rock the pickup until it came free of the tree and reversed it out back onto the drive. The whole time I watched the thing in the truck's rear view.

As we were pulling out of the drive, onto the main road, David called out, "It moved! I think it moved!"

I didn't look back.

16.

I drove straight to the police station and told Al Weaver everything. Everything, except I told him it'd been a bear that had attacked us. The truth could stay with my boys and me. He sent the hunting party that had been searching out by the cemetery, to our house to look.

They didn't find a bear when they got there, but after a search of the woods they did find Dad's body, and another that had been dug from the cemetery earlier that day. I overheard Ray talking to one of the hunters out by reception. Both bodies had had their faces removed.

"What about the other one?" I heard Ray ask, before Al caught me eavesdropping and suggested that his deputy and the hunter talk elsewhere.

"If that bear limped its way back into the woods after what you did to it, it's likely it limped back in there to die," Al tried to comfort me. "We'll find it, Ellie. It won't bother you or your boys again."

Al offered to have Dad reburied but I asked that his remains be cremated. That way, there wouldn't be a body for him to try and bring back again. That way, whatever deal he'd made with the beast would be done. Maybe, once his body was gone, his spirit would be free, maybe then the torture he'd endured all those months would end.

We stayed a few days with Jim and Sally before we moved back to our house. The hunters never found the bear. For the next three weeks I spent each night sitting at our dining table with a loaded shotgun, ready in case the thing returned. It didn't. Still, it would be a long time before I'd sleep soundly again.

I couldn't get what Ray had said that night out of my head. *What about the other one?* There was a third body that they hadn't recovered? What had the demon done with it?

What I did know was that my 'sensitivity' hadn't gone. Maybe it was Dad's passing had brought it back, maybe it had been there all along, but I would continue to know things, feel things and sometimes hear things that others didn't. Somehow, our encounter with the demon only seemed to sharpen those senses, focus them. I hoped I'd been wrong about Max, that he didn't share the same 'abilities', that I hadn't passed my curse to him.

About two weeks after the demon had attacked us, Max and I visited the library. On the way home I pulled into the cemetery car park. I told Max I had to pick something up from the pastor, but that was a lie. I left him reading in the pickup.

I headed up to the second cemetery and I walked among the graves. Dad's had clear signs it'd been refilled recently. I found a second grave and a third that had both been disturbed. I made a note of the names of the dead and headed back to the truck.

I was walking through the bottom cemetery when it began. At first I thought I heard someone crying, a recently bereaved mourner maybe. I couldn't see anyone and so I kept walking. As I crossed the cemetery I heard another person sobbing. Then I heard a scream.

The first scream was joined by another, and then another. I walked faster. The screaming grew louder, it swirled around me, it seemed to come from every direction. There were voices

187

begging for help, others wailing in agony.

THEY'RE UNDER MY SKIN!

THEY'RE EATING ME!

I broke into a run. Tripping, stumbling through the graves as the sound of the screaming grew.

I'M TRAPPED!

HELP ME! LET ME OUT!

Other voices were darker—ranting, screaming abuse— long ago driven to madness. The voices chased me to the pickup. I tore the door open and jumped inside.

I'd expected to find Max reading, but his book lay open, dropped in the foot well. He sat wide-eyed and terrified, his hands clamped over his ears.

"Please, Mum, make them stop! They're dead! Why are they shouting?"

Max and I never returned to the cemetery. We kept what had happened between us. We both knew that Tommy and David Jnr wouldn't understand. He'd inherited my curse, I was certain of that now. I would do everything in my power to protect him from the horrors that would bring.

A week or so later, as I was tucking him in, he asked me, "Mum, do they all scream like that? The dead. Do they all scream like the ones in the cemetery?"

I sat on the end of his bed and thought about what to say. And then I lied. I told him that most people, when they died, they went to heaven. Some, if they had unfinished business, stayed behind. If they'd died abruptly, if someone had wronged them, then they couldn't go to heaven straight away.

I think I said, "We all get there in the end, honey. It just takes longer for some people." And I stayed sitting at the end of his bed until he fell asleep. The truth was, that ever since that day in the cemetery, the same question had been haunting me. Was that what was waiting for all of us? Buried but somehow aware? Left, locked in a box, waiting for the maggots to consume us?

*

I made sure all three boys were asleep before I took my shotgun down. I kept it loaded at all times now. The second and third bodies the demon had exhumed belonged to Irma Grierson and Cole Burkitt. Irma's faceless body had been the other corpse recovered that night, but Cole—well, he was still out there. Had he done a deal with that thing too? Had the hunting party not found him because they were too late?

I stuffed more cartridges in my pockets and I headed out to the pickup. I'd found Cole's address in the directory and I had my shotgun, just in case.

THE RAMBLING MAN

They bathed Esme in water scented with lavender blossoms, rose petals bobbing on the surface. She smelled like a bride on her wedding day. Ma's voice was full of pride. "You're a beautiful girl daughter. The Rambling Man will be glad of you."

The women of the village fed her wine; much more than a child should drink. They dried and dressed her in a white linen smock. Ma put flowers in her hair.

They formed a line and Elder Ambrosina pressed open the bathhouse doors. Steam escaped like a winter breath, a ghost loosed into the sky on a cold April night.

Through the village and up the hill, to the edge of the woods, they strode. Elder Ambrosina leading with a torch that popped and spat embers into the air. She also carried the twine to bind Esme to the Rambling Man's post.

Stood alone, watching the woods, the post faced the forest like a man before a crowd.

"It's an honour to be chosen." Her mother had told her. No one knew how the Elders chose, but twice a year, a girl— who'd recently come of age— would be led to the Rambling Man's post.

"Such an adventure for you, daughter. The sights you'll see." Twice a year a girl would be led to the post. None had ever returned.

And the village's crops had never failed.

Once, twice Elder Ambrosina wrapped the twine around Esme's wrists. But the years had twisted her fingers—they were worse in the cold— and she found it hard to fasten the rope.

"Why must my hands be tied?" Esme had asked.

"So the Man can rescue you child." Had been Elder Ambrosina's blunt reply.

"He'll be here soon!" A woman called. Why didn't the women stand still? They shuffled from leg to leg, took little steps around the post. Why did they hurry? Why did they want to leave?

One by one they passed the post. Some left flowers, some wished Esme well. One took too long— "Don't dally child!" another had scolded.

And then Ma was the last one left.

"Goodbye daughter." She kissed Esme on the forehead. "When the time comes, close your eyes my love." She whispered before hurrying after the others.

*

Some said the Man was a prince. That he took the girls to a castle in the woods. *Why would I close my eyes?* thought Esme.

It was an honour to stand at the post. To face the woods. To have a chance to see what lay beyond the village. *Why would I close my eyes?* Esme watched the woods.

For hours she watched, waiting for the man to step from the trees, to untie her, take her away. The wine that had warmed her stomach, held back the cold, now made her mouth dry and her head pound.

Where did the Chosen go? Where did the Rambling Man take them? What did he do with the girls from the village? Esme watched the woods.

She watched till her head nodded, her arms screamed and she could not feel her hands. The post dug into her back. Why tie her up? What did she need to be rescued from?

When she was little her friends would dare her to: "Step into my woods child!" None of them did. That was where the Rambling Man lived. If you weren't Chosen you didn't enter *his* woods.

Cramp! In Esme's arm. A spasm jerked her hands apart. And the twine gave way! Free of the post Esme fell to her knees.

What now? Oh no! What should she do now? She was Chosen but the man hadn't come for her! Esme stood alone, facing the forest. She had to find him. Or the crop would fail. She had to go into the woods.

*

"Step into my woods child!" She remembered their taunts as she trod between the trees, finger branches snatching at her smock, reaching from the darkness to scratch at her skin. Why had the man not come?

She found the answer on the forest floor. It lay at her feet, a rotten thing, skin turned to leather, wrapped in filthy cloth. Had she found The Rambling Man?

The stench led her to its nest. Gnawed bones and bloody smocks, piled high, lining its filthy lair. How many children had it consumed? How many of the Chosen had it murdered?

Esme ran to the edge of the woods. She'd race back to town, tell the Elders what had happened.

Ma's words stopped her, "When the time comes, close your eyes my love." Had she known? Had they all known what would happen, what was waiting for Esme in the woods? Was this how they kept the crops from failing? They fed the thing she'd found in return for a fat harvest?

Damn them! Damn them all! She'd show them. She'd wait. She'd wait in the woods and watch their harvest fail. She'd watch as they sent new girls, one after another. She'd save them, cut them from the post and they'd join her, join her until she had an army.

Then, she'd march back down the hill, armed with the bones of those that had come before, she'd take the village for her own. She'd have her revenge.

*

But the crop didn't fail. The village didn't send more girls. Esme's once plump face became sallow and gaunt. Her smock grew filthy as she scavenged for food. She ate berries, roots that made her sick and, when the agony of starvation had consumed her mind, she gnawed on the dead things she found on the forest floor.

Only the need for revenge kept her alive until the Autumn offering came. And that night, when she armed herself with a bone, after waiting for the women to leave, she had no intention of saving the girl tied to the post. All she needed was to have a good meal.

Her transformation was complete.

CONNECT WITH ANDREW CULL

Thank you very much for buying BONES!
I hope you enjoyed the stories in my first collection.

For the latest news on my books and movies follow me on
Facebook:
https://www.facebook.com/OfficialAndrewCull/

I'm also on Twitter:
https://twitter.com/andrewcull

I love to hear from my readers so please feel free to get in
touch.

Printed in Great Britain
by Amazon

65414731R00125

Gay Love
& Other
Fairy Tales

Dylan James

Winnipeg, Canada

Published September 2018 by Deep Hearts YA, an imprint of Deep Desires Press and Story Perfect Inc.

Deep Hearts YA
PO Box 51053 Tyndall Park
Winnipeg, Manitoba R2X 3B0
Canada

Visit http://www.deepheartsya.com for more great reads.

Gay Love
& Other
Fairy Tales

Chapter One

Jordan

IT STARTED WITH MY family. The day before school started. Over dinner. At TGI Fridays.

I don't know why I chose to do it so publicly—but I don't know if I really had a solid plan in mind. I wonder how many people actually have a step-by-step plan and follow it. If someone is like me, it just…happens.

We had finished our dinner, the waitress had taken our dirty plates away, and we all sat back in our seats, sighing from being so full and still contemplating the dessert menu. There's always room for dessert. And, apparently, there's never a wrong time to come out as gay.

"Guys," I said, my mouth leading the way before my brain could fully catch up. Mom and dad and Bella, my sister, all looked at me. Maybe it was the weight in that word, how I said it so seriously, but it seemed they knew I had something important to say.

"I'm...I'm gay."

Around us, the noise of other diners seemed to hush and there was a clatter of dishes—almost like this was a conversation for the whole restaurant and everyone was scandalized. My palms went sweaty and my heart thudded irregularly.

Mom's eyes widened—I doubt it was surprise, but I guess it could have been. Dad looked like he was about to say something. Bella giggled into her hand—at eight years old, I'm sure any mention of the word "gay" is giggle-inducing.

"So, did you decide on dessert?" the waitress said as she came up to our table again.

Mom, dad, and Bella were all staring at me and I was staring back at them. No one said anything, no one acknowledged the waitress. The longer the silence went on, the more terrified I became. No one chose a dessert.

I felt my cheeks burning with shame. My eyes started to water. *Don't cry,* I told myself. If the silence went on even a second longer, I knew I couldn't hold anything back.

Just as the waitress was about to give up and walk away, mom said, "Can we get something big and sweet? We need to celebrate." A smile immediately spread across her face—a warm, genuine, loving smile. Relief flooded through me.

But there was still dad. I looked at him and he looked like he was still thinking, trying to process what I'd said. I mean, it couldn't have been a surprise, right? Every time he tried to engage me in sports or other masculine things, I always made lame excuses. I wasn't the boy he thought I'd grow up to be, I knew, but surely he still loved me. Right?

"Thank you," dad said, finally. "Thank you for sharing."

More relief flooded into my chest. I was at risk of crying still, but for a very different reason. Beside me, Bella still giggled.

Maybe it's because mom is a doctor and dad is a teacher—they both deal with all sorts of people and they know that being gay is normal. Maybe they're just nice people. Maybe they just love me so much that if I'd come out as sexually attracted to dinosaurs, they'd accept it.

I didn't think too much on it, I still don't, because it doesn't matter.

What does matter is that I got to start senior year of high school without hiding who I am. It wasn't like I rushed into having a boyfriend—there really weren't any gay guys at school I was interested in anyway—but it at least opened the door to the possibility.

Anything could happen, right?

Anyway, after dinner, I sent out a snap declaring my homo status and posted a similar thing on Tumblr. I got a few anonymous hates on Tumblr, but mostly I got love. Overwhelming love. Even though this is the twenty-first century, I was still surprised at how positive it all was.

Now, at late September, after about a month of being

out—of being *free*—I was still the same old Jordan Ortiz. Nothing about me was different, except the façade of liking girls, of course.

My friends were still my friends, my nemeses were still my nemeses, and those I didn't interact with just didn't care. I sometimes got called "fag", but I got called that before coming out. Like I said, same old Jordan Ortiz.

Well, I guess there's one change. I'm now co-captain of the cheer team. The other co-captain is a high-maintenance, self-obsessed girl by the name of Nikki Simms.

Nikki is the kind of person that lives for Snapchat and Instagram fame. It's like her life goal to get sponsorship deals or something. She's forever taking selfies, especially when she's got a Starbucks cup in her hand, and posting them. If she doesn't get enough likes, she deletes a photo and throws a fit. I'm pretty sure she wants to be the next Kim Kardashian. Really. It's exhausting working with her.

Or should I say working *for* her.

We're co-captains, but it's clear she thinks she's more *captain* than me.

I really don't care. I just like the cheer team. I love performing and launching people into the air. Plus, all the eye candy when we perform at football games is a nice added benefit. All those tight ends and whatnot.

I steal one more glance over my shoulder at the football team running a scrimmage behind us—I couldn't help indulging myself in that brief moment of unobtainable eye candy and very quickly found my gaze following Benjamin as he charged across the field, looking powerful as hell—and then turned back to the task at hand. Cheer practice.

Nikki takes charge again and orders us to run through our routine one more time. We're supposed to have a teacher supervisor coach us, but even she can't stand Nikki and has basically walked away. We're all at Nikki's mercy. But she does lead us into phenomenal routines.

I take my spot next to Alex, with my BFF Hannah in front of us. A moment later, music thuds from the portable stereo Nikki had brought along. I plaster a smile on my face and join hands with Alex to catch Hannah as she leans back, falling into our embrace. We lift and spin her once. She lands in our arms again and we help her stand, then a second later her left foot is in my hands and her right in Alex's—we lift her up, and, well, you've seen cheer teams before. We throw her in the air, spin her around, and have her soaring in every direction.

To my left are two more trios like us, performing similar routines. The one furthest from us is doing an identical routine. Between us is the trio featuring Nikki—with her naturally being the chick in the air—and her trio is doing the more complicated stunts.

Nikki, of course, is hoping that someone snaps or instas the whole thing and some cheer scout from college sees her. Or maybe she's hoping a hunky NFL player spots her and gets her to join his team's cheer squad. Or maybe she just wants a million likes.

If social media wasn't around—like if it was the dark pre-history of the internet back in the nineties—then she probably wouldn't even be on the cheer team.

The music comes to an end and so does our routine.

I throw my arms around Hannah and pull her into a giant hug. "You did great, babe!" I tell her.

Nikki, though, disagrees. She stomps over to us, fury on her face—fury, I discover, aimed at me. "You guys were pitiful. Alex, that backflip was totally sloppy and was a big disaster. All three of you need more strength and height if you want to keep up—if you want to stay on the squad. Better beef up, Ortiz, or else I'll get you off the team." She lowers her voice and narrows her eyes. "I won't have you make me look bad."

I glance at Alex and Hannah and they both look torn apart. Nikki doesn't get to me like she gets to them. I look back at Nikki and nod, hoping she'll just leave.

She can't kick me or Alex or Hannah off the team— only our supervising teacher, Ms. Hammer, can do that. Besides, how could Nikki see my performance if she was spinning through the air? She's full of crap and she knows it and she knows I know it. But she's just out to get me. She just doesn't like that she's *co*-captain.

She stomps away. "The rest of you were fantastic! Don't let Jordan hold you back." I have to bite my tongue to refrain from spitting a swear at her. She'd use that outburst to her advantage somehow.

She hurries off to give feedback to someone else—

feedback that I can clearly overhear is much more helpful than what she gave us—and so I pull Hannah and Alex into a quick huddle. "We all know she's full of BS," I say, and while I know they agree, it doesn't erase the anger and hurt on their expressions, "but if you want to get a little extra practice in, we could work on the throw. And, Alex, we could just practice backflips."

Alex nods and looks over his shoulder at Nikki, then back into the huddle. "I'll just practice at home; I just need to nail my landing. Thanks, though," he says.

"I don't think we need extra practice," Hannah says with a sneer. "She probably just thinks we're too good and stealing the spotlight."

Alex and I laugh, then Nikki's shouted voice cuts through everything, "Everyone, go home and rest. Homecoming is Friday!"

The cheer team claps for ourselves and then packs up their stuff to head to the showers and head on home. I pat Alex on the back as he heads away with the rest of them. I walk over to the bench at the side of the field and pick up the water bottle from my backpack, then sit on the bench and gulp it down like I'd just walked through Death Valley or something.

A moment later, Hannah plunks down beside me, similarly gulping her water.

"I don't know how you put up with that," she says, throwing a sneer toward Nikki's retreating backside. "I almost threw a punch at her."

"Meh," I say. "I don't let it bother me. My love of cheer team obliterates her bitchiness. Besides, you and Alex were awesome—she's just jealous." I gulp some more water. "I just feel sorry for whatever poor guy she ends up with. She'll have his balls in her fist and never let go." I chuckle when I picture the football captain, Benjamin, at her mercy. In a lot of the highly-staged photos Nikki posts, Benjamin looks a little...trapped.

Hannah laughs and then closes her water bottle, throwing it into her backpack and standing up. "You gonna change?"

I glance behind her to the football players. They're just finishing their practice and on their way to the change room. "Nah. I'll wait."

Hannah looks behind her and instantly understands. She blows me a kiss and then heads off, leaving me as the only cheer team person still out on the field.

I watch all the buff, muscular teens head toward the school and the change room in there. Even before I came out, I avoided changing when the footballers were in there. Being the wimpy and effeminate kid made me a target of bullying and teasing. I'd had more than my share of gut punches, locker slams, and backpacks thrown into the showers.

But to now be the wimpy, effeminate, and *gay* kid in a change room full of buff, macho, straight football players? That could only lead to a black eye. Part of my survival as a gay is to avoid putting myself in places where I'm in danger.

I pull my phone out of my backpack and check my social feeds. Of course, Nikki is sharing post-practice selfies that make her seem glowy rather than sweaty (like, seriously, how does she do it?) and scrolling a little further shows me that someone had captured the rehearsal for her on her phone. Of course, it focused entirely on Nikki flying through the air.

I just roll my eyes. I can only take so much Nikki in one day. I bring up Spotify, put on some hipster playlist that I don't like people knowing I like, and put it on the bench beside me. As the music blares, I lay back and stare up at the darkening sky. A few stars are starting to poke through the deep, dark blue.

As much as I love high school (despite Nikki), I'm eager for college next year. With more people, maybe there'll be more gays.

Maybe in college I'll get a kiss.

Maybe I'll even get a boyfriend.

But until then, I'm happy just being Hannah's gay BFF. It's not the same as having a boyfriend, but it'll do until then. I mean, it'll have to.

After I decide enough time has passed and that the change room has to be empty, I turn off the music, throw the phone in my backpack, and head into the school and to the change room.

Sure enough, the place is empty. Nothing to worry about.

I head to my locker, trying to avoid stepping in all of the puddles of water from guys' showers and all of the puddles that look like spit (seriously, straight guys are so disgusting). I open my locker, strip, grab my towel, and head around the bend to the showers.

And that's when I find out I'm not alone.

Fuck.

There's a guy in the showers. I freeze mid-step, trying to decide if I should wander in like I don't care or if I should turn and run and just shower at home. But by the time I get changed and get my shoes back on, whoever's in the shower will come out and it'll be just as bad as if I walked into the shower.

Before I can make up my mind, the shower shuts off. A few moments later, I hear the slap of wet footsteps. I'm still frozen in place, my heart thundering hard against my ribs, cold sweat breaking out all over. I worked so hard to avoid this very thing.

"Jordan?" came the voice. A friendly voice. Benjamin.

I breathe out a sigh of relief. "Hey," I say, finally forcing myself to look at him. He's muscular, buff, toned, and sopping wet with water rolling down his warm, brown skin and just a towel wrapped around his waist. I try not to make it obvious I'm checking out his biceps.

Okay, this isn't a disaster, I tell myself. Benjamin is the only guy on the football team I don't hate. He's captain of the football team—a fact that Nikki keeps swooning over—but more importantly, he's been my next-door neighbor our whole lives and we were friends until a few years back. Nothing really ended our friendship, we just drifted in different directions. Him towards sports and me towards academics and cheer.

I haven't heard a word from him since I came out, though.

"You guys were looking good," he says. I don't know if he actually means it or if he's just making conversation. I also don't know if he means he thinks *all* of us were looking good or just Nikki.

"Thanks," I say, deciding to take the compliment as it was likely intended. Despite the douches on the football team, Benjamin is a pretty nice guy.

Still, I don't know what to say to him at this point. Though he has to know I'm gay—who doesn't, after all—neither of us have actually acknowledged it. Now it's like that's an invisible wall between us.

"Well..." Benjamin says, struggling for conversation as much as I am.

"Yeah..." I say.

After another moment of awkwardly staring at each other, he smiles and nods and steps around me to head toward his locker. With him out of sight, I let out a breath I didn't know I was holding and sag against the tile wall behind me.

That was awkward.

But it was still better than it could have been.

Eventually, I step into the shower area and take off my

towel—but I'm carefully listening for sounds as I do so, like I'm worried there's another football player in here, one that wants to punch a fag. But there's no one else. I turn on the shower, rinse myself, dry myself, and return to the change area, finding that Benjamin is already gone.

When I get home much later, I find mom has made a late dinner so I'm not forced to warm up leftovers. We sit down and have a casual dinner as a family—and I'm reminded again of how lucky I am to have this family. These are the same kind of family moments we had pre-gay.

After dinner, I head up to my room to attempt the mountain of homework I have to do tonight. I sit at my desk by my window, turn on the lamp, and set to work. Some time later, in the depths of a pre-cal problem that seems to be getting the better of me, a light catches my eye.

Looking out the window and across the divide between our two houses, I see Benjamin in his bedroom. He looks out his window and spots me, then looks away for a moment, seeming oddly conflicted. Then he gives me that friendly wave that you give people you used to know but don't really talk to anymore. I give him the same wave and before I can even wonder at that conflicted look, he closes his curtain.

Chapter Two

Benjamin

"ALRIGHT, BOYS, IT'S GAME time!" coach shouts, his deep voice echoing in the concrete change room.

The whole team cheers, even me, and I can feel the energy and fighting spirit flow through all of us. It's the homecoming game—generations of Charlesburgh High students and alumni are waiting in the stadium—we need to kick ass!

"Let's give it one-twenty!" I shout.

Everyone around me shouts "One-twenty! One-twenty! One-twenty!" and pumps their fists into the air in time with their chants.

It's a silly thing, but it never failed to get the boys riled up. Other teams gave a hundred and ten percent—but we always give a hundred and twenty. I like to think it's helped

Charlesburgh High reach the number one statewide ranking last year. We need to do it again—I want my senior year to be number one. I want to go out with a bang and ride that success into college, maybe get some scholarships.

Around me, the chants of "One-twenty!" are being replaced with "Badgers!"—our school mascot. I join in, pumping my fist, shouting, "Badgers! Badgers! Badgers!"

The room thunders with our chants, and when coach's assistant comes into the room and we know it's time to make our grand entrance, our powerful energy only increases. I charge through the group—the captain leads the team—and we jog out of the change room and out of the school and across the small divide between the building and the school's football field.

Our thunderous chants are overwhelmed by the energy coming from the crowd, already cheering our entrance even though they can't see us yet. I lead the team down a passage and we burst onto the field and through a hand-painted paper banner held by Nikki and Jordan. The applause and cheers doubles—triples—and we take our place on the field, standing in formation.

The other team is already there, in formation on their side of the field. Between us, Viola walks up with a microphone. Viola's got sweet pipes and is the lead singer in the jazz choir.

"Please stand for the national anthem," comes a deep announcer's voice from the sound system. The cheering quiets and hundreds of men and women get to their feet, take off their hats, and put their hands over their hearts. A moment later, Viola belts out the anthem, really bringing it home at the end and firing us all up for the game.

With the anthem over, the teams run off the field to their respective sideline benches and the cheer team runs onto the field for a performance to open the night and fire us up even more.

"Ben," a voice says as a hand grabs my bicep. I'm pulled out of the game-ready headspace I was in and find Nikki's clear blue eyes staring into mine. "Good luck," she says. She looks at me like she wants to kiss me—or like she wants me to kiss her. But before I can decide to do it or not, she leans in and gives me a peck on the cheek.

I turn and watch her as she runs onto the field to join her team. Some pop tune I don't know echoes around the field and rebounds off the bleachers as the cheer team launches into their routine. I catch Nikki's eye and she winks at me.

But then my gaze shifts to the left…toward Jordan.

"Jordan," I whisper to myself. I've been thinking about him non-stop since we ran into each other in the change room. I mean, yeah, we see each other all the time at school, but that was the first time in a long time where it was just the two of us, even if only for a few seconds. It was nice. I like being alone with him. Even if it made me a nervous wreck.

We used to be such good friends as little kids, but we grew apart in high school—he went in his direction and I went in mine. He thinks the distance between us is just about that. But it's not. It's because—

"Ben!" coach snaps at me. I jerk out of my thoughts and hustle over to the bench. Coach is giving us another pep talk, but my mind is elsewhere—not on Jordan, though it often is. No, I'm looking at the rows of seats surrounding the field. The bleachers are packed. Homecoming is always our biggest game—everyone comes out to see us. Charlesburgh High is one of the oldest schools in the state, so even non-alumni come out for the game and the weekend-long party.

The crowd suddenly roars nice and loud again and I look to the cheer squad and catch the tail end of what looked like a really acrobatic stunt, with Hannah landing nicely in Jordan and Alex's arms. A moment later, the music winds down, the cheer squad waves to the crowds...and Jordan is beaming. I love his smile.

The squad runs off the field and I watch Jordan the whole time.

"Ben!" coach shouts at me, pulling me back to the game.

"Sorry, Coach," I mutter, staring at the grass between my feet. From the corner of my eye, I glance toward Devon, the guy sitting next to me, wondering if he'd caught me staring. Thankfully, he's focused on coach.

I try to force Jordan out of my mind and tune in to coach's pep talk and the remainder of our opening play strategy. But I can't stop thinking about Jordan. I have so much I need to tell him.

Once the whistle blew, my head was in the game. The Kelvin Tigers were putting up a stronger fight than I expected. By halftime, we were tied, missing the commanding lead we'd hoped to have at this point.

For halftime, we're in the change room and coach is pacing back and forth, alternately cursing and pep-talking. I stare at the tile floor beneath my feet. Right now, on the field, Jordan is in that slim-fitting cheer uniform of his, helping Alex throw Hannah high in the air. I love watching him in his element and doing what he loves most.

"Damn it, Ben!" coach yells.

I jerk my head up and see him glaring at me, face red like a tomato. Around the room, all the other players and the assistant coach are staring at me. I blink several times, trying to clear away the embarrassment, trying to pull myself back into the here and now.

"You can daydream about girls later," coach says, still furious but no longer shouting. "Right now, I need you to focus. Understand?"

"Yes, Coach," I say. He glares at me a moment longer and I can't hold eye contact anymore, so I look to the side. Soon after, coach goes on to point out all the things we did wrong in the first half and orders us to do better in the second half.

"You lose this game," coach says, voice strong and clear, "and you cast a pall over homecoming. No one's going to want to celebrate a loss."

The room is deathly silent. A couple of the guys shuffle their feet awkwardly.

I'd much rather be outside, watching Jordan.

After a quick break so we can all piss and grab some water, we line up to make our triumphant return to the field. We trot out in our double line as the cheer team bounces and prances off field. I try to look at Jordan, but can't force my eyes in his direction. I do catch Nikki's gaze, though, and she blows a kiss at me.

We're soon on the field and launching into the second half of the game. It goes better. Not phenomenally well, and nowhere near as well as coach is screaming at us to do, but it's better. With a minute left in the game, we're tied again—the Tigers had a touchdown and surprised us all.

The giant clock on the scoreboard counts down like the timer on an epic-fail-bomb. Moments later, Devon passes me the ball and I'm running around bodies, evading tackles, and doing my best to stay on my feet. I see two Tigers charging straight at me and I know I can't escape, but Randy comes up beside me—I pass the ball to him and he darts away from me, evading the rush of players heading in my direction.

With me no longer having the ball, most of the people chasing me move on to chasing Randy. And with less attention on me, I can evade the tackle attempt. But Randy isn't so lucky—nearly every Tiger on the field is about to pile on him in an epic tackle. I catch his eye and he passes the ball back to me a split second before he's sacked by three guys at once.

I dart to the side, evading a nimble Tiger, and then make a beeline for the goalpost. It's all I can focus on. I'm twenty feet away—fifteen—ten—five…

I step across the line—and less than a second later, the buzzer barrels through the stadium *and* a Tiger tackles me from behind. I'm lying on the ground, stunned, smiling, basking in the insane cheers of the crowd.

We won!

I'm laughing out loud, uncontrollably, full of joy. We won!

The Tiger pushes himself off me and stands up. He glares down at me as I push myself to a seated position, still laughing.

"Fag," he mutters. It's just loud enough that I can hear it over the thunderous chorus of cheers from the bleachers.

My laughter instantly dies and any hint of a smile is wiped from my face.

Fag?

Before I can even think on that beyond the shock of being called a fag, the Tiger walks away from me and heads toward his team. My team comes charging across the field to me and tackles me in a pile-on group hug full of cheers and whoops of joy. I'm buried and smothered in happiness and excitement, but I don't feel any of it.

Do I…give off a vibe or something? How the hell did he know I was…you know…?

My team climbs off me and then suddenly I'm hoisted off the ground and into the air on the shoulders of my buddies. Everyone in the stands is on their feet and cheering—well, everyone that wanted us to win.

I look over at the Tigers and quickly spot number seven, the kid who called me fag. He and his team are throwing their stuff around, clearly angry. Maybe he called me fag just because it was the first insult he could come up with. Maybe he didn't, like, *see* something in me.

I look to our side of the field, toward where my teammates are carrying me. The cheer team is bouncing around, joining in on the excitement shared by everyone. Jordan is beaming and looking right at me with those gorgeous, dark eyes.

I can't make eye contact right now. I avert my gaze, searching the bleachers for my family instead. Mom and dad are easy to spot with their big homemade sign with my name on it. They're jumping and screaming as much as the cheer team.

Finally, a smile breaks out on my face again. It's not a full smile. I still don't feel quite…

Fag. The word still echoes in my head.

This is supposed to be my moment of glory—football captain wins the homecoming game at the last possible second—but all I can think about is being called a fag. Is it possible he knows I'm—

Damn, I can't even say the word—not even to myself.

. . .

After doing my best to celebrate with the guys and then showering and changing, I'm now wandering aimlessly toward the now-empty stadium. Mom and dad had planned to head home after the game, knowing I wouldn't want them hanging around with me and my friends.

But I've never felt so alone as I do right now.

Over in the parking lot, I can hear tailgate parties going on. All of the alumni that came in for the game are catching up or whatever. It sounds fun, I guess.

I wander down the path through the bleachers and out onto the field, moving to the very center. I stare at the goal post, remembering again my moment of elation and then the absolute crash that came immediately after.

How does Jordan do it? How does he put up with all that crap?

I chuck my bag off my shoulder and drop it to the ground and I lay down next to it, staring up at the night sky. It's clear and dark and the stars are starting to shine through.

When did life get so complicated?

Life was easier before I realized I...well...before I realized I was...different. I watched Jordan do it, watched him come out, and I wished I had the same strength and bravery as him. I chuckle, laughing at myself with pity—me, the captain of the football team, a coward. I close my eyes and throw my arms over my face. I feel so trapped in life, so stuck.

I stay like that for a while, not even sure how much time passes by. Eventually, I hear the soft tread of footsteps across the grass, like the rustle of the bottom of a shoe brushing over upright blades of grass. I hope they walk away—I don't want to talk to anyone right now.

"Benjamin?"

Except him. I'll talk to him. I'll listen to that voice every chance I get.

I look up into Jordan's warm, brown eyes.

"You okay?" he asks.

"I don't know," I say. I have no idea why I didn't just say yes and pretend everything is fine so that he doesn't ask further questions. Sigh. If it was anyone else, I would have done just that.

He steps closer to me, towering over me, concern clear on his face. "You don't know?"

I want to reach out and touch him, grab his ankle or something, but I can't do that. As long as I'm straight, I can't do that. At least, not in the way I want to.

"I'm just having a rough day."

"After *that* game? Do you want to talk about it?"

Yes, I do. I want to tell him everything. But I can't. I can't tell him.

It touches me that he'd actually ask, though. None of my football buddies would ask. Though I barely talk to

Jordan, he cares more about me than my supposed friends do.

"No," I say, finally.

He looks like he's about to turn and head back to wherever, to meet up with his cheer friends or something. But I don't want him to leave. Not yet.

"Can you sit with me for a bit?"

He looks across the field again, then down at me. "Sure. People might gossip, though, the football captain and the cheer co-captain," he says, with a teasing smile on his face. He winks at me. "Scandalous."

I laugh, but at the same time I worry about that exact thing. Still, I don't want him to leave. "I'll survive," I say.

He sits down cross-legged next to me.

Unexpectedly, he starts giggling.

"What?" I ask.

He tries to stifle his giggles and look at me, but then a new wave of laughter takes over.

"What?"

"I'm sorry," he says, still laughing. "I was just remembering the first time we met."

"Oh no," I say, knowing exactly what he's talking about.

"Oh yes," Jordan says. "Remember the look on Mrs. Wilson's face after you ate that paste? And then when it dried before she could wipe it off, your lips got stuck together and you started crying."

He laughs again and I can't help but join in and laugh at my four-year-old self. "And yet that didn't tell you I'd be trouble as a friend."

Jordan guffaws. "As if you're the only trouble maker. Do you remember the Christmas concert in first grade?"

"Yes!" I exclaim. "You mooned the audience!"

Even though it was Jordan that brought this story up, he still blushes and covers his face with his hands. I ache with the need to reach out and touch him, but still I hold back. When his chuckles die down and the blush of embarrassment fades from his cheeks, he lowers his hands and looks at me. He tilts his head like he's trying to figure out what I'm thinking. The thought of him reading my mind is both terrifying and liberating—he'd know my secret, but then I wouldn't have to keep it a secret anymore.

"You okay?" he asks again.

"I will be."

Silence falls on us again and we just stare into each other's eyes.

I can remember the first time I felt something for Jordan that was more than just friendship. We were freshmen and assigned to work together on a science fair project. The project was something about the effects of pollutants on air quality—I can't remember the details of the project, but I do remember when we won the first place award in the school's science fair. Jordan hugged me.

In the weeks leading up to the fair, when we spent so many evenings and weekends together working on that project, I spent more time with him than I typically did. I slept over at his place sometimes and he slept over at mine, even though we live next door to each other. When the morning came, I didn't want to go back to my house—or if he was at my house, I didn't want him to go back to his. At the time, I had told myself that it was just me liking my friend so much and enjoying all the time we spent together.

But when he hugged me at the science fair—that's when I knew.

And it scared me.

And I couldn't tell anyone.

I couldn't tell Jordan, that was for sure. But I couldn't tell my brothers or my parents or anybody else. Some parts of my family are really homophobic—I don't know how my parents are on that, but I've heard dad make comments about gay scenes on TV. My brothers routinely call each other gay as an insult and mom just lets it happen.

So I buried it.

And to kill my feelings—or at least to *try* and kill my feelings—I focused more on sports. It would take me away from Jordan—away from the one person who made me feel strange.

Of course, that didn't stop anything. I see Jordan daily and we share a lot of classes, so I had to put more distance between us. Still, I pined for him. And being a jock now with jock friends, I'm surrounded by locker room talk, with the guys talking about tits and ass and who they want to bang. I have no interest in those girls, but I do have an interest in the hot jock friends of mine, especially when they're changing. But I'm into Jordan ten times more.

No matter how much I try to run and hide from this, it follows me everywhere and at every moment. I can't escape this.

"If you want to talk," Jordan says, pulling me back into the present moment, "I'm always here."

"I know," I say. And in this moment, right here and right now, I decide to come out. I can't go on much longer living this lie. I can't keep hiding my feelings for Jordan. But the silence lapses between us as I struggle to gather the courage to open my mouth and actually say the words. "Jordan..."

He looks at me. He can tell by the shift in my voice that this is serious.

I pause again, scrounging up more courage. Just as I'm about to utter the words, a burst of raucous laughter interrupts us, pulling our attention to the side of the field. A group of cheerleaders and football players are headed this way, all of them laughing at something or other. I can tell they're not laughing at us. They don't know what I was about to say to Jordan. They don't see that when they look at us.

Part of me is relieved. Part of me is devastated.

Jordan looks back at me and there's an uncomfortable grimace on his face. I know he doesn't like most of the football team and some of the cheer team can be bitchy to him. I look again at the group as they near us—Nikki is one of them, Jordan's arch-nemesis. I've seen her berate him at cheer practice and how he just takes it. I sometimes want to step in and tell Nikki to cool it, but it's difficult when she's my pretend girlfriend.

"I better go," Jordan says. Before I can protest, he's up on his feet, backpack slung over his shoulder. He looks down at me before heading off. "Offer's always open if you want to talk." He smiles and my heart swells. Then he walks away.

Moments later, the group of football players and cheerleaders reaches me. The people that are my "friends". The people who don't treat me as nice as Jordan does.

"Why were you hanging out with *him*?" Nikki asks as the group circles around me.

"None of your business," I say with a little more force than I intend. Before they have a chance to react or to imply something about me and Jordan, I hop to my feet and pick up my bag. "What're you guys up to?"

Nikki steps close and runs her finger down my chest, ending somewhere near my belly button. "We're headed to a party," she says. "Anthony's parents are out of town and he's invited a bunch of people over." Anthony is the youngest player on the team—he probably sees this party as an opportunity to build up some social cred. "You should…come," Nikki says, really drawing that out.

She wants to get me in some dark corner and get her hands in my pants—she's made that clear enough over the past year or so. I'm not stupid. She doesn't want me for me, she wants me for the status of dating the captain of the football team. *Insta-perfect*, as she might call it. Besides, even if she did genuinely want me for me, well, she's missing certain body parts I'm looking for in lovers.

But, of course, playing along with it, even just a little, helps keep those at bay who might question me. After all, who *wouldn't* want to get with Nikki? Like, among straight guys. I took her to a dance last year and after all the pics for social media were done, she was really a bore, and then on the car ride home she made me pull over in a quiet park so that we could make out. We fooled around a little bit, but I wasn't able to, uh, *rise* to the occasion. I didn't want her to spread rumors about me, so I faked a stomachache and I drove her home.

The next day, she was blabbing to everyone about how we had a hot and heavy make out session in Tillman Park. She didn't say we had sex, but she certainly implied it. All the guys on the team were slapping my back and congratulating me. What could I say? *No, we didn't do it. I prefer guys. Nikki is missing the necessary dick.*

Social suicide. That's what that would be.

So I played along. And since Nikki doesn't want to be known as the slut, she told people we were on-again-off-again boyfriend and girlfriend—that would allow her to explain away why we're not affectionate at school ("Ben's being a dick! I'm so over him!") but then it gives her the chance to make up a hot story whenever she needs attention ("Ben *begged* me to come over last night!"). I don't think she knows how much I'm aware of her stories, but it always reaches back to me because the whole school talks about it—which is undoubtedly her plan all along.

Nikki pokes me in the middle of my chest, reminding me of my predicament. "What do you say?"

"I don't know." I really don't want to go to a party. I glance past all of them and I see Jordan turn a corner and finally disappear from sight.

"Benny," Nikki begs, low and seductive. I hate that name—*Benny*. "It'll be fun. We haven't had a chance to *unwind* yet this school year."

Behind her, I see Devon elbow a couple of guys in the ribs. They think I'm getting laid tonight. If only they knew all of the lies in front of them.

I sigh. "Fine."

She squeals and I try not to wince from the assault on my ears. She grabs my hand and leads the way to her car, the rest of the gang in tow behind us, heading to their vehicles. Devon, my best bud on the team, comes up on my other side and throws an arm around my shoulders. He gives me a little shake, a silent congratulations for hopefully getting lucky with Nikki. He cares for me a lot, I know, but I wonder if he'd be the same if he knew the truth.

I really don't want to go to this party. But I know that if I don't want people to know I'm—well, *that*—then I need to make sure they know I'm straight. Sometimes I feel so trapped by all this, like I'm living someone else's life.

Chapter Three

Jordan

IT'S BEEN A FEW weeks since I sat with Benjamin in the middle of the football field and he's been avoiding me like the plague ever since. I still can't get that moment out of my mind—his voice, his face, his posture, the tension…those damn fine biceps, the way he pouted his lips for a moment, making them look soft and kissable. I have to mentally shake my head to get the image out of it. Focus, Jordan. Benjamin was about to unload a bombshell on me. I'm sure of it.

But what was it?

I tried to run through all of the obvious ones first.

Gay? No. Even if half of the rumors about him and Nikki were untrue, there was enough there to convince me that not only was he with her, he was dangerously in love.

There were enough pics on her Instagram to make that clear enough.

Drug addict? No. He's clean as a whistle. I've smoked pot a couple times, but I doubt he has. With two lawyers for parents, he's had the law hammered into him as something to obey or suffer the consequences.

Parents are breaking up? I've not seen or heard anything coming from the Cooper household that would indicate there was anger or unhappiness there. Other than Ben and his brothers roughhousing and it sometimes getting out of hand, they seem like a close-knit and loving family.

"Earth to Jordan," Hannah said, snapping her fingers, breaking through the flurry of thoughts in my mind.

"Sorry, Han," I mutter, then focus back on her. We're spending our mid-morning spare at school in our usual spot, the picnic table under the tree at the far corner of the school's lot. Almost no one hangs out at this table, which makes it our favorite place, even if it was a little cold for mid November. I can see my breath. Yeah, it's too cold.

"When did you tune out?" she asks. This is her thing. She knows I can sometimes drift off in my head and she accepts that, so she wants to know the last thing I remember her saying so she can continue from that spot.

"Some new kid?" I say.

"Yes! Kumail!" she says, sounding excited. I raise my eyebrow at her and she just sticks out her tongue. "He just moved here from somewhere in Kansas. Senior like us. Except he's deaf."

"Oh?" Even though I have no knowledge of where this story went the first time I supposedly heard it, I could make a few intuitive leaps. Hannah's younger sister is deaf too and so she's fluent in sign.

"He has an EA with him that translates everything, but Principal Moyer wants to jump-start his social life at school. He didn't say that directly, obviously, but I know that's what he was thinking. He pulled me out of first period to introduce me to Kumail." Seriously, when Hannah has a story to tell, her mouth can go a mile a minute. But I like it. I also like this other part of her, the part that wants to help those of us who are lesser in society. Like the gays and the deaf kids. She's verbally ripped a few people to shreds on my behalf before. "I invited him to join us for lunch," she says. I realize I've tuned out a bit again, but this time I've at least tuned back in with enough context that I don't have to ask her to repeat anything.

"Oh yeah?" I say.

"Yeah, you'll like him, I hope." I try not to read into that. Hannah has tried to set me up with a couple guys since I came out, but her gaydar is pitiful. Every guy she wants me to date is woefully straight. There are only a few gay kids here at Charlesburgh High that I'm aware of—and a few that I suspect will come out sooner or later—but all the guys Hannah has her eyes on for me don't even register on my gaydar as even a little bit gay.

Maybe she just means I'll like him as a friend. I hope that's all she's implying. Maybe she just wants this Kumail kid to have as many friends as possible. Not a lot of people know sign after all.

I know a little bit of sign. Hannah took it upon herself to teach me basic vocabulary over the years so that when I visit her house I can at least say hi to her sister. I've picked up a bit more than that over the years—not enough for a full conversation, but enough to hold my own.

The end of our spare is marked by a harsh buzzer cutting through the air. I groan and stand up, slinging my backpack over my shoulder. Hannah is a little less dramatic than me.

We head into school and part ways, her heading to English and me heading to math.

Benjamin is in math with me. It's been awkward. He ignores me, like looking at me is painful. I wonder again what he was planning to tell me. Whatever it was, it couldn't have been too important or else he would have told me in the weeks since that night.

Crap. That night. I saw the party he went to on Snapchat. Nikki was all over him. Even from the safety and security of my bedroom, far removed from the party, I felt cringey for all the partiers who had to watch those two tongue-wrestle all night. I hope they at least found a bedroom to take it private.

When I enter the classroom, my eyes immediately find Ben's and then he looks away. A slight red tinge warms his cheeks. What's that about?

I take my seat, which, to make things even more

awkward, is right behind him. See, at the start of the school year, we were talking to each other—even though we barely had anything resembling a friendship and the "talking to each other" was little more than the occasional hello—and with Ms. Barnes being a stickler for her seating plan, I was stuck behind Ben even when it seemed like he wished I wasn't even in the room.

"Hey," I mutter as I pass by. I always do that. Force of habit. Part of me hopes that one day he'll say "hey" back and we'll suddenly be back on speaking terms.

Seriously, I don't know what I did wrong to earn this silence. Even when I came out he didn't give me this much silence. Our low-key friendship changed, but not by much, and the silence he'd imposed then had only lasted a couple days before he started talking to me again and telling me some crazy story about his brothers.

As I sit down, I just barely hear him say, "Hey, Jordan."

I freeze when I hear his voice, half sitting in my chair, half still standing. Part of me wondered if I'd ever hear it again. And part of me wondered if I'd just imagined that whole thing. Then he glances half over his shoulder, to where I can just barely see the corner of his eye, and a gentle smile stretches his lips.

I decide to push my luck. "How you doing?"

He makes a noise that sounds like the middle ground between a grunt and the word "fine". Then he turns again so he fully faces the front. Well. That's good. I think.

I stare at his back as Ms. Barnes starts up her lesson. I

write down whatever she writes on the whiteboard, but, seriously, it's in one ear and out the other right now. I hope the next thing Benjamin says to me is an explanation for the past few weeks. And then the second thing he says better be an apology.

We decide that the day is just too cold to go and eat our lunch outside. The spare period was enough November weather for me. Hannah and I grab a table at the edge of the cafeteria, hopefully making it easier for Kumail to find us when he comes looking.

"Benjamin talked to me today," I tell her. I told her a little bit about what happened on the football field. I didn't tell her that I thought he was going to tell me some big secret—if he's having trouble telling me, his friend of more than a decade, that he even *has* a secret, he certainly doesn't want me blabbing about it to everyone I meet. But I did tell her that he seemed depressed and that something was bothering him. And then I told her about the silence.

Every week she'd pry and ask if I'd heard from him. When I would tell her, yet again, that the answer was no, she'd sometimes try to guess at what was going on. But I always tried to cut that off. I didn't want to think about all the things that could be bothering Ben—though we'd drifted apart over the years, he's still a friend and means a lot to me, and so I don't want idle speculation on his many theoretical faults.

She puts down her yogurt cup and leans so far forward

that she's almost crawling on the table to get to me. "What did he say?"

"Just 'hey'."

"Hey?"

"Hey."

"And?"

"And then I asked him how he's doing. He just grunted." I unwrap my sandwich and take a bite. "That was it," I say with a mouth half full of sandwich.

"Huh," she says, picking up her yogurt cup again and scooping some out. She puts it in her mouth and swallows it down. "It's a start, I guess."

She doesn't really know Ben, certainly not like I know Ben. When Benjamin and I went our separate ways a few years ago and I found myself as a freshman member of the cheer team, I met Hannah. We were both awkward and out of place and so we bonded pretty quickly. I wasn't out at that time, but I think she sensed that something was different about me, which played into her need to bond with the outsiders and outcasts.

A few moments later, we're interrupted by a tall and skinny kid with a lunch tray. I've never seen this guy before but it doesn't take a leap to assume this is Kumail. He looks at Hannah with a big smile, then Hannah signs to him. Yup, Kumail.

Have a seat, she signs.

He nods, then sits next to her.

I stumble through my words. *Hi. My name is Jordan.*

His already-big smile broadens even more when he realizes I can sign too. He introduces himself, spelling out his name with individual letters. Hannah then launches into a conversation with him that I can only partly follow—their hands are moving far too fast for me. But I think she's asking him how his first day is going. Judging by the exuberance in his hand motions and the smile on his face, it's going well so far.

I guess because I'm not able to follow the conversation, I find my mind drifting as I continue eating my lunch. With Thanksgiving around the corner, we have our final performance for the cheer team and the final game for football—Charlesburgh puts on an exhibition game with Kelvin, our arch-rival school. Once that's over, then I'm free from the tyranny of Nikki, at least as far as the cheer team goes. I've still got the rest of the school year with her and we share a few classes. Plus, it's hard to not be annoyed by her at any major school event, what with the endless posing for photos.

"We'll make sure it happens!" Hannah says out loud. I look to her and find her looking at me.

"What's that?" I ask.

"Were we going too fast?" she asks me, signing for the benefit of Kumail.

"A little," I say, also signing.

"I was telling Kumail about prom and he said he doesn't go to school events because they're never deaf-friendly." She looks at Kumail and he nods, following her words via her hands. "So I said we'd make sure it happens, that prom is deaf-friendly."

I smile so broad that I feel like my face is going to crack. That's classic Hannah—and that's why I love her. She finds out that one person feels left out because of who they are, and she takes it upon herself to change the world so that person fits in.

"So you're going to join the prom committee?" I ask. I stumbled with my signing. How do I sign "committee" again? I end up just spelling it for Kumail. If he's going to have lunch with us on the reg, then I really need to brush up on my sign. I can't spell everything—conversations would take forever.

"I saw something about it on the notification board. I think it starts up next week," she says.

I'd seen the poster too. I tried not to sneer at it. Prom is such a hetero thing. Prom king, prom queen, happy hetero couples dancing to sappy music. I'll go, yeah, but not with a date. And I won't dance. Except with Hannah—if she wants to dance with me, I'll begrudgingly oblige.

"Sounds fun," I say, sarcasm heavy in my voice. I overemphasize my facial expression for Kumail's benefit. I don't know how to sign sarcasm. Can someone sign sarcasm?

"It *will* be fun," she says. She then bursts into another flurry of sign with Kumail and I'm lost again.

Maybe prom will be better than I expect with Hannah involved in planning. Not only would she make sure it's deaf-friendly, given her friendship with me she'd make sure it's homo-friendly too.

I pull a sachet of fruit snacks out of my lunch bag—a holdover from elementary school that I'm still not ready to give up on—and open it up. Quickly dividing them by color, I gobble down my least-favorite flavors first, then move on to the better-tasting ones. All while watching Hannah and Kumail.

I can't make out what they're saying, except for a word or phrase here or there, but I'm not really paying attention to the content of their conversation. Instead, I'm focusing more on body language. Particularly Kumail's body language.

I hope Hannah has no plans on setting me up with him because, cute as he is, I'm pretty sure he's straight. And he's attracted to Hannah. It's pretty obvious. But I can't tell if she's into him. She likes him, yeah, but does she like him enough to match what I'm pretty sure I'm seeing from him? That I don't know.

"Kumail is cute," I say as Hannah and I walk home. She lives a few blocks over from me, so our route is pretty similar.

She giggles and bumps her shoulder into mine. "I'm still getting used to you talking about guys like that," she says.

It's not often I call guys cute. While I might be a little bit stereotypical gay, I don't guy watch and gossip with her about hunks and I'm not into drag queens or anything like that. Like I told my parents when I came out—I'm still the same Jordan I've always been, just, you know, not into girls.

"You two have hit it off," I say. "It was nice of you to invite him to lunch."

"I like him—he's got a great sense of humor," she says. I can tell she's holding back, trying to not say something. Then I sense a change in her physical stature, like a wall inside has broken down. "He *is* cute, isn't he?" she asks.

I put my arm around Hannah's shoulders. "He's *damn* cute," I say. "And I think it's awesome you're going to make prom accessible to him."

"I want to do a fairy tale theme," she says. "Like, for prom. I wonder if I can convince the committee to do that."

"Hannah," I say. "I've found that you can do *anything* if you set your mind to it."

Chapter Four

Benjamin

OUR THANKSGIVING GAME IS against the Kelvin Tigers again.

We're in it to win, of course, but it doesn't carry the same weight as homecoming. That isn't stopping the Tigers from trying to humiliate us in our own stadium, though. And Tyler Stamets—I found out that's the name of the guy that called me fag at homecoming—has it out for me in particular. I still don't know if that was just the first insult that came to mind or if he somehow *knew*. But if he knew, then it's obvious he can't stand that a...a guy like...a guy like me bested him.

Shit. I still can't say the word, even in my head.

I'm going to have to say it one day. Jordan did. It's almost hilarious in a funny sort of way—me, the big alpha male football captain is a coward compared to the skinny little cheer guy.

But if he can do it, so can I. Today just isn't that day.

"Badgers!" coach shouts, trying to work us up into a frenzy as we prepare to run out of the change room and back onto the field for the second half.

"Badgers!" half the team shouts as coach shouts it again. *Get your head back in the game, Ben,* I tell myself. "Badgers!" I shout. I join in with the rest of the guys, pumping my fist in the air, shouting "Badgers!" over and over again. We quickly build up until we're like a tightly-coiled bundle of energy, ready to launch into the stadium and implement destruction on the Tigers.

The assistant coach throws the door open and I lead the charge, all the guys hot on my heels, running into the stadium. The cheer team is finishing their routine—and I lose my breath for a moment when I see Jordan athletically and nimbly throw his legs and arms around in front of him as he and his teammates try to work the crowd up into a frenzy. Devon bumps into me and I nearly fall over, but I catch my footing and continue leading the team forward, desperately hoping no one noticed what I'd just done, how I'd just reacted. Maybe if someone saw, they'll think I was breathless because of Nikki.

The cheer team runs past us, vacating the field, and I catch Jordan's eye as he runs past me. He seems almost surprised I'd made eye contact. I don't blame him. I've treated him like dirt for weeks now—not because of anything he'd done, of course, but because of my own stupid insecurities. Because of my cowardice.

Moments later, we're sitting on the benches at the sidelines and coach is pacing back and forth in front of us, giving us a last minute pep talk and reminders of the strategies he laid out over halftime. In my head, I try to shove all thoughts of Jordan out. I need to focus on the game. I need to evade Tyler Stamets. I need to ensure the Badgers win and that the Tigers are sent away to lick their wounds.

The ref blows the whistle and we head onto the field, taking our positions. In a flurry of jostling bodies, the second half starts. The Tigers have the ball—Tyler Stamets—and I charge after him. My need for revenge, to show him that this...sigh...this fag is better than him. Power and strength that surprises even me flows through my legs, carrying me ferociously across the field.

I leap, soar through the air, and crash into his waist, tackling him to the ground. We both grunt when we hit the ground, the air being forced out of both of us. Before either of us can recover and I can push myself off of him and stand above him with a gloating grin on my face, he shouts at me.

"Get off me, fag!" Tyler shoves me off him and I roll to the side.

I see red. I'm so furious. I jump to my feet at the same time as him.

"What the hell, man?" I demand. The cheers and jeers from the crowd flow through me, making me impulsive. I'm about to launch at him, but a ref comes between us, obviously cluing in on what's about to happen.

I stalk away and before I'm out of earshot, I hear Tyler mutter, "Cocksucker."

Tyler and I manage to avoid each other for most of the second half. But then all of a sudden I have the ball and I have a clear line to the end zone—I make a break for it, trying to summon the same strength and speed as when I tackled Tyler Fucking Stamets.

The roar of the crowd spurs me on faster. They see what I see, that the end is in sight, that we'll win this one like we won homecoming. But then a new cheer ripples through the crowd—and it's coming from where the Tiger fans sit. That can only mean one thing: a Tiger is hot on my heels.

And I know exactly who it is.

I try to summon even more speed and strength than before. My lungs and legs are burning. Really, I'm seconds from crossing that distant line—and that distant line is really not so distant—but with Stamets somewhere behind me, probably very close behind me, it seems so epically far away.

Suddenly that distance seems to shrink and I'm no more than five running steps from the end zone. The end is in sight. Victory is in reach.

And then it all comes crashing down in a whirlwind of pain. Someone tackles me, taking my legs out from under me, and I collapse to the ground underneath him. A scorching, searing pain slices through me, coming from my right shin. I scream out in pain. The guy on top of me pushes himself up, scrambling off me, and that movement sends a wave of pain through me, starting in my leg and ending in my gut, almost making me vomit.

Lying still again, I'm still in excruciating pain, but I'm not on the verge of barfing and I'm able to not scream. But I can't do anything else. I try to push myself to a seated position, but another wave of pain crashes into me and I just fall back to the ground.

I'm aware of people above me, of shapes around me, but I'm having trouble seeing anything or focusing on anything with all of this pain crashing into me.

My leg is broken. I don't need someone to tell me—it's obvious.

When that dirtbag Stamets tackled me, he broke my leg.

Everything is a blur. I'm aware of someone hovering closer to me—maybe a ref, maybe coach—and then there are two people I don't know who somehow move me onto something flat and firm. A stretcher, I realize. The stadium is filled with deafening silence. That much I'm aware of.

I watch the rapidly-darkening sky above me as the stretcher is pulled off-field. Each jostle of the stretcher sends a mini-burst of pain and nausea through me, but I manage to keep my lunch down.

Mom and dad meet me at the ambulance. Mom frets over me while dad gets the details from the EMTs. Mom climbs into the back of the ambulance after my stretcher is loaded in. She sits on the side next to the EMT and she holds my hand. I'm seventeen, almost an adult, but it's holding mom's hand that gives me strength. I try to swallow down my panic, try to ignore my pain, and I hold mom's hand really tight.

Thanksgiving sucked.

I found out much later that we had lost the game to the Tigers. And it *was* Tyler Stamets that tackled me and broke my leg.

Thanksgiving dinner was low-key this year, with everyone fretting over me and my leg. Dad's big concern was what this would mean for football scholarships. Not, you know, how I'm doing. Mom did her typical mom thing—constantly making sure I'm comfortable, fretting over me to the point where it's annoying. And because of all of this, she cancelled the big family dinner.

So the five of us—me, Mom, Dad, and my brothers Brayden and Daniel—had a giant turkey and some Stove Top Stuffing, along with steamed veggies. The turkey had been thawing in the fridge before the broken leg, so it had to be cooked. Seriously, Thanksgiving was a week ago and Mom still pulls containers of cooked turkey out of the freezer.

I might have hit my turkey limit for my lifetime.

Thanksgiving morning, Devon came over to hang out a bit, doing his best friend duties, but really all we talked about was the game and that was the last thing I wanted to think about. My leg was a painful reminder of how awful that game ended. After it became too much, I faked being tired and he gave me a bro-hug and went home.

On the first day back to school after the long weekend, I got the hero's welcome. Everyone wanted to give me a mini pep talk—"You'll be back to normal soon!"—but once the novelty of that wore off, I just felt...isolated.

All my buddies just hung out without me. I mean, we always play sports when we're together, even if it's just tossing a ball around, and I can't really do that while I've got this stupid cast on my right leg. Because the break was so bad, the doctor didn't give me a walking cast, so I'm hobbling around on crutches, making a fool of myself. Devon tried to include me as much as possible, but it just became too much of a hassle—both for them and for me.

I want to just skip school until the cast is off, but mom has taken pity on me and drives me to school and picks me up every day—so I have to go. While mom might feel sorry for me at home and get me extra ice cream, she won't put up with me faking a sick day. Even if she felt that much pity for me, she wouldn't let me take six to eight weeks of sick days.

I sit back in my chair at the desk in my bedroom, craning my neck from side to side. This homework is brutal. Some pre-calculus nonsense that I'll never use in real life. I check my answers against the ones in the back of the textbook and—surprise, surprise—they're wrong. I throw my pencil down on the desk and push myself up to stand on my good foot. Shuffling slowly, since I found trying to hop on my good foot ends up jarring the break in my bad leg, I make my way over to my bed and collapse onto it and stare up at the ceiling.

My life is a mess.

My friends have abandoned me, daily life is a struggle with this cast, and I can't even confess to myself my deepest, darkest secret. I can't even say the word—not even in my head. I mean, I can say it when it applies to other people, but I can't say it about myself.

Jordan is gay. See? I can say the word.

Me? I'm...ugh.

And if I can't do that, how can I tell Jordan how I feel about him?

I pick up my cell and scroll through my feeds, looking for anything to distract myself with. But I quickly realize that's an epic fail. I'm seeing all the posts and photos and snaps of my supposed friends living it up without me. We got our first dusting of snow today—the kind of snow that will probably melt tomorrow—but my feeds are full of my friends having snowball fights or building miniature snowmen.

And then there's Nikki. With me being the lame football captain, no longer a status symbol for her to cling to, she's moved on to Winston, captain of the basketball team. Basketball is a second rate sport at our school, far behind football. But with me no longer adding to her social cred, she's hoping to find some through him. In all the pics she posts, though, he's got this bewildered look in his eyes, like he's stunned that Nikki is even giving him the time of day, never mind the kiss that seems perfectly photographed and hashtagged to death.

As soon as I'm back on my feet and back into sports, Nikki will come crawling back. And pitiful me will take her back—at least in the sense that I'll allow her to claim we have a relationship—if it means I can hide my secret a little longer.

I scroll deeper into my feed, wanting to escape the vapidity of Nikki and the hurt of my former football friends. And then a picture of Jordan pops up. I check the account, it's posted by Hannah, and it shows her with Jordan and that new kid, Kumail. But the only person I really see is Jordan.

He's got that broad grin on his face, the one that almost splits him in half and shows off his near-perfect teeth. It's the smile that lights up my day and warms my heart. It takes me a moment to realize that I'm caressing the image on the screen like he's here in bed with me.

Damn, I'm thirsty for that boy.

And instantly I feel terrible again.

Jordan is the one friend that hasn't abandoned me—but I've abandoned him. Well, not *abandoned* him, but certainly pretended we weren't friends. I'd like to say it's all Tyler Stamets's fault—I can still hear him calling me "fag" and "cocksucker"—but if I'm honest with myself, I'm the one at fault. One hundred percent.

I'm so desperate to keep this secret that I'm putting my friendship with the guy I...the guy I like...at risk.

I shut off my phone. I can't look at that gorgeous face anymore. I toss the phone out of reach so that I can't just reach over and pick it up and put myself through that torture again. I know I need to get back up on my good foot and shuffle back to the desk to tackle that last bit of homework, but I just don't have it in me right now.

Instead, I look out my window at the dark sky above. A light flicking on catches my eye—Jordan's bedroom. I prop myself up on my elbows so I can get a better look. Did I tell you I was thirsty?

He's not alone—he's got Hannah and Kumail with him. His friends sit on the bed together and he takes the chair in front of his desk. If I didn't know better—and really what do I know—it looks almost like there's something going on between Hannah and Kumail. Maybe it's because I can't hear what they're saying and I have to go entirely by body language that I'm making these assumptions. They're sitting super close to each other.

And suddenly all three of them are waving their hands around, signing. Oh, right, Kumail is deaf. I don't share any classes with the guy, so I don't know much about him other than the fact that he's deaf. Some of the school bullies had tried to pick on him a while back, but Hannah wouldn't have any of it and she confronted them. She's got a lot of balls.

Jordan spins around in his chair and starts up his

computer and brings up something that looks like a PowerPoint for some presentation they're all working on. Their conversation, lively and with hands flying all over the place, continues. Although it might sound kind of creepy, I wish I knew sign so I could figure out what they're talking about. It would at least allow me to fool myself into thinking I have friends talking to me.

Then Jordan glances out the window and over in my direction. I quickly fall back down to the bed, hoping I got out of the way before he saw me. A few moments later, my phone chirps with a text. Careful not to raise my body above the windowsill, I shimmy down the bed and then crawl across the floor on my good knee to retrieve my phone.

My heart feels like it stops when I see it's from Jordan.

JORDAN: Wanna come over? I mean, we're signing and working on homework, but if you're looking for company...?

Crap. That means he saw me. But he wasn't repulsed, wasn't put off that I was spying. He knows I'm lonely and he's reaching out. I want to go over, but I also know I shouldn't. One, because I need to finish this pre-cal and, two, because I still don't know what to say to Jordan, especially with his friends in the room. What if he asks me what the deal is with the cold shoulder?

I text him back.

BENJAMIN: Thank you for the offer—seriously—but I gotta get this pre-cal done.

I feel a cold sweat peppering my forehead. Is he going

to take this as a brush off? Is he going to say he's done with me?

My phone chirps.

JORDAN: Understood! This polynomial stuff is melting my brain. Good luck!

Relief floods through me. He didn't take it the wrong way. Then, a moment later…

JORDAN: We should hang out sometime.

I type out a reply, delete it, type something different, delete it, make a third try, delete it. What the hell do I say? Yes, and can we hang out without pants? I agree, like, maybe on a date? Let me come out to my parents first?

Sometimes I hate myself.

In the end, I type:

BENJAMIN: Agreed! Back to homework now, tho. G'night!

Then I turn off my phone—like, *completely* off—before he has the chance to text back and I slide it along the carpet under my bed to where I can't easily get it, not with this gimp leg. My heart is thudding against my ribs, threatening to break through. All I can do is lie on the floor on my back, arms splayed out, and stare at the ceiling while I try to calm my breathing and my racing heart.

Next time I get Jordan alone, I have to tell him the truth.

Chapter Five

Jordan

BENJAMIN: AGREED! BACK TO homework now, tho. G'night!

I smile at the text. Benjamin and I used to be such good friends and even when we drifted apart, we still caught up now and then. The past couple months of utter silence have been torture. It's felt like a big part of my life has gone missing.

So when I saw him watching Hannah, Kumail, and I through the window, I took my chance and texted him. I'd seen in school how his friends had abandoned him. They all signed his cast and helped out as much as they could in the first couple days after Thanksgiving, but then they disappeared. Some friends they are.

I'd been looking for a way to open the lines between us again. Like, I mean, I couldn't just text him out of the blue or walk up to him at school—he wanted distance between us and even though I didn't understand it, I had to respect it. But then I caught him creeping.

When I asked Hannah and Kumail if I could invite Ben over, Hannah gave me a skeptical look but agreed. Kumail doesn't know Ben, so he just shrugged. I texted Ben and while he didn't come over, it at least opened that door again. Maybe he'll eventually tell me what he wanted to say at homecoming.

I probably have the stupidest grin on my face now as we work through our social studies project. Benjamin is back in my life—that's awesome! We used to be such good friends and I miss his company. I suddenly get this weird feeling of butterflies in my stomach at the thought of hanging out with him again, but I quickly squash that down.

As we work on our social studies project, I also pay attention to Hannah and Kumail, like, attention to what's going on between them. They've been growing closer and closer as the weeks passed by. Anytime I ask Hannah about it, she asserts that they're "just friends". Yeah, back in junior year I was "straight". I've seen that sort of denial before.

The three of us work well together and so we've already got all our parts prepared, this work session is just a matter of pulling all the pieces together. I finalize the PowerPoint and then we rehearse the presentation together. Hannah and I sign as we speak—or at least I do my best—and as Kumail signs, Hannah practices interpreting for when we're in front of the class. After we're done, we do it one more time.

I think we've got it down, Kumail signs.

I nod and Hannah says, *I think so! Nervous?*

A little. Kumail grimaces. *I've never actually done a presentation before. At my old school they let me skip assignments like this and write an essay instead.*

Hannah gives Kumail a side-hug. *You'll do great! And if you make a mistake, I'll cover for you,* she teases.

He gives her a playful punch in the shoulder and then the two of them are signing faster than I can keep up with. My skills have really improved with Kumail in the picture, but I'm still worlds behind the two of them. They know they lose me now and then, so I don't worry about it. They'll slow down and pull me back in if they want me to hear something.

I slowly swivel in my chair, facing the window again.

There's Benjamin.

He's sitting on his bed, pencil in hand, probably working on that pre-cal. I catch his eye and he smiles at me, giving me a friendly wave. He looks more casual and at-ease than he has in a long time. Whatever wall had built up between us, maybe it was starting to crumble. His smile briefly gets wider—maybe he's thinking the same thing— and my heart does a little pitter-patter. I love that smile of his and the way it puts little dimples in his cheeks.

I know he's straight and I have no chance with him, but it's moments like this that I wish that wasn't the case. But if he's straight, what the hell does he see in Nikki? Then again, judging by her Instagram, she's moved on to Winston—and Ben hasn't seemed too heartbroken. Maybe it wasn't quite the match made in social media heaven that I thought it was.

Ben will make some woman very happy one day, as long as he finds the right woman. If he finds another Nikki, we're going to have a talk, *mano-a-gayo*. Then I have some deviant thought of that *mano-a-gayo* talk revealing that Ben isn't quite as straight as I think and what that would mean for our friendship...

"Jordan?" Hannah says.

I spin around in my chair, jolting out of some daydream that was quickly turning sexy. I nearly fall out of my chair due to an over-spin. "Uh, yeah?" I can feel my cheeks warming with a blush.

Out of habit, even though Hannah is talking to me, she signs since Kumail is in the room. "You okay?" She glances out the window and obviously sees the person who had entranced me so. Before I can come up with some sort of lame excuse, she adds, "Were you crushing on Ben?"

There's a teasing gleam in her eye. She knows I don't really like talking about the guys I'm into—whether or not I'm actually into the guy and with Ben I'm *not* actually into the guy. Even if he's got that killer smile. And I'm totally *not* into him even though I saw him wrapped in just a towel by the showers. And I'm definitely not into him even though he sometimes makes my heart skip a beat.

Damn.

I'm into Benjamin.

This is going to be awkward.

"No, I'm not into Benjamin," I say. Belatedly, I sign the words for Kumail. "Besides, he's straight."

I don't know if she buys my denial. I'm a terrible liar.

A couple weeks later, I still haven't hung out with Benjamin. But that doesn't stop Hannah from teasing me about it.

It's our morning spare period and we're hanging out in a corner of the library since it's far too cold to hang out at our favorite picnic table. We're loosely doing some research for our English papers, but really we're just chatting about various things.

Inevitably, she brings it up. "How's your boyfriend?" she asks. She keeps her voice low, though, because she knows I wouldn't want anyone else to overhear that. She also doesn't want to start rumors about Ben. She might tease me, but it's an ethical tease.

"How's yours?" That's the best I can come up with. Teasing her back about her and Kumail. I really need to be a more sassy gay. The only fault in that comeback is that they might *actually* be boyfriend and girlfriend soon. I don't know if either of them have acknowledged it to themselves or to each other, but it's obvious to anyone that looks at the two of them interacting.

"Oh!" she exclaims, backhanding my chest. When she

realizes how loud she was in the library, she winces and mouths "sorry" to the librarian on the other side of the room. She picks up her backpack and pulls out a plastic folder.

"What's this?" I ask.

"Prom plans!"

Hannah did get on the prom planning committee. Truthfully, it couldn't have been that hard—the committee consists of Hannah, two students I vaguely know, and a supervising teacher. It's not exactly high competition. Everyone wants to go to prom, but no one wants to plan it.

She lays the folder out on top of our textbooks and opens it. The first thing I see is a roughly-sketched poster concept. I pick it up and bring it closer to me, and as I do so, Hannah clasps her hands in front of her mouth, like she's waiting for me to assess her life's work.

"Fairy Tale Dreams," I read from the poster. "Join us for an evening of magical wonder in the land of fairy tales. Fancy dress required. Tiaras optional." I smile. It's so Hannah.

"What do you think?" she asks in a hushed whisper.

"I think it's awesome," I say, and I mean it. Hannah's touch will make this really special.

"Kumail drew the picture," she says.

I focus more on the picture behind the words and I see an intricately-drawn image of an attractive prince at the base of a castle tower with what appears to be Rapunzel high above, her golden hair spilling down and lining the bottom of the poster.

"*Kumail* drew this?" I ask, incredulous. It's not that I don't believe Kumail is capable of such a thing, it's that this is the first I've heard of him being able to draw more than a stick figure.

"We worked together on it all weekend," she said.

Ah, so that's why she was evasive when I texted her to hang out. She was working on this...with *Kumail*. Potential boyfriend-girlfriend confirmed. I think they still don't know it, but it's real and I'm so happy for her.

Last year, she showed me a few of her diaries from when she was younger. She was big into fairy tales and Disney movies and would regularly write about wanting a prince to come and sweep her off her feet. I'd watched her go on date after date after date with none of those guys measuring up to her high fairy tale standards. There was even one time we went on a date, back before I realized I'm gay. It was awkward. We chalked it up to us being best friends and that adding a romance angle was not right. It wasn't until shortly after that that I realized it's because she doesn't have a wiener.

Not that my developing feelings for Ben have to do with his wiener. I mean, it's a benefit, I'm sure, but Benjamin is...*Benjamin*. He's athletic, attractive, smart, friendly, just an all around good guy. And he treats me so well...when he's not avoiding me like the plague.

Seriously, why am I crushing on my friend? Is this some

sort of "best of a bad lot" sort of thing? With no real gay prospects in this school, I'm just attracted to an unattainable straight guy? Maybe if I fap some more to it, I'll burn my way through this infatuation.

"I'm thinking of adding 'Where dreams come true' to the bottom of the poster," she says.

"Isn't that, like, a Disney slogan? For Disneyworld or something?" I ask.

"Oh." Her smile suddenly falters as she thinks it through. "I want to get it across that it's a magical night where anything can happen. Any girl can find her prince." Her voice takes on that mystical tone again as she's lost in her mental image of this fairy wonderland she's concocting.

An unexpected bubble of cynicism rises to the top. "Not *every* girl will find her prince."

She looks at me, giving me the side-eye. We both know what I'm talking about. *I* won't find *my* prince. Not at prom anyway. This fairy tale dream thing is for straight people.

"Anything can happen, Jordan," she says with absolute conviction.

She believes wholeheartedly what she says—and that's yet another reason I love her and keep her as my bestie. Her eternal optimism and her belief that there's someone out there for everyone—even me—keeps me going when being one of the only gay kids at Charlesburgh High weighs heavy on my shoulders. All I have to do is get through high school and then go to NYU—a giant university in a giant city will instantly lead to more prospects in the romance department.

Maybe I'll even lose my cherry next school year.

The thought of sex is both arousing and terrifying. I mean, I see the stuff on Tumblr and I fap to it, but, like...*yikes*.

"Earth to Jordan," Hannah says, pulling me back to the planet. I have to stop doing that, drifting off in thought, especially into sexy thoughts while in a public place. I shift my legs, hoping to hide my physical reaction to the thoughts I'd just been pulled from.

"Sorry," I say. "Last thing I heard was 'anything can happen'."

"I said that we *will* find you a date for prom. Even if we have to go through all the dating apps." Like with her conviction that there's someone for everyone, she says this with the same conviction. If it came right down to it, she would download all the apps and find me a date. That terrifies me. Not that Hannah would do it and not that someone would date me, but the *actual* date. Having no fellow gays to fool around with at school—at least none that I *want* to date of the ones that are actually out—I'm able to put aside all thoughts and worries about dating as something to worry about later, at NYU.

"Um," I say, trying to sort out my words and my thoughts. "Let me worry about it. I'd, uh, I'd rather go to the prom with you and Kumail as your chaperone than with someone I met online."

There's a slight twitch in her eyes when I mention the possibility of me being her chaperone. If I didn't know better, I'd say it was disappointment—but I'm unclear on if it's disappointment at me not wanting a date or disappointment at intruding with what will surely be a full-on date with making out between her and Kumail.

"Prom is still months away," she says. "We have time to sort that part out."

If I could choose, and if I didn't have to worry about the gay or straight thing, and if I couldn't go with Hannah and Kumail, I'd go with Ben. But Ben will be going with some hot girl, no doubt, maybe even Nikki.

Maybe I'll just go alone. Or maybe I'll stay home.

Hannah won't like that, but she'll have to live with it.

Christmas break is stupid so far.

Mr. Empaces assigned us to write a five-page research paper for English class over the break. It's seriously due on the day we're back. Way to wreck Christmas, Mr. Empaces.

I try to make the best of it, but it still sucks. Since Mr. Empaces also teaches history, our paper has to be on an historical event of personal significance to us, and we have to include a personal reflection on how that historical event impacts who we personally are today.

Hannah is doing hers on some war in the Philippines, which directly led to her family immigrating to America. Kumail is doing his on how the inclusion of deaf people in mainstream society changed over the years, and how that means he's in a public school and not in some mental institution or something. I meant to ask Ben what his paper's about—we're not in the same English class, but he also has Mr. Empaces, so I know he has the same assignment—but never got around to it.

Christmas came and went. Our little nuclear family is small—mom, dad, Bella, and me—but mom's side of the family is huge and dad's is bigger still. So we had four Christmas dinners spread over the day before Christmas Eve through to Boxing Day, with one of them being held here. I've had enough of family now.

I did get some sweet gifts, though. Mom and dad got me a new iPad and Hannah got me a really cool sweater. I gave Bella concert tickets to some boy band she likes (and whose name I can never remember) and promised to go with her. I think I won the best Christmas gift award with those tickets.

But now with Christmas over, I have less than a week to come up with a paper topic, research it, write about it, and reflect on it. I had floated some ideas past Hannah, but she shot down each and every one of them—they were too broad (history of this state), too narrow (history of Charlesburgh High), or not related to me (history of trains). I know what she's pushing me toward, but for some reason I don't want to do it.

I don't want to be the gay kid that researches gay history.

Then again, that is sort of the point of this assignment. Hannah is Filipino and researching a war in the Philippines. Kumail is deaf and researching the history of deaf kids in school. I really *should* do something on gay history.

I pull up Google and type in "gay history" and skim through results—bar raids, Stonewall, Harvey Milk, trans rights. There's so much to pick from, but it wouldn't be hard to narrow it down to one topic. The problem, though, is that I feel like I'd be revealing something too personal by tying who I am to this historical event. Yeah, I'm gay and everyone knows it, but I still don't really talk about it much. If someone missed my big coming out on Tumblr and didn't hear about it in the school gossip, they might not know I'm gay.

It's not that I'm hiding or semi-closeted. I just don't like to put it in people's faces.

But this paper isn't putting it in people's faces—this paper is just going to be read by Mr. Empaces. I click on a link at random and end up at a website detailing the Stonewall Riots in New York City. Okay, I could do this— history of gay liberation, which directly leads to me being able to be an out gay kid at school. I don't have to hide who I am for fear of jail or worse.

Swallowing down my weird discomfort with the whole thing, I read on and start making notes on a scrap piece of paper. I follow link after link and find pictures and biographies and detailed historical accounts. Yeah, this will work. And I can easily see how I can tie the personal reflection piece into this.

If it wasn't for these people—led by a trans woman of color—I might not be able to be gay today. Well, I'd be gay no matter what, but I might not be able to acknowledge it or proclaim it. At least not safely.

My phone dings with a text, pulling me out of my research. I realize that the place is shrouded in darkness. I'd started this right after dinner and it was now after midnight—I hadn't even turned on a light or gone to take a piss in all that time. I'd been working in the light cast out by my computer monitor.

I pick up the phone. It's Benjamin. I lean to the side, looking across the short distance between our houses. He waves at me, waggling his fingers.

I smile. He's cute. Then I blush for thinking of him as cute and I'm thankful I'm in near total darkness because he can't see the blush and can't ask me what it's about.

BENJAMIN: How's your break? How's the paper?

JORDAN: Break sucks because of the paper. But I think I got it now.

BENJAMIN: What's your topic?

JORDAN: Stonewall riots and LGBTQ liberation

There's an awkward stretch of silence after I send that message. I lean to the side again and look across the expanse between our bedrooms, wondering if he'd somehow fallen asleep in the middle of our text messages. No, he's still sitting on his bed, looking across at me. The light from his phone illuminates his face like he's telling someone a ghost story around a campfire.

JORDAN: And you? Your break and your paper?

BENJAMIN: Christmas is a quiet affair, at least

compared to yours. I saw all those people on xmas Eve. LOL

BENJAMIN: My paper's about the slave trade. My ancestors came over on the boats.

Suddenly I feel so foolish for thinking that writing about the Stonewall Riots as being too personal or deep of a topic. With us both researching such troubling histories, I feel a need to change the topic, to move us away from that and to something lighter.

JORDAN: Plans for NYE? Party with the team I assume?

BENJAMIN: No—no plans. I don't talk to the boys much any more

BENJAMIN: Not since the leg

BENJAMIN: Sorry if I got you down. What are your plans?

JORDAN: You didn't get me down

JORDAN: I'm planning to avoid my family. Like my extended family.

JORDAN: Probably hanging out at home. Watch music videos, make nachos, watch the ball drop.

BENJAMIN: Sounds nice :)

I think back to when we texted last, about how we had said we should hang out and then we never did. Is he fishing for an invite? Whether he is or not, a New Year's hangout might be a good follow up to those texts.

JORDAN: You wanna come over for NYE? I can make nachos for two.

JORDAN: We can probably steal some beer from my dad's supply

There's another of those very long stretches of silence that again has me wondering if he's fallen asleep mid-conversation. Again, I lean to the side to look through the window, but before I make it all the way, my phone dings.

BENJAMIN: That'd be great.

BENJAMIN: What time should I be over?

JORDAN: 7? Sound okay?

BENJAMIN: Def. See you then buddy.

BENJAMIN: :)

Chapter Six

Benjamin

T HAT TEXT CONVERSATION WITH Jordan was two days ago, but I kept checking it like every ten minutes since it happened. Is this...a date?

No, not a date. A date means both parties need to know it's a date. Jordan has no idea I like him and he has no idea I'm...he doesn't know it's okay to like me.

But...it's a friend hang out, something we haven't really had since that awkward hug in freshman year that made me realize the truth about myself. Sometimes I want to kick myself. I've lost out on three years of solid friendship with Jordan—potentially even more than just friendship—because of my utter cowardice.

He came out so he could be his true self for senior year—at least that's what he said on his Tumblr post, which I still have bookmarked and which I read every once in a while. I sometimes wonder if I should do the same, but then I think of all the ways it could possibly go wrong.

I would probably lose my football friends more permanently than I have right now. And who knows how my parents would react—they can be weirdly conservative in ways. I know my grandparents, at least on dad's side, won't accept it. They live, breath, and eat Catholicism and whenever there's a gay news story I always hear one or both of them mutter something about "the gays".

Speaking of. My parents and brothers are going to *that* set of grandparents' house tonight—there's a family board games gathering for New Year's Eve. And if my grandparents have their way, it'll end with a midnight prayer for the return of God's holy kingdom to America or some bullshit like that.

Dad comes knocking on my door and lets himself in.

"Last chance," he says. "We're packing up to go to grandma and grandpa's place. It'll be fun…" His words trail off with a lilt, like he's trying to convince a five year old. He doesn't know I have a date tonight—*a hangout,* I tell myself, *a hangout.*

"I'm not feeling up to it," I say, indicating my still-encased leg. This goddamn piece of plaster is due to come off soon and I won't miss it one bit. I know that excuse can only go so far, so I give him a bit of the truth. "I might go next door and hang out with Jordan, watch the ball drop."

As soon as dad's expression changes, I know I've said the wrong thing. He doesn't approve of Jordan's "lifestyle choices". Well, dad, did you know your son is a flaming homo too?

Holy crap.

I just called myself that word. I called myself a homo.

That's one step closer to calling myself g—

No, still can't do it.

That word still carries a lot more baggage with it. "Homo" almost sounds scientific, academic, but the…the g-word is somehow more personal.

I'm such a coward.

"I'd really prefer you join us for board games," dad says, leaning forward and lowering his voice, like he's trying to intimidate me or order me to come along. He'd never *actually* order me, though. I know my dad. He's just trying to guilt trip me into going along. Any second now he'll say something about "family". "Ben, it's not quite a family gathering without you."

Cue the guilt trip. The guilt trip that I'm skipping out on.

"Sorry, dad, but I'm really not up for it," I say. I try to make my voice as firm as his, to show him that I won't be intimidated into being the good little hetero Christian. That bothers me too. I know Jordan's parents are religious and I don't think religion has ever come between them on the topic of Jordan being gay.

"We'll take our time putting on our boots," dad says, "in case you change your mind. I hear grandma made those cinnamon rolls you love so much."

I don't say anything in response. I just wait for dad to leave.

"Don't disappoint your family, son," he says, then finally leaves me be.

I fall back on my bed and mash a pillow in my face—I want to scream, but this pillow-face torture it just barely managing to help me hold it back. Maybe me not coming out isn't a cowardice thing—it's a family pressure thing. Or it's both. It's probably both.

I can tell my blood pressure is high—I can feel the blood rushing through every vein and artery in my neck and they all throb with my pulse. I listen as the four of them clatter about loudly, putting on boots and coats and packing up some games. I wouldn't be surprised if dad is making extra loud noises just to further guilt me into coming along.

"Benjamin?" dad calls out. He only says my full name when he's disappointed. "Last chance. You coming?"

"Not up for it," I shout. Then, as if it makes everything better, I add, "Sorry!"

I hear an exaggerated and exasperated sigh from dad and then a few moments later the door opens, they all tromp out, and the door is shut and locked. I stay where I am, lying down in bed, and I wait for my blood pressure to fall. With every beat of my heart, the pulsing in my neck diminishes just a little bit and the sensation of feeling every blood cell move along its path starts to fade. My breathing, which had become tense and strained during the makeshift-argument with dad, slowly relaxed too.

When I feel like I'm back to normal, I pick up my phone to look at the time. Five o'clock. That gives me two hours to prepare to go to Jordan's place. I sit up and look across the space between our houses, but I don't see him in his bedroom.

I close my curtains, strip naked, and hobble into the bathroom. With this cast, I can't really shower or bathe easily, so I've let myself get a little stinky lately and that won't do for a date-slash-hangout with Jordan. Taping a plastic bag around my leg to keep the plaster dry and sitting on the edge of the bathtub, I run the shower and angle the head so it cascades down over me. The floor is getting a little wet, but smelling nice is worth the mess. Finished with the shower, I hobble out, dry myself off, shave, brush my teeth, and use mouthwash. I stand in front of the mirror and flex a bit. Does Jordan like muscles?

Even if nothing happens, I'm looking forward to this. Even if this is purely a platonic hangout and we watch music videos, eat nachos, and watch the ball drop and I go home, it's still exactly where I want to be tonight. I look down in the mirror and see that I've grown with my thoughts of Jordan. I ignore it for now, even though I want to fap so badly.

I realize I still have my plastic bag taped to my leg. I quickly tear it off and then grab the washcloth and wash my toes on that foot. I don't think those toes have been washed since the cast went on. I don't want them to stink tonight.

Hobbling back to my bedroom, I pick out clothes that

make me look good, but don't make it look like I'm trying to impress him. You know, like, "Oh, this old thing?" kind of nice. I pick out jeans that have a slight rip on the inner thigh—give him a tease of skin—and a shirt that is uber-casual, but clings to my biceps nicely. It's the shirt that Nikki wants me to wear when she's got some social media agenda in mind for me and her.

I roll my eyes at the thought.

Jordan is on social media—who isn't?—but at least he's not obsessed with his online image like Nikki. I don't think I could be with someone who's that obsessed about meaningless crap like that. She keeps talking about getting Insta-famous, but half the people on Instagram are aiming for the same thing and no one is going to make it.

I struggle into my jeans—the cast makes it difficult. And when I put on the button-up shirt, I spend an awful lot of time debating if the top two or top three buttons should be undone. In the end, I decide on three open buttons for the casual factor, but also so I can show a little more skin.

Almost as if on cue, my phone chirps.

JORDAN: I just put nachos in the oven—come over any time!

BENJAMIN: Nachooooos!

I immediately regret sending "Nachooooos!". That's a little too dude-bro. I need more of a could-be-friends-could-be-more vibe.

BENJAMIN: I mean... Ooo! Nachos! On my way! :)

JORDAN: LOL it's ok to get excited about nachoooooos!

I want to send a text in return that's witty or cute, but my mind freezes over and my fingers don't move. In the end, I give up and just hobble down the stairs to the front door to put on my boots—one regular boot and one giant-sized fit-over-the-cast boot—and my jacket, though I don't zip it up.

I'm feeling incredibly nervous. And sweaty. Nervous and sweaty. And anxious.

God, I'm a mess.

I walk down my sidewalk, around the fence between our two yards and up his sidewalk. He's at the door, holding it open, when I hobble up his front steps.

"Hey," he says.

"Hey. Thanks for inviting me," I say.

"No prob. I've been looking forward to it." And I can tell from his voice that he means it.

I enter his house—I haven't been in here since before I put distance between us in freshman year—and already the spicy aroma of nachos wafts through the air and greets my nose. I shuck off my coat and boots and hobble behind him toward the kitchen.

"Do you need a hand?" he asks, looking over his shoulder.

"Only when we get to the stairs," I say. "Unless you don't mind me scooting down on my butt."

He laughs. "We'll figure something out." He walks into the kitchen and when I catch up, he's opening the oven, checking on the nachos. He closes the oven door. "Just a little longer," he says. He comes to the kitchen island between us and leans on his forearms. I can see down his shirt. "Did you finish that paper?"

"Yeah," I say. "It was a bit rough to write the reflection part, but I guess that was the point. You get yours done?"

"Yeah. I know what you mean—the reflection is way tougher than the research part."

Part of me really wants to ask to read his paper, to find out more about the riots and, more importantly, his personal reflection. But part of me is also scared, scared that I'll see a lot of myself in that personal reflection, scared that it'll be even more personal to me than the topic I wrote about.

"So," I say, coming toward the kitchen island. I lean my hip against it and rest my hands on the countertop. My heart is pounding my chest and all my blood is rushing south. What would he do if I leaned across the island and kissed him? "What's the plan for tonight's festivities?" I already know the plan, of course, because I've re-read those texts every ten minutes since he sent them to me two days ago. But I need to distract myself with something.

"Well," Jordan says, hooking a thumb over his shoulder, "the nachos are almost done. I thought we could watch some music videos or something—maybe play some video games if that's more your thing—and then watch the ball drop in New York." An evil smirk crosses his lips—his kissable lips—and it looks just as cute on him as his grin. "And I think we could grab a few beers without my dad noticing."

"That'd be sweet," I say. Maybe a beer will calm me down. I had my first drink last year at a party—kind of late compared to when most of the guys on the team had their first drink. I didn't like the taste and I didn't like how it made my mind fuzzy—but that fuzzy mind is kind of what I need right now. I just have to be careful that I don't do *something* if it lowers my inhibitions. "I could go for a beer or two."

"Great," he says. "Want one now?"

"Sure."

He turns around and goes to the fridge. I try not to ogle his butt when he bends down and opens the bottom drawer of the fridge. When he stands up and turns around, he's got two cans of Bud Light in his hands and he passes one to me. I take it from him, thankful that the beer gives me something else to focus on, even if only for a brief moment.

I pop the tab and it hisses at me. When Jordan does the same, we tap our cans together and wish each other a happy new year, then I take a swig. I struggle not to cough from the god-awful taste. I take the can from my mouth and press the back of my hand to my lips. My eyes are watering.

Jordan is struggling too. At least I know he's not a raging alcoholic.

"Your first time?" I ask when I can finally summon the strength to speak.

"No, but pretty close," he says, then coughs. "And you?"
"Same."

A timer dings and Jordan returns to the oven, bending over to pull out the nachos. Again, I do my best not to ogle his butt—and I fail miserably. When he stands and turns around, I quickly look down at my beer, hoping it's inconspicuous enough. I look up when he brings the nachos to the island and puts it down on a towel.

"They smell amazing," I say and it's true.

"Thanks," he says, giving me a wink. He goes and gets a big plate from a cupboard and I help him transfer the nachos to the plate. Then I follow him as he takes the plate and his beer and heads toward the basement stairs and the rec room down there. I grab my beer and trail behind him, cradling it against my chest as I awkwardly shimmy down the stairs.

The rec room is exactly as I remember it. The walls have an outdated wood paneling that somehow works and there are a couple old but super comfy couches all facing a giant flat screen TV with an assortment of equipment and consoles on the shelves beneath it.

A bit of an uncomfortable silence descends and fills the room, but thankfully we have nachos and TV to focus on, so it doesn't feel quite as awkward.

Of course, MTV doesn't show music videos anymore, so we back out of that and he turns on the Apple TV and we browse YouTube, distracting ourselves with videos we've never seen for songs we both know by heart from them being so overplayed all over the place.

When the nachos are done and my beer is almost drained, Jordan turns to me and asks me the one question that I was hoping he would never bring up.

"You know back at homecoming and we were sitting on the field...you were going to tell me something. Can I ask what it was?"

I avert my gaze and stare at the music video on TV—it's full of half-naked women grinding each other and it does nothing for me—and I feel my cheeks heating up. "I, uh..." is all I can manage.

"It's okay," he says in a rush. "You don't have to tell me."

I fiddle with the tab on my can of beer until it snaps off completely. "Thanks."

The music video ends and YouTube auto-loads another and we're just sitting here, staring at nothing, trying to recover from the awkwardness we've both brought upon this hangout. I drain the last of the beer and look around in every direction except for Jordan's. Then I spot his old Nintendo Wii.

"Mario Kart?" I ask, finally looking at him.

His eyes flare with excitement. Mario Kart used to be our thing when we were younger. We'd have sleepovers and play almost until sunrise. It's a bit of nostalgia to help us continue until midnight.

He hops off the couch and goes to fiddle with the Wii

and the TV settings and a few moments later he hands me a Wiimote. I don't think I've played this since I was last here. And no more than five minutes later, the familiar opening music and Mario's voice come from the sound system.

My Mario Kart skills are a little rusty, especially compared to his. He's obviously played this more recently than me. He easily wins first place for the first few races with me at, or very close, to the end. But by the time we hit the fourth race, I start to get back into the groove of it, quickly finding myself in second place, right behind him, with a red turtle shell. I let loose the shell and he bounces around from the hit—and he squeals in surprise and I find it adorable—but then I zoom past him on the track and cross the finish line.

"It's on now," he mutters as he starts up a fifth race.

I grin. Jordan was always weirdly competitive with video games, but never took it too seriously. So when he says "it's on", I know that he's determined to make me lose, but he'll also have a great time if I end up winning. It's one of the things I like a lot about him—he's competitive, but winning isn't everything.

With football, winning is everything. We *must* outdo the other team. It's so high pressure and it sometimes makes football not as fun as it should be. But with Jordan and Mario Kart, it's a nice change—I can compete, but it doesn't ruin my day if I lose. Jordan makes this a lot of fun.

After several more races, we decide to shut off the Wii and scroll through the cable channels, looking for some sort of New Year's party to watch. Mario Kart helped ease the awkwardness and I'm comfortable again—and I'm pretty sure Jordan is feeling the same. We eventually find our way to coverage of the street party in Times Square. The ball is still about an hour from dropping.

"What are you doing next year?" I ask. We haven't really compared plans for university yet and it just occurs to me that if we go in separate directions, then my crush on him is all the more difficult because there'll be a separation in the fall. I'm suddenly very nervous for his answer. I know he was thinking of NYU, which is where I'm going, but he also had a bunch of other options in mind.

"NYU," he says, and I feel a crash of relief—and a rush of hope. If I *were* to come out to him and if he *were* as into me as I'm into him, then *maybe* we have a hope in hell of something happening and lasting beyond the school year. "And you?" he asks.

"Also NYU." I get this very sexy thought. "Maybe we'll be roommates."

His eyes light up. I don't know if it's with a similar thought or if it's just happiness at already knowing someone at his future school. But the only way I could live with him, whether it be a dorm room or a crappy apartment, is if I come out to him and tell him I love him and he tells me he loves me too. I don't think I can do this closeted thing much longer, especially if I'm living with him. And I couldn't live with him if he rejects my feelings for him.

"That'd be sweet," he says. And there's a slight

hesitation in his voice. Is he maybe thinking I'd be the straight roommate in the way of him bringing home a guy? Thinking of him with another guy makes me feel like I've been punched in the gut. "Another beer?" he asks, wiggling his empty can.

"Definitely," I say. The first beer had loosened me up a bit, but I still wasn't as relaxed as I wanted to be. Another one would probably hit the spot perfectly.

He rushes up the stairs and is out of the room for several moments. I take stock of how I'm feeling and what I'm thinking. I'm filled with this weird nervous energy and I know for certain that I want *something* to happen tonight. I don't know if that something is me coming out to him or just a hug at midnight or something else. All I know is that I can't go home knowing I didn't at least move this a tiny bit forward from where we are right now. But I'm also very terrified to do anything—I'm so used to making sure everyone knows I'm a hundred percent straight and I'm so dude-bro. I don't know if I even know how to move this forward.

Maybe that second beer will help. Jordan rushes back down the stairs with two more cans of Bud Light in his hands. I pop the tab and take a big gulp. Jordan watches me like he's trying to figure out what's going on—like if I'm just that thirsty or if there's something else. With half the can already drained, I give him a smile and he chuckles.

A burst of music from the television pulls us back to it, someone I don't recognize is belting out some song I've never heard. I'm sure she's famous. Whoever she is.

"Would you be okay with a hug?" I ask, staring hard at the TV. "Like, it's tradition to have a kiss to ring in New Year's, but we could, you know, hug or something. I'm okay if you don't want to. You know what, never mind, forget I asked." I want to kick myself. Coward.

He puts a hand on my forearm to stop my negative rant—and it also clears the dressing down I'm giving myself in my head—and instantly it feels like heat blooms from that touch of his hand on my arm. My only regret is that I'm wearing long sleeves and I can't feel his hand on my bare skin.

"A hug would be great," he says.

My heart beats and it's like my whole body pulses with it. I can feel it throbbing in my neck. He's going to hug me. I'm going to hug him. I sip my beer slowly as I watch the clock in the corner of the TV—they've displayed a countdown to midnight.

Twenty minutes.

Twenty minutes until my hug. Twenty minutes until I have Jordan in my arms.

Nineteen minutes and thirty seconds.

I can't keep counting down like this. I'm going to drive myself insane. I'm going to kill the mood if I'm glued to the clock. I hear some rustling beside me and I see that Jordan has pulled out his phone and he's scrolling through Instagram. He suddenly angles his phone away from me.

"What?" I ask.

He hesitates, then says, "Nikki's posting pics of her and Winston."

"I'm not her boyfriend," I say automatically. I've never actually said that to anyone. I've always just let people make their own assumptions and I was happy to play along with it. "We were never together."

"Really?" Jordan asks, raising an eyebrow.

"I make her look good in photos, but I have no interest in her," I say. I can feel a bead of sweat forming at my temple.

He scoffs. "You put on a good act then." He goes to her profile and scrolls down until he finds pictures of me and Nikki. Together. Kissing.

"That's exactly what it is. An act." My heart is beating so hard it feels like it's going to punch through my ribs.

He looks at me like he's assessing me. "She's gorgeous," he says. It's like he's pushing me, like he knows what I want to say, even though I don't think he has a clue. "She's a control freak sometimes, yeah, but she's gorgeous."

"Not my type," I say.

"Oh?" He shuts off his phone and tosses it on the couch between us. "What is your type?"

You. You're my type. But can I say those words out loud? Hell no. Coward.

Instead, I turn my attention to the TV. Fourteen minutes left.

"I'm still figuring that out," I say.

He seems to accept that as an answer, or at least accepts

that I'm not ready to talk more about it. We silently watch the rest of the countdown and inwardly I'm kicking myself again—way to ruin the mood right before the hug! I'm saving my last mouthful of Bud Light for midnight, so I'm just sitting here idly holding an almost-empty can of beer.

Finally, what seems like ages later, we're down to less than a minute. Slowly, the energy in the room warms up. I lean forward, like getting closer to the TV is going to somehow make this more exciting. Beside me, Jordan does the same.

"Ten!" he says out loud, joining the cheering people on the screen counting down.

I join in with him. "Nine! Eight! Seven! Six! Five! Four! Three! Two! One! Happy New Year!"

I take that final swig of beer, letting the alcohol give me a burst of courage. I stand up and hold my arms out and Jordan stands up and comes into them. I wrap my arms around him, holding him tight.

"Happy New Year," I whisper.

"Happy New Year," he whispers back.

I know I should let go, end this hug, because it's getting too long—it's past the limit of how long friends hug. But I don't want to let go.

I never want to let go.

Jordan feels so right in my arms.

But there's something I want even more.

I loosen my arms a little bit and he backs up just an inch or two and he looks up at me. His eyes sparkle in the light and I can see a question behind those clear, brown eyes. He knows something is different.

With the alcohol pushing my decisions, I angle my head in and kiss him.

He puts his hands on my chest like he's ready to push me away, but I keep kissing him, even though he's not moving his lips, even though he's as still as a statue. Panic starts to rise in me and I can feel myself starting to shake. Jordan isn't responding.

Chapter Seven

Jordan

WHAT THE HELL IS happening?

Benjamin has his lips pressed against mine. Straight Ben is kissing me. How drunk is he?

Then it occurs to me that he's not drunk—at least not *that* drunk—and that this is probably what he was trying to tell me on the football field at homecoming. And this is probably what the wall of silence was since then.

Shit. I'm overanalyzing this. Benjamin is kissing me. Benjamin!

I've had so many wet dreams about him.

Kiss him back, idiot, I shout at myself. I can feel Ben's lips faltering, like he's coming to the realization that I haven't kissed him back yet. It's time to fix that.

I move my hands from the front of his chest around to his back and I pull him in tighter and open my mouth a little and kiss him back. He moans and almost seems to sag into me and oh my God I'm kissing the captain of the football team! I'm kissing Ben and Ben is kissing me back!

Benjamin is gay? Or bi? Or heteroflexible? Or is he just experimenting? Crap, I can't take it if he's just trying this out and doesn't mean this. But someone doesn't kiss *like this* if they're just trying it out, right? Ah, what do I know? This is my first kiss—well, my first *real* kiss, since that one from Suzie Rocco in grade two doesn't really count.

Ben pushes his tongue through my lips and into my mouth and holy this is amazing. I brush my tongue against his and start rubbing my hands up and down his back, feeling his powerful muscles. If this is *real*, if he *means* this, then this is amazing—incredible!

Slowly, but far too fast in my opinion, he breaks from the kiss. I look up at him with half-lidded eyes, hazy with all that just happened, and he looks down at me with a cross between lust and confusion.

"Benjamin..." I murmur, soft and low.

His eyes suddenly widen and in our tight embrace I can feel his heartbeat kicking up a notch. He suddenly looks like he's in fight-or-flight mode, like all of this has terrified him, the gravity of what he's just done is sinking in. And it's all too much for him.

"Benjamin," I say, stronger, clearer, trying to reach past that fear I see in him.

"I need to go," he says. He holds me for a moment longer, then lets go of me and starts hobbling toward the stairs. He trips as he reaches them and turns around to sit on the bottom stair and scoot himself up, one step at a time, watching me the whole time, panic in his eyes.

I want to chase after him, to grab him and hug him and tell him everything will be okay, but I know that if I do that he'll just get even more scared, he might even push me away—and I don't know if I can take being pushed away. I do follow him, though, up the stairs and toward the front door.

"Benjamin," I say, pleading once more. "Please stay."

"I need to go," he says again. He nearly trips when he tries to put on his boots and I grab his arm to stabilize him, but he looks down at that hand like it's made of fire or something. I let go and he puts on his jacket and grabs the handle of the door. Before opening it, he pauses, and without turning around, he says, "You won't tell anyone, will you?" There's genuine fear in his voice.

"No," I say. "It's a secret."

"Thank you," he says. "I had a nice time tonight."

Before I can tell him that I did too, he opens the door and hurries out. I stand there in the open doorway and watch him hobble down my sidewalk, around the fence between our houses, and up his sidewalk. He never looks at me once. He enters his house and I can't see him anymore.

I close the door, lean against it, then sag to the floor. I reach up and touch my lips. If they weren't still buzzing from that kiss, I could almost believe I imagined the whole thing.

What the hell was that?

Whatever it was, it was *amazing*.

The next morning, I texted Hannah. But, like, I couldn't tell her anything about what happened the night before.

JORDAN: How was NYE?

HANNAH: Uh...Kumail and I might be official...?

JORDAN: Whaaaat? Details!

HANNAH: We had a hangout, he kissed me at midnight, we didn't stop kissing till several minutes later. We're gonna hang out again today.

JORDAN: Wow! Hot! You two are cute together! :)

HANNAH: Thx! And you? Your NYE?

JORDAN: Boring

HANNAH: Wasn't Ben coming over? The big friend reunion?

JORDAN: Yeah he came. It was good—not exciting like yours tho. He left right after midnite.

I wanted to tell her everything and ask her what she thought it meant. Like...Ben is gay and maybe into me? I still can't wrap my head around it. I didn't hear from Hannah for the rest of the day—I left her to fuss over her date with Kumail. I'm happy for them. But I miss confiding in her when I need it most, even though I wouldn't tell her what happened. If word got out, it would only push Ben away—I could trust Hannah to keep a secret, but you know how these things are, they somehow find a way to get out.

The next day was our first day back to school after Christmas break.

As much as I want to hunt down Hannah, pull her into a quiet corner of the library, and tell her everything—I want to pull Ben into a corner even more and demand he explain everything. Or make him kiss me. That would do. Well, kiss me and then explain everything. And maybe kiss me some more.

Shit, I need to get the kissing thing out of my head.

Now I understand why Ben avoided me so much since homecoming—whatever he was going to tell me or if he was just going to outright kiss me like that, the only way to not let it control his whole body and mind would have been for him to ignore me. I know because that's what I'm going to have to do to him if I have any hope in hell of getting through the day without trying to seduce him.

The biggest problem is math class.

I manage to avoid crossing paths with Ben and mostly avoid thinking about him, but when I step into math class and our fricking assigned seating, I know I have to spend the next period staring at his back—his beautiful, muscular back. My heartbeat speeds up and my hormones go crazy as I see him staring down at his open binder, studiously avoiding looking in my direction. I walk toward my seat, doing my best not to stare at him as I near him and then pass him. But when I sit down and that back is in front of me, it's all I can look at. Just a few days ago, I had been running my hands up and down it while our lips were pressed together.

I bite my lip pretty hard, desperately trying to pull myself back from this edge I'm on. I can't dive into thoughts of him—not here, not now, and there's a chance we'll never follow up on New Year's Eve, no matter how badly I want to.

I open my backpack and pull out my binder and a couple pencils. When I put them down on my desk, the gush of air from my movement hits Ben's back and rebounds to me, carrying his scent straight to my nostrils.

Goddamnit, I'm thirsty for him.

Ms. Barnes starts up the lecture and I write down all the notes, but none of it is sinking in. I'm gonna have to review all of this when I get home. I don't even know what topic we're learning because I can't even focus my attention long enough to read the words I'm writing on the paper. I hope they make sense when I read them tonight.

But having Ben in front of me is like having a boulder in front of me. He barely moves, he definitely doesn't look back, and there's no warmth or welcome coming from him. I want to touch him. But I can't.

Somehow, I make it through class and find Hannah and Kumail at our lunch table. They're already doing cute couple things like sharing their lunch and swapping desserts and I know that under the table their feet are touching and when a hand disappears beneath the table it's touching a thigh or something. I could have all that. With Benjamin.

That's what's weird about this whole thing.

I never imagined any of this until Benjamin kissed me. Yeah, I knew that gay love happens and there are couples and, yeah, I want that for myself. But I didn't think it was *possible*, at least not here at Charlesburgh High. I mean, I know of some of the other gay kids, but we're not in the same social circles and even if we were I'm not attracted to them.

Benjamin is the anomaly. He's the one gay kid in my social circle that I'm attracted to. And I want him.

That's the other thing—I'm pretty sure he's gay, not bi and not experimenting. He said that Nikki does nothing for him. Even me as a gay boy, even me as hating her guts, I can see how attractive she is. If I were straight, even if I still hated her guts, I wouldn't be able to say she does nothing for me.

And him having that pretend relationship with Nikki…that's like a classic closeted move. I tried dating girls and let people think it was more serious than it was, all in order to deflect attention from my boy-loving secret.

"Jordan?" Hannah says, pulling me from my mental spiral. Her hand is on my shoulder, giving me a shake. I don't think that's the first time she tried to get my attention since I sat down, but it's the first time her voice has penetrated my whirlwind of thoughts. "What's going on?" She signs as she speaks.

"Nothing," I say, signing as well. Kumail watches both of us, but doesn't jump in. Maybe he feels he doesn't know me well enough to jump in like Hannah is no doubt about to do.

"It's not nothing," she says.

"But I can't talk about it."

She gives me a look that tells me she's disappointed—but I give her a look back that says I definitely don't want to talk about it. Kumail stays out of it.

"Is Ben ignoring you again?" she asks. There. She hit the nail on the head. She knows me far too well.

"No," I say. I don't bother signing that word. I'm sure Kumail can read lips well enough for that word—and if not, I'm standing up and leaving anyway. He can figure it out.

I shove my lunch back in my bag and grab it and walk out of the cafeteria without looking back. I go to my locker and grab my jacket, then head outside to our picnic table under the tree. It's far too cold to really stay out for any length of time, but I don't care. I need to be alone.

There's a light dusting of snow everywhere—it must have come down during morning periods—and I brush it all off from the seat before sitting down. The cold wood instantly freezes my ass, but there's no way in hell I'm going back inside right now. I put my lunch bag on the table, but don't pull any food out. I'm not hungry.

My phone buzzes in my pocket. I pull it out, weirdly hoping beyond hope that it's Ben. It's not.

HANNAH: What the eff was that about?

I turn off my phone and shove it in my pocket.

• • •

It took a lot of apologizing, but Hannah forgave me for being so rude to her. She knows something is up, but she's stopped pestering me about it, though she knows that whatever it is, it has to do with Ben. Kumail continues to stay out of it. Hannah and I have been friends for far too long to let one pissy day damage our friendship—and she can read me way too good to not know the Ben connection. Though Hannah says she didn't know I'm gay before I came out, I'm pretty sure she did. She's just that good at reading me.

By the end of the first week back to school, it's gotten a little easier to be around Ben and not be constantly pining over him. I can actually pay attention in math class again…though I do still get distracted frequently.

Benjamin still hasn't looked at me, at least not that I've noticed. I haven't seen his eyes since he ran away from me on New Year's Eve.

The part that I find hurts the most is that he keeps his bedroom blinds closed now. He used to keep them open, like, ninety percent of the time. It's not like I want to creepily stalk him or want to catch him half-naked when he's changing (though I certainly wouldn't mind), but it's more that I like to look up and see him—or at least his room and the things that remind me of him, like all the sports trophies on that shelf by the door—as a moment to ground myself when I'm being overwhelmed from homework or just the stresses of being a teenager.

Even when we drifted apart, I still found comfort from looking through the window and seeing him or his football posters or something like that. If I caught his eye, even if we weren't really talking at the time, he would always give me a friendly wave. It was like I had a constant friend, even if we weren't really friends for a while.

But now with his blinds closed, that's all gone.

It's Friday night and I should be out having fun, but Hannah and Kumail are seeing a movie, Ben's not talking to me, and my parents are shopping with Bella. I'm home alone, sitting at my desk, with nothing to do but math homework.

Life sucks.

A light catches my attention. I look through my window and across to Ben's window. The blinds are still closed—I haven't seen them open all week—but the lamp on the other side of the blinds is on. It wasn't on when I sat down. Ben is in his room.

I feel an urgent need to talk to him—like, so urgent that if I don't, I might die.

I pick up my phone and text him. I haven't texted him since he ran away from me.

JORDAN: Hi

Because we both have iPhones, I see that he's read the message less than a second after I sent it. But he doesn't reply.

JORDAN: Can we talk?

Again, he sees it within a second. Then a very long minute or two stretches where nothing happens and there's no reply. Then all of a sudden those three dots pop up that tell me he's typing something out. But those dots disappear pretty quick. He must have deleted what he typed out.

They show up again, but disappear once more. This happens over and over for what seems like forever but is probably more like just a couple minutes. He's trying to figure out what to say to me, that much is clear. I try to imagine what each of those attempts were. Was he going to give me a positive response? Maybe a negative one? Maybe a noncommittal "hey"?

I could go for a noncommittal "hey" right now. I'd take anything. Well, maybe not a negative response. After a kiss like that, I don't think I could take the "Never talk to me again" text.

Finally, those dots appear again and a short while later an actual text comes through.

BENJAMIN: I'm not ready yet. Sorry.

My heart breaks a little at that. It's not as bad as "Never talk to me again", but it's pretty close. But then I latch onto the word "yet". That means he'll talk to me eventually, just not right now. Right? Or am I reading too much into this?

I want to text him back—now that I've gotten a response, I want to try to get another one. But if Hannah were here, and if she knew the whole story, she would tell me to hold off until Ben is ready. I mean, if I were hearing someone else tell me this story, I would tell them to hold off too. So, like, I get it. But I also want to talk to Ben.

It takes all of my willpower to put the phone down and not text him. But I can't get back into my math homework. Instead, I just stare at his closed blind for a long time.

When I hear noises from downstairs—mom, dad, and Bella are back—I head down to say hi and find out how their shopping went. They were looking for a new couch for the rec room. Apparently, Mom wants to renovate the basement so that it doesn't look quite so 1980s.

I ask about what they found and mom pulls out her phone. "I took pictures of my favorites. I think I like this one best," she says and shows me a deep red couch that really seems to be an odd color choice for her. "But your father prefers this one." She swipes her finger and shows me a black leather couch that looks so big and deep that you could sink into it and get lost forever.

"They're both wrong," Bella says. She's at the age where she's starting to get into fashion and other girly things, so she has opinions on everything. Generally, though, I find her instincts bang-on. I like her choices. She makes mom show me a photo of another couch with a rather bold pattern on it—but it looks like it's a great size and the seat looks comfy. "It doesn't match right now, of course," she says, explaining the couch, "but if the walls get painted blue and if that ugly carpet gets torn up, this could really work."

"But the leather couch…" dad says, as if the leather is reason enough alone. It might be a straight guy thing. I don't know why, but I picture straight men dad's age all having leather couches.

"Bella's right," I say. "She always is."

She smirks proudly. "I knew you'd agree."

Mom sighs and I think it's because she knows that Bella is right and it's just taking her a while to come around to accept that. Dad makes a weird whimper sound and clutches his head, obviously distraught at not having a leather couch.

I can't help but already mourn the loss of the couch we have. While Ben and I didn't have our first kiss *on* the couch since we were standing up, it was on that couch that we hung out the whole night leading up to the kiss. It's special to me. And with Ben not talking to me, I want to hold onto that couch for as long as possible—I don't want to replace it with a red couch, a leather couch, or the perfect couch that Bella picked out.

Our conversation quickly moves on to other things, meaningless things, and I grab an apple and head back up to my room to continue with my homework. When I get there, I instinctively look out my window toward Ben's and find that the light is off. And the blind is still closed.

It still hurts, but it hurts a little less. Yet—he said yet—which means eventually he'll be ready to talk.

I just hope he still wants to kiss me when that time comes.

Chapter Eight

Benjamin

I DIDN'T KNOW WHAT I'd feel when my cast comes off, but I don't think I ever considered glee. Relief, maybe? Sure, I'd be happy. But *glee*?

As the doctor takes a small motorized saw to the plaster and slowly cuts into it—and as I try to ignore the instinctive fear that his hand is going to slip and he's going to cut into my leg—I feel glee.

My life is going to go back to normal. Well, as normal as it can be after New Year's Eve.

I can hang out with my football friends again. Really, I could always hang out with them, but now I can keep up with them. I won't be left in the dust anymore. We play a lot of sports throughout the year, so to not be able to run, never mind having trouble standing, makes it super tough to keep up with them when there might be an impromptu street hockey game.

With the cast cut, the doctor breaks it the rest of the way open. My bare leg looks strange, almost like it doesn't belong to me. It looks dirty and grimy—and considering I haven't washed it for two months, that's not surprising. And it looks skinny. Like, skinnier than my other leg. I put my legs together, side by side, and the dirty, grimy leg is definitely thinner.

"You've lost some muscle mass in your leg," the doctor says, obviously knowing what I'm looking at. "But you're young and fit—being gentle at first and exercising regularly, you'll be back to normal before you know it."

Beside me, dad puts his hand on my shoulder and gives me a squeeze. I look up at him and he's beaming down at me. He's happy to have his son back to normal.

With the appointment over, we head out and he takes me to Wendy's for a burger and fries to celebrate me being back on my feet and crutch-free. Walking suddenly feels weird, so I take it slow at first. I grab a table and he brings the tray loaded with food. With two parents and two brothers, it's not often that it's just dad and me. I'm already having a good time.

We talk about football. Of course. What else? But I like football and I like talking with him, so it's fun. He's obviously concerned about my prospects for scholarships and football at NYU, because he's already talking about a training regimen and maybe even getting a personal trainer.

I know why he's pushing so hard on this—with three sons, college and university are going to be super expensive if we all go, so every scholarship helps.

As we finish up our lunch and I sit back for a moment to let the burger settle before I stand up and we make our way to the car, dad says, "You should call up Devon and the guys when we get home and see if they're up for a hangout. Would be good for you."

Something about how he says that sounds off to me. I don't think he means it's good for me *only* in the sense of seeing those friends again and maybe running around a bit. No, there's something else there. Some deeper meaning.

It has to do with Jordan.

It's the kind of comment I would normally let pass and just ignore it—but lately, especially since Jordan came out back in August, it's like each and every one of these kinds of comments leaves a little mark on my soul. It's like I have a suit of armor and each comment about Jordan, every homophobic joke about someone on TV, every sneer dad throws at gay couples he sees in public, it's like a pebble hitting my armor. One pebble doesn't do any damage, but if you have hundreds or thousands of pebbles repeatedly pelting your armor, it wears thin. It breaks.

"What do you mean by that?" I ask, unable to keep the irritation out of my voice.

Dad kind of glances around and then looks at me again. He doesn't say anything for a very long moment. I don't think he's used to me challenging him on something like this. He knows I know what he meant.

"You shouldn't spend so much time with Jordan," he says. His words are a whisper but to my ears they sound like a screaming accusation. He stares at me intently, like he's trying to impress on me how important this is.

"Why?" I ask. I know why. I want him to say it. I want to hear those words come from dad's mouth. He's danced around the topic since Jordan came out and implied it clear enough for years before that. But I haven't heard him say it explicitly.

"You know why." He glances around again, then back at me. The tension between us is thick. The silence is deafening.

"I want to hear you say it."

Dad suddenly looks angry, like I've pushed him too far. "Why does it matter?"

Because I'm g—

"It just does," I say.

Dad leans in closer. To anyone looking at us, it might look like a casual conversation between father and son and the leaning in closer is to share an embarrassing story about a sibling or something. But to someone within earshot, this is an angry showdown.

"Listen, Benjamin," he says, using my full name, "we're Roman Catholic. We're *good* Roman Catholics. That should be explanation enough."

Jordan and his family are Catholic too. Dad knows this. That's why he emphasized "good".

"I still want to hear you say it." I'm not letting this one go. Even if it means I have to walk home because he leaves me here or something. I somehow need to hear it, like I need to know for sure where the lines are drawn for when I...when I...

"Benjamin..."

"It's because he's gay," I say. And I say it loud. I notice a few heads turn our way, but I don't break my glare at dad. He glances around, though, and does that awkward smile and mini-nod that people do when they're put in a situation like his.

But then he looks back at me and that smile disappears. Last time I saw dad this mad, I was setting off firecrackers in the basement at midnight. Yeah, I did that once. Only once.

"Let's go," he says, voice like ice. He stands up and doesn't even glance at me—he just heads to the exit and on to the car.

I stand up and follow him, but before getting in the car, I fantasize about just walking away. I'd make my way home before dinner, but it'd make him realize how badly he's screwing this up. But then I think better of it. I know dad. He'll just call me juvenile and make this into a lesson I have to learn about being a responsible adult.

And if I'm going to come out to him and the rest of the family eventually, I need to deal with this homophobia now.

I get in the car and buckle my seatbelt. Dad is so silent that the clatter of the buckle sounds harsh and loud in the confines of the car, even though it's just a soft click. I wait for him to start the car up and take us home. But he doesn't.

"What the *fuck* was that?" dad asks. He almost never swears. That tells me how mad he is.

"You know what that was," I say. I'm not backing down from this one.

Dad grips the steering wheel hard and his knuckles start to go white. "Listen...I know you're friends with Jordan and I'm sure he's a great guy, but I can't accept his *lifestyle*." Dad still can't say the word "gay". Like father, like son, I guess, just for different reasons.

"I'm not going to stop being his friend because he's gay," I say.

There's another long silence between us. Dad loosens his death grip on the steering wheel. He sits back in his seat, but still doesn't look at me.

"I pray for you."

His voice is so quiet that I almost wonder if I imagined he said it. But, no, he did.

"What do you mean?" My heart is quivering in my chest. I feel like I'm going to crumple and collapse.

"Ben..." he says as he finally turns to look at me. I notice he's back to calling me Ben and not Benjamin. "Are you...?"

He can't say it. Neither can I.

I struggle to breathe. I struggle to hold back tears. I struggle not to die right here and right now.

"Would you still love me if I was?" I can barely get those words out.

A tear suddenly gathers in the corner of dad's eye and it rolls down his cheek. "Of course, Ben. Of course. I would never stop loving you."

I want to believe him. I'm desperate to believe him. But how can someone go from the dad I saw in Wendy's to the dad here in the car? How can that be the same person? You either accept gay people or you don't.

"Ben," he says again, "are you gay?"

I take a deep breath and I try not to shudder. Now is the moment.

"No." I can't do it. I can't come out. Not yet. Not now. Not here.

I'm such a coward. Such a fucking coward. I'm ashamed of myself. I'll never have Jordan's strength. Goddamnit. I'll never have Jordan either.

I just want to cry. I just want to dig a hole, hide in it, and cry.

"Can we go home?" I ask.

Dad looks at me a moment more, like he wants to say something, but I turn my head and look out the passenger window. I stay as still as I can, not wanting to let on that tears are streaming down my face. He starts up the car and pulls away, driving us home. We don't say a single word.

Returning to school cast-free is like being a celebrity. Suddenly everyone is my friend again or they want to be my friend. Even Nikki.

Her Instagram and Snapchat have been nonstop photos of her and Winston, to the point where I was wondering if they had something real. Their photos looked so much more genuine than the ones with Nikki and I. Plus, Winston's feed had filled up with similar pictures of him and Nikki. If they weren't the real thing, then he had the same drive to be Insta-famous like Nikki. In some ways, they're perfect for each other.

Nikki is clinging to my arm as we walk down the hall to third period. She's babbling about something, but I'm not even listening. I don't think she cares that I'm not listening. This isn't about a genuine relationship; this is about status.

As we walk from one end of the school to the other, taking the most visible route, of course, we pass two people looking at us and my heart breaks for different reasons with each person. One of them is Winston. The other is Jordan. Both of them look like they've had their heart broken. I don't know if Nikki notices either one.

I'm gonna have to talk to Winston later. And Jordan.

When we reach chemistry, our shared class, Nikki points at the poster on the wall just outside the door. "Have you seen this?" she asks.

I look at it. It's for senior prom and it's got Rapunzel letting her hair down for her prince. "Prom's coming up," I say, stating the obvious.

"Duh," she says. "But what do you think of the stupid theme? Fairy tales? Like, that's so sixth grade. I hear they're even changing it from prom king and queen to prom prince and princess." The disdain is clear in her voice.

I look at the poster again. "I don't see anything wrong with it. It might be fun." I'm too worn out and exhausted to deal with her bullshit. I can sense the coming storm of her reaction and know she's going to rip me to shreds for not agreeing with her. To prevent it—hopefully—I try to pander to her way of thinking. "You'll probably get some great snaps and pics for Instagram," I tell her. "All the formal attire, all the decorations. Might go viral."

While I don't look at her, I can practically hear her jaw drop open as she gasps in surprise. Somehow, she hadn't thought of that. Her hands find mine and her fingers intertwine with mine. "Anything you want to ask me?" Her voice is sickly sweet, like ice cream with chocolate sauce and caramel sauce and added sugar on top. I know what she wants. She's not the most subtle person I know.

I turn to her and hold her hands between us. "Nikki," I say and her eyes light up. "Did you finish the chem homework?"

I can't help but laugh—and I kind of feel bad for leading her on like that, only to smash her hopes. Her cheeks redden slightly and she slaps my chest. "Yes, but you can't copy." She turns on her heel and struts into class.

Sighing, I follow after her. It's just a matter of time, I know, before I ask her to go to prom with me. I need someone to go with and she wants to go with me.

I'd rather go with Jordan. But I can't do that.

As we take our seat in chemistry, Nikki pulls out her phone and snaps half a dozen pics before the buzzer rings. She shoves her phone back in her purse. I have no doubt at least one of those will be all over social media at lunchtime.

When class starts up, I do my best to pay attention to Mr. Roe, but my mind is elsewhere. It's going to be a miracle if I survive this school year and actually graduate with how often my mind has been on other things.

Specifically, my mind is on my dad. That awkward and terrifying Wendy's parking lot conversation was on Friday afternoon. It's now Monday. We haven't spoken a single word about it. I don't know if he bought my answer that I'm straight.

Part of me is shocked that he'd even ask—I don't put out any vibes, do I? Besides, isn't it supposed to be up to me to decide when and where to come out? How does it work if your parents actually ask you straight up if you like dudes? It's so complicated.

And I still don't know how dad will react when I do finally come out. One moment he seems super homophobic and the next he's crying in the car and telling me that he'll always love me. Which side of him will I get when the time comes? Or will I somehow get *both* sides? Like that "love the sinner, hate the sin" crap that I hear churchy people saying? If someone is gay and you hate their "sin" of being gay, then I'm sorry but you can't really love them if you don't accept them.

And what about the rest of them? I'm sure mom would

get over it, but it might take some time. I doubt my brothers really care—they'll tease me, of that I have no doubt, but it'll be brotherly teasing. My grandparents are another matter entirely. They're like dad's homophobia times ten.

Suddenly I feel very tense and anxious.

Beside me, Nikki shuffles her chair a little bit. In chemistry, we have these big tables instead of desks so that we have space to do experiments. She inches closer to me, trying not to be too obvious about it. Her foot touches mine. Then her thigh touches my thigh.

I need some air.

My hand shoots up in the air. When I get Mr. Roe's attention, I ask, "Can I go to bathroom?"

Mr. Roe sighs and hitches his thumb toward the door. I take that as the cue to leave. I can't get out of there fast enough. As soon as I'm out in the hallway and the door is closed behind me, I feel a little bit better. It was the pressure of having people around me and of Nikki and her damn expectations that pushed me over that edge.

I have a few minutes before I have to be back in class. I figure a short walk will help and since I asked to go to the bathroom, I just walk toward there, but, like, not the closest one. I don't want to get back too quickly.

My path takes me past the library and I glance through the large windows on the doors and see Jordan. My breath catches. Then he looks up and sees me.

He's with Hannah and Kumail. He says something to them and starts getting up.

I don't want to talk to him right now. But I can't walk away. I stay here, stuck on the spot, not wanting to be here but not wanting to be anywhere else.

When he comes out of the library, I start walking again, heading toward the bathroom. He follows close behind. When we're in the bathroom and we check for feet under stalls and find that we're alone, I finally speak to him.

"Hi," I say.

"Hey," he says.

Those are the first words we say to each other after days of not talking to each other. We'd texted that one night, but we haven't spoken out loud since New Year's.

After a long stretch of silence, he says, "Aren't you in class right now?"

"Yeah," I say. "I needed some air. I have to go back soon."

"Do you want to talk about the…the kiss?"

I feel my cheeks burning with a blush and I can't look him in the eye. I want to talk about it—more than that, I want to grab him and push him up against the wall and kiss him again. I want to have my hands on that body of his, feeling his arms and his chest. I want to breathe him in. I want to have his arms around me. I want to have a moment frozen in time, just like New Year's Eve.

But at the same time, my hackles go up.

Everyone wants to talk to me about stuff I want to keep private. First it's dad asking if I'm gay and then it's Jordan asking about the kiss. I want to talk about both of these things—I do—but I'm just not ready for it. I need to have a conversation with myself before I can have a conversation with other people.

"Ben?" Jordan says. I realize I haven't answered his question yet. Do I want to talk about the kiss?

"No," I say, before I can even really decide. "Because it never happened." I don't know why, but I'm retreating into full defensive mode, just denying everything. I can see the change in Jordan's eyes, the hurt that suddenly springs loose there. It hurts me that I've hurt him. "And you're not going to tell anyone," I say, putting far more threat into my voice than I intend to, and I take a step forward.

Jordan's eyes widen and he steps back and he genuinely looks afraid of me. Why the hell am I doing this? Why am I intimidating the love of my life? Why am I throwing away the one person who I *know* won't judge me for my secret? Why can't I just own up to who I am and come out?

I don't have the answers.

All I know is that I'm not ready to do any of that and my automatic response is to throw up walls. I need to separate myself permanently from Jordan, even if it will kill my heart to do so. Maybe when we're both in NYU, he'll forgive me. I'll have to grovel and beg for forgiveness, but if I can just explain it then, maybe he'll understand.

But now is not that time.

I realize that at some point in all of this my hands have balled into tight fists. Jordan's noticed. He's looking down at them and back up at me, his eyes wide and terrified and bouncing between my fists and my face.

"I won't tell anyone," he says. His voice is shaking. Why am I doing this? I hate myself. I really hate myself.

"You better not," I say, and the *or else* is implied. I can't take it anymore. I can't take what I'm doing to Jordan. I can't take that I'm destroying everything we have and everything that could develop between us. And it's all because I'm a coward.

Tears start to form in my eyes, but I don't want Jordan seeing me cry. I go into a stall and slam the door closed and lock it. I wait for Jordan to leave. There's a squeak from his sneakers as he turns and bolts.

I put my face in my hands and I cry.

Chapter Nine

Jordan

WHEN I'M OUT OF the bathroom and in the hallway, I freeze. I don't know where to go. I can't go back to the library—not yet, not when I'm this shaky. But I can't stay here because Ben will come out any second now.

I dart down the hallway, heading in the opposite direction of the library, on the assumption that Ben will head back the way he came. I find a stairwell and push myself against the crash bar and through the door. I go down half a flight to where it doubles back on itself and goes down to the next floor.

And I just press my back against the corner.

I'm gulping in breaths and sweat is breaking out all over and my heart is thudding and I'm filled with panic. What the *hell* was that?

One day he's kissing me and the next he's threatening me?

I get that he's conflicted. I get that he's got a lot of crap going on and it's probably too much to deal with. But, like, what the *fuck*?

Someone bangs against the crash bar and opens the door from where I just came and my heart goes into overdrive and I'm suddenly in fight or flight mode—but it's not Ben, it's some kid I don't know. He looks at me like I'm crazy and hurries past me.

I need to get back to the library.

Surely, Benjamin is gone. He said he had to go back to class.

I climb the steps as quietly as I can, each soft squeak of my shoes sounding like a horrible screeching to my ears. I pause before I grab the handle, listening for any noise at all. I push my face to the glass and try to look down the hall. Benjamin is not there.

Gently, I open the door and enter the corridor. I ease it closed behind me, flinching at the click it makes when it closes. Again, I wait, but still no Benjamin.

I walk slowly and quietly down the hall. When I near the bathroom door, I go even slower, listening for sounds as I pass, but I hear nothing. Once I get past it and it's behind me, I walk as fast as I can without running, making a beeline for the library.

I come to a sudden stop before entering the library. I need to compose myself. I can't let on to Hannah or Kumail that anything happened…whatever that was. I take several deep breaths, smooth out my clothing, and run my fingers through my hair. That's about all I can do.

Entering the library, I feel like all eyes are on me and accusing me of something—and I'm jumpy, like I'm expecting Ben to pop out from behind a bookcase and start wailing on me. But it's all my imagination.

Hannah and Kumail look at me, yeah, and the librarian whose name I don't know nods a hello to me, but everyone else is absorbed in their own thing and Ben is not here. The closer I get to the table, the more concerned Hannah and Kumail are—they know something happened. I can't hide it, not from my bestie and her boyfriend.

Are you okay? Kumail signed.

"Yeah, don't worry," I say, signing as I speak.

Hannah and Kumail exchange a look. They don't believe me. I wouldn't believe me either. But I'm not going to explain a thing.

"I'm always here if you want to talk," Hannah said, signing too.

I wave my hand dismissively. "I know. No worries. Thank you—both of you."

Both of them smile, but Kumail's looks a little more genuine. Hannah knows me well enough to know that I'm dealing with some serious crap, even if she has no idea what it is. It won't be long before Kumail can read me as well as Hannah can.

I push my attention to my math assignment I've got

splayed out before me. I need to get my attention on that and hopefully get their attention off me. A few moments later, rapid hand movement catches the corner of my eye and I know they've moved on and they're having their own conversation.

I just hope it's not about me.

Cautiously, I glance up. When they don't look back at me, I take the opportunity to eavesdrop on what they're saying. My signing is getting better now that I practice daily with Kumail, but I still can't move at the speed those two go. I can pick out fragments here and there and I know they're deep into prom conversation.

Hannah roped Kumail into joining her on the committee—though I doubt she had to try too hard. He goes anywhere she wants him to. They're actually quite cute together. Kumail told me once that he was used to being bullied at his old school and expected more of it here, but with no bullies and a friend and a girlfriend that can sign, he's taking advantage of everything he can in his senior year, including helping organize prom. That way he can also be sure it's accessible to people with disabilities.

Those two really have no idea how special they are. And every day they're more and more adorable together.

Why can't I have that?

Why did Ben have to be such a dick?

That could be Ben and I, but no, he has to go and be a self-hating homophobic dick.

Until the bathroom, I could have totally seen Benjamin

and I like Hannah and Kumail. I could have even seen us going on double dates and hanging out together. I could see us making out on the couch when my parents are out of the house. All of this, of course, if and when he comes out. I know he wouldn't want to do anything while he's closeted.

But all of those dreams and fantasies were now shattered and destroyed. He's a dick. He's a douchebag. And I need to forget about him and move on.

I realize then that Hannah and Kumail had started looking at me while signing. They wanted me in the conversation. They'd been doing this now and then, having a conversation entirely in sign, to get my skills stronger.

You could bring your friend, Hannah says. I blink several times. I missed something important.

What? I sign.

To prom, Hannah says. *You could bring your friend and come with Kumail and I.*

I look from Hannah to Kumail and back again. I'm lost. *What friend? You two are my friends.*

A slight blush warms Hannah's cheeks and Kumail shoots her a look of concern, one that seems to ask her if they should have even brought this up.

You've got a crush, don't you? Hannah asks.

It's my turn to blush. While earlier today the blush would have been of embarrassment, of having been called out at having the hots for a cute boy, now it's a blush of shame, of having fallen for a problematic guy like Benjamin. I want to leave the library and leave this conversation.

No, I say.

Hannah squints her eyes like she doesn't believe me. *You haven't been ogling a certain someone?*

I can feel my own anger rising. Now I know where Benjamin gets it from—these questions somehow seem far too personal. The difference between him and me, though, is that he will lash out at those that care about him and I won't. I swallow, trying to force that anger back down.

No, I say again.

Hannah pauses and again looks like she doesn't believe me. Kumail puts his hand on her forearm and she looks at him and he gives her a look that suggests she stop asking questions. But that won't stop Hannah. I know her too well to hope for that.

But the theme of prom is fairy tales. You need your Prince Charming on your arm. She smiles like she's hoping she's appealing to my romantic side. Hours ago, I would have pictured Ben on my arm. Now, I don't. I can't. He's not in the picture at all anymore—except maybe in the background, taking a selfie with Nikki.

I'm not bringing anyone, I say, my signing motions harsh and jerky. *I don't get a Prince Charming. I don't get a happy ending. Life isn't a fairy tale.*

Now I know I've gone too far. Hannah's eyes get watery and I know I've pushed too hard. I've upset her and she's doing her best to not let it show.

Kumail shifts his body slightly away from me and signs something to Hannah quickly and discreetly. I look away—

this is like whispering for them. I give them their privacy, even if only so I have a few moments to cool down. And the longer I wait for them to have their private little whispers, the more terrible I feel.

I had basically destroyed Hannah's fantasy of a magical prom that is for *everyone*. I pretty much told her that gay kids don't get happy ever afters—even though I want one even more than she does.

That's the thing. I *want* a happy ever after. I *want* a Prince Charming. I want a guy to sweep me off my feet and carry me away. I want a strong man to wrap his arms around me and protect me.

And until today, I had hopes that Ben would one day be that man. I had figured that with time he would come around—he'd come out to his family and he'd kiss me again and we'd be boyfriends. I had even wondered if that's what he had implied when he said he'd hoped we'd be roommates at NYU.

But now that's all gone. That's all dead in the water.

I feel so crappy.

I finally turn back to Hannah and Kumail. We stare at each other. Everyone is waiting for someone else to be the first to talk. I was the jerk in all of that; I know I have to be the one to talk first.

I'm sorry, I say. And before I can stop myself, I start babbling, my hands flying around in front of me as fast as my thoughts come tumbling through my head. *I did have a crush. We…we kissed. But he's in the closet and dealing with all that. He basically broke up with me and told me to piss off.*

I watch Hannah's expression as it changes through that story. She grins when I tell her I had a crush, her face lights up when I tell her about the kiss, and she looks almost as hurt as I feel when I tell her about the incident in the washroom. I don't give her any details or anything that could be close to a detail. Even though I hate Ben right now, I don't want to out him. I still care for him too much to do that.

Is there a chance he'll come back to you? And that he'll be your Prince Charming? That's Hannah for you. Ever the optimist.

No, I say. *He made it clear it's not changing anytime soon.*

Her face falls. *I'm so sorry, Jordan.*

I'm sorry too, man, Kumail says.

Thanks, guys.

Hannah suddenly smirks. *Was he cute, at least?*

I feel a new blush warm my cheeks, but the good kind of blush. *Of course. I don't kiss ugly boys*, I sign, giving my hand motions a bit of a dramatic gay flair.

I can still remember that kiss. It rocked my world. Even though it ended badly, that was a *damn good* kiss. Of all the ways a first kiss could go, that was amazing. First kisses are supposed to be awkward, terrifying, clumsy. They're supposed be rushed and giggly. But my kiss with Benjamin was mind-blowing, passionate, and genuine. This wasn't the experimentation of two curious guys—this was a kiss between two men who had real feelings for each other. I know now that he had a crush on me and it was obvious in how he kissed me.

You still like him, don't you? Kumail asks.

I look at him for a long moment before I answer. *Yes. Does that make me a bad person?*

Absolutely not! Hannah says. *The beauty loved the beast. It only took time for things to turn around.*

If me and Benjamin are beauty and the beast, then the beast is being a real douchebag.

He's back to ignoring me so hard that it's like I don't even exist. And when he did that before, it was out of a need to fight his feelings and I could sense that he wanted to talk to me, wanted to acknowledge me and have me in his life. Now, though, he's giving me such a cold shoulder that I know he wants nothing to do with me.

The worst part of the day is math class, where I sit right behind him. It's like we're in different universes or something, like not only is he ignoring my existence, but it's so effortless of a thing that it's like I actually *don't exist* for him. This is a whole new level of being ignored that I didn't really think was possible.

Now that his cast is off, he's fully back in with his sports buddies and his football team. They roam the halls in packs and hang out like a pride of lions during lunch and before and after school. At the center of it, like he's the king of the pride, is Benjamin. And at his side, more often than not, is Nikki.

It's like he's establishing his heterosexuality and his dominance.

But every time I look at him, I just want him more. And I hate him just a little bit more too. It's a weird headspace to be in. I want him and I don't want him at all.

Maybe I just want another kiss from him. Maybe I could tell from the kiss if there's still a chance for us or if he's over me completely.

As I enter the cafeteria, the lion pack is there again, in the same spot as always. Ben and Nikki are sitting *on* the table, which is against the rules of the cafeteria but none of the school staff say or do anything about it, and the rest of the football team, a couple other jocks, and half a dozen arm candies are gathered around, sitting on the benches or standing alongside them.

Every time I look at them, I wonder if it's a hierarchy of some sort. Ben and Nikki on the table make them the leaders of the pack—but are those who get to sit near him higher ranking than those who are forced to stand to the side? I shake my head and almost laugh to myself as I picture them hissing like feral cats, trying to sort out who ranks higher.

I'm lost in my head, but I'm pulled out when I hear a raucous chorus of laughter. And among those laughs, I *clearly* hear the word "gay".

My blood suddenly runs cold. I stop walking and I look at them. Half of them are looking back at me and they're all laughing. I know that whatever the joke was, I'm the butt of it. My gaze inevitably travels to the leaders of the pack, to Ben and Nikki. He has his arm around her waist and they're laughing as hard as the rest of them.

Only the laughter doesn't reach Ben's eyes. I can tell he knows this is wrong, but he's doing it anyway.

"What're you looking at?" one of them says taunting. I don't know his name, but he has a pug-like nose and a cheerleader is sitting in his lap.

I feel like closing the distance between us and breaking that ugly nose of his. But it's me versus all the jocks, so my self-preservation keeps me rooted to the spot.

"What's your problem?" another one asks.

My eyes are pulled toward Ben again. I look at him and he's looking at me.

"Get lost," Ben says, sneering.

That hurt. More than anything else, that hurt.

All of my instincts to fight and stand my ground suddenly dissipate. I turn on my heel and walk away from them, quickly finding Hannah and Kumail. The laughter of those jocks and their entourage erupts again and follows me as I go. Hannah's eyes immediately find me and they're filled with worry; she signs to Kumail what just happened.

"Don't listen to them," she says when I sit down. I can't even look her or Kumail in the eye. "They're idiots. Not worth your time."

I know it all. I've heard it all before. I've told myself all those platitudes. But it still hurts when someone mocks me for being gay. It's something I don't know if I'll ever get over.

When I was confronted with it, I had strength. It was that old fight or flight thing, and I was ready to fight. But now that I'd walked away and was now sitting down, the echoes of that taunting laughter won't leave my ears. And the fact that Ben had been involved in that just made it all the worse.

"I know," I say. Belatedly, I sign it for Kumail.

Kumail catches my eye before he signs something. I still can't bring myself to look him in the eye, but I can at least look at his hands.

At my old school, I was teased mercilessly, Kumail says. Beside him, Hannah makes a pained whimper sound, no doubt feeling terrible that someone would tease her boyfriend. But not everyone is as loving and accepting of differences as Hannah is. *It's why I transferred here. It was really bad.*

Kumail, I'm sure, is refraining from telling us the whole story. While I can't look him in the eye, I catch enough of his facial expressions in my peripheral vision that I can clearly see the pain. There's that shellshock on his face that is surely on my face right now.

That pain from being mocked and bullied might never leave you, he says. *Being both deaf and brown meant I got double the bullying. No matter how many times my parents complained, the teachers couldn't stop it.*

Hannah puts her arm around Kumail's waist and pulls

him closer. He smiles, but the hurt is still in the tightness around his mouth.

"I'm sorry," I say. "I'm sorry that you had to go through that."

I'm not saying that being deaf and brown is the same as being gay, he says, *but if I could survive that, you're strong enough to survive this.*

I fold my arms in front of me and rest them on the table, then lay my forehead on my arms. I breathe out a long breath and then suck another one in. I can't even tell them the full extent of the hurt, not without telling Ben's secret.

Fingers stroke my head, weaving through my hair. Hannah's comforting touch seems to break down a last wall holding back the upset inside me. I let out a shuddering sigh, close my eyes, and rest for just a moment, trying to calm and center myself.

Eventually, I feel ready to lift my head again.

"It gets better," Hannah says, repeating that oft-repeated piece of advice for LGBT kids. It's a nice saying, but at times like this, it certainly doesn't feel true. Yeah, high school is over in just a few months and then after a summer of being lazy, I'm heading to NYU. But confronting crap like this isn't restricted to only high school and to only smaller cities. I'm not stupid enough to believe that big cities and big universities are gay meccas.

"I know," I say, giving Hannah the answer she wants, even if I don't believe it myself.

"Everyone gets that fairy tale ending," she says. This is

her personal spin on that "it gets better" advice.

Hannah and her fairy tales. I don't want to destroy it for her, but not everyone gets that happy ending. I said it before and I would say it again. Not right now, though, because I don't want to get into an argument and I don't want her feeling as bad as I do right now.

I look over my shoulder at Ben and his posse. They're laughing about something else now. Ben suddenly turns his head and sees me. Our eyes lock and our gazes hold. I see hurt in his eyes, as well as something else. It takes me a very long while to figure out what I see in his eyes and it's not until after we both turn away that it clicks.

Self-hatred.

Suddenly, I feel sorry for Benjamin. I'm not ready to forgive him for his part in whatever homophobic teasing was going on, but that doesn't stop me from feeling sorry for him.

Chapter Ten

Benjamin

MAYBE IF I TRY a little harder, I could just *not* be gay. Perhaps if I have sex with a girl, it'll all make sense and I'll figure out I'm actually straight. And, possibly, I could just choose to ignore whatever I'm feeling.

But as much as *I don't want to be gay*, I know it doesn't work like that.

I've tried to deny it for almost four years now. Ever since that hug, I've tried to pretend it didn't happen, that I don't have these feelings, that I like girls, that Nikki is the one for me. But with every strategy I've tried, every time I tried to force myself to be straight, I just end up back at square one—gay, depressed, and lonely.

Wait.

What?

Did I just call myself...I did.

I'm...gay.

I'm gay.

What a fucking time to have this realization. Why couldn't I have been able to call myself gay when I kissed Jordan? Why did I have to deny it then?

Still, acknowledging I'm gay doesn't mean I actually have to *be* gay. I can still try to be straight. I sigh with disgust at myself. A gay guy can't just *be* straight any more than a fish can be a bird. No amount of wishing, hoping, denying, and refusing makes any of it true.

"That'll be $6.74," a voice says, punching through my identity crisis. Of all the places to have this realization, I'm at the Trader Joe's just down the street from school. "You guys got a barbecue or something?" says that same voice.

I fish into my pocket for my wallet, feeling disgusted with myself. "Yeah," I say, and hand over a ten-dollar bill. I wait until the cashier gives me my change, then I grab the two packs of hot dogs and head out the door to meet up with the rest of the guys.

My stomach feels like it's tied in knots. Like one wrong move and I'm going to double over and hurl. Everyone else is laughing and giddy; I just want to crawl in a hole and die.

"You okay, Ben?" Devon asks.

I fake a smile and I nod. "I'll be fine."

All fifteen of us bought two packs of hot dogs.

Anthony saw a sign at Trader Joe's about a hot dog sale. One thing led to another—someone came up with this stupid idea, I don't even know who it was anymore or if it was some idiotic group effort—and now we're all-in on a prank for the Charlesburgh High gay kid. For Jordan.

It's the day before spring break starts and they want to give him something to remember.

I want to vomit.

Laughter ripples through the group. Fifteen guys. Three hundred and sixty wieners. See where this is going yet?

As one, the group starts walking toward school and I follow like the sheep I am. Everyone thinks this is hilarious. Not me. I did...before coming out to myself. Even then, it wasn't true hilarity—it was the "this is awful and I feel disgusting but laughing about it might let me hide from my feelings" kind of hilarity. I went along with it. Now I regret it. Now I want to run away. But as the captain of the football team, the guys expect me to lead in this prank.

I still remember that day in the cafeteria a few weeks ago when Jordan walked past and someone made a cocksucker joke. I laughed. I admit it. I hate myself for it, if that makes any difference. But it's not like I did anything to make up for it or to even make the guys go easier on Jordan. I can still hear my own voice, clear as a bell, telling him to get lost.

The pain I saw in his eyes made me feel lower than dirt. He'll never forgive me.

Especially after what the guys are going to do. Even if I back out, everyone will know it's the football team and everyone will know I had a part in it. Even if I had no part, I'd be guilty by association.

So I keep following them like a sheep.

What's that thing parents always say? If all your friends jump off a bridge, would you do it too? Right now the question is if all your friends pull off a homophobic prank, would you do it too?

I follow my "friends" into the school. Are they even my friends anymore? Were they ever my friends? What would they do if I tell them I'm gay? And that I like Jordan?

We're here super early and the place is almost empty. We make a beeline for Jordan's locker and somehow Bryce jimmies the lock open. I feel like we're violating Jordan's personal space. *We are,* I tell myself. This is *his* locker. We're in it without his permission. Someone starts rifling through the contents of the locker. I feel like I can't breathe, like my throat is closing.

"Hey," Devon says. "Leave his stuff alone." Devon, the one guy who seemed reluctant to take on this prank, seemed to still have a shred of decency in the face of the shit we were about to pull. I silently thank Devon for pulling the guys back from the edge—even if only a half step.

I can almost hear the smart-ass reply to Devon on the tip of the guy's tongue, but he leaves Jordan's stuff alone. I'm not even aware of who reached inside—the blood is pounding through my head and my vision has narrowed and my hearing has diminished. All I'm aware of is that we are in Jordan's locker and we're about to pull a prank that will absolutely ruin his day. And that he'll never forgive me.

All around me, guys start ripping open their packs of hot dogs.

"At least put a bag down...protect his stuff," I manage to say, my voice sounding choked.

I can almost sense someone wanting to say something along the lines of "You a fag lover or something?" But everyone wisely keeps their mouth shut. A couple guys throw their plastic bags in the locker, lining the bottom, before everyone starts ripping open their packages.

Suddenly, hot dog after hot dog is piled on top of the plastic bags. Between us, we have three hundred and sixty hot dogs.

I drop my two packs of hot dogs. They make a weird crinkle-splat sound when they land on the floor. I can't do this. I can't. Not to Jordan. Not to anybody. I back up a few steps.

"Ben? You okay, man?" Devon asks. He actually looks like he's concerned about me. Nobody else cares.

"No," I say. I back up a few more steps. Like meerkats at the zoo, one by one each guy turns their head to look at me, frozen mid-locker-stuffing. "I'm not okay," I say. I turn and run toward the bathroom.

When I turn the corner and I'm out of sight, I hear the laughter again. I'm already forgotten and mocking Jordan is the only thing those guys care about. It's all that matters to them—picking on the gay kid.

I come crashing into the bathroom and lock myself into

a stall. I sit on the toilet and I'm shaking. What if they knew I was gay and they stuffed *my* locker with wieners? I'd feel violated, hurt, angry…and if I knew someone important to me was part of that prank, like Jordan, I'd feel betrayed.

I pull my phone out of my pocket. My hands are shaking. I type my text to Jordan and then correct all the typos—it takes forever with my shaking fingers.

BENJAMIN: I'm sorry, Jordan. I'm so sorry.

BENJAMIN: I couldn't do it. I didn't do it. I'm sorry, Jordan.

I wait for him to respond, but I get nothing. It still says "unread". I wait and wait and wait for him to read the message and reply. Then I start freaking out that it might not have reached him, that it just shows as being sent on my phone but it never actually reached his.

BENJAMIN: Jordan? You there?

I wait forever and he still doesn't read the message. I'm still shaking, trembling, quivering. I still feel like I need to blow chunks. If anything, it's worse now.

I need to go home. I need to hide under my blankets and pretend the world doesn't exist. Pretend that I didn't just participate in the world's crappiest prank. Maybe if I go home now, I'll leave before Jordan gets here and he won't think I'm part of it.

It won't be hard to tell people I'm sick—I feel like crap and I'm sure I look like it.

I get up and exit the bathroom, speeding my way down the hall. I need to go home. Now.

When I round the corner between the bathroom and Jordan's locker, I hear his voice. My heart feels like it's stopped, like I'm dying right here and now. I freeze in my tracks. Jordan, Hannah, and Kumail are gathered around his locker. He pulls off a note taped to his locker.

"Wiener lover," he says, reading it out loud.

I want to tell him to stop, to not open his locker, but I'm helpless. I can't move, can't shout, can only stand there and watch. He spins the combination lock on his locker, not seeming to notice anything out of the ordinary, and opens it. A second later, hundreds of slimy wieners come raining out of his locker, most of them slapping against him before pooling around his feet.

From the far end of the hall, horrible, mocking, screeching laughter fills the air. The football team and their entourage of wannabes and hangers-on are pointing and laughing, throwing taunting comments at him.

Jordan's face is beet red and he looks more upset than I've ever seen him. He turns away from the football team and that's when his eyes lock onto mine. I see hatred there. Pure hatred.

Jordan stomps over to me, nearly wiping out on a hot dog and eliciting more laughter from my former friends. He stops when he's a foot away from me. I try to tell him it wasn't me, that I'm sorry, that I tried to text him to stop him from opening his locker—but even I know it's too little too late. Besides, I can't even get anything more than a pitiful squeak out of my mouth.

He cocks his fist back, preparing to strike me. I see the slightest fear and hesitation in his eyes, like he's worried I'll hit him back. But I could never hit Jordan. Never.

"Jordan Ortiz! Put that fist down!" comes an authoritative shout from across the hallway.

Neither him nor I move. Neither him nor I even glance in the direction of the shout.

"I'm sorry," I finally manage to say, my words barely a whisper. "I didn't do it. I couldn't."

Jordan looks like he's considering again if he should punch me and it looks like he's going to do it. I brace myself, ready to take it. I deserve it. I deserve worse. But I'll take it.

"Jordan Ortiz—final warning!"

Jordan huffs, letting out a sharp exhale through his nose, his nostrils flaring. Slowly, he lowers his fist.

A moment later, Mr. Empaces's hands are on our shoulders, leading us toward the principal's office.

I spent all morning in the principal's office, but when I explained my role in the prank—specifically, how I realized how very wrong it was and that I backed out—I was let off with a warning. The rest of the guys were in his office until late afternoon. I don't know what their punishment is; they aren't talking to me right now. I betrayed them. But it's not like they were secretive about having done it, what with them standing there and laughing, mocking Jordan as he was pelted with wieners.

Jordan's not talking to me either. I don't know if he'll ever talk to me again.

Spring break is almost over and I spent the entire thing in my room, partly because my parents grounded me and partly because I had no energy or interest to do anything other than lie in bed. My brothers thought the prank was hilarious, until they got a stern lecture from our parents, and now they just think it's hilarious when mom and dad are out of the room. I don't know how convincing their lecture was anyway. I still don't know where mom and dad stand on the whole gay thing. Like, do they actually think the prank was wrong? Or do they secretly think Jordan got what he deserved?

And what would they think if they knew I'm gay and someone pulled that prank on me. Is it different if the gay kid is your own kid? Or are all gays immoral?

"Benjamin!" mom calls from downstairs. "Dinner's ready!"

I don't want to eat. I have no appetite. I've barely eaten anything all spring break. But if I miss out on another meal, that's just going to give mom more reason to pester me to demand to know what's wrong. She's been relentless all week. I think at first she thought I was moping just because I was grounded, but she's starting to realize that there's something bigger going on.

I don't know how much longer I can stay closeted. It's killing me.

Reluctantly, I push myself out of bed and up onto my

feet. I shuffle out of my room and down the stairs. When I get to the dining room table, mom, dad, Brayden, and Daniel are already there and loading lasagna and garlic bread onto their plates. Mom forces my brothers to take some salad too. Mom and dad exchange a look with each other when I sit down and then mom passes me the plate full of garlic bread.

I take a piece and put it on the edge of my plate, then take a small slice of lasagna and some salad. I cut off a small bite and shove it in my mouth. It takes some effort, but I chew and swallow. I go on repeat: food in mouth, chew, swallow, food in mouth, chew, swallow, food in mouth, chew, swallow.

My brothers are talking about some video game or something, entirely immersed in their own world and oblivious to the silence on this side of the table. I choose not to look at mom and dad, but I know they're looking at me. If they're not looking at me, they're looking at each other and surely exchanging silent telepathic comments about me.

There's a sudden clatter of dishes to my left. Brayden and Daniel are done.

"Can we go back to our game?" Daniel asks.

Normally, mom doesn't like any of us to rush off after dinner, rather she prefers that we stay and talk about the day. But today isn't a normal day.

"Of course," she says with a smile. Brayden and Daniel hurry off to the rec room, leaving mom and dad and I in total silence.

After a very long time of not talking, after I manage to eat a whole piece of lasagna, mom says, "Benjamin, you know you can talk to us about anything, right?"

I finally look up at her and meet her eyes. "I know," I say, but I don't offer anything more than that.

After I finish off the salad and garlic bread, part of me wants to go back to my room, but part of me wants to stay here and have *the conversation* with mom and dad. But I have no clue how to start that conversation. How did Jordan do it?

I think mom knows I'm not ready to go back to my room, that something's eating at me, because she asks me to help her and dad with the dishes. I dutifully stack up the plates and cutlery and follow them into the kitchen. Mom fills the sink with soapy water and I grab a towel.

She washes, I dry, and dad puts things away, as well as packing leftovers into containers. When we're nearly done, and my heart is racing at what has to be hundreds of beats per minute, if not thousands, I finally say, "Mom...dad...I need to talk to you about something."

She keeps washing the last of the dishes and dad waits patiently for me to dry a plate and hand it to him. They obviously know the seriousness and gravity of what I'm about to tell them, even if they don't know *exactly* what I'm going to tell them, and they're just waiting patiently for me to say the words.

"About the...the Jordan thing. The hot dogs." Remembering that incident is almost physically painful. "I want you to know why I backed out, why I couldn't go through with it."

"Because it's wrong," dad says, offering his understanding. "It's wrong to tease or bully anyone about something like that."

"It's…it's more than that."

Mom hands me another dish—the last of the plates— and I dry it completely and let dad put it away in the cupboard before I continue.

"Mom…dad…" My lips are quivering. My hands are shaking. What if they kick me out? Would Jordan's family take me in? I take in a shuddering breath. I can't do this. I can't.

Mom takes my hand in hers, stilling it, warming it. Dad puts his arms around my shoulders. Both of them are holding me. Both of them are giving me strength. I only hope that they'll accept me for what I say. I hope they're still holding me when I'm done.

"Benjamin," dad says. "We will always love you, no matter what."

Mom starts rubbing her hand up and down my forearm as she still holds onto my hand. We're not usually a family for such expressions of love and comfort, but this is exactly what I need right now. I only pray that it doesn't end when I say the G-word.

"I'm gay."

Mom pulls me into a hug and I sob into her shoulder. Dad hugs me from behind, sandwiching me between them, surrounding me with love.

"We love you, Benjamin," mom says, murmuring into my ear. Dad squeezes me a little tighter.

How could I have thought they would ever stop loving me?

BENJAMIN: Jordan?

BENJAMIN: I understand if you don't want to talk to me. Or if you never want to talk to me again. But I wanted you to know that I came out to my parents today. They know I'm gay.

BENJAMIN: I don't know how you did it. You're so strong. I really look up to you.

I open my curtains and look across the space between our houses. Jordan's curtains are closed and his light is off. I look down toward the first floor—their dining room is below Jordan's bedroom—but the lights are off down there too. Maybe he's not home.

I sigh and throw myself back on my bed and scroll aimlessly through my phone. Every few minutes, I check back in my text thread with Jordan to see if he's read my message or if he's typing a response, but there's nothing. Anxiety rises in me and I struggle to keep it at bay; this long silence is eating away at me, even if I know that "unread" means he hasn't even seen it yet.

Part of me hopes this is my chance to get Jordan back, to repair all that's gone wrong between us. Maybe it'll lead to me kissing him again. I hope it does.

There's a soft knock on my door and then it's pushed open. Dad pops his head in.

"Hey, Ben…you got a minute?"

"Yeah," I say. I sit up in my bed and put my phone facedown on the nightstand. If I keep it in my hands, I'll be obsessively checking it.

Dad comes in and he closes the door, then comes and sits on the bed. He puts his hand on my feet. "I wanted to say again, son, that I love you and your mom loves you. You being gay doesn't change that in the slightest."

I'm suddenly able to stare only at my thumbs as I twiddle them in front of me. Dad and I don't usually have such heart to hearts and I'm still not quite used to this gay thing. It's all too much.

When I don't reply, dad says, "Anyway, I just wanted you to know. And I wanted to thank you for trusting us to tell us."

I still can't reply and I still can't look up from my thumbs. Dad lets out a sigh and stands up. Just as he's about to walk away, I blurt out the question that's been burning on my mind. "Dad…back at Wendy's the other day…you didn't want me hanging out with Jordan because he's gay. But now you're okay with me being gay." Okay, maybe it isn't a question. But it's what's been bugging me.

Dad sits back down on the bed. He balls his hand into a loose fist and bumps it against my knees. He's feeling awkward, I can tell. There's something he doesn't want to say.

"Are you really okay with me being gay?" I ask. I'm not sure if I want to know the answer.

"Ben..." Dad lets out another sigh. "I haven't been the best father when it comes to you being friends with Jordan. And...yeah...I *did* have a problem with gay people and I didn't want you to be gay."

I feel like he's stabbed a knife in my chest and started twisting.

"But that day at Wendy's...I clued in that you might be gay. And I realized that I'd made a huge mistake as a father. I wasn't letting you be free to be *you*." Dad's eyes get watery. We're not normally criers, despite that numerous tears we've all shed today and back at Wendy's. "One thing I haven't ever really told you about my work as a lawyer is that I help a lot of families who have lost their kids—to disease, to accidents...to suicide. The number of times I've worked with a family that's lost a son or daughter to suicide because they were gay or lesbian or something...I've lost count." The tears start rolling down dad's cheeks. My own tears aren't far behind.

"When we were at Wendy's," dad says, "I had this horrible vision that you would be next, that if I wasn't careful, you'd be the next gay kid that takes his own life. And as a parent, you never want that. Never. Ever. As a parent, you want your kid to grow up happy and healthy. That's all. There's nothing in there about who your kid loves—because that doesn't matter as long as your kid is happy and healthy.

"So I took a hard look at myself and realized I'd done you wrong, kid. I did some real bad things, setting you up for...for all of this...this pain and uncertainty. I wasn't providing the safe and happy home that I thought I was. I resolved right then and there—whether or not you were gay, I wasn't going to put that kind of pressure and stress on you. I'm no longer going to try to control how you live your life. I just want you to be happy and to know that you're loved. And I had failed at that one job."

My own tears finally spill from my eyes. I wipe them away quickly, but they're soon replaced.

"I'm sorry, Ben," dad says. I hug him. I hold him and we both gently cry. "I love you, Benjamin."

"I love you too, Dad," I say and I hug him tighter.

Dad takes a deep breath and he tries to get his crying under control. I wipe at my face and brush away the last of my tears.

"Thank you," I say. "Thank you for telling me everything."

The truth from my dad is probably far more important than he could ever know. I've been walking on eggshells ever since Wendy's, not wanting to accidentally do something that would make him question me again and then have everything blow up. But with this heart to heart, I now know that he really does love me.

Chapter Eleven

Jordan

DAD LETS US INTO the house and I head upstairs to my bedroom to plug my phone in. It had died when we went out for dinner and a movie and I need to charge it up again.

Spring break had been pretty quiet—Hannah and Kumail were mostly doing the things that couples do, but they did invite me to a few hangouts here and there. Other than that, it was mostly staying at home and watching Bella while our parents were at work.

I'm almost weirdly ready to go back to school on Monday. But then I get a flash of memory of the last day before break, of all those wieners waterfalling down on me. Normally I can take a little bit of bullying or teasing in stride—I've got a thick skin—but something about that just pushed me over that line, to the point where I could only see red. I'm not sure if it was having the whole football team and their entourage laugh at me, or if it was knowing that Ben had a part in it.

But, of course, Ben *wasn't* part of it. Although he was originally going to be. Shit, it's so messed up. I don't know if I should be mad at him for even considering being a part of it or if I should be glad that he saw the light and backed out. Either way, I'm not ready to talk to him.

My phone suddenly beeps with an alert. I pick it up and see texts from Ben.

BENJAMIN: Jordan?

BENJAMIN: I understand if you don't want to talk to me. Or if you never want to talk to me again. But I wanted you to know that I came out to my parents today. They know I'm gay.

BENJAMIN: I don't know how you did it. You're so strong. I really look up to you.

Oh…my…*God*. Benjamin came out?

I open my curtains to look at his window. His curtains are open too. Was he hoping to see me? Probably, especially if he's texting me like this.

I leave my light off—he doesn't seem to have noticed me yet and I don't want to draw his attention right away. I peer through the darkness. The sky is dark and it looks like Ben's only got a lamp on, making his room pretty dark too. He's on his bed and hugging his dad. Now they're both wiping their faces, brushing away tears.

I've never seen him cry, I realize. It's kind of sweet to know that he's sensitive enough that he can cry over something. I pick up my phone again and look at the timestamp on the texts; he sent them about ten minutes ago.

I watch as Ben and his dad talk a little bit more, and then his dad leaves the room. Ben picks up his phone, looks at it, then immediately looks across to my window. Maybe he noticed that I've read his texts now. Even though my room light is off, he spots me right away and a smile blossoms on his face.

Picking up my phone, I send him a message.

JORDAN: Congratulations. That's a big step. Did it go well?

BENJAMIN: Yeah. You see my dad hugging me?

JORDAN: Yup :)

Benjamin looks at me for a very long time. Then he starts typing on his phone. I see the dots appear, but then disappear, appear, then disappear. Finally, they appear one more time and a text shows up a moment later.

BENJAMIN: I'm sorry

BENJAMIN: For the hot dog thing

A sudden pall falls over me. My happiness for Benjamin and his coming out, for what this might mean for repairing our friendship…what this might mean for another kiss…all disappears, smothered by memories of wieners. I look at him and he looks back at me and I know he's waiting for a response. He's waiting for me to tell him it's okay, but I don't know if I'm ready to say that. I still don't even know if I should be mad at him.

But I need to tell him *something*.

JORDAN: Thank you

That's the best I can do right now, thank him for the apology. He seems to accept it because he gives me a weak smile. But I kind of want to leave this conversation. I still need to do some processing and thinking about this. I'm pretty sure I'll forgive Ben, but I still need time.

I turn my head and pretend I'm listening to Mom calling me.

JORDAN: Sorry—mom's calling me, gotta go

I give him a little wave and then rush out of the room before he can reply. I head down the stairs and find Mom sitting at the kitchen table, playing some game on her iPad. I sit down with her and she looks up at me and smiles, but when I don't say anything, she turns her attention back to the game.

I watch her play for a bit and then she looks up at me again. "You okay, Jordan?" she asks.

"Mom…can I run something by you?"

She shuts off the iPad and puts it aside. Something in how I said that must have told her how serious I am. "What's going on, honey?"

She knows about the hot dog thing—though she doesn't know about Ben's possible involvement in it—and so I'm sure she's thinking this is what this is all about…and it sort of is…but it's more than that.

"Back at homecoming, Benjamin wanted to tell me something, but we were interrupted." From there, I tell her *everything*—homecoming, the silence afterward, the kiss on New Year's Eve, the repeated silence, the almost-but-not-quite threat in the bathroom, and the hot dog incident, including Ben's aborted involvement in it...and then I tell her that Ben just came out to his parents. "But don't tell anyone about Benjamin," I say and she nods. "But, like, I don't even know what to do now. Do I forgive him? Do I not? Do I move on from him and forget any of this ever happened?"

"Jordan...before *you* came out, what do you remember of what you were like?" mom asks. The question kind of catches me off guard. I don't know where she's going with this.

"I don't know...wasn't I like I always am?"

Mom chuckles in that way that moms do. "Oh, honey, no. You were *miserable* for the months leading up to you telling us you're gay." She smiles, but it's a tight smile, like the memory of me was unpleasant. Looking back, like, I do recognize that I wasn't really *happy*. "I knew *something* was bothering you, but I didn't know what. Then when you came out, I was, like, ooohhhhhhhhh...I get it now. And in the matter of a few moments, you changed completely. Miserable Jordan was gone; the happy-go-lucky Jordan I've known his whole life was suddenly back."

I feel a slight blush warm my cheeks. I guess I had known I was a little difficult during those months, but I never realized that other people thought I was miserable.

"I mean," Mom says, continuing, "you know more than I do, but I think during those miserable months, you were probably sorting everything out in your head and deciding when and where to come out and realizing that you couldn't pretend to be someone else anymore. It had to be torture."

"So the stuff Benjamin's been doing..." I say, connecting the dots she's laying out before me.

"Were *probably* him dealing with his own issues. He needed to come to this point on his own and it was a rocky journey to get there—rockier than your own journey, maybe, since he's captain of the football team and all," she says.

"So I should give him another chance?" I ask.

"That's up to you—and only you can make that choice. Some people would say that what Ben did doesn't allow for forgiveness. Others might say that understanding where he's coming from explains his behavior. He didn't *actually* threaten you in the bathroom, as you said, but he was angry and you took it as a threat. He didn't *actually* put the hot dogs in your locker, even though he was along for part of that. And you said he did try texting you before you got to school." She pauses like she's collecting her thoughts. "I can't tell you what to do—it's not my place—but I can help you see the possibilities and the context to help you make the right choice for you."

So, maybe I should forgive Benjamin. Back in elementary school, like grade one or two, I had a friend named Chad who used to always pull Stephanie's hair, a girl he clearly liked. It's not the same thing, no, but I can see how someone dealing with tough emotions might lash out at the person they care for. I thank my mom and head back upstairs—she's given me a lot to think about.

I *want* to give Benjamin a second chance. I like him, he's a good guy, even if he made a few mistakes. I think I've already forgiven him, even if I'm not totally over what's gone on between us. But…maybe the first step to getting over it is to give him that second chance.

When I get back to my room, I look out the window and find Ben still sitting on his bed, fiddling with his phone. I turn on my light and catch his attention. He looks over at me and I smile. I walk to my desk and sit down and pick up my phone.

I look at him one more time before I text him. I take a deep breath—I feel calm…this is the right thing to do.

JORDAN: I'm sorry I rushed out—I was a little surprised by everything is all

I look up at Ben. He glances up at me and a small frown turns his mouth downward, but it's a frown of contrition. Even through two windows and the space between our houses, that remorse is clear.

BENJAMIN: I'm sorry again. If I could take back all the shitty things I said and did, I would.

BENJAMIN: I just want to start over with you

JORDAN: I'd like that too

• • •

It's Saturday, two days before we head back to school and spring break is finally over.

And I'm on my first official gay date.

Ben borrowed his dad's car and drove us to a park on the other side of the city. It's a sunny day, surprisingly warm given how early in spring we are, and the park is filled with families and couples. I walk beside him as we meander down a beaten walking path that skirts the boundary between the main part of the park and the surrounding woods. It allows us some privacy.

Benjamin is nervous. Even if I didn't know him for almost my whole life, I'd be able to tell he's nervous. He hasn't said much since we got out of the car.

"So," I say, struggling to come up with a topic. "What are you going to study at NYU?"

"Law," he says. "Following in the family's footsteps, I guess." He chuckles awkwardly. With both his parents being lawyers, it's not surprising he would go on the same career path. "And you?"

"Political science and literature." I laugh to myself. "I don't really have the defined career path that you do. I'm not quite sure where those studies will lead…but I want to do them."

"I think that's cool," he says. "Sometimes you gotta do what you really want to do. You know, damn the expectations of others." I know he's talking about more than just my university-with-no-career-plan thing. He's also describing *us*.

The path meanders to the right and dips a little deeper into the woods, trees now on both sides of the path and hiding us from the people in the park. I take this opportunity to reach for his hand and take it in mine. When I touch him, he jerks his head around and looks at me with a panicked look in his eyes. But when I fully take his hand in mine, that panicked look disappears, though he does glance around, as if ensuring no one can see us.

We keep walking, silence filling the space between us again. His overwhelming nervousness is apparent even in how he holds my hand. He's holding me too tight and his fingers twitch now and then—and his palm is sweaty—but I'm just glad to be holding his hand that those things don't really matter to me. And I totally get where he's coming from. He's been out less than twenty-four hours—and he's only out to his family and me and no one else—whereas I've been out for months now and everyone knows. It'll take time for him to be more comfortable with it—and I'm willing to be patient with him, to let him move at his own pace.

"Are you looking forward to going back to school?" I ask. I want to kick myself; can't I ask questions that aren't about school in one way or another?

He chuckles nervously. "Not really," he says. "You know…"

I nod. He hasn't told me yet if he plans to come out at

school or not—either way, going back on Monday has got to be terrifying. He's either hiding a secret he's fully acknowledged to himself now or he's going to start coming out to people, including possibly the football team. If he does, there's no way that can go well.

Some noise from ahead interrupts us and a moment later we see a cyclist on the path heading toward us. Ben immediately lets go of my hand and shoves his in his pocket, then steps to the complete other side of the path, putting as much distance between us and allowing the cyclist to pass between us. But when the cyclist is gone, he doesn't move back to my side.

It hurts that he's put distance between us again, but I try not to let it show on my face. He's new to this. It takes time. I get it. It doesn't mean I have to like it.

I take the initiative to close the distance between us, slowly migrating to his side of the path as we keep walking forward. He looks over at me and smiles, but he keeps his hand in his pocket, not giving me the chance to reach out and hold it. I step closer and bump my shoulder against his like a playful hello—and a step later, he does the same to me. I let out a soft chuckle and he does the same.

"I'm sorry," he says, voice so quiet I almost didn't hear him.

"For what?" I ask.

"For not...for not being a good date." He glances behind us, like he's making sure we're alone. "I want to touch you, but...you know, I get nervous."

I smile—and it's a genuine, full smile. *This* is what I want. Honest, heartfelt talk, not mindless chatter about school. Even if it's him confessing he's scared to do gay things in public, it's still him speaking from his heart.

"There's no one around," I say, glancing behind us and ahead to ensure we are, in fact, alone. "No one will see us, and we can act straight if we hear someone coming our way."

He stops walking and chews his bottom lip. I can see the conflict in his eyes—his desire to touch me and his absolute terror at being caught and outed. "Fuck it," he mutters, and he finally takes his hand out of his pocket and puts his arm around my shoulders, pulling me close and tight against his muscular body.

Giddiness swells in my chest and I can't stop grinning. I put my arm around his waist and hold him just as tight, and then we continue walking.

"This is nice," he says. "I like this."

"Me too." I put my other hand on his chest as we walk and I can feel his heart pounding against his ribs. He's still incredibly nervous—or maybe he's excited? Or maybe it's both.

Ben is a good six inches taller than me and with our vast differences in sports preferences, he's bulky and muscular, whereas I'm trim and toned. With this difference in size, I'm loving the feeling of being protected and cocooned by him.

We walk for a good five minutes with our arms around

each other and it's glorious. It's amazing. It's incredible. Like, seriously, I feel all warm and fuzzy inside. I've never felt this before—but then I've never been on a gay date before, never had a boyfriend before. Wait. Back up. We're not boyfriends. Not yet, anyway.

The path through the trees starts to veer to the left and the trees on that side thin; it's taking us back into the main part of the park. To make all of this easier on Ben, I let go of his waist and start to separate from him, so that he's not always the one breaking contact when others are nearby.

But before I can completely disengage and disentangle from him, he pulls me closer and plants a kiss on my forehead. Then he lets go of me and continues walking like he hasn't just totally made my day. I hurry to catch up to him and when I do I see a goofy grin on his face.

"What was that?" I ask.

"What was what?" he says, feigning ignorance. His grin only gets wider.

"If I didn't know better, Mr. Cooper, I'd say you like me," I tease.

He looks at me and his eyes are full of warmth. "I'm terrible at keeping that secret." The path takes us a little further into the park and away from the trees. "Ice cream?"

I look ahead of us and see an ice cream stand—it must have just opened up for the season recently because it's barely ice cream weather. "Sure."

We make our way to the ice cream stand and Ben buys us both a treat. I get some ice cream thing dipped in caramel and then dipped in hard chocolate. Ben gets a Drumstick. We keep walking on the path, mostly keeping some distance between us and keeping our conversation limited—we're near other people and I know Ben wants us to look like friends rather than two guys on a date.

But then the path goes back into the trees and all of the other people in the park fade into the distance. We keep ourselves apart a little longer because we hear a jogger heading our way. But after she passes and rounds a bend and is out of sight, Ben puts his arm around my shoulders again. That warm and fuzzy feeling comes back.

Ben finishes his Drumstick and balls up the wrapper in his hand. A moment later I finish my treat and put the stick in the wrapper and shove it in my back pocket. Benjamin looks down at me and smirks.

"What?" I ask.

"You have ice cream on your lips." I reach up to wipe it away, but he grabs my hand. "No. Let me."

Ben stops walking and turns toward me, putting a hand on either side of my face. He pulls me close and kisses me, his lips warm and hard against mine. Then he swipes his tongue across my lips and laps up the ice cream—though I'm not entirely convinced I had ice cream there. Damn, I must be nervous. Focus on the kiss, focus on the kiss, focus on the kiss.

I moan and my knees seem to sag, but Ben just moves one of his hands to my back, both pressing me against him and holding me up. I try to move my lips with his, to sync with his kissing. It's clumsy, but it's magical, and I wouldn't trade it for anything. I don't want it to stop—I never want it to stop. I could do this forever.

It's like the world stops.

Ben holds me tighter and I can even feel his heartbeat pounding against my own. Both of ours are racing. I let my hands roam up and down his muscled back as I sag into the kiss. He starts leaning forward, arching over me, pressing into the kiss. It's mind-blowing.

And then a bicycle bell interrupts and shatters the moment. Benjamin instantly stops kissing me and lets go of me and I almost fall backward onto the ground, but manage to catch myself just in time. I feel a blush burn my cheeks as the cyclist passes by; I avoid looking at him in case he's giving us judgmental eyes or something. When he's gone, I can't help but giggle.

Then I notice that Benjamin isn't laughing. He looks mortified. He crosses his arms and looks down at the beaten path; he's avoiding my eyes.

"Hey," I say in a soothing voice. I put my hand on his bicep, but he turns away, forcing me to drop my hand.

"I'm sorry," he says.

"You don't have to apologize," I say. It sucks that being caught kissing a guy—even by a total stranger who's already gone—is making him close off and clam up like this. I understand, like, on some level, but it still hurts to be given the cold shoulder right now.

This is almost like a repeat of New Year's Eve.

At least he's not running away from me right now. I guess that's a win.

Still, the date is clearly over. Almost as if on cue, Benjamin shudders and rubs his arms.

"It's getting cold," he says. "Maybe we should head back."

"Sure."

We leave the circuitous walking path and head straight across the park toward the parking lot. Benjamin walks fast, like he's late for something—or like he's running away. I have to hurry to keep up. He unlocks the car with a beep and we get in.

Before he starts up the ignition, he puts his hands on the top of the steering wheel and then leans his forehead against it, his eyes closed. He lets out a long, heavy sigh. I know he's disappointed and angry with himself.

I put my hand on his back and pat him gently.

Chapter Twelve

Benjamin

THAT KISS HAD BEEN so amazing.

It had taken me all day to build myself up to it. And then that biker had to come by and I totally lost my cool and all those feelings of shame and guilt came rushing in and taking over. Jordan had told me that it would take time for me to be as comfortable as him—and that he doesn't think less of me for being uncomfortable—but I still feel like a complete and total loser. Why can't I just kiss him and not worry about what other people might think?

I rest my head against my hands on the steering wheel. A moment later, I feel Jordan's hand on my back. It's comforting. It feels natural—like his hands belong on me—but it still doesn't bring me out of my sinking spiral of self-hatred.

I want to be out and proud, but right now I just can't.

Turning my head slightly, I rest my temple on my hands and open my eyes. Jordan is disappointed, I can tell, but he's trying to hide it. Damn it, I've gone and ruined our date and I've failed at impressing the man I want to be my boyfriend.

This was my chance to make up for all the crappy things I've said and done and it was going *so well*...but then I had to go and blow it. I want to say sorry again, but he's already told me to stop with the apologies.

"I really enjoyed our date," I say, "you know, until..."

"Me too," Jordan says, though the disappointment doesn't completely disappear from his eyes.

"I'd like to do this again," I say. "Date you, that is." I'm suddenly nervous again. Maybe I'm worried I've blown my chance and he's going to turn me down. I feel like I'm walking on eggshells.

"I'd like that too," he says. While relief floods in because he wants to see me again, I still feel like I'm at risk of doing an epic fail and losing it all. If I freak out again, that might be the end for him.

"I'm sorry," I say again, even though he's told me not to.

He pats my back again. "It's okay. I understand."

I lean forward and give him a quick kiss on the lips before my anxiety can work itself up again and before my nerves can overwhelm me. The kiss must catch him by surprise because he gasps into the kiss, but then his lips close and he kisses me back.

Don't look around, I tell myself as I back up from the kiss. *Don't look around.* The last thing I want or need right now is to look around like I always do, scoping out if someone saw us, just putting my shame and embarrassment further on display and spoiling the kiss.

It takes almost all my force of will to not crane my neck around and look in all directions like some paranoid owl. I start up the car, pull out of our spot, and drive us home. When we exit the park, I breathe out a sigh of relief—I had, in fact, managed not to look around.

One step at a time.

When we got back home, we didn't kiss—even Jordan didn't feel right kissing in my driveway in clear view of both my house and his. I'm grateful he didn't push me for a kiss, but I would have given it to him because I don't want to risk disappointing him—and, really, I *want* to kiss him. I want to kiss him and never stop. But it's those damn feelings of guilt and shame that are always ruining everything.

We didn't go on a date on Sunday—with it being the last day off before school, we both had homework to catch up on, and Jordan always goes to mass on Sunday with his family.

And that brings us to Monday.

My first day at school after having come out. Even though I haven't come out to *anyone* at school—other than Jordan, of course—I feel like everyone's eyes are on me. Like everyone can see a rainbow flag painted on my face or something.

I pass Devon in the hallway. I put my hand up to give him a high five, but he just turns away from me, a look of disgust on his face.

Panic instantly takes over. What does he know? Was he at the park?

It takes a long moment—a very long and terrifying moment—to realize his dislike of me is because I basically ratted the whole team out to Principal Moyer about the hot dogs. I don't know if I should be upset or relieved that I've likely lost all my friends, even if only temporarily, because while it sucks to have lost my friends, right now I don't want to talk to them. The whole hot dog thing proves they're homophobic and right now I just can't deal with it. And I don't want to have to lie to them about everything that happened on spring break—but I'm certainly not telling them the truth either.

I pass a few other of my buddies—former buddies, I guess—and they all ignore me like Devon did. I'm sure they think they're punishing me, but, really, I couldn't be more relieved.

I open my locker and throw my jacket in there and grab a textbook. When I shut the locker, I nearly jump out of my skin—Nikki had snuck up and was hiding behind the door to surprise me. Obviously, she's not ignoring me like everyone else in our group, though I kind of wish she was.

"How was spring break?" she asks. She squeezes her

arms together in front of her, pushing her boobs out a little bit. Not that I'm into boobs. But I guess she doesn't know that. Yet.

"It was okay," I say.

"I tried snapping you," she says. She pouts because I never replied to any of them.

"I know. Sorry." I sling my backpack over my shoulder. "Spring break was…busy." I start walking toward first period—a class we share—and she follows along beside me.

"Benny…" she says, using that nickname that I've told her countless times I hate, "are you avoiding me? Did you already ask someone else to prom?"

Prom…damn. She's fishing for a date.

"No, I haven't," I say. I try not to get her hopes up that I'll ask her. Honestly, I don't know what to do. I want to go with Jordan—and I *know* he'll want to go with me—but that's too big of a step for me right now. I have enough trouble getting through a date where we're almost entirely alone in the woods—never mind a date surrounded by our friends and classmates and frenemies.

"Well," she says, sweetly, "I'm still holding out for the right guy."

"I'll keep that in mind." I give her a small smile. It's forced, but I hope it doesn't look forced. I know she wants me to ask her, but I don't want to go cold and harsh and deny her when I can't give her a valid reason why I don't want to ask her.

She makes a noise that seems to be a cross between a

giggle and a squeak. I take it to mean she's happy.

"But what about Winston?" I ask.

That question seems to catch her by surprise. "What about Winston?" There's some strain in her voice.

"I'm sure he'd love to ask you to prom." Maybe I can get out of this if I set up the match made in social media heaven between those two.

"He...he did," she admits. "I told him I had to think about it."

I look at her and she's looking ahead of us, but, like, with an unfocussed gaze, like she's lost in thought. It's then that I know for certain that she has feelings for Winston, but she's all caught up in this Insta-famous social media wannabe celebrity thing. And in her mind that means the cheerleading captain and the football captain on a date at prom. I'm honestly shocked that even her feelings for Winston couldn't break through that obsession.

Before I can offer her any support or encouragement in the Winston direction, the bell rings. We're already late for class on our first day back.

After class, Nikki was caught up in gabbing with another cheerleader and I got to escape without more pressure on the prom situation. For the last period of the morning, it was time for a class that both excited and terrified me.

Math. Because Jordan sits behind me.

I get to class first, as I usually do, and take my seat.

When Jordan comes in, my eyes instantly lock with his and it's like time stands still. I allow myself a small smile in greeting, but I can't do anything more than that, not if I want to keep my closeted and assumed-to-be-straight status.

Jordan walks past me—"accidentally" brushing his hand against my shoulder and sending sparks of electricity through that touch and rushing straight to my core—and takes his seat. I can almost feel his presence, just inches behind me, like his body heat is radiating toward me and my chilled skin is soaking it in.

It's going to take everything I have to get through this period. The start of class bell rings and Ms. Barnes starts by asking us to hand in our homework from the break. As per usual, students hand homework down the rows from back to front, adding theirs to the pile as it's passed to them.

Jordan taps on my shoulder—that damned electricity sparking from his touch again—and I turn around to take the papers from him. I'm captivated by his eyes.

"Thanks," I murmur, if only so I can look at him for half a second longer. A small blush reddens his cheeks and makes him look adorable, but then I turn around because I need to keep up the Straight Benjamin Cooper thing. I add my homework to the pile and pass it on to Annie in front of me.

I happen to glance to my right and a few rows over I spot Kieran—linebacker and part of my now-former friend group—glaring at me. Then all of my joy at being next to

Jordan comes crashing down and burns to ash.

The homophobic football players are no doubt looking for any excuse to get back at me for ratting them out. And if they find out I'm gay, I'm pretty much as good as dead. They'll pull something far bigger than some stupid hot dog prank.

I breathe in a deep breath and then slowly let it out.

If I can get through coming out to my family, I can get through this.

Maybe it'll blow over with time. Their attention span can be really short sometimes—all it takes is for someone else to piss them off and they'll be ready to forgive me and let our differences die in the past. But do I really want that? I mean, I don't want to be a target, but if they forgive me, then that would mean they'd want me back in their friend group.

Could they deal with a gay friend? Could they accept a gay football captain? I mean, football season is over and my career in high school football is over too, so I'm technically not their captain anymore. But, still, there's that status thing—they're lower status than a *gay* captain.

Some might be able to handle that, like Devon, but others would never get over it. Kieran is one of those guys.

Ms. Barnes begins her lesson and I do my best to follow along and take notes. But every few moments, I find myself glancing over at Kieran. I never catch him looking at me, so his anger toward me is probably forgotten, at least for the duration of the period, but that fact doesn't make me feel any more safe and secure.

Kieran is stronger than me. He likes to show off in the weight room and he lifts things I can't even contemplate. He also has a quick temper. If he were to get so pissed at me that he tries to take a swing at me...

I'd survive, I mean, he won't kill me. But he could do a number on me before he backs off or before someone pulls him off.

School is no longer safe.

And I can't let any of them know about me and Jordan.

But I can't just ignore Jordan at school and put up that wall of ice between us again. No, I need to give him a heads up about it first. He'll understand, I'm sure, but he won't like it.

And now I feel horrible for more reasons. I'll be asking him to deny that we like each other while simultaneously I'll be dating him—if he'll even still have me after me asking him if we can ignore each other at school.

I struggle through the period and at least copy down all the notes. I'll read them again at home and it'll all make sense, I'm sure. Or maybe I can have a study date with Jordan and he can teach it to me.

I smile to myself at the thought of the two of us sharing a bowl of popcorn, cuddled up on the couch, going over our math assignment. I'd demand a kiss for every question I answer correctly. When I look up from my desk, something catches my eye—Kieran is looking at me and scowling.

Once again, my daydream of fun and romance with Jordan is instantly destroyed. If anything, Kieran knows *something* is making me happy and by the scowl on his face, he wants to bash my face in and make me as miserable as him.

When class is over, I quickly pack up, give Jordan a quick glance so I don't ignore him, and I hurry out of class before either him or Kieran can catch up to me. With it now being lunch, the halls are packed with people and the noise level is at a hundred. I quickly melt into the crowd and move through it as quick as I can, hoping to continue to evade Jordan and Kieran, as well as avoiding all other football players.

I reach the stairwell, dart down to the first floor, and head outside. It's a little chilly today, so almost no one is outside. My breath fogs in front of me.

Heading to the football field, I dart around the bleachers. I pause and I listen for any voices, in case anyone has followed me. When the coast seems to be clear, I poke my head around the corner. I breathe a foggy sigh of relief when I confirm that no one followed me and no one else is within sight.

I pull out my phone and text Jordan.

BENJAMIN: Meet me on the football field? We need to talk

JORDAN: Ok. Be there soon

I shove my phone in my pocket and rub my arms, trying to get warm. I really can't stay out here long, but I need to talk to Jordan in private and I need to do it now and this is the only place I can think of that works.

A few minutes later, Jordan comes around the corner.

"Hey," I say and I give him a smile.

"Everything okay?" He's nervous, I can tell. I can't blame him—my text sounded ominous. I get mad at myself for making him worry.

"Sort of," I say.

He closes the distance between us. I want to reach out and touch him, but...someone will see. Even just being caught here with him is enough for people to suspect I'm gay. I mean, me having a private conversation with the openly gay kid? If I was still in my pre-coming-out stage when I was stupid and self-hating, I would've probably spread such a rumor if I'd caught someone else here with Jordan. Sometimes I really hate myself for what I used to do.

"What is it?"

Fuck it, I need to touch him. He looks cold, so I put my hands on his arms and start rubbing up and down, hoping the gesture is both warm and comforting.

"I'm having some difficulty, like, with the football team." His expression softens a little bit—I hope he knows already that I'm not asking to break up and he hasn't done anything wrong. "I think some of them are out to get me since I ratted on them to Principal Moyer. They're looking for any opportunity to put me in my place."

"Oh," he says. He looks at my chest like he's deep in

thought. Then he looks back up at my eyes. "Can you tell Principal Moyer?"

I shake my head. Jordan can be so innocent sometimes. "That'll only make it worse."

"So what can you do?"

I let out a breath and I'm suddenly fearful. "I think we need to hide *this*," I squeeze his arms, "a little more than either of us want to."

"It's a secret, I know," he says. There's disappointment in his voice. It hits me like a knife stabbing into my heart.

"More than that. We need...I need for us to ignore each other completely. Like, back when I was being a douchebag." I blink several times, trying to prevent my eyes from watering. I'm picturing Jordan telling me I come with too much baggage and that we need to be separate until I sort out my shit.

But then he sighs heavily and says, "Fine."

"I'm sorry," I say. "I wish I could make it up to you somehow."

He looks thoughtful for a moment. "Kiss me."

"What? We're at school."

"There's no one around." He glances in all directions to verify his statement. I don't look around—I need to trust him and he needs to know I trust him. "A kiss would prove to me that you still want me and this isn't some stupid ploy to go fully-closeted again and be straight again." He's mad. That feeling that he's stabbed me in the heart? Now it feels like he's twisting the knife.

"I don't want to be straight again," I say. "I'm gay." Wow, I said it out loud. Again. It's no easier this time than it was when I told my parents. "And I want to be with you."

"Then prove it. Kiss me." He's not going to let this go.

I fight valiantly against the urge to look around, though I do glance behind him to the passage between the bleachers. If anyone would wander in, it would be through there. No one.

I pull him close and press my lips against his. I kiss him and he kisses me. I move my lips a bit, feeling his, exploring his, and it feels *so good*. I feel my whole face warming with pleasure and delight. I'm kissing Jordan—and he's kissing me. I'll never get over that.

Then I break the kiss. We can't keep at it forever, not when we're at school and we can be caught at any moment. When I pull away from Jordan, I see that his eyes are closed and he's got this cute grin on his face. He opens his eyes slowly and they look hazy with delight.

"Thank you," he says.

"No, thank *you*, you're putting up with this bullshit about me and the football team."

The euphoria on his face dims a little bit, but he doesn't look angry or upset. "There's only a few more months of school left."

"Thank you," I say. "And to make it up to you, I want to date you like crazy. Go out with me tonight?"

The euphoria returns full force. "Definitely."

Chapter Thirteen

Jordan

I'M CRUSHED THAT BEN wants to continue to pretend we have nothing to do with each other, though I'm not really surprised. I know he's not out and doesn't want to be—at least not yet—and of course that means we can't be all kissy-kissy at school. That wall of ice and silence again? That's going to take some getting used to.

But the promise of a date tonight immediately lifts my spirits. I can deal with pretending we aren't totally head over heels for each other when we're at school if it means we can do the total opposite after school hours.

To give Ben some discretion, I walk across the field and take the exit on the other side, letting Ben return to school several minutes ahead of me. I saw some of the dirty looks he got this morning; I don't know how he's doing with his friends. I'll have to ask him tonight.

My phone buzzes in my pocket.

HANNAH: You coming for lunch?

JORDAN: Yeah—on my way!

I catch my reflection in the window as I head into the school and I find I'm grinning stupidly. I try to make my face more neutral, but then I think of why I'm so happy— *Benjamin*—and that stupid grin just returns. *Think of something less cute than Benjamin,* I tell myself. I try to picture things like horrible news stories, sick puppies, and an ice cream splattering on the ground. None of it really works, but it's the best I can do.

I head toward the cafeteria. When I enter, I find Benjamin *not* with his football friends, though the football team and their entourage is again at their claimed table, spread out like a pride of lions. Though I don't like them, nor do I like who Ben is when he's with them, I do feel bad for Ben not being part of his friend group. He's probably feeling pretty lonely and dejected right now.

I hurry past the team and their entourage—given that they're all in deep crap because of a prank they pulled on me, I'm sure they'd take the chance to call me a fag or something if I linger too long in front of them. They're still smarting from all that—their cold shoulder to Ben is enough proof of that.

As I make my way through the cafeteria to my regular table with Hannah and Kumail, I spot Benjamin sitting at a table with people I don't know, just staring vacantly into space as he eats his lunch. I wish I could invite him to join me at my table.

"What took you so long?" Hannah asks as I sit down, signing for Kumail's benefit.

"Sorry. Bathroom break," I say. I want to tell her and Kumail *everything*, but I can't. I don't even want to tell her an anonymous version, like telling her that I have a crush on someone who I can't name, because I don't want her to start guessing who it might be. If she were to guess Ben, then I might give a tell, like a twitch or something, and she'll know she's guessed right.

No, for Benjamin's privacy—and for mine, really—I need to keep this absolutely silent.

There's something different about you, Kumail says.

"In what way?" Hannah asks. After signing the question, her hand goes under the table and I can tell she's resting it on Kumail's thigh. They've gotten really close and I like it. I know they spent nearly all of spring break together. They had invited me along as the awkward third on a couple of their dates, but I felt so out of place that we didn't repeat it after the second time.

He's glowing, Kumail says.

My cheeks, which must have already been red, burned hot with a blush, surely getting much redder. I try to distract myself by unpacking my lunch, and maybe if I'm rooting around in my backpack, the redness of my cheeks might not be so obvious.

"You're right," Hannah says. "He's also...super happy."

Though I'm still fake-digging in my backpack, I glance toward Kumail to catch his reply.

Reminds me of me after our first date, Kumail says. A stupid grin starts forming on his face, the same one I tried to get rid of back when I saw my reflection.

Hannah gasps loudly, causing a few heads to turn in our direction, then she leans across the table, looking up at me with wide eyes. "Is it true?"

I sigh and put my backpack down on the floor, placing my sandwich and yogurt on the table. Folding my hands in my lap, I sit back in my chair, putting a bit of distance between her and me.

"No," I say, doing my absolute best to lie. I forgot to sign it for Kumail, so I repeat myself in sign language.

She squints like she's examining me under a microscope. "I don't believe you," she says.

"My love life," I say, picking up my sandwich, giving my hands something to do, "or lack thereof, is private." Again, I forgot to sign it, so I put my sandwich down and repeat myself. This being questioned is making me flustered.

Hannah leans back in her chair and turns to Kumail. They have a quick conversation in sign, their hands flying around. My skills are getting a bit better and I can mostly keep up with them. They're deciding whether or not to believe me, with both of them leaning toward *not* believing me.

"Well," Hannah says. "If you're non-existent and totally imaginary and super-fake boyfriend wants to take you to prom, which he totally should, tickets go on sale on Thursday."

I sigh, both in frustration and relief. She's not going to let this go, but by referencing prom, she's given me an opening to change the topic. I suspect that's intentional; Hannah knows that if she keeps questioning me that I'll only put up more walls.

"And how is prom coming?" I ask, remembering this time to sign as I talk.

"Good," Hannah says. "Almost everything is set in place. The committee is doing some final decorating choices this week so that we can still order what we need in time."

I glance to Kumail, almost feeling embarrassed to ask this question, but I just go for it. "How are you making it...accessible for everybody?"

She knows what I mean and I have no doubt that Kumail does too. How are they going to make an event that largely relies on being able to hear music accessible to Kumail?

She looks at him and smiles; he smiles back. "We're going crazy on the lights and the bass speakers. Syncing the lights to the beat and getting just enough bass to vibrate the floor lets Kumail keep the beat, you know..." she looks at him, "if he wants to dance with *someone*."

I see a brief look of fear in his eyes that he quickly tries to hide. I try to contain my laugh—seems Kumail is like me in that he can't dance. If *someone* were to ask me to dance, I'd be terrified too.

I would love to dance with you, Kumail says.

"You're a terrible liar," Hannah says with a smirk, "but I'm going to take advantage of it. I'm making you do *one* slow dance with me."

Kumail smiles, likely thankful she didn't make him commit to dancing the whole night. *Deal,* he says.

"*Everyone,*" Hannah says, looking straight at me and examining me again, "deserves a slow dance with their sweetheart at prom." It's like she's waiting for a response from me, like she's expecting me to suddenly bust out the gay gossip attitude and tell her all about my new man.

I won't give her the satisfaction.

We move onto far more neutral topics, though I know it's taking all of Hannah's self-control to not pester me with more questions. Instead, we talk about various homework assignments, the teachers we hate, and some of the cute Hannah and Kumail stories that only serve to make my heart ache because I want to be able to tell similar stories about Benjamin and me.

After dinner, I help mom take the dishes into the kitchen and load them into the dishwasher. I know she wants to talk to me because she specifically asked *me* to help her and told dad and Bella to go pick a movie to watch.

"Saturday," Mom says.

"Saturday," I repeat. While I'm more inclined to give

mom the details on my love life, I still feel awkward opening up about such a thing. It was one thing to come out as gay and have them accept me and keep loving me—not that I really had any worries about that—but it's another to now talk to her about the man I'm falling in love with.

Wait...falling in love?

Not just, like, really strongly appreciate?

I get this weird flutter in my heart like this means something.

"You know what I'm asking," she says.

"We...went for a walk."

"Come on, Jordan, you have to give me more than that," she says, her scolding mom voice coming out. The voice I've been trained since I was toddler to always obey.

"We went for a walk at Keystone Park," I say. I find I can talk about this if I just look at the dishes instead of at mom, so I fully take over loading the dishwasher. Mom rests a hip against the counter and just waits for me to continue. "We had ice cream, we talked, and we came home."

She laughs. "I'm sure that was all," she teases.

Like I'm going to tell mom I had a super hot kiss in the woods and it gave me a boner. "Some things need to stay secret," I say, teasing her right back.

Her chuckle soon dies and she gets a more serious expression on her face. "Those things we talked about on Friday...the stuff Ben said and did to you before he came out..."

Ah, that's where this is going. Again, I focus on the dishes as it makes talking easier. "He's really different now that he's come out," I say. "Though he's not out at school—and I respect that—but he's not doing crap there anymore."

She doesn't reply. It's a mom trick for conversation that I know too well—she's really good at letting silence stretch so that I feel compelled to share more. As much as I know what she's doing and I want to fight against it, my instincts kick in and I tell her more.

"I think it's like you said, it was anger inside at what he was doing, like he couldn't accept himself. He's not out at school, but he's out to himself and his family, so a lot of that anger I felt in him before is gone." I hope I don't sound like a foolish kid. I've seen those teen dramas on Netflix—there's that kid, usually a girl, who's in a bad relationship with someone with a temper. I think mom is making sure that's not the case here.

"Good," mom says, finally breaking her silence. She smiles warmly. "If that ever changes or if he does something you don't like, don't feel nervous or scared about talking to me about it, okay?"

"Okay," I say. I put the last of the cutlery in the dishwasher and close it. I glance at the clock on the microwave. "I should go." She knows I have a date, which is probably why we're having this talk now.

She comes to me and hugs me. "Have fun, Jordan. I love you and I'm so happy you've started dating. Just remember, if you have sex, use condoms."

"Wow. Way to make it awkward, Mom."

She breaks the hug and puts her hands on my shoulders, looking me right in the eyes. "I'm a mother and a doctor. Get used to it. And if you need protection, just ask."

My cheeks are burning and I'm sure I'm as red as a tomato. "Yes, Mother," I say. She hates being called mother, so it's my way of getting back at her.

"Smartass," she says. "Go have fun."

Before I even get my shoes on, the doorbell rings. I'm all giddy and fluttery inside when I rush to answer it. Benjamin is standing there. He looks gorgeous. He's got a buttoned-up polo that hugs his chest in all the right places, and black-as-night jeans that somehow make him look taller than he already is.

"Ready to go?" he asks. He smiles, big and bright.

"One sec," I say and I quickly pull my shoes on. "Ready!"

We walk to his car like we're just friends—no hand holding and lots of space between us—but as soon as we're in the car, I grab his hand and hold it.

"I'm so glad you're here," he says.

"Me too."

Before I can even process it, he leans across the console between us and gives me a quick kiss on the lips. When I'm recovering from the fact that Benjamin Cooper just kissed me again, he starts up the car and pulls out of his driveway.

"I thought we'd go bowling," he says as he navigates

onto a busy street. I put my hand on his leg, wanting to touch him but to also not distract him from driving.

"That should be fun." I haven't bowled in years. I think the last time was my tenth birthday party. I tell Benjamin that.

He laughs. "I remember that. I got my first strike ever."

I vaguely remember that. Ben had been overjoyed about something and me being ten years old, I didn't quite understand how exciting it was. I was just too into having fun and hanging out with my friends for my birthday, but with Ben growing up to be a jock, it makes sense that the athletic achievement of his first strike would be significant.

After a good fifteen minutes of driving, I realize we've already passed two bowling alleys. "Where, exactly, are we going?" I ask as I watch the second bowling alley grow tiny in the passenger side mirror.

"United Lanes," he says.

It takes me a moment to figure it all out. United Lanes is on the clear other side of the city, like further out than Keystone Park. I get one of those moments again where I'm kind of disappointed that we have to go through such lengths to make sure that no one sees us together, but I'm also just overjoyed to be on a date with a guy I really like. I try to push the disappointment away and just focus on the overjoyed part.

A short while later, we pull up at United Lanes and head in. It's one of those glow bowl nights where everything is lit by black light and there's loud disco music pumping through the speakers. The shoes are uncomfortable and my game is no better now than at my tenth birthday party. But I'm having fun. Ben seems so calm and relaxed and…himself. I remember the carefree Ben from years ago and I had figured that when that carefree nature faded, it was just him taking sports and school more seriously, but now I wonder if it was a byproduct of him working so hard to hide a certain side of himself. Like, if he would be too carefree, someone might figure out his deepest, darkest secret.

Like, seriously, Ben on a date is a completely different person than Ben at school or Ben from the last four years.

Ben sends his ball down the lane and even from my seated position behind him I can see that he's got fantastic aim with this shot…it's rolling right for the center. I stand up, trying to get a better view. Ben is both tense and excited, waiting and hoping for a good shot. With a loud clatter, all ten pins go crashing down.

"Strike!" he shouts, pumping his fist in the air. I whoop and clap and jump a couple times. And then Ben comes running to me, and picks me up in a hug, spinning us around in a circle. For a moment, I feel like we're going to kiss and even I'm uncomfortable with how public this would be.

Why does it have to be so difficult to be gay? Straight people would kiss right now, no hesitation, but we both can't bring ourselves to do that celebratory peck on the lips.

He puts me down and lets out another whoop.

"Your turn," he says, giving me a wink. "Knock 'em all down!"

I stick my tongue out at him. "I'll try."

The first few frames had been so relaxed and fun, but now with Ben having gotten a strike and with him watching me, I feel like the pressure is on to do as good as him. I take a calming breath, focus, center myself, step forward, and send the ball down the lane. My aim isn't as good as his, but I'm damn near close.

The ball strikes just to the side of the head pin, obliterating everything on the left hand side—but then a few of those pins spin into the ones standing on the right, knocking almost all of them down. The final pin, the one in the far back corner, is struck by a spinning pin and starts wobbling side to side. I get excited, but then I realize it's settling back into its standing position…until another pin rolls over and hits it at just the wrong time, knocking it over with the others.

"Strike!" I shout and I spin around.

Ben comes running up to me and he picks me up in another of those spinning hugs. Again, I want to kiss him, I want to celebrate us both getting a strike by pressing my lips to his—but we can't. I hug him back—that'll have to do in place of a kiss—and then he puts me down so he can take his turn.

When I sit down to watch him take his turn, I glance over in the next lane and I spot some random woman staring at us with a smile on her face. She winks at me before turning back to her own game. I think she knows we're on a date and she approves. Somehow that makes me feel kind of giddy—someone other than our parents know we're on a date and approves of what they see.

I'm ludicrously happy right now.

The thumping disco song on the overhead speakers reaches its end and in its place, a slower and more romantic song comes on. Ben is oblivious to the change in music; he's lining up his next shot, hoping for another strike, I'm sure.

But as the song continues, all I can think about is what Hannah said at lunch. *Everyone deserves a dance with their sweetheart at prom.* My heart suddenly aches with how badly I want that. I want to dance with Ben to some sappy love song, hand in hand, chest to chest, getting lost in the music, just having a moment of closeness and romance.

Benjamin would never go for it. Not in public anyway. But a slow dance in my basement rec room isn't as romantic or special. Benjamin won't even go with me to prom, I realize. He'll either go by himself or skip it or, worse, take a girl. Probably Nikki.

My moment of elation and joy deflates like a balloon with a leak. As long as Ben is closeted, we can't have many of those special moments that couples have. And I can't ask him to come out at school in time for prom—it's up to him to decide when he comes out and to who and I have no say in it.

It sucks that we can't have those special couple moments.

"Yes!" Ben shouts, punching the air again. "Strike number two!"

I do everything I can to smother my disappointment and share in his elation.

Chapter Fourteen

Benjamin

AFTER BOWLING, OUR DATE was over, but I wasn't ready to take us home quite yet.

"Where are we going?" Jordan asks when I turn off the main road.

"The scenic route," I say. Our city is surrounded by a few hills and one of them, as dad pulled me aside to tell me, has a little parking area that offers an amazing view of the city. I reach over and grab Jordan's hand, holding it in mine. This feels right. This feels *perfect*.

The road climbs as it goes up the side of the hill. Near the top, I spot the sign that Dad said would be there. He'd told me about it quite a while ago, hinting I should take Nikki here, though I never did. I'd much rather have Jordan here with me anyway. I turn on my blinker, and turn into a small rest area. There are no other cars here; it's just us.

"Wow," Jordan says, looking out at the city. With the sky being so dark, the city is lit up and sparkly. "This is nice."

I raise his hand to my mouth and kiss it. "*This* is nice."

"I had a really nice time," Jordan says. "I like being with you."

As cozy and as wonderful as this is, I'm still longing for something even better, like the couch in Jordan's basement. But if we want some time alone, this will do. I pull the lever and lower the back of my seat so I'm reclining a bit; Jordan does the same. I reach across and put my arm over his shoulders, then he tries to snuggle closer, both of us leaning awkwardly over the console between us. Jordan pulls out his iPhone and turns on some music, setting it down on the dash.

This is perfect. Jordan and I along with this amazing view of the glittery city and romantic music flowing around us.

"Do you like dancing? Slow dancing, I mean," Jordan says.

My brows pinch in the center. Where did this come from? "With you, Jordan, I'd do anything. Especially slow dancing. I mean, getting to hold you close, swaying our bodies to the music...it'd be romantic."

He sighs like he's imagining it—and like he likes it. It makes me smile that he would like to just hold each other on the dance floor. Then it's like ice goes through my veins when I realize where this might be leading.

"Jordan?" I ask.

"Hmm?"

"Why are you asking?"

He doesn't respond for a moment, almost like he hasn't heard my question. Then he turns a little in his seat so that he can look up at me. He's searching my eyes like he's hoping to find something there.

"No reason," he says, then turns back to looking out the window and over the city.

"You...weren't wanting to go to prom together...were you?"

He tenses slightly. I can feel the stiffening of his muscles against my arm. "No," he says. After a very long moment, he adds, "I mean, it'd be really nice if we could. But I understand that's not possible with...you know, with you not being out."

I get this weird feeling that this is more important to him than he's letting on. I need to salvage this; I can't let him be disappointed in me this early into our...our what? Our relationship?

"Since I can't take you to prom," I say, "can I take you out on another date soon? Preferably very soon?"

The tension in his muscles eases when I ask my question and some relief fills me. I've salvaged this, but I can already tell that this prom thing will be an issue that we'll have to deal with eventually. And with prom being only a few weeks away, we'll have to deal with it sooner than I want to.

"I'd like that." He settles down further into the crook of my arm, getting comfier. I like holding him like this. "I can treat this time; it shouldn't always be you. Want to go for dinner on Thursday?"

"That's so long," I say. I want to spend every single day with him. Every. Single. Day. "But you're worth the wait." I kiss him on the top of the head and he lets out a contented moan.

We sit there for a few more songs and by the second one, we're full-on making out. He's a good kisser and I hope he thinks I'm a good kisser too.

By the time Thursday rolls around, I'm still not talking to my old football buddies. I found out what their punishment was—they had to come in on spring break and help the custodians wash the floors in the entire building—and the guys are still apparently angry with me for having ruined their spring break.

They don't seem to comprehend that *they* ruined their spring break, not me. It's not like they would have gotten away with it if I hadn't confessed everything; they weren't being secretive, what with standing there, pointing, laughing, and gloating as hot dogs rained down on Jordan.

I think Devon's close to coming around, though. He had texted me last night, just with a simple "Hi", but when I responded, he didn't text back. Kieran, though, the one who gives me angry glares in math class, hasn't eased up at all. I still feel physically unsafe in math class and it's only confirming the intense need to hide what Jordan and I have.

If push comes to shove, I can take a beating from Kieran. I'd give back almost as good as he gives me, though I know he'd ultimately win. But I don't want Jordan drawn into this. It would devastate him if he knew that me getting beaten was because of me being gay and me being with him. Plus, I don't want him to see me with a bruised eye and a bloody nose; I don't want him to have that memory burned into his mind.

At lunch, I head to my now-usual table where I sit by myself. Really, I'm not totally by myself as a few other kids I don't know sit at the other end, but I'm not sitting *with* anyone. So I'm alone.

I glance across the room and see Jordan with Hannah and Kumail. Hannah and Kumail are holding hands under the table and all three of them are in an animated conversation in both spoken word and sign. I wish I could join them. I wish I could sit beside Jordan and hold his hand under the table. He could teach me sign so I could keep up with Kumail.

A roar of laughter pulls my attention behind me. The team and all the girls that cling onto my old buddies are in the middle of some laughing fit. They've probably insulted someone behind their back. Maybe I'm the butt of the joke. I wouldn't be surprised.

When I turn my attention forward again to watch Jordan some more, a body interrupts my view. I look up and see Devon.

"Hey," he says. He sits down across from me and puts down a plate of fries he bought from the cafeteria. He points at the fries. "Wanna split?"

"Uh, sure," I say. I don't really want fries, but I want things to return to normal. Well, mostly normal. I mean, it can't go completely back to how it used to be—it can never go back to that. Not if it means pretending I'm straight again.

Devon shoves the plate to the middle of the table and I take a couple and shove them in my mouth. While most of the cafeteria's food is pretty crappy, their fries are amazing.

"How you been?" Devon asks. He doesn't look at me, but he doesn't look at the guys behind me either. He just kind of stares at the table. It's that awkward talk that guys sometimes have.

"Okay," I say. "Been keeping busy."

"Haven't seen you much lately."

"Wasn't sure I was wanted."

There's a silence then. It only confirms that, no, I wasn't wanted. We both eat more fries. It's silent and awkward, but I'm also thankful to have him here.

"Why'd you bail?" he asks when we're half finished the fries.

Because I'm gay and what we were doing was homophobic? I can't say that. Because Jordan was your target and I love him? I can't say that either. Wait...love? Wow. Can't think about that now.

"Jordan's an old friend," I say, finally settling on a

reason that I can say out loud. "It didn't feel right."

Devon chews a few more fries and swallows, seeming to be deep in thought. "Okay," he says. Then he adds, "Despite what Kieran is telling everyone, you ratting us out doesn't change anything. We would've been caught soon enough. There's a camera in that hallway."

Devon is one of the more levelheaded guys. He doesn't hold grudges and he's smarter than most of the guys. An odd thought passes through my head that I should come out to Devon—tell him I'm gay—but I'm still not ready for that. But I think Devon would accept it and it wouldn't change our friendship.

"I'm having a few people over tomorrow," he says. "You should come."

I turn my head slightly, peering back at the guys at the end of the room. "Is Kieran invited?"

"No," Devon says. I didn't think he would be—Devon and Kieran don't exactly see eye to eye. "But Nikki is."

"Great," I say, not even bothering to put excitement or interest into the word. "I mean, I'm looking forward to it," I add, trying to sound more interested. I *am* interested in hanging out with Devon, it's the Nikki part that I'm not a fan of. She's nice, but she wants something from me that I can't provide.

Devon eats the last fry, then wipes his hands on a napkin and tosses it on top of the empty styrofoam plate. "I gotta go," he says. "Tomorrow at seven." He gets up and leaves. I don't think he made eye contact once during that entire talk. He's obviously a little angry, even if logic is telling him he has no reason to be.

I look across the room to Jordan and he meets my gaze. Our eyes lock temporarily and I see an expression in his eyes that I can't figure out. He's got an opinion on me talking with Devon, I bet, and he probably disapproves. I don't blame him, given what they did to him. But I can't just abandon all my old friends.

Jordan picked Sarah's, a café on the far side of the city, for our date.

"I've never been here before," I say as I pull into a parking spot.

"Neither have I," he says, "but the reviews on Facebook say they have good food at cheap prices."

I lean across the console to give him a quick kiss. "I'm looking forward to it."

The interior is quaint—wooden tables and chairs all crammed together in a tight space that's half full of people. We're seated in the corner and handed menus. I don't know how much I can eat; my stomach is fluttering with both excitement and nervousness at being on another date with Jordan. After the waitress brings us water and takes our order, Jordan takes a sip of his water and I can tell by his body language that he wants to ask me something.

"What is it?" I ask.

He looks up at me over the top of his water glass, then he puts it down. "I saw you talking with Devon at lunch," he says. I knew we'd be talking about this.

"Yeah, he was checking in. He invited me to his place tomorrow night." I try not to sound defensive. Jordan hasn't accused me of anything yet.

"Are you going to go?" he asks.

"Yeah. I was planning on it."

He looks me in the eye and I see hurt in his. "Even after that crap they pulled."

I swallow. Why can't our dating ever just go smooth and easy? "I'm going to see how it goes. If he and the others are still dicks, I don't have to stay their friends. But I *was* good friends with them until the...that crap."

His lips twitch for a moment, like he's about to say something, but changes his mind. I know he's struggling with the idea, but I hope he can see my point—I can't just cut them off, even if we ended on bad terms before spring break. I at least need to tell them our friendship is over if that's where this is all headed.

"Okay," he says. "I don't like it, but I trust you."

I reach across the table for his hand; he puts his hand in mine and I wrap my fingers around it. It's so warm and soft and comfortable. "Thank you," I say.

Slowly, a rather goofy-looking grin spreads across his face.

"What?" I ask. "What's so funny?"

"Not funny," he says, "just surprising." He squeezes the hand that's holding his. "You did *this* in public."

I look down at our hands, then toward the rest of the

people in the restaurant. No one seems to have noticed. Or if they've noticed, they don't care. In other words, the world hasn't ended now that Benjamin Cooper has done something gay in a public place.

A few moments later, our sandwiches arrive and I unfortunately have to let go of his hand. But I have every intention of holding it again once our meal is over.

We talk about the things that couples talk about—school, friends, movies, music, video games...all of it...except prom. We're still skirting around that topic. That's fine with me, though, because I'm not ready to talk about it.

When the bill comes, Jordan pays, and then we head out to the car. "Let's go to Keystone Park," Jordan says.

That was where we had our first date and we walked along that path. "Okay. It's not far from here."

The evening is starting to get dark, with just a little bit of light left in the sky. I park in the lot and we get out. Jordan leads me toward the center of a field and he lies down in the grass. I stand and look down at him, arching my eyebrow.

"The stars will be out soon," he says.

I lie down next to him and watch the sky above us. He reaches for my hand and holds it. This is my new favorite thing, holding hands in public places.

Above us, the sky darkens and the color deepens, turning almost to a deep purple before darkening fully to black. One by one, the stars start poking through the dark.

"Wow," I say. "I've never really done this before, you know, just enjoying the stars."

"When I was younger, my family used to go camping in the summer. I used to lie on the ground with my dad and watch the stars come out. He knows all the constellations and would point them out. That's the Big Dipper," he says, pointing toward a series of stars. I think I can see the shape. He points at another one, "Little Dipper. And those three stars are Orion's Belt."

"That's nice," I say. I roll over onto my front and prop myself up on my elbows. "But you know what is nicer?"

He looks at me, his eyes glistening in the near dark. "What?"

"This," I say, then I kiss him. I hook my leg over his body and straddle him, pressing my chest against his, pushing the rest of my body against his. He feels amazing under me and it's like electricity fires everywhere that our bodies touch—with most of it happening at our lips. I like kissing Jordan even more than I like holding his hand. He wraps his arms around me and puts his hands on my back, pulling me closer to him.

I moan in pleasure. I want more. I want to be closer to him.

But then his phone starts blaring.

"Sorry," he mutters. He pulls his phone out of his pocket and answers it. "Mom? Yeah, almost done. We're heading back soon. Bye." He ends the call, puts the phone on his chest, bangs his head against the ground, and groans.

"She says I'm out too late for a school night."

I laugh. "It *is* a bit late."

He gives me a mock accusatory look. "Not you too."

"I guess I'm the responsible one." I roll off him and look up at the sky again. I exhale long and slow. "We should go, but we should make plans for another date very soon."

He rolls onto his side, propping his head up under his arm. "Since you're seeing Devon on Friday, how about Saturday?"

I roll to my side, facing him, my lips so close to him. "Perfect." I kiss him, deep and hard, then stand up. "Your mom is waiting," I say with a smile and my best "responsible adult" voice.

Jordan groans.

I feel really nervous when I walk up Devon's steps—like, almost as nervous as when I told my parents I'm gay. Maybe it's because I'm leading even more of a double life now and it's eating away at me. I want to be who I am in my whole life, but I know I can't.

It only takes Devon a moment or two to open the door after I ring the bell. "Hey, man," he says, opening the door wide for me to come in.

I take off my shoes and throw my jacket on the floor near the door. "Am I the first one here?"

"Yeah, Nikki and Andrea texted to say they're late and Stuart and Robbie are stopping at McDonald's before coming over. Come on," he says, turning and leading the way to the kitchen. I follow him and find that he was in the middle of getting a bunch of snacks ready—bowls of chips and a few bottles of pop. He comes around to the other side of the kitchen island and leans over it almost conspiratorially. "Unfortunately, my folks are home—they're upstairs—otherwise we'd have slightly different drinks."

I've had alcohol a few times—I don't do well with it, unless it leads to kissing Jordan. The rest of the guys can hammer back a couple beers and they're still sober, or at least they look like they are. For me, it's like a mouthful is all it takes to make the room spin. I'm kind of glad Devon's parents are home.

We make some idle chatter as we open bags of chips and pour them into bowls. It's like we're back to how we used to be. Yesterday at lunch must have been him assessing how things are and now that he's done that, things are good.

"So what'd you do last night?" he asks as he counts red plastic cups.

"I, uh, just stayed home. Did homework." Again, I have this urge to tell Devon everything. He would understand. I know he would.

"Me too," he says. "I'm having trouble with all the dates in history, so I made up some flashcards."

"Devon," I say, my mouth moving before I can really think about what I'm going to say. "I have to tell you something."

He glances up at me, then back at the cups. "What's up, man?"

"I'm...I'm—"

The doorbell rings.

I let out a breath, both in exasperation and relief. I want to tell him, but I also don't want to. Why is this so freaking hard?

Devon hurries out of the kitchen and toward the front door. I follow him and when he opens the door, Andrea and Nikki come in. Nikki's eyes immediately find mine and she smiles in a way that seems to indicate she's genuinely happy to see me. I smile back, hoping it's convincing.

Then Andrea and Devon start kissing. When the hell did this come about?

Nikki steps around them and comes to me. She leans in for a kiss and completely out of reflex I pucker up. We're not kissing as passionately as Devon and Andrea, but then I think they're in love—or something close to it—whereas I love Jordan and I'm pretty sure Nikki secretly loves Winston. It's only because of her desire to be a social media celebrity—somehow former football captain is higher status than current basketball captain—and my stupid ongoing need to have people think I'm straight that has the two of us kissing.

She breaks the kiss and smiles again. Devon and Andrea are now tongue-wrestling.

"When did this happen?" I ask Nikki.

Her hand finds mine and we lace our fingers together.

"On spring break at Jenny's party." When she realizes that I wasn't invited to that party—in fact, I knew nothing of it until now—she kind of looks at me awkwardly and then looks away. I know I wasn't invited because the guys wanted nothing to do with me.

Whatever.

Will those two ever stop kissing?

Would I be the same if Jordan was here and we felt comfortable enough to kiss in front of other people? Would we make that much of a spectacle of ourselves? Maybe. But I wouldn't care because I'd be kissing Jordan.

The doorbell rings again and finally those two horndogs stop kissing. Devon opens the door and Stuart and Robbie come in. They exchange dude-bro handshakes with Devon and say "hey" to both Andrea and Nikki. I'm the last person they both greet and I get a subtle nod from each of them and not a single thing more.

I'm okay with that, I guess.

Devon leads us all through to the kitchen and we each grab some snacks and drinks and carry it all down into the rec room in his basement. I sit on one end of the large couch and Stuart and Robbie sit as far away from me as possible, sitting instead on the loveseat that's at a ninety-degree angle from this couch. Nikki, of course, sits beside me, with Andrea on her other side and Devon at the far end, next to the loveseat with Stuart and Robbie.

I feel so trapped. Nikki's hand is in mine again and I know the pressure from her is going to be high tonight. I still haven't asked her to prom. And the other side of the room is happy to pretend I don't exist.

As a group—well, Devon, Stuart, and Robbie—we decide to watch something on Netflix. Within a matter of minutes, some horror film I've never seen before but promises to be super gory is playing. Nikki uses this as an excuse to get even closer to me—she cuddles up against me so she can hide her face against my chest if there's a scene she can't watch. I put my arm around her—it's the right thing to do, but I also can't be a rigid cardboard cutout of myself. I need to act straight. I need to be dude-bro like the rest of the guys.

Nikki snuggles even closer and rests her hands on my thigh, very close to my crotch. That's not accidental, I know. But it makes me uncomfortable. I shift like my leg is falling asleep and just need to reposition myself—thankfully, her hands move off my thigh, though one of them does half-snuggle under my butt. That's a little better maybe?

I'm not a fan of horror movies, but I get through this one without looking away, even though it gets really bloody and gross at certain points. The acting is terrible. We all mock the actors throughout the movie and this seems to ease up the group a bit—Stuart and Robbie don't seem quite so hostile to me, even though they're not exactly welcoming.

Afterward, Devon throws on MTV and there's some stupid reality show playing, but no one is watching. Devon and the guys are talking sports, Andrea and Nikki are gossiping about something or other, and I'm sitting here, fiddling with my phone, wishing I could text Jordan without someone looking over my shoulder.

Nikki's hand is suddenly on my thigh again, cupping the muscles there, her fingertips far too close to my crotch for comfort. "Benny," she says, again using that nickname I hate and I've asked her so many times not to call me, "you still haven't asked me to prom." She pouts like a wounded puppy.

"Oh, right…" I say. What else can I say?

I instantly feel so stressed and conflicted. I want to go with Jordan—but I can't. Nikki wants so desperately to go with me and I know Jordan wouldn't like it—but it's not like we'd have sex or anything, and I'm sure Jordan would come around eventually to understand that my cover as a straight guy requires this. But that's a crappy excuse. Even I can see that. But if I *don't* ask Nikki—if I don't ask any girls at all—then it would be a big scandal and there'd be so much gossiping and rumors and inevitably people would start to wonder if I'm gay or something, because weirdly that's people's first assumption.

"If you're going to ask me," she says, still pouting, "I need to know soon so we can coordinate outfits. I already have my dress, but you would have to have a matching bowtie and order me a corsage that goes with the dress."

Andrea leans over and injects herself into the conversation. "You two would be so cute together," she squeals. "You'll be prom king and queen for sure!"

Nikki's pout disappears and it's replaced with

something akin to disgust. "It's prom *prince* and *princess* this year, apparently. It's that awful fairy tale theme."

Though I'm not friends with Jordan's friend Hannah, I feel like I need to defend her. She's my boyfriend's best friend. Wait, boyfriend?

"I think it's a great theme," I say.

Instantly, Nikki changes her reaction. She's like a goddamn chameleon. "We can make it work—we can make it *magical*."

"See," Andrea says, "it'll be a night you'll always remember."

Nikki turns back to Andrea. "Oh my God, I could have my dress altered to look like a princess—with a tiara, of course!"

"And Ben could have a princely tux with long coattails," Andrea says, catching on to Nikki's newfound enthusiasm.

From there, their words come a mile a minute and I'm feeling very overwhelmed. The two of them are making plans upon plans upon plans, all of which involve me in more and more elaborate tuxedos that sound more like outright costumes. And all I can think of is that if I *do* take Nikki to prom, Jordan will be furious with me, but if I *don't* take Nikki to prom, all sorts of hell will be unleashed on me.

The biggest problem, though, with turning Nikki down and not asking her to prom is that we'll be the gossip of the whole school and it wouldn't take long for everyone to start wondering if I'm gay. And I can't have that. I just can't.

I know I was about to tell Devon before the girls came

over, but any resolve I thought I had is now long gone. Any thought I had of stepping a toe outside the closet is now so long dead and gone and I'm so deep in the closet right now that I can't even see the light under the door.

"It's settled," Nikki says, turning to me again. She puts her hands on my upper thigh, her fingertips touching me in a place I only want Jordan to touch. "I'll get daddy to pay for modifications to my dress and buy some sparkly jewelry, and you'll wear a retro tux with long coattails and a ruffled shirt and your bowtie has to match my dress color—I'll help you pick it out." She hugs me and kisses my cheek. "I'm so excited!" she squeals.

When did I say I was taking her?

My heart is racing so hard and fast in my chest that I don't think I could summon the strength or will to tell her I'm not taking her—that I don't *want* to take her. Because if I turn her down…what the hell will she do? Hell, she might even start the "he's gay" rumor herself.

NYU. I can be gay at NYU. I need to be straight at Charlesburgh High.

"You can get our tickets on Monday," she says, "okay?"

"O-o-okay," I say. It's a struggle to get that one, short word out. And with it, I feel like I've killed whatever I have with Jordan. Whatever it was going to evolve into, all of that is gone now.

But I can't tell him now. I need to ease him into it. Maybe I can still salvage this.

I just have to be careful.

Right now, though, I feel like passing out. My head is swimming and my heart is still racing and my whole body is shaking.

Nikki lets go of me and immediately turns around to make even more plans for my outfit with Andrea. I glance over at the guys and they're happily in the midst of some conversation and ignoring us. I kind of curl up into a ball in the corner of the couch. I pull out my phone—I can't text Jordan, not now, but having it in my hand is like having a piece of him with me. I clutch my phone to my chest, like it will somehow magically make all of this go away and let me just be with Jordan.

Chapter Fifteen

Jordan

EVER SINCE BEN GOT back together with some of his buddies, it's like I've only had *part* of him with me. When we go out on our dates or just hang out at each other's place, he's there *physically*, but it's like the rest of him is gone off somewhere else.

When I walk into the cafeteria on Monday at lunch, my heart breaks a little. Ben is sitting with his posse of football players and their hangers-on. I slow my pace when I spot him, but I don't stop walking because I don't want to draw the attention of his "friends". But I make eye contact with Ben and his eyes seem to apologize to me.

Like that makes any of this better.

But I had hung out with Ben last night and we kissed a lot and cuddled on the couch. If he's back with his friends, he's not quite back to how he used to be. I have to hold onto that—the knowledge that Ben might be back with the guys, but he's not back to how he used to be. Benjamin is still mine. Benjamin is still gay.

I stroll past them, doing my best not to look at Ben again, nor to look at anyone else and draw their attention. They've mostly left me alone since coming back from spring break, but I see the dirty looks they send me sometimes. It was entirely their own fault for getting in trouble over that stupid hot dog prank, but of course they blame both me and Ben. Though it looks like they've forgiven Ben.

I sit down at my table and say hi to both Hannah and Kumail. Digging my lunch out of my backpack, I open my sandwich and start eating, not really tasting anything and not even really aware of anything.

I'm torn by this two-sided nature to Ben. When we're not at school, we cuddle and kiss and have such a wonderful time together. But when we're here, it's like he's still straight. He's leading a double life because he's closeted—and it means I lead a double life too. I'm happy and overjoyed when I'm with Ben and when I'm at school I have to pretend that nothing special is going on in my life.

I'm jolted out of my headspace when I feel a tap on my forearm. I focus my eyes and my attention and see Kumail looking at me.

You okay? he signs.

It takes a moment for that to all sink in, for my mind to process what he's asking. Both him and Hannah are looking at me with concern on their faces.

I put down my sandwich. "Yeah, I'm fine. Don't worry about it," I say and sign. I glance over my shoulder at Ben—while he's with his gang, he doesn't look like he's having a good time. It makes me wonder if he's as unhappy with his double life as I am.

And what's with the change in personality since he hung out with Devon on Friday? Yeah, we cuddled and kissed on the couch last night, but it wasn't quite the same as what it was before. It was like he was holding back somehow...like he wasn't completely with me.

I mean, it could've just been a bad day and he didn't want to talk about it, but the paranoid side of me is terrified that there's something bigger going on, like he's self-questioning his decision to come out and date a guy. I don't want to lose him.

When I turn back to the table, Hannah and Kumail are still looking at me.

Out with it, Hannah says, deciding to only sign and not speak the words out loud. I realize that this is because she knows I might say something confidential and, as far as we know, we're the only three people in the cafeteria that know sign. We can talk about anything we want and no one can eavesdrop.

I sit back in my chair and tap my fingers on the table. I don't want to tell anyone about Benjamin, out of respect for his privacy, but at the same time, bottling all of this up inside is hard. While I can talk to mom about some things and she knows about Benjamin, I don't really want to bring my dating problems to her.

My non-existent boyfriend, I sign, referring to back when I denied I was head over heels for someone, *isn't so non-existent.*

Hannah's face lights up and she claps frantically, a habit I've always found endearing when she's excited about something. Kumail grins widely.

Who is he? Hannah demands.

Sorry. Confidential. I take a moment to breathe and think. How much do I want to say? *We've been dating a few weeks, but this has been a while in the making.*

You should bring him to prom!

No, I say, adding extra emphasis to my hand motion. *He's not out. It's secret.* I feel my smile falter—my fake smile—and Kumail seems to catch on quicker than Hannah.

What's wrong? he asks.

I want to turn around and look at Ben again, but I know I can't. *I don't know,* I say. *Maybe I'm just being paranoid and things are fine.*

Do you want to talk about it? Kumail asks. Though we've been friends now for several months, I'm still touched that he makes such an offer.

I sigh. *No...I don't think so.*

Hannah looks disappointed, but thankfully she doesn't press for details. From there, our conversation returns inevitably toward senior prom. Hannah and Kumail are discussing some last-minute details about decorations and set-up. With it only being two weeks away now, the pressure is on.

And I still don't know who I'm going with.

I don't even know *if* I'm going.

I want to go with Ben—more than anything—but I know that's not possible. I wonder what Ben's plans are?

Come with us, Hannah says.

Huh?

To prom, she says. They must have been talking about the very thing I was thinking about. *If your non-existent boyfriend won't take you...come with us.* She smiles and looks hopeful.

While I know Hannah would be okay with it and she genuinely wants me there, I glance at Kumail to get his take. I don't want to intrude on their special night. But he seems just as keen as Hannah does to have me along.

Are you sure? I ask. *I don't want to be a third wheel.*

Yes, we're sure! Hannah says.

We'll be busy most of the night anyway and could use your help, Kumail says. Then he gives Hannah a rather thirsty look. *Though I might steal her away for a little bit.*

Hannah blushes, but I know she likes the thought. I get a little pang in my heart—I want Benjamin to steal me away at prom for a few minutes of private, sexy fun.

But, seriously, you should come with us, Hannah says, signing fast to, I assume, hide her blush and embarrassment.

I think of Benjamin once more. What are the chances

that he'll ask me? Pretty non-existent, I'd think. *Okay,* I say. *Thank you.*

Now to tell Benjamin. Actually, he might like this idea because it takes the pressure off him to ask me.

After school, I head straight home. Mr. Empaces had given us far too much homework and I want to get started on it right away. I have to read a chapter of *Great Expectations* and write a personal reflection essay on the chapter. With all the time I've been spending with Ben lately, I've fallen behind in our novel study—I've been able to keep up when needed, but tonight's homework will require not only reading the chapter, but also the three chapters before it that I didn't get around to reading.

Some time later, after finishing a chapter, I notice a text on my phone.

BENJAMIN: You stuck with that chapter paper too?

JORDAN: Yeah—gonna be busy all night. Sorry I can't hang out with you...unless you want to do our homework together?

BENJAMIN: I think if we do our homework together, we'll just end up making out and not get anything done ;)

JORDAN: LOL Yeah that's a risk

JORDAN: Ben...I need to tell you something...

BENJAMIN: Yeah?

I glance out the window and across the space between our houses. He's on his bed, looking at me. He's got a worried expression on his face.

JORDAN: If you're not going to take me to prom, I'm

going with Hannah and Kumail...you okay with that?

I glance at Ben again and he looks a little relieved. However, he still looks like he's holding something back. Part of me wonders if that's just me being suspicious, like I'm looking for something to be wrong when there's actually nothing wrong.

BENJAMIN: That's okay. Thank you

I'm a little hurt that he doesn't seem upset about it, like, he doesn't even say, "I wish I could take you". He just says "okay". I try not to let my frustration show on my face because I know he's probably looking at me.

JORDAN: I really need to get back to this

BENJAMIN: Me too

BENJAMIN: Text me when you're done—if it's not too late, I'd love to see you again

JORDAN: :)

As the week progresses, I've become more and more okay with our prom arrangement. We're both going and we'll both have fun—me with Hannah and Kumail and Ben with...his buddies, I assume. He still hasn't told me his plans. Maybe he doesn't have any yet?

He still hangs out with his friends in the cafeteria at lunch. He's told me that things are starting to get better with him and the guys, though he still worries about Kieran. Apparently, he holds a grudge for a long time.

Twice I've seen Nikki hanging on his arm. He swears up and down that there's nothing going on and he's not encouraging it—she just does it. While it makes me angry to see her getting so close to him, I don't doubt that she's pushing herself on him. I know what she's like. She's the boss bitch back when we were in cheer practice—she always got her way, to the point where the cheer coach gave up and walked away.

I wish this was all just over. I want the school year to be over so that we don't have to deal with this bullshit of him appearing straight all day and me denying the existence of my happiness. I want us to both be at NYU already, free from all of his friends who think of him as straight, so we can just *be*. We can be closer, we can be more open, we don't have to worry about who might see us or what people might say. It'll be amazing!

For now, though, I just have to content myself with our dates. At least with these dates, I get to see the real Ben— the romantic, fun, and spontaneous Ben. The Ben that always tries hard to make me smile. The Ben who has a cute butt.

And I'm staring at that cute butt right now.

For tonight's date, we drove across the city to the Magic Puttz mini-golf complex. We're halfway through the game and I'm *absolutely destroying* my athlete boyfriend at this game. That's an unexpected turn of events. I think it's because football is a game of strength and with mini-golf, you have to be gentle. He's consistently over-hitting the balls—either sending them way past the hole or, far too often, hitting the edge of the course and bouncing out of bounds.

I try not to laugh too hard when this happens. He's a good sport, but he's getting frustrated with his consistent lack of luck. He's been over par on every hole, sometimes as much as double of par, whereas I've been at par or lower on all of them and I even have two hole-in-ones.

He lines up his shot—being less than a foot from the hole, most people could make this, but I suspect Ben will overdo it. He swings the club back, then hits the ball—and, yeah, he hits it way too hard. I try not to burst out laughing as it *almost* goes into the hole, but instead the momentum carries it around the rim of the hole and then shoots away, rolling until it hits the little barrier around the putting green. It's now more than a yard away.

Ben looks like he's about to swear, but when he sees me barely containing my laughter, he lightens up. He sticks his tongue out at me and goes to the ball to line up another shot. I've already sunk my ball quite a while ago, so it's just him struggling to keep up. He carefully lines up the shot again, swings, hits the ball—and this time it goes much nicer, though for a moment I suspect he hasn't hit hard enough, as it's slowing down before reaching the hole. It almost stops right on the edge, but then does a little wobble and drops in with a satisfying clatter of the golf ball against the hard plastic lining of the hole.

"So…twelve," I say, writing down his score. I had sunk my ball in four strokes.

Ben bends down to pick his ball up and I sneak a glance at his butt. "You know our bet," he says with a gloating tone to his voice. Once it was clear who was going to win and who was going to lose, Ben decided that the loser gets to demand something from the winner as a sort of sympathy prize for losing. He's already told me about what he wants to do to me when we get back into the relative privacy of the car.

"Oh, I haven't forgotten," I say, almost trembling with anticipation. It isn't sex that he wants—and, honestly, I don't know if I'm ready for that yet—but it's something almost as good. He wants a hot and heavy make out session with him on top of me, basically pinning me down.

Our make outs over the last couple weeks have gotten more intense and I feel like sex is going to come up eventually, but until then, I'm just enjoying these more *enthusiastic* kissing sessions.

After a few more holes, we finish our game. He has more than double my score, making me the clear and easy winner.

"When do you…want your prize?" I ask, voice husky.

His nostrils and eyelids flare with desire, but then a tease seems to come over him. "Later," he says. And I swear he's about to kiss me right then and there. But then he looks past me. "Milkshake?"

"Uh…what?" I ask. I'm so lost in the idea of having him on top of me that the word "milkshake" just sounds like nonsense to me.

"Do you want to split a milkshake?" he asks, with an evil grin. He knows exactly what he's doing to me and my desires and he knows exactly the effect his teasing is having on me.

It's moments like this that I can *almost* forget everything that's changed since he got back in with his friends. *Almost.*

"Come on," he says. He grabs my hand and pulls me toward the concession stand. Magic Puttz is in a large year-round golf complex with a tee-off range on one side, the mini-golf course on the other, and a small concession stand with tables and chairs in the middle.

I follow dutifully while being totally enamored by the fact that he's again holding my hand in public. He orders us a large chocolate milkshake and we take a table while we wait for it. The table and chairs are basically plastic patio furniture. It's not the most romantic of places, but I'm here with Benjamin and it's a date, so I love it.

He reaches across the table and holds both my hands in both of his. This is a step beyond holding my hand while we're walking—this is more romantic and also more obvious to those around us. The fact that Ben is comfortable doing this both amazes and pleases me.

A few moments later, the server comes by with our milkshake and puts it on the table with two straws. She has a funny grin on her face, like she thinks we're a cute couple or something. I hope that's what she thinks. I like that other people think that about us.

Ben puts our straws in the milkshake and then puts the drink between us. Like we're in an *Archie* comic book, we both drink from the milkshake, staring into each other's eyes.

"It's good," he says.

I smile. "It's better with you." It's a cheesy line, I know, but just being here with Ben really does seem to make this the best milkshake ever.

He reaches across the table and swipes his thumb across my bottom lip, scooping up a little bit of milkshake, then he puts that thumb in his mouth. Oh, God, I want him so bad.

I reach across the table to take his hand and when our hands make contact, there's just the slightest and briefest flickers of discomfort on his face. However, I know it's not the discomfort of doing something gay in a public place—I know *that* look. This is something different—something that's only come about since he hung out with his friends last Friday.

"Benjamin," I say, before I can back down from what's on my mind. "What's wrong? You haven't been the same since your Friday night hangout."

There's a conflicted look that passes over his face, like he's trying to decide if he wants to tell me the truth. Then there's a hardening of his features and I know I'm going to get a lie. I now recognize that as the same hardened face he gave me when he was ignoring me before Christmas—he's not ignoring me now, of course, but there's a similar thought process going on in that head of his. Maybe it's the belief that if he doesn't acknowledge the existence of something, then it's not true, so he doesn't have to worry about it.

"Nothing's wrong," he says. "I think I've just been tired lately."

I take another sip of the milkshake. I don't particularly want a mouthful of it right now, but by taking the drink, it's giving me a moment where I can't speak without thinking. When I swallow it down, I say, "So what did you guys talk about on Friday? What'd you do?" I hate being the nosy boyfriend—I trust Ben, or at least I should—but if he's not going to tell me something that he most certainly should, then I'm going to have to get it out of him somehow.

"Nothing much, really, we just watched a scary movie and then shot the shit after. Had a few snacks, then headed home." He talks quick and his words are clipped. There's something he doesn't want to tell me. I don't think he'd outright lie to me, though, so I know if I keep pushing and if I ask the right question, I'll hit on what's troubling my man.

"So it was you and Devon and…?"

"Stuart and Robbie," he says, then he looks away from me. That's a guilty look if I ever saw one. When he glances back at me, I hold his gaze. I don't say anything, waiting instead for him to supply the information I'm pressing him for. He cringes for a moment, then says, "Andrea and, uh, Nikki were there too."

I feel like ice is suddenly coursing through my veins. He

hung out with Nikki and didn't tell me. I know Ben wouldn't initiate anything romantic or sexual between them—but I certainly didn't trust Nikki to behave. And if she tried to do something, Ben would feel obligated to let it happen in order to preserve his precious heterosexuality, especially if his straight football buddies were in the room.

Goddamnit.

I'm seething with anger, but trying to contain it. I think I'm failing, though.

"Sorry," Ben says, looking at the table between us. He sounds like he's genuinely sorry, but is he sorry for not telling me he spent time with Nikki or is he actually sorry for whatever happened between him and Nikki? Like, is he actually sorry or is he sorry he got caught?

"What happened?" I ask. He starts to stutter out a reply, but I interrupt and say, "Tell me everything. I need to know."

He cringes again and is still staring at the table. "Nothing, really. We watched a movie. She was beside me on the couch and might have hid her face against my chest during the gory parts. But that's it. She spent most of the night talking with Andrea and I just sat there wishing I wasn't there."

The hardest part about that story is that it's entirely believable. Nikki doesn't really love him, at least I'm pretty sure she doesn't. She just wants to be seen with him—especially on social media—but she really has no genuine interest in him that I've been able to see. And I know that

Ben doesn't have feelings for her either. Should I really be jealous of this thing that's *totally not* happening between them?

"Did you know she was going to be there?" Somehow, this is important to me.

"No. Devon just told me he'd invited over some of the guys. He didn't mention Nikki at all." He finally looks up at me and for a moment I feel like he's giving me the full and unvarnished truth. But that still has me worried that the things he said before looking up at me were not entirely true.

I hate that I feel this way. I hate that he's *making* me feel like this.

"And you swear nothing happened between the two of you?"

He glances at the table when he says, "I swear."

That bastard is keeping something from me, something he knows I will hate hearing.

I want to demand that he tell me everything, but I can see in his eyes that a door has slammed shut, a wall has been put up, or whatever the hell metaphor you want to use. If I push him now, it'll go nowhere. What is it dad always says? Angry arguing never works. It's not until right now that I really understood that saying of his—I know that if I just get angrier and demand answers right now, it'll drive a wedge between us. But if I wait until tomorrow and we've both calmed down, maybe he'll tell me more—and maybe we can sort this out.

"I want to go home," I say. If I don't want to argue while I'm angry, then I can't be on a date anymore with him tonight.

"Fine," he says. He gets up and puts the half-drunk milkshake on the order counter and I follow him toward the exit.

Between the main indoor golfing area and café, there's a narrow hallway that bypasses some offices and banquet rooms, with the exit on the other end, just around a corner. As we near the exit, we suddenly hear some very recognizable and very loud voices joking around with each other as they enter the building.

Some of Ben's football friends are here.

Shit.

I'm frozen in fear, rooted in place. I need to run and hide, but I can't.

Ben's head is clearer. He pushes me to a door beside us—the men's room—and we wait in there, holding our breaths, hoping beyond hope that they don't come in here. All they have to do is walk past us and go to the golf area or the café—then they'll be out of sight and we can make our escape.

"Yo, man," one of them says, just outside the door, "I gotta take a piss. I'll catch up."

My eyes shoot wide and my pulse quadruples. Ben shoves me to the side and I clatter into a stall. Right as I hear the door open, I lock the stall door and sit down, pretending I'm just a guy taking a crap.

"Ben?" the guy says.

"Oh, hey, Devon," Ben says. He sounds so calm and cool, like he wasn't almost just caught on a secret gay date.

He's the closeted one, not me, yet I'm the one that's petrified with fear. I don't think I'm breathing. Why am I not breathing? In. Out. In. Out. In. Out.

"What are you doing here?" Devon asks. His footsteps go around the corner of the stall I'm in, to the urinal on the other side of the wall. I stare at his feet in wide-eyed fear.

"Just played some mini-golf with my cousins. They just left, I'm heading out too," Ben says. Does he even have cousins? I suddenly feel bad that I don't even know that about him.

A moment later, Devon flushes the urinal and goes to wash his hands. "I hope you had a good time on Friday night," he says.

"Yeah, for sure," Ben says. "It was great to see you and the guys again."

"Nikki was glad to see you too," Devon says with an exaggerated suggestion in his voice.

"It was nice to see her too," Ben says. His voice is quieter now, though, like he knows I'm listening and he knows I don't want to hear this.

"She says she hasn't seen much of you lately. Like, you used to hang out on weekends or something, but now you're always too busy."

"Yeah," Ben says. Devon and I seem to both be waiting for Ben to say more, but he doesn't.

"Well...she's certainly over the moon that you asked her to prom. It's all that her and Andrea talk about."

Ben...asked Nikki...to prom?

That's what he was keeping from me.

Suddenly, it's like I can't breathe. But it's not the same "can't breathe" that I felt when we were almost caught. This is different. This is the "can't breathe" because I just found out my boyfriend has a date with someone else. This is the "can't breathe" of my heart breaking.

"Yeah," Ben says, sounding almost like he's at a funeral.

"You okay, man?" Devon says.

Ben clears his throat. "Look, Devon, I'm just tired, okay?"

Ben asked Nikki to prom. The most important and most romantic event of high school and my boyfriend is taking someone else. I mean...I guess I knew he couldn't take me, not if he's not ready to come out, but Hannah's stupid fairy tale thing had me secretly hoping that Ben would somehow make it happen, that he would be my Prince Charming.

I'm an idiot. I'm a complete moron. I'm so incredibly stupid for thinking that I get that happy ending that Hannah won't ever shut up about.

"Whatever, man," Devon says. A moment later, the door clatters as he leaves.

I watch under the stall door as Ben's feet come closer. He stands just outside the stall; the door clatters as he thumps his head against it.

"Jordan," Ben says, whispering.

I can't even form words. I can barely breathe. Ben took my heart and ripped it in half and then stomped on it.

"Jordan, please talk to me," Ben says.

I take in a deep, shuddering breath. "Go to hell."

"Jordan…" he pleads. I can hear shakiness in his voice too. I hope it fucking hurts.

"When were you going to tell me?"

"Jordan…please open the door."

"When were you going to tell me?" I demand again, my voice stronger and louder.

Ben doesn't have an answer for me. All I get from him is silence.

"That's what I thought," I say. I'm so disgusted with him right now.

"Jordan…I'm sorry."

"Go," I say. "Go away." He starts to say something, but I interrupt him. "Go home. Leave. I'll find my own way home."

"Jordan…*please*…" he begs. His voice is even shakier now.

"I said *go!*"

He stands there for a very long moment—far too long—and then sadly shuffles away. When the door clatters as he leaves, that's when the first tears fall. I try to hold back my sobs, but it takes a few moments for me to rein it in. I pull out my phone and ignore the apology texts I already have from Ben and instead send a message to Hannah.

JORDAN: I need you to pick me up. I'm at Magic Puttz

HANNAH: Uh…I'm on a date

JORDAN: Please. I need you. I told my boyfriend—ex-boyfriend—to f off

JORDAN: I'm stuck here

HANNAH: OMG

HANNAH: Kumail and I are on the way

JORDAN: Text me when you're here. I'm hiding in the bathroom

I try to make myself presentable—or at least a little less miserable looking—and then duck out of the bathroom. Thankfully, no one is in the hallway. I hurry out the door and to the back seat of the waiting car.

Hannah turns around in her seat. "Jordan, honey, what happened?" She doesn't sign for Kumail, but he's staring at her lips, likely reading enough of her words to know what she's asking.

"Not now," I say, also not bothering to sign. I don't have the energy.

"Jordan—"

"I said not now! Take me home! Please." I cross my arms over my chest and try to sink into the seat. I stare out the window, away from them. I love them and I'll thank them later for rescuing me, but right now I just want to go home without anyone talking to me.

Thankfully, she can take a hint. She starts up the car,

signs something or other to Kumail, and then pulls out of the parking lot.

But Hannah being Hannah, she can't keep her questions to herself. Halfway home, she starts talking to me again. I sigh and try to bury my hurt and anger, to bottle it all up.

"Jordan…what happened?"

I'm grateful that she doesn't look at me over her shoulder and that Kumail doesn't turn around to read my lips or hope that I'll sign. I don't want anyone looking at me. She'll fill Kumail in later, no doubt.

"He's taking someone else to prom," I say. Then I give her a very terse and edited version of what's been happening, leaving out all references that could tie the story to either Ben or Nikki. "I knew this might happen, that he might decide he has to still look straight and take a girl. But I guess part of me was hoping he'd be brave and take me."

"Jordan, honey, I'm so sorry." After a moment's silence, she adds, "Maybe he'll come around. Maybe you'll still get your fairy tale ending."

"No," I say, rejecting that idea before it has a chance to grow roots.

"But it could happen," she says, determined to make her point. "He could ditch her and still take you."

"No," I say again. "It won't happen. It doesn't happen for guys like me."

"Nonsense," she says, still set on whatever fantasy she's got playing out in her head. "He'll come around and he'll sweep you off your feet. I *know* it."

"No, Hannah!" I say, nearly shouting at her. "No, it doesn't happen for guys like me!"

"What do you mean guys like you?" she shouts back at me.

"Gay guys, okay? Gay. Us gay guys don't get happy endings. Life isn't some stupid fairy tale, okay? I don't get a Prince Charming. I don't get any of it. Life isn't fair—it's just not fair." Tears are streaming down my face and I'm shouting at my best friend and I don't know what's happening. I just want this day to end. I want to go to sleep and pretend that none of this happened, that I can just rewind the clock to before Friday and I can beg Ben to not go to Devon's house.

But that doesn't work either. I can't undo what's happened.

I just want to dig a hole and hide in it until school is over.

There's tense silence in the car now. Hannah is focused on driving so hard that it's like I'm not even in the car. And Kumail is rigid in his seat and staring straight ahead—though he couldn't hear it, I'm sure he felt the angry energy around us, saw how furious we were.

Silently, without a word, Hannah pulls up to my house. I get out, slam the door, and run into my house and up to my room, ignoring my parents. I slam the door and quickly yank my curtains closed, then collapse on the bed, burying my face in the pillows.

Chapter Sixteen

Benjamin

I CAN'T GO HOME. Not yet.

Going home means going to my room—and seeing Jordan's room from my window—and I'm not ready for that.

When I get in my car, I consider just waiting there. Jordan has to come out eventually. If I could just talk to him—apologize again, explain how I got forced into asking Nikki, explain how I can't go with him even though I want so badly to do so…but I know it's not a good idea. I know that will get us nowhere.

He's too mad at me—and he has every right to be, I know that.

I screwed up. I screwed up royally.

I watch the door to the golf center, hoping beyond hope that he'll come wandering out of it, looking for me, willing to give me a second chance.

"No," I tell myself out loud. "No, I should go." Jordan doesn't want to see me.

I turn the key and start up the car. I glare at the doors once more, still hoping that magic happens and Jordan comes out and we make up and I take him home and we're happy again. But even the most hopeful part of me knows that won't happen. I'll be lucky if I ever get him back.

I shift into drive and stomp on the gas, peeling out of the parking lot with a spray of gravel behind me. I don't even know where I'm going, I just let the road and the car take me wherever they decide to take me. Before long, I find myself on a road rising along a hill.

It's the lookout point where we made out.

I turn on my signal and cross the road and into the little parking lot that has that spectacular view over the city. It looks as bright and sparkly as last time, but without Jordan by my side, it's meaningless. I turn off the car and let the silence settle over me.

What the hell do I do now?

My heart feels like someone's stomped on it—and the longer I sit here, the worse the feeling gets. It feels like someone is sitting on my chest—it feels heavy. I'm having trouble breathing. I force myself to take a deep breath and let it out slowly. Everything hurts.

I realize here and now that I love Jordan. Like, with all my heart. I think I've known all along that I love him, but I've been too scared to admit the full truth to myself. But now that I've lost him—maybe forever—I realize how much he means to me.

I have to win him back. Somehow, I have to get him back.

But this determination to win back the man I love does nothing to ease the crushing weight on my chest or the feeling that I've been shattered into a million little pieces and I can't put myself back together.

I start the car up again—I need to go home, even if it's just so I can hide in my bed until all of this hurt is gone. As I pull back onto the street, tears gather in my eyes and the road is blurry. I swipe those tears away—crying will get me nowhere.

I clench my jaw so tight that it feels like my teeth might crack, but it gives me the strength and resolve to make it home without crying. God, I've never cried as much as I have this past year.

I get in the house, close the door, ignore mom's questions about how the date went, and climb the stairs to my room. The first thing I see is my window—and Jordan's window...with the blinds drawn. He hadn't really closed them in weeks, only shutting them when he went to bed, so that we could always look over at each other. But with it being only eight in the evening and his curtains closed, it's very clearly an intentional sign. He doesn't want to see me.

I close my blinds too. Staring at his will only make me feel worse.

Sitting down in my chair, I feel like I'm stunned, like I

don't know what to do or say or anything. My mind goes numb and I just sit there and breathe and try to think about anything but Jordan telling me to go away. It takes me a while to even realize that I'm sitting in the dark, staring at the wall.

Some time later—it could be minutes or it could be hours, I don't know—I hear footsteps behind me as someone comes into my room.

"Ben?" mom says. "What happened?"

It takes me a long time to even think of the answer, and then even longer for my mouth to form the words. "I screwed up."

Her hand is suddenly resting on the top of my head and then a moment later she hugs me from behind. It's nice, but it's not the hug I want most. It's not Jordan.

After the hug, she retreats from the room and I hear my door click as she pulls it shut.

And I just sit there, letting time pass by, numb to it all.

For once, my parents let me pretend to be sick and stay home. Maybe they've suffered heartbreak before. Maybe they've screwed up as badly as I have. Maybe they understand.

I still haven't told them the epic depths of my failure. They don't yet know that Jordan broke up with me because I'm taking Nikki to prom.

Nikki. She doesn't deserve this.

As much as her quest for social media stardom irks me,

and as convenient as it is for me to go to prom with a girl, this isn't right. Especially if what I suspect is true—that her and Winston are a secret item.

I wonder if Winston knows that Nikki is going to prom with me. I wonder if he's dumping her because of it.

I pass all of Friday with these same thoughts swirling in my head—Jordan, Nikki, Winston, and my overwhelming cowardice. I want Jordan back, but I don't know how to do it—and I don't know if he wants me back. If he's moved on, or determined to do so, then it might be that no amount of work on my part will get us anywhere.

Somehow, as I'm mired in all of these thoughts, the entire weekend passes and I find myself back at school on Monday morning. I manage to get to school without seeing Jordan and navigate the hallways without running into him. But then it's math class and our damn assigned seats.

I stare down at my desk when I see him come in. I want to look up at him and his gorgeous eyes, but I can't stand to see the anger, hurt, or hatred that might be there. My chair jostles as he sits at his desk and it bumps into mine. It's like that wall is between us again. We're only inches apart, but at the same time there's the Grand Canyon between us.

I happen to glance to my right and I find Kieran *still* glowering at me. He looks less rage-filled and serial-killer-like than right after spring break, but it still looks like he wants to rip me to pieces. He's been skipping the lunch hangouts with the guys; obviously it's because he hates my guts.

Join the club.

I dutifully copy down the notes and do an attempt at a few questions, but know it's hopeless. My brain is mush right now.

When the bell rings, I stay seated and staring at my desk while everyone else—including Jordan—gets up and leaves. When he's out of the room, I start packing my bag. When I do up the zipper, I sense someone staring at me. I look up and see Kieran.

He glances to the corner of the room where I know Ms. Barnes is at her desk, then says, "I gotta ask, man, why'd you turn on us?" There's some menace in his voice, but not nearly as much as I expect, despite the anger clearly written on his face.

"It...it wasn't right. Jordan is special to me," I say. My words are quiet and pitiful, like a weak whisper.

"*Special?*" he says, stressing the word. He eyes me up and down, like he wants to ask if I'm a fag and then offer me a beat-down. But then that starts to evaporate and he looks a little more like his normal still-slightly-pissed-off self. "Huh."

"I'm sorry," I say, and slip my pack onto my shoulder.

"We woulda been fucking caught anyway," he says with a laugh.

"Kieran," Ms. Barnes says from the corner of the room, "language."

He jerks his head toward the door and I head out into the hallway with him. "I also gotta ask about the punch.

You stood there and he was gonna clock ya."

"I deserved it," I say. "Even though I abandoned you guys halfway through, I was a part of it. I helped hurt him, it was only right that he hurt me."

Kieran looks me up and down again. He thinks I'm gay, I'm sure of it. He's figured it out. I'm not exactly being as discreet as I used to be, not as protective and obsessively straight. How many straight bros describe a guy, especially a gay guy, as being "special" to them?

He suddenly holds out his hand between us. I stare at it for a long moment before I realize he wants to shake hands. I put my hand in his, squeeze, pump, and let go.

"Truce," he says. "But if there's a next time, I won't let you off so easy."

"Deal," I say.

He turns and walks away, melting into the frantic rush of fellow students as they hurry to the cafeteria or whatever other lunch plans they have.

Did I…just come out to Kieran?

Each day gets a little better and a little easier—with the very obvious exception of math class—and every day my heart hurts a little less. I'm eating full meals again and I'm doing my homework—except for math, where I'm still hopelessly lost because all I can think about during class is how Jordan is right behind me and how much I want to pull him aside, apologize, and kiss him.

I still dream about his kisses. I fantasize about holding him again.

And every time I peek out my window, his curtains are still closed.

It's now Friday afternoon and it's just over a week to prom. I know Jordan won't talk to me and I might have lost him forever, but I still have to do right by him. Even if we never get together again and I'll forever feel like I've lost something special, I need to show him that I can do the right thing.

So, halfway through lunch, I leave the guys in the cafeteria and go in search of someone I need to talk to.

While the football team likes to hang out in the cafeteria, claiming a giant table as our domain, the basketball team is usually playing pick-up in the gym, despite their season already being over. Sure enough, as I approach the gym, I hear the repetitive bouncing of balls against the hardwood floor.

As I approach the door and grab the handle, my heart is thudding in my chest. My palms are sweaty. I ask myself again why I feel the need to come out to Winston.

Before I can talk myself out of it, I open the door and slip in. There are half a dozen guys on the court, running around and passing the ball. Winston, tall, athletic, and with a mop of curly, red hair, ducks past some guy who's name I don't know and launches toward the basket. Man, that guy can jump! He *almost* touches the rim of the basket as he drops the ball in.

The ball bounces away as Winston high-fives everyone—both those on his team and those who aren't. Then he sees me and his smile disappears. I wave at him like I want to talk to him. The other guys look over at me, then back at Winston. He says something to them that I can't hear, then he jogs across the gym toward me.

"Hey," he says.

"Can we talk?"

He eyes me up and down, just like Kieran did on Monday. "Guys, I'll be right back. Don't let them score any points." Then he steps past me and pushes through the door and into the hallway.

I follow him. The hallway is empty—it's just Winston and me.

"What do you want?" he asks. He paces around like a caged animal, one hand on his hip and the other behind his neck. The last thing he wants to do is talk to me, the guy who's taking his girl to prom.

"I need to talk to you about Nikki," I say. I clench and unclench my hands over and over. My heart is still racing.

He eyes me, but keeps pacing. "What about her?"

"I'm going to tell her I'm not taking her to prom."

Winston stops pacing. He has his back to me and he looks over his shoulder. "Why?"

There goes my thudding heart, racing even harder. Tell him I'm gay. Tell him I'm gay. "Because I'm sure she'd rather go with you. And you'd rather go with her."

He scoffs. "Maybe. But you know what she's like.

Basketball captain doesn't quite have the same appeal as *football* captain."

I don't even want to ask why he's okay with her going with me. Jordan flipped and dumped me; I don't know why Winston hasn't done the same with Nikki.

"So you *are* dating her?" I ask. Part of my plan hinges on this being a fact.

He sighs and turns around, swinging his arms out to his side. "Yeah. What of it?"

"Why haven't you guys been more public with it? There was some stuff on social media back in December, but that was it. You've been dating all this time?" God, why can't I just tell him I'm gay?

"Look, Ben, we both know she wants to go with you for image. When your little evening is done together and you do a few dances, she's going home with me. That's what matters." He starts pacing again and avoids looking at me. "I don't like that she's going with you rather than me, but if she *actually* hits it big as a social media celeb, then there's big money in it. I don't like it, but I knew going in that all this was part of the package."

"So when I tell Nikki I can't take her, you'll step in?" I ask, trying to get this back on track.

He eyes me, finally looking at me again. "Why are we even talking about this? You know how she is—she gets what she wants. She wants *you* to take her to prom. The deal was I get to take her to the grad dinner and dance. So have your *little date* and let's never talk about this again." He heads toward the gym doors.

As he grabs the handle, I open my mouth and say the words I meant to say this entire time. I didn't think I'd actually have the strength to say them.

"Winston...I'm gay."

He pauses, door open a couple inches, and looks at me. He lets go of the door, letting it close, and steps toward me. I have this sudden flash of fear that he's going to punch me or something. Even though I'm stronger than him, I'm still scared.

He towers over me. "You're what?"

"I-I'm gay."

He chuckles. "That explains it."

My heart is threatening to break through my ribs. "Explains what?"

He suddenly steps away, returning to pacing, but the scowl is gone from his face. If anything, he looks relieved. "The only reason I caved and let Nikki go with you is because she told me you're not into her. You guys have never slept together. You've done nothing more than the fake kisses for Snapchat. Didn't realize it's because you like dudes," he says, his voice way too loud.

I step closer to him and he stops pacing. He eyes me suspiciously as I say, "Can we...can we keep that fact secret between us?"

"You think I'd tell everyone that you're gay?" he says, still far too loudly. He must see the panic in my eyes because he glances up and down the hall and then leans in, lowering his voice. "I got a brother that's gay. I might not know what it's like to be gay in high school, but I've got a decent idea." He squeezes my shoulder. "Your secret is safe with me, Ben."

And my furiously pounding heart suddenly slows to normal speed. I let out a long breath I didn't know I was holding. "Thank you." When it no longer feels like my head is swimming, I add, "So I'll tell Nikki I can't take her and then send her your way...?"

Winston smiles. "I appreciate it, man."

He bumps fists with me, then heads back into the gym. Just one more person to track down. I pull out my phone.

BENJAMIN: Meet me in front of the trophy case by the gym?

NIKKI: Be right there Benny!

Even seeing that nickname in text irritates me. I let it slide, though.

I lean against the wall next to the trophy case, waiting for her to find me. I'm antsy. I can't stand still. Pushing away from the wall, I start pacing the hall just like Winston had done. It seems like every thirty seconds I'm pulling my phone out of my pocket to check the time. What's taking her so long?

Then she finally comes around the corner, her perfectly styled hair swinging behind her. Everything about her is picture perfect, from the amazing hair, to the flawless make-up, to the clothes that hug her body in all the right places.

"Benny," she says as she comes up to me. She grabs my hands and holds them, then leans in to kiss me on the cheek.

Rip the bandage off. That's what I have to do. This might be painful, so doing it quicker is better. Right?

"Nikki...I can't take you to prom. I'm sorry."

Her hands fall from mine. "Why?" she asks. Red spots start blossoming on her cheekbones.

What's that saying? In for a penny, in for a pound. Hopefully, she can keep a secret.

"Nikki...I'm gay. And I know you're dating Winston. You should go with him. I'm going to...I'm going to go alone." I realize I'm staring at the floor between us; at some point I decided to avoid her eyes and look down. I force myself to look up at her.

Her eyes are wide, like she's both surprised and frozen in fear. Her cheeks are still red with the apparent sting of my rejection.

"You...you know about me and Winston?" she asks. It doesn't escape my notice that she's more surprised by that than by the fact I'm gay.

"Yeah. I asked him about it," I say, and nod toward the gym doors, "and he told me I was right." When she doesn't say anything for a while, I ask, "So...you're not surprised I'm gay?"

Her eyes seem to focus on me, like they were focused elsewhere a moment ago. "Not really," she says. "I mean, I've tried flirting with you so many times and you just don't respond. I mean, if you just weren't into me and you liked another girl, you'd make your move on her...but that never happened. I mean, I wondered, but, you know, just didn't feel right asking." She turns her head to look at the gym doors.

"Nikki," I say, and I reach out to grab her hand. She looks at me again. "Thank you for understanding. I've already talked with Winston—I told him everything—and he'd love to take you to prom."

She lets out a sigh that sounds suspiciously like relief. "Thank you, Ben, for telling me who you are. We've spent a lot of time together, and I feel like it's just now that I'm starting to know you."

"And, uh, I feel weird asking...but you'll keep the gay thing a secret?"

"Of course." She hugs me and plants a kiss on my cheek. "You're a special guy, Ben, and I hope one day you'll find a guy to help you see how special you are."

"Thanks, Nikki." I hope I haven't totally lost my chance with Jordan, the one guy who thinks I'm special, the one guy who makes me feel all sorts of good.

It's the night of prom. And I don't have a date.

But I don't want a date—not if I can't have Jordan as my date.

My heart still hurts at that thought. I pause in adjusting my bowtie and lean back so I can look out my window and across the gap between our houses. It had taken a week, but

Jordan had started opening his curtains again, tearing down one of the many walls between us.

There was still the big one—my betrayal and secrets. I've sent him half a dozen apologies through text and Snapchat and other things, but he hasn't responded to any of them. I told mom what's going on and she told me that I've made my apologies and I just have to hope that Jordan comes around. Trying to apologize more won't help—it could even make it worse.

Still, my fingers itch to type out an apology every time I have a thought that involves Jordan. It isn't easy holding back. But it was a couple days after my final apology that he opened the curtains. So there was some success, I guess.

Math class is still tense, but not as tense as it could be. There's still this barrier between the back of my desk and the front of his. We can't speak across that barrier, nor can we interact.

But it's not all hopeless. A few days ago, Jordan started meeting my eyes in the hallways at school and nodding a polite hello. It's a very tiny step forward, but one that suddenly made me feel a whole lot less lonely and much less of a failure. I made a mistake—I know that—but it seems it might not be a fatal mistake.

I wanted to ask him to prom. I talked to Mom about that one first and she told me not to. If he somehow says yes, but the date is a disaster, then we're stuck together for the night and we ruin any happy memories we could have of prom. The strategy, she says, is to go without a date to prom and try to run into Jordan at the punch bowl.

My heart suddenly lurches into my throat and it feels all constricted. Jordan steps into his room and he's wearing a tuxedo. Damn, he looks incredible. He must have had it custom tailored, because it hugs his slim frame and narrow waist, just highlighting how fit he is, which in turn makes him look very masculine, despite his smaller size.

But more than that, he's *gorgeous*. Even from this span between our houses, I can tell that the deep red bowtie plays against his brown eyes, making them look so large and luminous.

He glances up and catches my eye. He freezes for a moment, then he smiles a very small smile—and that makes me melt. I step into full view of the window and hold out my arms to either side in a "well, what do you think?" gesture. I do a slow spin on my heel. When I turn around to face him again, he's still smiling, but there's a little bit of hurt in his eyes. And that makes me sad. He nods, trying to hide that hurt, trying to tell me he approves of my outfit.

I do a spinning motion with my fingers and he does what I did—hands out at the side and a slow spin around. Holy crap, he's amazing from all sides. But when he faces me again, that hurt is still in his eyes.

I give him two thumbs up.

We stare at each other awkwardly for a moment, then he turns his head like someone's calling him from downstairs. A moment later, he heads back out of his room.

I stand there for a long time, watching his window,

hoping he'll come back, but he doesn't. Eventually, I turn back to the mirror and finish adjusting my bowtie. In the back of my mind, I hope that Jordan found me as attractive in a tux as I found him.

"Ben! Are you dressed yet?" mom calls from downstairs. "We want photos!"

I roll my eyes. Mom always wants a million photos of every major event in any of our lives. I just wish this major event was shared with Jordan on my arm, by my side, in my heart. I swallow down the rising sadness, put on my best face, and head to the top of the stairs.

"Runway music, please!" I announce. This is all mom's doing—she picked some thumping electronic song on YouTube and wants to video me coming down the stairs like a fashion model.

A moment later, that loud, pounding music is thumping through the air. Dad and Brayden and Daniel all come to the bottom of the stairs and point flashlights at me—they've all been roped into mom's plans. Beside them is mom, holding up her phone.

I strike my best debonair pose, then shift between fashion catalogue positions, pretending to check my non-existent watch, pretending to point at something in the distance, giving a moody look over my shoulder. The music swells and I start coming down the stairs, taking each step slowly, pausing to pose as the mood hits me. When I'm at the bottom of the stairs, mom squeals and pulls me into a big hug, planting a kiss on my cheek. Soon after that are the million and one photos—with each family member individually and then as a group and over and over and over.

I'm relieved when I get a text from Devon that they're on their way. I'm hitching a ride to prom with Devon and Andrea in their rented limo. I managed to talk mom into *not* making Devon pose for another million photos with me and the limo—but the compromise was that she would follow me out of the house and take a video. A few moments later, the limo pulls up and I head out, mom hot on my heels. The chauffer comes around and opens the door for me—and Devon peeks his head out and waves for Mom's camera—and then I'm safely cocooned inside the limo and being taken away.

"Hey," I say. "Thanks for letting me bum a ride."

Devon squeezes my shoulder. "No problem, buddy. I'm just…still surprised you didn't bring Nikki."

I haven't told him about the whole liking guys thing yet. Other than Winston and Nikki, I haven't told anyone. Oh, and Kieran seems to know, but I haven't said it in words to him.

"It just didn't feel right," I say. "I know she likes Winston and he likes her. Might not be as Insta-perfect as the cheer team co-captain and the football captain—but they're better together than me and her."

Devon looks at me strangely. I try to draw his attention away from me and my mysterious dating life. "Don't take this the wrong way, bro," I say, "but that suit makes you look fly."

He grins and tugs on his jacket, striking a pose similar to the one that I did at the top of the stairs.

"You think Andrea will like it?" he asks. He leans back into the seat and his fingers start drumming against his knee. He's nervous.

"She hasn't seen it yet?"

"No, not yet. I haven't seen her dress either. Nikki made sure we're color-coordinated." He stares out the window, fingers still drumming against his knee.

I suddenly feel weirdly bad that I came out to Nikki and Winston, but not to Devon...and Devon is the closest thing to what I'd call a best friend. I consider coming out here and now, just to get it over with, but then I throw that notion away when I realize what spectacularly bad timing it would be. This is *not* the time to tell him I'm gay.

The car pulls to a stop in front of a house I've never seen before. The chauffer opens the door for Devon to come out and the chauffer and I watch as Devon hurries up to the door and disappears inside. Several minutes later—likely after Andrea's mom's million and one photos—the door opens again and Devon and Andrea step out onto the front steps of the house.

She is *gorgeous*. The blue of his tie absolutely plays off against the lighter blue trim of her dress. They look like a perfect match, a couple made for each other. I scoot over on the seat to make room for Devon and Andrea. She comes in first and greets me, I say hi back and smile as Devon follows her in.

Then the car pulls away from the curb and Devon and Andrea are basically ignoring my existence and I've never felt so awkward in my life. I slip my phone out of my pocket and check my feeds. I stumble across a post from Jordan—a photo of him, Hannah, and Kumail having a great time in what looks like a limo. Looks like he's also pulling the third wheel thing, but having a better time with it. I do my best to ignore the other people in the car—especially now that they've started kissing—and stare intently at my phone as the car takes a roundabout path through the city and to the hotel where we're holding prom. The scenic route was lost on us with those two focused on each other and me focusing on my phone.

When the car pulls up at the hotel, we all get out of the limo and I let Devon and Andrea head on in. I hold back a bit, not wanting to cling onto them the whole night. Our limo pulls away, heading off, and another limo pulls into the spot. I step aside, watching to see which of my classmates would step out of this one. The chauffer comes around to this side of the car and opens the door...and Hannah and Kumail come out. A moment later, so too does Jordan.

Hannah and Kumail spot me and give me a funny look, almost like they know something. Hannah looks over her shoulder at Jordan and he nods at her. She and Kumail walk up the steps of the hotel and into prom.

Jordan walks over to me.

"Hey," I say.

"Hey."

"I know we sorta said it through our windows, but you look great tonight," I say. I step back to get a good look at him. Man, he's hot.

"Thanks." He smiles—a genuine smile. "You do too."

I look up the steps, to where Hannah and Kumail had gone. "Do they...?"

He shakes his head. "They know that we're not getting along right now. That's it." He looks around like he's searching for something or someone. "You really did it? Nikki's not with you?"

"No, she's with Winston." I bite my lower lip, unsure of how far to go forward. "Listen, Jordan...I know I said it, like, half a dozen times, but I'm sorry."

"I know," he says and he looks down at his feet. "I forgive you, but it's going to take some time to get over it." I want to say something, but I think he wants this conversation to end, because he looks up at the stairs again. "Let's head in." He starts walking up.

I follow behind him. He forgives me. That's a huge step—way bigger than him opening his bedroom curtains again. I can't help but smile. But when we get into the hotel and find the ballroom, he walks away from me like he doesn't know I'm behind him. My smile disappears.

I watch as he threads through the tables to catch up with Hannah and Kumail. I hear Devon call my name and I spot him on the other side of the room, sitting down with Andrea and a few guys from the team and their dates. I sit down with them and try to participate in the table conversation while we eat our dinner, but for the entire evening, my attention is fully on the other side of the room.

A hand on my shoulder pulls me out of my reverie. I look up and find Nikki and Winston. They look fantastic together—both of them look amazing, but together they just look stellar. And there's an energy surrounding them, of overwhelming happiness and love.

I stand up and turn around, taking a step back so I can get a good look at both of them. "You two look *incredible!*"

Nikki blushes—actually blushes—and Winston smiles. "Thank you," she says. She reaches for Winston's hand and their fingers easily and comfortably interlock. "Thank you for pushing me to do what I should've done all along."

Winston lets go of her hand to slide his arm around her shoulders. "No date tonight, buddy?" Winston asks. I think because I've given him his happiness tonight, he wants me to have happiness too.

I shake my head. "No. Flying solo."

When I glance past them, I see Jordan heading for the punch bowl. I excuse myself and slip around them, timing my pace so I arrive at the bowl at the same time.

"Hey," Jordan says when I come up beside him and pick up an empty glass. There's still some sadness in his voice.

While he scoops out his punch, I turn and take in the venue. "Hannah and Kumail did an incredible job," I say. The dance floor is made to look like an enchanted forest, with a few potted trees along the edges, along with some sheer white fabric to look like fog and fairy lights lighting the fabric from within. Each of the tables were draped with table cloths in royal colors—reds, blues, purples—and the centerpieces held twigs and more of that white fabric.

"Yeah, they did," he says and turns around to scope out the room too. He takes a sip of his punch. I turn to fill my glass.

When I turn back around to face the room, I feel like an odd and uncomfortable silence has settled between us. I need to break that silence. "It's really good to see you—and even better to be talking to you again."

Jordan has some sort of immediate reaction to my words—his face twitching into an expression that I can't figure out—then he smothers that and puts a neutral look back on his face. "Yeah," he says, staring out at the floor, taking another sip. As I'm about to think of something else to say, he suddenly looks down at his glass of punch and says, "Look, Benjamin...I like you. Like...a *lot*. But the past few months have made it very clear that I can't be with someone who isn't out. It's too painful for me...having to hide everything and denying our feelings when other people are around." He looks up at me, tears gathering in the corners of his eyes. "I'm sorry, Benjamin."

I feel like my heart has been ripped out of my chest. I'm stunned—immobile, speechless, emotionally numb. Jordan apologizes again and walks away, returning to his table.

Kieran seems to appear out of nowhere, bumping into me as he scoops out some punch for himself. He turns around and takes a sip, staring out at the tables and dance floor.

"Listen, bud," he says, low and discreet, "I saw you and Jordan just now. It doesn't take much for me to put two and two together. He walked away—I walked past him, he's hurting, it's obvious—but sometimes you gotta chase the one you want."

I slowly turn my head to look at him. My mind is still fuzzy, trying to recover from the stunning rejection I'd just received. "What?"

Kieran leans in, like he's telling me a secret. "Sometimes you have to fight for what you want."

I blink several times. His words still aren't really sinking in.

All I can hear is Jordan's words. *I can't be with someone who isn't out. It's too painful for me…*

Just as I'm about to pathetically say "What?" again, the squeal of a microphone pulls my attention forward. Hannah is at the mic, with Kumail at her side.

"Good evening, Charlesburgh High!" she says into the microphone, signing the words for Kumail as she says them. The crowd cheers back. "I said *good evening, Charlesburgh High!*" she says, louder. The crowd cheers back louder. "The DJ is ready to go and we're about to open the dance floor, but we wanted to first announce this year's prom princess and prom prince!" Another cheer roars through the room.

Rippling throughout the room, moving like a wave, students and friends start drumming their tables, imitating a drumroll. Kumail hands a big, glittery envelope over to Hannah.

"As you know," Hannah says, "you voted last week on who you wanted as your princess and prince. Kumail tallied the votes and kept them secret. Your princess and prince are..." she pauses as she opens the envelope and slides the paper out, "Nikki Simms and Benjamin Cooper!"

The crowd cheers and everyone is looking at either me or Nikki. I'm still stunned. Jordan broke up with me. I mean, I guess it wasn't a surprise, but now it's official. I want Jordan, but he doesn't want me.

Kieran nudges my back and I'm jolted back to the present. Everyone is clapping and staring at me. Nikki is already on the dance floor, waiting for me. I walk forward, putting one foot in front of the other, not really aware of anything around me.

I can't be with someone who isn't out. It's too painful for me...

I slow to a stop when I reach the center of the dance floor and stand in front of Nikki. Hannah and Kumail come up behind each of us and place a crown on our head. Everyone cheers. The DJ starts a song—a slow, romantic song—and Nikki steps closer and puts my hand around her waist and takes the other hand in hers. We start dancing. Beside the DJ booth is a large panel of lights that flash and make patterns in time with the music—a feature I'd heard made it possible for Kumail to enjoy the music.

But all I can think about is Jordan.

I drag my eyes down to look at Nikki, but she's not looking at me. She's looking at someone behind me. I turn us around in our steps and I see who she's looking at—Winston. And behind Winston is Jordan.

I can't be with someone who isn't out. It's too painful for me…

I look down at Nikki again. I know she wants to dance with Winston right now—to have this special first dance at prom with him. And I want Jordan. What was it Kieran said? *Sometimes you have to fight for what you want.*

I lean forward, closer to Nikki. "I'm going to make this right," I say. "Trust me."

We turn around in our dance again and I see Winston and Jordan again. Winston is watching us with the same pain in his eyes that I see in Nikki's. He wants this dance with her; he doesn't want to watch someone else dancing with his girlfriend. I look behind him to Jordan—Jordan is upset too. Those tears that had gathered in his eyes when we were at the punch bowl now threaten to fall. He hurries out of the room and my heart breaks again.

"What do you mean?" Nikki whispers back, her eyes still on Winston.

"We both want to dance with someone else. I'm going to make it happen."

Chapter Seventeen

Jordan

*O*F COURSE BENJAMIN AND Nikki get voted prom prince and princess. She's cheer co-captain and he's the football captain and everyone thinks they're madly in love.

The fact that it was inevitable doesn't make it any easier to watch. I want Benjamin so bad—so goddamn bad—but I know that as long as he's not out, it's just too painful. I've had my first love, my first kiss, and my first boyfriend, and I couldn't tell a soul about it—not Hannah, not Kumail, not anyone! Telling mom is not the same as telling my friends.

And then to find out that he had asked Nikki to prom? That had killed me.

The fact that he had then broke that date off didn't make any of this easier.

To watch him on the dance floor, his hands on her,

their bodies pulled close, romantic music filling the room...it was too much. I wanted to be in her place.

Watching them felt like my heart was being crushed.

So I left.

I didn't go far. Just outside the ballroom doors. But it was far enough. I can't see them now. I can still hear that crappy romantic music that I want Ben to kiss me to, but I can't see his hands on her anymore.

I rub the heels of my hands against my eyes, trying to rub away the tears. I'm so pathetic sometimes, crying over some boy.

The sudden squeal of a microphone and the collective gasp of everyone inside the ballroom pulls me—momentarily—out of my self-pity. A moment later, the music stops, cutting off mid-song. Then I hear a voice. I can't quite make out the words, but I know the voice.

Benjamin.

What the hell is he doing?

I swipe my hands across my eyes once more and hope that it doesn't look like I was crying, then I approach the doors to the ballroom. They've been propped open, so I can stand and watch without fully entering the room.

Ben is on the stage, microphone in hand. Everyone around looks like they're gossiping and whispering to each other—probably trying to figure out what Ben is doing. Then Ben sees me and our eyes lock.

"I have a secret," Ben says, never taking his eyes from

me. The gossiping and whispering of our classmates dies down. "I'm in love."

My heart starts racing, throwing itself against my ribs. What's he doing? I put my hand out and brace it against the doorframe. For some reason, my knees feel weak. Ben's eyes still haven't left me. I can feel the heat in his gaze from across the room. I want to dig a hole and hide until this is all over.

The gossiping in the room rises in volume after Ben's declaration that he's in love. But it goes apeshit when Ben clarifies and says, "But I'm not in love with Nikki. She loves someone else. And so do I."

Don't do it, Benjamin. Don't do it. Don't come out because of some stupid crap I said. My gut wrenches with the thought that I'm forcing him to come out, that he's not ready for it but he's doing it because he thinks it's what I want.

But it *is* what I want. Isn't it? I still love him—I can't deny that, I can't lie to myself anymore—I still love him with all my heart. But it's him being closeted that makes this so hard. It's us having to deny our feelings whenever we're in public, it's us having to have our dates on the other side of the city, it's him asking Nikki to prom so that he can stay "straight", it's me not being able to tell my best friends what's going on in my life…it's all of that and more. Love is supposed to be happy, wonderful, joyful, and we're supposed to glow and everyone's supposed to see how much we're in love—and we have to smother all of that. We have to hide it.

"Three and a half years ago," Ben says loudly, leaning into the microphone, silencing the gossipers, "I worked with my best friend on a science fair project." He laughs, seemingly lost in the memory. He breaks his intense eye contact with me for just a moment, and when he brings it back, it's not filled with heat—it's filled with love and happiness. "We were measuring air quality in different parts of the city. Every day after school, we'd hop on our bikes and ride to a different part of the city to collect an air sample. We had so much fun."

I remember that like it was yesterday. Ben had been so carefree then—so relaxed, so easygoing—and those were some of my happiest memories of him. Other than the memories that involve him kissing me, of course. We'd had such a great time on that project. He taught me how to ride with no hands on the handlebars—I'd always been so terrified I'd fall over and hurt myself, but he rode right next to me and made sure I was okay.

"The day of the science fair came," Ben says. The room is super quiet now. I see some guy I don't recognize pull out his phone to record Ben—but then Kieran approaches him and with a few whispered words, the guy puts his phone away. Benjamin laughs again at another memory. "We got first place. We hugged. And it was in that moment I realized I had feelings for my best friend."

It's like my whole world collapses and focuses on that

one instant in time. I barely remember that hug. I mean, I was excited to have won first place—I remember jumping around and I guess I hugged him. I feel weirdly bad for not remembering that hug. It was so important to him, a changing moment in his life, but I can't even remember it.

The murmuring in the room starts to get louder. I can't make out any of the whispered words, but I know what they're saying. Everyone is trying to figure out who his best friend in grade nine was. A lot of the people in the room were our classmates back then.

One person looks at me. Hannah. I see her through the crowd. She's looking at me with what I can only describe as a mix of emotions—I see hope, hope that this is true and it's me, and I see hurt, hurt that I didn't tell her this already, but also concern. She knows that it didn't end well with the anonymous person I was seeing.

I give her a quick nod. I hope it tells her everything—that this is true, that Ben was my boyfriend, that I'll be okay.

Suddenly, a few other heads start turning my way as people catch on to who Hannah is looking at and start putting everything together.

"I've loved you, Jordan Ortiz, for a very long time," Ben says. The room fills with gasps, but then everyone hushes. "I'm so sorry for being a dick. I'm so sorry for putting you through the hell I've put you through. You said you couldn't be with me if I was closeted—if I was pretending to be straight. Well...now everyone knows I'm gay."

Everyone is looking at me. And the people standing right in front of me have parted, clearing a path between Ben and I. My sight gets blurry as tears fill my eyes—crying *again*, damn it. But then I realize that all my fear for what Ben was doing has all melted away. What's left is love. My heart is swelling with love. All I can see is Benjamin.

He holds a hand out to me, even though we're separated by half the ballroom. "Jordan Ortiz...will you do me the honor of having this dance?"

I furiously try to wipe away all the tears. The entire senior class is looking at me and I'm sobbing. But I don't care. Benjamin loves me—and he's proclaimed it to all of our friends. There's no more hiding. There's no more denying any of this exists.

I finally start walking forward, toward Benjamin. Every step brings me closer to him and makes my heart swell a little bit more. He steps down from the little stage and meets me in the middle of the dance floor. I put my hand in his—it feels damn good to have him hold my hand again. His fingers are soft and warm and almost send a shiver down my spine.

"I'm sorry," Ben says. "I know I've said it so many times already, but I'm so sorry. I'm sorry for putting you through all that. I'm sorry for asking someone else to prom. I'm sorry for being a dick. I don't know if I can ever make this up to you, but I hope this is a start."

I wipe away a few more tears and inhale sharply, trying not to let my nose run. Benjamin is so adorable when he's apologetic. All I feel for him now is love and happiness—all of that hurt and hesitation is gone. It's gone. Totally gone.

I realize I haven't answered him yet—but I don't know if I have the mental capacity for words right now. I'm such a mess and this is all overwhelming. So I give him an answer without words. I wrap my free hand around the back of his neck and pull him close for a kiss.

God, it feels good to have these lips pressed against mine again. All of the emotions I'm feeling right now come pouring out as I kiss him. Everything that's been pent up comes rushing out. Benjamin loves me. I love him. And everyone knows it.

I'm vaguely aware of the clapping from our classmates.

When we finally break our kiss and stare deeply in each other's eyes, I notice something new. The old Benjamin is back—that carefree, fun-loving Benjamin of our science fair. There's a subtle change in his eyes and in his face, something that almost no one would notice, but I see it plain as day. Now that he's out and he's no longer hiding any part of himself, he's no longer wearing a mask. He's no longer pretending to be someone he's not.

"Let's have a change in program," Hannah says from the microphone. I don't take my eyes off Benjamin's. "Instead of this being the prom princess and prince dance, let's make this a dance for all the couples and lovers here tonight."

Around us, everyone starts pairing off with who they came with, and then that same sappy love song starts playing again from the start. Only it's different now. I'm not watching Nikki dance with Benjamin—it's *me* dancing with Benjamin.

It takes several moments before I can bring my feet to start moving. I'm just rooted in place, hugging Benjamin, staring into his eyes. And I love it. Eventually, we start shuffling our feet, awkwardly dancing to the music, our hands and arms never leaving each other's bodies. I pull myself closer to him and rest the side of my face on his hard chest. I can hear his heartbeat.

As we dance and slowly turn, I see Hannah and Kumail, dancing almost as close as Benjamin and I. With them, I can see Kumail staying aware of the wall of lights on the stage, keeping beat to the music, so he can dance with Hannah. She's absolutely in love with him—I can tell just by the contentment on her face. And Kumail is just as content and happy—and I bet part of it is even just happiness that he can even do this. If Hannah hadn't made this prom accessible for him, he wouldn't be able to dance as well as he is. Almost as one, they catch me watching them and they both grin widely. No doubt they're overjoyed that my romantic saga with my mystery man has reached a happy conclusion.

We turn a bit again, my ear still to Benjamin's chest, my heartbeat syncing up with his, and I find myself watching Nikki and Winston. I remember when Benjamin and I hung out on New Year's Eve…we'd wondered if those two were hitting it off. As aggravating as Nikki was when we were on the cheer team, I *am* really happy to see her with Winston...and not just because she doesn't have her hands on my man anymore. Everyone deserves love and it's something Benjamin just can't give her—but Winston can. She rests her head on his chest much like I'm doing with Benjamin, and then she closes her eyes as they keep dancing. They look so peaceful and in love.

And as we keep turning, I see Benjamin's friends, Devon and Andrea. They're talking intimately to each other as they dance, breaking out in giggles now and then. Then Devon glances our way and I can feel Ben stiffen up at the glance, like he's expecting some sort of smart-ass comment. Instead, Devon throws on the biggest smile and gives Ben a thumbs up. Beyond them, Kieran is dancing with a girl I don't know—and I'm pretty sure Kieran winked at Ben. And then we make the full circuit and I see Hannah and Kumail again.

I take my lead from Nikki and I close my eyes, just letting the music and the moment and the magic all take over. Benjamin and I sway together as one, like we're two halves of the same whole.

Ben lets go of me, moving that comforting arm off me. I whimper and open my eyes, looking up at him. He's taking off that crown that Kumail had put on his head when he'd been crowned prom prince. He looks at it, smiles, then slips it onto my head.

"Looks cute on you," he whispers, then hugs me tight.

I rest the side of my face against his chest again and

catch Hannah and Kumail looking at me again. By the way they've both got an identical smile on their lips, I know that they shared some secret thought about me.

I discreetly sign them. *What?*

Fairy tales come true, Hannah signs back.

It takes me a moment to make the connection. But then I feel the weight of the crown Benjamin had put on my head. He was the prom prince—so my prince *did* come and sweep me off my feet.

Mom wants a bunch of photos. Not as many as I know Benjamin's mom wants of him, though.

I adjust my black graduation gown, trying to get it to hang properly on my shoulders. She waves her fingers at me, indicating for me to hold my diploma higher. I do and she snaps a bunch of photos.

"Now let's get you and your sister," she says, then pushes Bella forward. She's wearing a blue dress at mom's insistence. My sister hates dresses.

We do some goofy poses—thumbs up, tongues out, pretending to strangle each other—and then we get the nice family photos that she wants. Some helpless soul wanders close by and she gets him to take a photo of the four of us— me, Bella, mom, and dad. When she gets her phone back from the random guy, she starts looking around.

"Where's that boyfriend of yours?" she mutters.

"Mom, we don't need to do that." I don't want to drag Benjamin into these family photos—and he's already told me to not get involved in his photos or else his mom will be snapping pics until the sun goes down.

"Nonsense," she says, then starts walking through the crowd. Graduation had been in the football stadium and all of the families were now gathered around the stadium exterior, taking photos, hugging, and celebrating.

"Nancy!" mom calls out as soon as she sees Benjamin's family.

When we reach them, Benjamin immediately pulls me into a hug and kisses me. I have to admit that it took me a little while to get used to how *freely* Benjamin expresses affection now that he's out. But I can never resist his kisses.

Then begins the onslaught of photos—the two of us together, then with his brothers and my sister, and then with both our families. And when Hannah and Kumail come wandering by, all of this happens all over again with the two of them joining us in all the photos.

When I came out at the start of senior year, I had no idea that this was where it would lead. All I wanted was to no longer be in hiding, to no longer fear that someone would find out my secret. Yeah, of course I wanted to find love—who doesn't? But I don't think I ever honestly expected it to happen.

And I certainly didn't expect or even hope or even dream that it would be Benjamin. I had no idea what roller coaster of emotion had laid ahead of me for my final year of high school. There was a lot of pain and there were a lot of tears—but every single moment of heartache was worth it for where it got me.

As I put my arms around Hannah and Kumail for another round of photos—this time with their parents—I marvel at how senior year has turned out for both of them too. Hannah had finally met a guy that could keep up with her, that loved her for all of her passions and interests, and for every aspect of her being. And Kumail had spoken a few times of his old school, of being excluded and bullied, of always feeling alone and an outsider. And now not only does he have friends in myself and Benjamin, but he also has a girlfriend.

Soon, a number of other people come our way and join us for a large group photo. These are all new friends—some of them former enemies—who have all come together because of the choices that Benjamin made. When I mentioned this to Benjamin last night, he said it's all because of the choices *I* made. He says he only had the strength to come out because he saw me come out.

With Nikki and Winston behind Benjamin and I, Devon and Andrea behind Hannah and Kumail, and the rest of the football gang and their girlfriends crouching on the grass in front of us, we all smile widely for the phalanx of parents snapping photo after photo after photo.

And then it's almost like everything evaporates. The photos die down, people start heading home, and Benjamin and I are left. We'd turned in our caps and gowns and were now just in our nice black pants and dress shirts.

In some ways, the end of high school is the end of an era. And with NYU ahead for both of us, we're stepping into a brave new world. But with Benjamin at my side, I can do anything. No challenge is too big, no new day too scary.

I put my hand in Benjamin's and we walk to the school's parking lot.

Benjamin's parents had left one of their cars for him, figuring we'd want to drive home together. When we get in the car, he leans over the console and kisses me. I almost melt under his touch.

"Congratulations, graduate," he says.

"Congratulations, graduate," I echo.

Then he kisses me again.

He starts up the car and shifts into gear, then holds my hand as he drives us away from the school. He's taking a scenic route, not heading anywhere near our houses. Then we're suddenly on a road that's starting to rise and I realize he's taking us up the hill with the lookout point. Sure enough, when we reach that magical spot, he turns into the little parking lot that overlooks the city.

In the late afternoon sun, the city is bathed in a burnished gold color. It's magical.

Benjamin turns off the car and silence settles in. It's a comfortable silence. I lean across the console and rest my head on his shoulder, sighing with contentment. He kisses the top of my head, then leans his head against mine.

"I love you, Benjamin," I say.

"I love you too, Jordan."

About Dylan James

Dylan James believes love is for everyone, and through writing gay young adult romances, he hopes to get that point across to younger readers. Dylan is a lover of books, Star Trek, and animals. He lives in Canada with his husband and two cats.

Dylan also writes adult gay romances under the name Cameron D. James.

Follow Dylan on Twitter (twitter.com/DylanJamesYA) and Instagram (instagram.com/DylanJamesYA).

More by Dylan James

Gay Love and Other Fairy Tales
Gay Love and Other Christmas Magic
Thunder
Frankenstein Builds a Boyfriend
Drag Queens, Emo Teens & Big Dreams (September 2020)

Acknowledgements

A book is never the result of one person's efforts, but rather the results of a team. *Gay Love and Other Fairy Tales* is no exception to this.

This book started as a seed of an idea after watching the movie *Love, Simon*, and quickly blew up not only into a full novel, but into Deep Hearts YA, a young adult imprint of Deep Desires Press (of which I am co-owner and publisher).

Thank you to Ethan for being a sounding board for ideas when I was in the development stage. Thank you to fellow authors Jessica Collins, Marie Fox, L.B. La Vigne, and Siryn Sueng for being my go-to for this Canadian boy who needed American references—and sorry if I missed someone! (Thank you, especially, for explaining the difference between homecoming and prom!) Thank you to my beta readers, Ethan (again), Maddie, and Mariëlle. Thank you to my team at Deep Hearts YA, Ave (for the cover), Ethan (yet again, this time for marketing support), John (senior editor…and my husband), Lizette (editor), and Margaret (proofreader).

Most of all, thank you to John, my husband, for being part of this exciting journey. We met at a writing workshop and now we're partners in life and partners in business. (And I should probably also thank my cats, Wizard and Shyger, for forcing me to take cat-petting breaks now and then.)

More From Deep Hearts YA

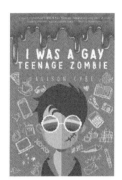

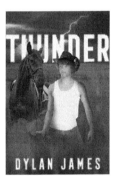

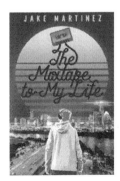

Find out more at deepheartsya.com
Twitter/Instagram/Facebook: @DeepHeartsYA

Printed in Great Britain
by Amazon

46916011R10156